FROM DARKNESS TO GLORY

J. R. Biery

ABOUT THIS BOOK

From Darkness to Glory is a western romance about the journey and adventures of a mail-order bride who leaves her job and family as a factory girl to travel to Montana and marry a gunslinger.

DISCLAIMER

DEDICATION

Dedicated to Jerry, my patient and loving husband, who has always supported and encouraged me to follow my dreams. Also, thanks to the members of Cookeville Creative Writers' Association who prodded and nudged me forward. Special thanks to Lisa Brown and other members of Cookeville Creative Writers' Association.

PROLOGUE

1875-Helena, Montana

Phillip Gant stood hip to shoulder with Shorty and Banes, the trio elbowing their way through the crowd of men waiting for the stage. All the way from New York to Montana, that's how far Johnson's new bride had traveled. Every man in the crowd was stirred by the same anticipation that had left the big bald man embarrassingly disabled. Two of the miners held him to his feet as the Overland stage pulled in front of the delivery office.

The crowd became hushed as the stage doors opened. A woman stood in the open doorway, but not an ordinary woman. No one could ever mistake her for the mother or sisters they had left behind back east, nor an Indian squaw like some of the men had settled for marrying. No, she was something special indeed.

Phillip saw the woman's eyes flicker across the crowd and light upon him. She smiled, the wintry blue of her eyes warming as she gave him a seductive grin. Banes giggled next to his ear and Shorty swore, then shouted. "Look at what a woman Johnson's got."

Irritated by the smell of whiskey from his drunken friend, Phillip stepped back from the crowd, clearing space so his hands could rest securely on his guns. His head hummed from the many toasts they had shared with the intended bridegroom; his thoughts rapid and jumbled.

Angry voices turned to yell at Shorty, but the tall goddess

smiled at him and Johnson suddenly straightened and blushed proudly. In awed wonder, the men watched the tall woman look at the bald miner, taking in his fresh scrubbed face and new suit. She smiled slowly. Gracefully she descended the stage steps and stepped forward to take his hand. A giant in his own right, Johnson smiled down at the perfect white moon of her face.

A noise like the humming of a swarm of bees replaced individual comments. Awed, the crowd followed them to the assay office and waited tensely outside. But as they peered through the doorway, the same thought was on each man's mind. They could have been the one to place the ad.

No one noticed when the unsmiling but handsome gun fighter in their midst swiveled on his heel and walked across to the telegraph office.

Phillip scribbled the message, then scratched through the words, looking around for inspiration. A yellow sheet was tacked to the wall behind the counter, the ads for brides set in bold type. Some of the notices described the prospective grooms, one as a rich miner, and another as a handsome cattleman. One ad boldly stated, 'wanted young woman, good natured, healthy breeding stock, free of disease.' The fool must think he was ordering a cow.

What Phillip wanted to order was a willing woman. It didn't matter if she was as beautiful as Johnson's bride; most women who answered these ads were homely at best. But he wanted a woman who would be willing, no eager, a woman who would be eager to hold him through the cold night, to surrender her soft sweet body to block the terrible shadows of the men he had killed from his dreams. He also wanted a woman who would do what she was told and like it. He wadded up the second sheet.

The message he sent was brief.

CHAPTER ONE

1875-Outskirts of Boston, Massachusetts

Lynne McKinney held her empty lunch tin so that it bumped against her thigh. Cautiously she placed one short booted foot down directly behind the other as she crossed on the narrow board over the stream of waste water. The air was misty sweet as the large cloud of vapor from boiled linen and starch gushed out with the other smells from the factory behind her. She swung her arms and shoulders to loosen them as she walked with the other girls and young women who trudged home from the long day at the mill.

For a moment she feared the rest of the world might not exist, that there was only this daily trek along the muddy ditch between her mind-numbing job and the chaos of their crowded apartment. If there were another kind of life, it might remain shrouded in mist and mystery from her forever. Three years she had worked in the shirt factory, moving from the looms and starch vats to the thunder of the sewing machines. At least she was nimble and quick and still had the use of all her fingers. However, the $1.30 that she had painfully tied in her empty napkin didn't even make a clank in the empty pail and she had to stop for food.

The group of women turned the corner in unison and the mist was left behind. The air was suddenly sharply cold and clear in the fading afternoon light. She turned to look at the others for reassurance. Her two closest friends from childhood walked on either side of her. The three girls had gone to work at the plant the same year. But Lynne was the oldest and she couldn't help but shake her head as Claire, six months younger, bobbed her golden curls and giggled.

"What kind of clothes are you going to spend your pay on this week?" Lynne asked.

Claire held out her latest copy of the _Lowell Offering_ to point to an ad for a new corset. On the other side, Bonnie, only a month younger, dropped a hand to her swollen stomach and said, "I wish there were a corset strong enough to make this flat."

Lynne grinned in sympathy as she straightened. Well it could always be worse. The tall, idle men outside the pub raised their voices in invitation to the young women, who either giggled nervously or stomped coldly past. Bonnie dropped out to wait for the worthless man who would have her pay drunk up before morning.

Lynne couldn't help but cast a last pitying look at the dark-haired girl, as she searched amid the crowd for her tall, young husband. She whispered to Claire. "A year ago, Bonnie dreamed that devil would take her out of all this. Well, a few more months and the bairn will come and she will be out of the mill for good. Then what?"

Claire rolled her eyes and giggled. "Well, for a bull like Tarn Micheals, an uncertain future might be worth it. Look at those dimples."

Lynne didn't look back at the approaching man who could only be described as tall, dark, and handsome. She remembered those dimples all too well. After all, he had flirted with her first but she had been too terrified to show any interest. Then he tried Claire, who he claimed giggled too much, before settling on quiet Bonnie.

She could remember feeling jealous when Bonnie gushed on and on about Tarn, what he said, and what he did. But then the dark-haired girl had told them she was in trouble, and Claire and Lynne were bridesmaids for a once more silent Bonnie. Now she was glad she had ignored his glib tongue.

"All men are trouble, but one like Tarn is worse than most. I heard whispers on the floor the other day about the devil slipping around behind Bonnie's back," Lynne whispered.

Already the women were on the last block before the tenements, and most hurried away toward home, leaving the two young women behind. Claire's babble rose a notch and Lynne tried to shake her gloomy mood and listen. "Oh lord, read this, would you read this."

Lynne tried, but she couldn't get her to hold the rattling sheets still. "For goodness sake, what is it now you goose, a new type of hat?"

"No-oo," Claire stuttered, "It's an ad from a firm out west. It's a list of men who want wives. Oh, oh, look at this one. 'Tall well-formed veteran without vices. Needs bride willing to settle in Montana on 640 acre horse ranch.' Oh Lynne, wouldn't you love to just see him?"

Lynne snorted and added emphatically. "Certainly not. It doesn't give his age or anything. And what type of description is that? He's probably an old goat with one leg or one eye who's tried his hand at mining, failed, and stayed behind to try ranching on a Federal land grant."

But Claire argued with her. "No, I don't think maimed men can be called well-formed, and if it isn't the truth, it wouldn't be in the paper."

Lynne shook her head as she stepped up onto the boardwalk in front of Sanders, the small grocery. "What kind of man do you know, Claire that would ever place an ad for a bride? Besides, they'll run anything to sell papers. That's disgusting. Your lady's journal is no better than the yellow-sheets." She inhaled the sharp tang of apples and oranges in the open barrels at the front and wished she dared buy one. They'd had oranges at Christmas and just the smell made her mouth water.

"Oh, it is in the *Globe,* not the *Lowell.* But, well, I think it sounds dreamy and I'm going to save it for my hope chest."

Lynne stared at her friend, taking in the wide blue eyes and silly grin, before smiling indulgently. She dampened the handkerchief that was still tucked in her sash and leaned across to dab a dark streak from beside the blushing blonde's cheek. Sometimes Claire seemed more like her younger sister than a woman of seventeen like herself. "Your hope chest is bulging, but I think saving descriptions of desperate men is going too far."

Claire pouted prettily, stuffing the folded yellow sheet into her drawstring purse as she turned her back on her. "Well, I'm to hurry home mum said, so shop by yourself, you old scowl." She twisted as she neared the end of the walk to call back to the serious woman in the broadcloth shirtwaist. "Your problem, Lynne McKinney, is you don't know how to dream. See you Monday."

Lynne nodded in silent agreement, and then bent to find something cheap but filling. She had to hurry home as well. Her mother wasn't feeling well and her small sister and young brothers would need their supper. She splurged and added tea, sugar, and a single lemon to the box holding a large sack of potatoes, two cabbages, dried beans, and flour. She would make a dessert for them and serve her mother tea with lemon. Maybe it would help restore her. How was anyone supposed to dream when the only thing between her family and starvation was the money she earned; especially, now the mill was talking about cut backs again?

She paid for the goods, adding a small piece of fatback to the bulging box. Hope was for fools and dreamers, so she would leave it for Bonnie and Claire. She had to hurry home in the dark to reality.

The tenements rose like noisy bird cages, surrounding the cold, dark street. Lynne quickly entered the last building to climb the stairs with her food box. Normally the boys and Mary Anne would be waiting on the landing watching for her, but tonight it was the sounds of other families quarreling and talking that seeped through the thin walls to fill the stairwell. Just like the scamps, Tom and Jim probably saw her coming up the stairs and ran to hide. Breathlessly, she shifted her heavy load and rested on the second landing before calling for them.

A dog barked frantically and a baby began to cry. A large, angry woman stuck her head out of the door and yelled. "Quiet, now, don't you know we all are sick here tonight."

Lynne joggled the box on her knee to get a better grip and shook her head. "No, I'm sorry Mrs. Garretty. Do you know if mother and the children are sick?"

But the woman didn't answer before slamming the door and Lynne pounded frantically up the remaining stairs to their own landing. Mary Anne opened the door for her with a small finger to her lips. Seven and small for her age, Mary Anne could have been described as the quiet child in a house full of noisy people, at least before '73. But the cholera outbreak had claimed four noisy McKinney's that year, the two babies younger than Mary, as well as her father and older brother. Now there were only the ten-year-old twins, Mary, Lynne, and her mother.

The twins came up on either side, leaning against her and then fussing over who would take the box to the kitchen. Solemnly Mary Anne leaned closer to warn her. "It's mother; she's been sick all afternoon."

Lynne caught her breath and removed a glove before laying a cool hand against the brow of each of the children to feel. All submitted without protest, as frightened by the specter of another fever as she was. "Go on, lads, put the food away. Mary Anne, pump water for the kettle and put water on to boil."

The children disappeared and Lynne stripped her shawl and other glove before pushing the curtain back. The curtain divided the large room into areas that served as kitchen, living, and dining rooms, from the corner that held her mother's large wooden bed. The other room in the apartment was divided with a similar cord and curtain, with a big bed the boys shared and a similar one she and Mary slept in. But their room was empty except for the quilt-covered beds and the pegs above them where their clothes hung.

Her mother's room could be called anything but empty. It had a complete bed suite made of burled walnut, the top of the bed curving like a sleigh over her head. A marble topped dresser sat against the wall, an ornate carved frame holding the wavy glass of its huge mirror. A tall wardrobe sat against the other corner, its doors carved to match the dresser. Lynne's mother had always been proud that they once had a lovely house of their own, full of fine furniture, not just the things in the living room and her bedroom suite. But that was before the Civil War, when her father had worked as a carpenter and had two good arms.

The sour, sweet smell of sickness frightened her before she

even peered around the curtain. For over a week, her mother had felt out of sorts, unable to work without exhaustion. The laundry from neighbors that she would have washed and ironed had been returned with an apology. The laundry made little difference on the bills, but it covered their rent and brought them cast-off clothes to wear and odd things they could use around the house like the quilts on all the beds. Since her father's death, Lynne had brought home the only money. How they would have managed without her mother paying the rent and keeping them in clothes, she couldn't imagine.

"Mother, how are you feeling?" she whispered the words soothingly as she approached the high bed, searching for her mother's slight figure among the covers.

"Wretched," the voice was a raspy whisper that sounded behind her. She turned to see her mother painfully rise and close the commode chair. There was no doubt where the odor was coming from.

Lynne moved forward to help her over to the bed. "The chamber pot has to be emptied. I'm sorry child, I didn't have the strength to do it, and I hated to send the children out with it."

Lynne carefully lifted the covers and smoothed them, before letting her mother sink down into the down mattress. "Don't worry. I'll take care of it." She covered her carefully, then frowned at the sight of her mother's beautiful face, gaunt and ghostly pale. She put a hand down to test for fever, but drew it back in shock at the clammy dampness.

Her mother's teeth suddenly began to chatter. "It's a bad fever, darling. Maybe you should take the children..." but her voice trailed off as she let her head sink backward into the pillow.

There was nowhere to take them, no one to turn to, and no money to use to leave. Tenderly Lynne poured water in the basin by the bed, then dipped, and wrung out a cloth before gently sponging off the cold sweat on her mother's face and neck. "Roll over mother, and I'll bathe you."

"No, darling," but Lynne ignored her protest and rolled the slight figure forward. Tenderly she lifted the gown and sponged the back of her legs and bottom clean. When she rolled her mother back and pulled up the covers she was shocked to see tears in her mother's eyes. She discarded the rag and leaned down to kiss her forehead, surprised by how warm and dry the skin suddenly felt. "Don't cry mother, it's nothing."

But her mother gripped her hand tightly and tilted her head to kiss her cheek. "Dearest."

"It will be all right. I'll send one of the boys for the doctor and he will bring something to make you feel right as rain."

The hand gripped her tighter and tugged so that Lynne was sitting beside her on the bed. The panic in her mother's eyes made her lean closer to hear. "No darling, not the doctor. You must use the money to pay the rent."

Lynne stared down at her, perplexed. "Nonsense, Mr. Huntmeister seems like a tyrant at times, but he'll wait for the rent payment. You're sick Mother. I have to send for the doctor."

"No, you have to listen," but suddenly she was crying so hard that Lynne couldn't understand her. She knew her mother was embarrassed by her helplessness, frightened because she was ill. Now was not the time for the stiff-necked pride that had made her turn away offers of handouts from the neighbors since her husband died.

She might have to beg the ugly landlord for time. Surely, even a fat pig like the rich German wouldn't throw out a woman and four children in the middle of winter. They would forsake their pride and beg. She would do it for her mother. With the job at the mill risky, they would have to ask for help from others.

She filled a glass with water and raised her mother to take a sip. "Rest mother, we'll talk later. I need to take care of the children for now and start supper. Relax, it will all work out for the best."

But as she carried out the basin and cloth she hesitated. Her mother was still crying weakly, and for the second time today, Lynne wondered if there was some other dimension to reality besides desperation and misery.

She opened the window to toss out the dirty water before pumping water into the basin again to clean it and the rag. She added a pinch of carbolic acid, the potion her mother swore by, before rinsing the rag thoroughly and cleaning the pan to toss the water again. Angrily she turned to look at the two pans on the cold stove. "Mary Anne, I thought I told you to boil the water."

The pale blue eyes looked up at her in the dim yellow glow of the kerosene lamp before the child crumpled. Just like her mother, she buried her face in her hands and began to cry. Lynne started to go to her, instead turned to the stove, and checked. There was one small lump inside, none in the coal box. It was late, dark, and if the signs were right, it would rain or snow again tonight.

All of Boston was awash with rainwater. An article in the Globe had suggested that the cause of the fevers that ravaged the slums each year was the incessant rain. The article claimed it was the flushing of the outhouses and privies of the fine city that led to the epidemics of dysentery, cholera, and typhoid each spring.

"Tom, Jim," she called softly, then walked out to the landing and called loudly. "Thomas and James McKinney, if you boys don't come here this minute." She heard the clatter of their brogans on the stairs and their anxious voices. "Is she all right, Lynne? Is mother going to be all right?"

The first one to reach the top anxiously buried a face at her waist and she held her arm open until the other boy had muttered his questions. "Do you wish us to fetch the doctor, sis? Do we need to go now?" then she folded him in against her.

She hugged them tightly, aware of the distant sound of Mary still crying, or was that her mother's sobs? "We'll make sure she's all right." She spoke gruffly, trying to reassure them all. "It's late out and a bad city, so stay close together. Take the cart and drag it to the coal yard. Here," she unpinned the draw bag from her skirt and pressed it into Tom's hand. "Buy all the cart will carry. Then run by the doctor's and give him the rest to come see mother." She bent swiftly to kiss each hot face before shooing them away. "Hurry now, and be careful."

Mary stood in the doorway, her small fist stuffed into her mouth to stop her tears. Tom saw her and turned to give her a hug first. "Don't be a baby, now, Mary. Go sit with mother." Jim reached out a hand to cuff her hair and then both solid little boys thundered down the stairs to the sound of dogs barking and tenants yelling.

Only when the criers were safely settled did Lynne see to the unpleasant chore of dragging the full chamber pot down the stairs and out to the privies behind the tenements. Before climbing the stairs again, she looked around the yard and managed to scoop up a broken limb and three small lumps of coal to carry inside.

CHAPTER TWO

Boston

She had scrubbed her hands and boiled water for them to drink and prepared potatoes and cabbage over the carefully tended fire by the time the boys returned, wheezing. The grumpy doctor reluctantly helped them lift the coal cart up the stairs.

"Lynne McKinney, this had better be important, dragging me out on such a night when all the city has been raging with fever and me tired and ready for my supper." He paused to catch his breath inside the door and she leaned up to kiss the cheek of the man who had delivered all of them. "She is very ill. I've plenty of supper cooked for you to share when you've had a look see."

He nodded, and then disappeared behind the curtain. Mary Anne came slipping out and backed into Lynne. Both boys stood anxiously, their cheeks bright red from the sharp cold of the night.

"Great, now you three come to your supper. Mother will be fine now the doctor is here."

She served up three plates of potato and cabbage, wishing she had butter for the potatoes or something besides salt and pepper for the cabbage. She had used a tiny piece of bacon fat to sizzle and season each vegetable, but children needed meat. Well, it was better than some would have tonight. She handed each a piece of coarse white bread with their plate and smiled.

After the blessing, Tom wanted to tell them about their trip.

"Old Mac was closing up the coal yard when we arrived." The twins had a flare for imitations and they all anticipated the story.

Jim interrupted, "Yeah, he was mad and blessed us out for keeping him from his supper."

"Quiet, I'm telling it. Anyway, we loaded the cart like you taught us, putting big chunks in first and filling with small, then big ones, and on and on till we had about twice what the cart should hold."

"How much did he charge you for it?" Lynne interrupted.

"Thirty cents."

She gasped. With the forty she had spent at the grocer's that left sixty cents for the doctor. Surely, Dr. Krantz hadn't taken that much from the boys.

Jim piped in. "Yeah, but we also filled our pockets and he nipped our ears and yelled at Tom. Said 'if he was to charge just by weighing Irish boys before and after they came into his yard, he would be rich.'" They all laughed at the broad brogue and brusque imitation of the old man.

"Yeah," Tom added. "But Jim squealed so when he tweaked his ear and told him our mum was bad sick. He tied up a sack and helped us fill it; it's there by the stove. See?"All eyes turned from the table to the large burlap bag resting against the full coal box. "So, he really ain't that worried about the money."

Tears bit at her eyes for the first time today as she rose sharply from the table. "You told him that. You let him offer you pity, and you a McKinney."

Both lowered their eyes toward their plates and the room was quiet. She stacked her plate in the sink and held the sides. Pride, stupid Irish pride. She would have to let it go. She turned to stare at the huge supply of coal. Why not be grateful and just accept the gift? They didn't have money or time for pride. She turned her head back at the three solemn children. They were good, as good as any children anywhere. Why had she had to make them share her shame?

She cleared her throat and smiled at them. "I brought a lemon and some sugar home. Would you rather have it in your tea, or as lemonade?"

"Lemonade," they piped and she laughed. "Fine, then finish your dinner and talk to me while I make it."

She carefully sliced the lemon and prepared a pitcher. Winter or no, it would taste good. It was like a miracle to see it in the store, but lately there were all kinds of fruit on display. It must be the trains running across the country that made it possible.

"Oh, I almost forgot to tell you what pretty Claire was talking about today."

Mary Anne looked up expectantly. Claire was her idol. She dreamed that someday she would work in the mill and make enough money to buy pretty bonnets and dresses like the girl who was more an aunt than her sister's friend.

"You know how she's always shopping by reading the papers and her magazines. Well today, she found one that runs ads for future husbands, and she decided she needed a young rancher in Montana."

"A cowboy, a real cowboy?" Jim asked.

Mary Anne looked entranced. For a moment, Lynne wished that she could dream of escaping to marry a cowboy. Tom saw it the way she had this afternoon. "What a goose."

Mary yelled at him, "No, it's romantic."

The children were so busy arguing that she didn't hear the doctor until he cleared his throat. When she offered him a plate, he shook his head, then motioned for her to join him outside on the landing.

"She is sick, but how sick I'm not sure. I've dosed her with sulfa drugs and magnesium hydroxide, but until we know for sure whether it's dysentery or typhoid fever, I have to ask that you and the children remain quarantined inside."

His voice was kindly, but he wanted her to understand. "If it's just the usual, she will be herself in a couple of days. However, I want you to check for a rash of small red splotches over her chest and stomach. Send for me if it shows up. With early treatment, there's a good chance. Oh, and force liquids. She's to have water, tea."

"I just made lemonade."

"Right, that would be good. But she needs broth. Just boil bones, then add salt to the liquid."

Lynne swallowed. "But, I've just bought the food for the week, and with the coal and…"

Dr. Krantz stared at her, then shook his head. "Here, the boys gave me this, but I think they overpaid me. Use what's left and get some good beef bones."

He opened the tiny cloth purse, withdrew the few coins, and hesitated. He pocketed two and forced one of the quarters back on her. "Get some meat if you can. Keep the children warm and well fed. It looks like a bad winter."

He was already descending the stairs when she saw the Garretty's door open again and knew they would try to force him in there for a few minutes. "If it is the fever?"

"If it is the fever, you'll just have to stay home and nurse her."

"But my job."

He scowled at the large woman who barred his way. "Hang the

job. Your mother needs you, girl."

Before she closed the door with a thud, she heard the stricken plea from the harsh woman below. "It's the baby, doctor, he's so pale, doctor, please come see."

She stared across to where the boys had cleared the table and now sat playing checkers with flattened bottle caps on the checked oilcloth while Mary Anne washed up the plates. It looked so normal, so routine. They were all safe. Her mother's soft voice called hoarsely and she ducked behind the curtain. A candle flickered on the high dresser beside the bed, casting shadows across the faded quilt pattern. Lynne crossed to her mother, clucking softly, noticing the glass was empty again. "Here, I'll take your glass to Mary to clean and bring you back fresh. We have lemonade and it will make you feel better."

Her mother reached out a hand to wave feebly in the flickering light. Lynne wanted to ignore it, to walk out and talk with the others, but instead she caught it in her own small hand and sat softly beside the slender form in the big bed. The feather mattress had packed down into a thin layer near the edge and the high wood of the bed panel pressed into her thigh. It felt ordinary. The room was the same as a hundred other times, warm now the fire had been burning in the kitchen stove. But her mother's eyes gleamed feverishly and she knew it would never be the same again.

"What did he say?" Her voice was so hoarse; Lynne turned and called over her shoulder. "Hey out there, someone bring lemonade for mother."

Both boys darted in through the curtain, Jim climbing between Lynne and the small figure of his mother. Lynne pushed him back off the bed and took the glass from Tom. She could see her fears in their faces and gruffly said: "That's it. Now take this dirty glass back to Mary Anne and finish your game. Mother and I want to talk awhile undisturbed."

Both stood there a moment, reluctant to leave. Lynne watched as her mother gave them a sweet smile. "Here, kiss me good night then and off you go, my darlings."

Mary had slipped like a shadow through the curtain and stood with her hands tightly held in the air, one gripping the wet wrist of the other. Her mother motioned her forward and sighed. "And you, too, baby girl. My good helper."

Only when they were alone again and she had held the glass for her to drink did Lynne look at her mother's face. She lifted the quilt, tucked it smoothly over her mother's folded arms and thin shoulders, and bent to kiss her dry forehead. She didn't want to hear this, to talk about what would have to be said. Lynne folded her hands in her lap and waited.

"You paid the doctor and bought coal. That's good, but you must listen to what I have to …to confess."

Lynne watched as her mother's gray eyes darkened with tears again and her voice broke. Anxiously Lynne leaned forward to smooth the silky tangle of dark hair back from her face. Her mother was still young, thirty-five, and still a beauty, although this fever had left her gaunt and pale.

She had always been proud when her father bragged that she looked just like her mother. How she had loved to hear him tell the story in his lilting voice of how he and her mother met on the boat to America. He a starving, out-of-luck Irishman, and her a beautiful French lady. They had loved each other dearly, so dearly. Lynne's throat tightened at the memory. Her handsome father was gone. He and Sean would never come laughing up the stairs again. Both tall, broad-shouldered, handsome men, her brother tall and manly from fifteen years on until his death at seventeen. They had worked hard and the family had plenty to eat, done so well. Then the fever came.

Her mother pulled a hand from beneath the covers to clutch at her. "Stop it. Listen to me."

Lynne looked down at her mother, shocked by her fierceness. "I'm sorry, I was just…"

"Dreaming! It's the damn Irish in you. You'll always be a dreamer like your father. But you must be strong." She coughed and Lynne offered her a sip of lemonade again.

"That's funny. Claire told me today I don't know how to dream."

"That goose," and a pale smile flickered across her mother's face. "If anything happens to me, Lynne, you have been so good and so strong, but there are things I haven't told you."

Lynne started to argue but her mother held a hand to hush her. "Listen." Her eyes darkened, but this time her voice didn't falter. "It's about the rent."

"Mr. Huntmeister has had an arrangement," her face paled and Lynne saw the tears stream down her cheek. "Don't be a fool like I was. Beg from the neighbors, the church, even your friends. Get the money to pay the rent."

The boys stuck their heads through the curtain, Tom's higher than Jim's. Mary Anne slipped through the curtain, then twisted so that her head was behind the tightly clutched drape. It was their favorite pose, the terrible two-headed McKinney girl. She shifted impatiently from foot to foot and Tom spoke in a high-pitched voice. "We need to go now, can we come in please, please."

Both women turned and laughed at them. Lynne looked at the normal accommodation and shook her head. "No, put on your coats and caps. I'll be out to walk you down in a minute."

Her mother sighed and turned her wet face toward the pillow. Whatever the terrible secret her mother had wanted to confess would have to wait until tomorrow, nature couldn't wait. She leaned forward but her mother turned away to hide her face in the shadows. Lynne pulled the covers snug. "Don't worry mother. Everything will be all right."

The only answer was a soft sob of despair.

CHAPTER THREE

Montana

Phillip slapped the neck of the big black horse, even knowing the stallion needed little urging now he had the scent of the mares. All morning the cowboy had worked to barricade the entrance with dead wood and brush. Now, if they were fast enough, they would pin the small herd in the box canyon before the scruffy mustang leader spotted the trap.

As soon as he watched the horses file through the gap in the brush, Phillip dropped from the saddle to throw the rails into place. Laughing, he stood trying to count the swirling herd as the two stallions whistled at each other over the slim logs. Phillip caught the reins and led Diamond to the outer corner of the canyon to a tree that he had left for just this purpose. He tied him securely, having to cuff the excited animal when he tried to bite him. He didn't intend to let these two fight, his horse was too valuable, and the mustang too old to be worth breaking. Once Diamond was secure and out of harm's way, he walked back to lower the top rail.

The roman nosed dun looked at him suspiciously, then bunched himself to jump the two lower rails. As soon as he flew over, Phillip slammed the top rail back into place in front of the anxious mares. Yelling, waving his hands while avoiding the kicking heels, he hazed the mustang out through the opening.

Diamond screamed his challenge but the horse was man shy enough to skedaddle. With luck, the brawny bullet head would have another string by spring and they would come back to take them away again.

Wearily, Phillip built his campfire just inside the canyon to cook his beans and boil coffee. When the stallion continued to complain and pull at the reins, Phillip removed the saddle and bedroll, then the halter and lowered the top rail for his big horse. The mares screamed and he heard the solid thud of kicks as they protested the new leader.

Phillip whistled happily as he watched the tall horse working the small herd, nipping at mares and moving them where he wanted. By daybreak, the stallion should have things settled. He just needed them docile enough to herd back to the ranch. The breaking would take time, but there were plenty of horses in the twenty that would bring him good money.

After pouring his funds into completing the cabin, cash was something he needed. Ordering and shipping a bride was expensive.

CHAPTER FOUR

Boston

Day dawned bright and cold. Lynne awoke with Mary Anne's little head curved over her arm and the boys brown curly heads like bookends on either side of her own. Stretching, she remembered calling them into her bed when they had tossed restlessly, unable to sleep. Maybe it was the occasional noise from the other room, or her fears, but she had been all too aware of the boys twisting and turning. They were too old to ask her permission to climb in, but last night she had invited them, as in need of their presence as they were of the girls.

She argued to herself that by sleeping together, they could share body heat, as well as the quilt from the other bed. But, she had really wanted to feel their firm young bodies beside her own, the strong beat of their hearts beneath her hands. She knew if her mother weren't so sick, the children would have crawled into bed with her for the same reassurance.

Carefully she untangled herself, then slipped from the warm pile of bodies, wincing as her foot touched the cold floor in the bedroom.

After dressing, she checked on her mother, relieved to find her sleeping soundly. Cautiously she moved around, stoking the fire into a blaze, then putting water on to boil for tea and porridge. Feeling the quarter in her purse beneath her belt, she pulled out the salt pork to slice for bacon. Still, she only sliced four pieces. She couldn't help but remember the breakfasts they used to have, with real bacon and eggs, warm rolls and fruit jam. She searched and pulled the tin of blackstrap from the cupboard and set it on the stove to warm. When they sat down, there would be no time to wait for the molasses to pour.

The food was on the table and church bells were chiming in the distance when the children finally crawled from the bed and dressed. Lynne was grateful. It had given her time to tend to her mother's needs. She had already filled the washtub, ready to suds out the dirty linen. She would have to hang it inside by the stove to dry since it would merely freeze on the line today, but it would allow her to change the bedding if her mother was as sick today as she had been yesterday. When Lynne remembered how feebly her mother had pushed her and the breakfast away; she couldn't help worrying that today might be the same.

She smiled brightly to greet them, but was surprised at how slowly the children moved. "Come on, get the lead out. Your oatmeal will get cold if you don't get a move on." Worriedly she stared at Mary Anne's listless gait toward the table. Was it just a week ago that her mother had felt tired and lethargic? The boys were little better, merely stirring the oatmeal after she added the molasses.

After she managed to get them to eat, she finished the porridge off and ate the two remaining strips of bacon before putting the pot and dishes to soak. "Come on, this is ridiculous. Who wants me to read them a story?"

The boys finally decided on one of her father's favorite books. She held the well-thumbed copy lovingly in her hands, smiling as she wondered if her father had been disappointed in America. Had the young Irish immigrant expected to see Iroquois sneaking around the forests near Boston?

She read the last of James Fennimore Cooper's *Deerslayer* yet again, disappointed that they had to stay inside. Mass would have been reassuring this morning, and the clear sky might be the last for a while. The winter had been strange this year. Warm and wet far later than usual. Now that it threatened to turn cold, everyone was too sick to enjoy the snow it might bring. She wondered what she would do on Monday if the children couldn't return to school and her mother was too ill for her to return to work.

She checked her mother again, this time forcing warm tea down her. Nervously she strode through the apartment, tending to small unnecessary chores. The old sofa and fainting couch were occupied by the children, the boys thumbing through the book they had just read, studying the etchings that illustrated it and arguing about whether anyone could actually walk through a forest without causing even a twig to snap. Mary Anne lay quietly against the faded tapestry of the one-armed couch, idly turning her doll back and forth, and humming to herself.

The knock at the door startled them all. Lynne patted her hair in place, then fastened the top two buttons on her shirtwaist. She was aware that the apartment smelled of coal and last night's cabbage as she walked to the door. She was surprised when Mrs. Garretty forced her way inside.

"I'm sorry," Lynne cleared her throat and waved toward the children. "Everything is rather a mess and the doctor has ordered the children to stay inside and not have contact with anyone for a few days." She hated to use the word quarantine. It made her remember last spring and the darkened doors where "Scarlet Fever --Stay Away" signs had been posted. Fortunately, she seemed to be resistant to most of the fevers that swept the tenements. Of course, typhoid fever hadn't been here for a number of years. Perhaps it would be one of the things she would catch.

Mrs. Garretty rubbed her bright round face, brushing at her red, teary eyes. "I know your mother will see me. She came to our place last week to help with my babies. Please, can I see her?"

Lynne started to argue but Mary Anne rose from the couch and pointed a finger at the large woman. "She gave Mom the fever."

Lynne stared at her sister. The child's face was a study in calm from her pale blue eyes to the soft brown of her hair. Her mouth was tightly pursed and she still held her arm out in judgment.

Mrs. Garretty burst into tears and then tried to force her way past. "You've got to let me…"

But Lynne barred her way and the twins ran up beside her. "My mother is ill and needs her rest. Haven't you done enough?"

"Let her come in." Her mother's voice, weak, and quavery, stopped the commotion. Angrily, Lynne pushed the boys back to sit beside Mary Anne, then followed Mrs. Garretty into the room with her mother. She expected her mother to chase her out, but instead she merely whispered softly, "Bring our guest a chair and some tea daughter."

Obediently Lynne turned to carry one of the strong kitchen chairs into the bedroom. Two were frail little caned chairs that could never bear the weight of their enormous neighbor. Impatiently she returned to the kitchen stove to wait for the tea to boil. Whatever they were talking about was none of her business, but still she wanted to listen in.

Her mother had been overwrought since she came home last night. With her weak and sick, she needed to be left alone, not worried with other people's problems. But then her mother had always been the one the women in the building turned to for advice. Beautiful and educated, they were at times pettily jealous of her, at others in awe of her wisdom. No wonder her mother had always been too proud to go to them for help. Lynne couldn't help wondering what it had cost her mother to take in laundry from the likes of a woman like Laura Garretty.

As Lynne poured the tea, she debated carrying the sugar in as well. No, her mother was too sick and the sweetness would only make her bowels weepier, while the other woman would probably fill her cup with the precious grains. She did place two slices of plain bread on the tray. Her mother would be more upset if she were inhospitable than if she had to go without bread at supper.

Lynne entered the room quietly, pretending to not listen as she carried the tray to her mother's dresser top. Carefully she pushed aside the silver backed brush and comb, treasures her mother had carried from France, to make room for the tray.

"Harold died last night. I know you understand how I feel. But, James says we cannot afford a religious ceremony. He says if we bury him in the pauper's field, the city will pay for it and provide a minister to read over him. I am beside myself with worry."

Lynne poured the tea and offered the crying woman a cup. She wanted to be hard and ignore her, especially when she saw her mother sagging sideways against her pillows in fatigue. Carefully she raised her mother up and plumped her pillows to prop her into a sitting position. She poured a second cup and held it to her mother's lips, hearing the bleakness in the voice of the woman who was making demands on her, even now when she was sick and helpless herself. Lynne wanted to tell her to leave, take her woes away, but again her mother's soft voice stopped her.

"Your James is wise. Your other baby is two isn't he?"

"Aye, just two years, but he isn't that sick yet."

"I remember the winter of '73, do you remember it?" She didn't look at her guest and Lynne wasn't sure if she was talking to herself or to the woman waiting on her advice. "I lost two babies that February. It was cold and rainy, like it is now. I thought I would die then, but John wouldn't let me. There were the other children to care for, and then he and my older boy Sean came down with the fever. Do you remember my handsome husband and son?"

Again she didn't look up, didn't see the woman nodding. "They were so big and strong, only sick a little while, then back out to work. But when the scaffold fell, they were too weak, too slow, to get out of the way." She paused for breath, leaning back against the pillow to close her eyes.

Lynne felt the tightness around her own heart, tasted the pain and tears of that bitter winter. But Mrs. Garretty hadn't come to hear their woes, to share their tears. In a loud, complaining voice she began again. "I know life has been hard for you, Mrs. McKinney, but now, now my baby has died, and I cannot go on in life if he is buried like some dead beggar in unconsecrated ground."

Her mother opened eyes as gray and stormy as the winter sky outside. "Do not be a fool? The child is gone, the others live. You must always do for the living, God will look after the souls of the dead."

Mrs. Garretty stood so abruptly, the chair scooted backward and Lynne had to spring forward to keep it from crashing to the floor. The big woman crossed her hand over her chest and muttered an oath. "'Tis fine for a nonbeliever like yourself, burying your bairns and men in such a place, but I be a good Catholic and ..."

Lynne watched as her mother's face flushed scarlet and she swayed forward, her eyes swimming in tears. Angrily she stepped between them and urged the larger woman backward. "That is more than enough. My mother has had more than enough of your problems." But again her mother's voice cut through the commotion and Lynne heard the painful voice with clarity. "What matters your conscience when you have the lives of your children to care for? Leave it in God's hand. Spend the money on the living while you still have them."

Furiously, Lynn backed the big woman out, then returned to her mother who was shaking with coughs, her face strained and her fists clenched into the bed. "Damn," she gasped. "Oh, Lynne, look what I've done now?"

Only when she had helped her mother to the commode and stripped the soiled bedding, did Lynn stop shaking. "How dare that woman? How dare she? Why did she come for advice and help, then yell at you like that?"

But her mother merely coughed weakly. Lynne heard the boys calling anxiously and her mother shook her head, "Shh, don't frighten the children. Bundle them up and send them out to play until we get the mess cleaned up."

Frustrated, Lynne stopped and stared at her mother, coughing painfully as she held her soiled gown out from her body. She started to tell her the doctor had warned her to keep them isolated from the others, but couldn't stand to upset her anymore. Reluctantly she bundled them, catching the boys to her as she stared at Mary Anne's gray face. "Stay inside the building, play on the landings and the stairs quietly. I'll call you when you can come back inside.

Remember, keep, Mary Anne with you."

Satisfied that there was nothing else she could do, she returned to the mess inside. She had restored order, padding the bed with towels and remaking it with the sheets from the boy's bed. She already had the dirty linen and her mother's gown in suds while her mother trembled and shivered as she sponged off. Satisfied that she had them clean, Lynne left the sheets to soak in the sink and returned with a clean gown for her mother. Suddenly she shook in horror, moving to numbly help her mother pull the fresh cotton over her red splotched body.

Only when her mother was asleep, the laundry hung from lines around the kitchen, and supper cooking, did Lynne sit down at the table. She brought a hand to cover her mouth to keep from crying, but couldn't keep the sobs from shaking her shoulders and the tears from falling. When she had cried the last hot tear, she rose to follow her mother's advice. She had to be strong and tend to the living.

They came when she called, slowly climbing the stairs. Lynne's guilt washed over her for the time she had wasted crying and feeling sorry for herself. Even though they were bundled up and dry inside the stairwell of the building, they hadn't been warm. The cold wind howled through the thin boards at the front and back of the tenement, making inside little warmer than outside. The same sickly sweet smells of sickness permeated the entire building, not just their apartment, as many of the tenants placed full slop jars outside their own rooms onto the landing.

Well, she couldn't undo the tears. Instead she held out her arms and welcomed them to her, pulling them into the warm apartment with enthusiasm. "Come on into the warmth, you sluggards. Suppers ready and I've sugar and lemon rind. Who wants to help me make tea cakes?"

◇◇◇

Monday it rained. Lynne left the children sleeping in the bed, unwilling to wake them and try to entertain them again when her mother was so sick. At least now she could go and fetch the doctor. She would visit the butchers along the way. Maybe if she hurried, she could even see Bonnie or Claire and have them take a message to the foreman, though lord knew if it would make any difference to him why she missed work.

Frantically she retraced her steps of Saturday, exhausted despite the day off from the mills. Even though the work day had been shortened to ten hours, the six day week left little time for the dozens of things at home. She had never realized how hard her mother's lot was with laundry and cooking, besides all the work she took in from the neighbors.

Well Lynne could at least do that one thing now she was stuck at home. They wouldn't have to send back the work baskets like last week. If she worked hard, the family would have what her mother normally earned to pay bills this week. And if she managed, and the doctor would come without charging, and …

She waved a handkerchief at her friends, stepping up on the boardwalk out of the worst of the downpour. Bonnie smiled grimly, holding her rain slicker tight against her but Lynne thought she saw a dark streak on the usually pale complexion. If that devil had laid a hand on her she would tell Tarn Michaels where to go. It was Claire who stopped and called to her. "Hurry up, it's cold but you won't melt in the rain."

Lynne leaned forward, holding her cape high to deflect the cold drizzle. "I'm not going to be there today. Tell the foreman my mother is sick with fever, and the children and I have been quarantined."

Claire's brow puckered and both women stared anxiously at her as others crowded past them down the muddy pathway. "Good grief, Lynne," Bonnie called, "It's not a good time to be missing work."

Lynne wanted to yell I know, I know, but obviously Bonnie appreciated how tenuous their positions were or she would never have been going to work in her condition. "Are you all right this morning? Has Tarn gotten out of line again?"

Bonnie stood still, her eyes as dark as her hair in the cold drizzle. "I've left him and gone home to mother. If he doesn't straighten up, I'm through with him."

Lynne leaned forward. There was so much to talk about, so much pain in her friend's voice. She wanted to ask her about the baby, about work, whether he hit her before or after she told him she was leaving. But there was no time. The girls could be sacked if they were late to work.

Claire looked up the path at the backs of the retreating women, then whispered something to Bonnie. Lynne watched as the other waddled cautiously forward after the departing group. "I've got to be going too, Lynne. Perhaps I can come by this evening with news."

Lynne waved at her, "Go on, hurry, but don't bother about tonight. There's sickness in our building, you'd best stay away. I'll come back this afternoon to talk from here if I can."

She snapped the rain from her cloak before she walked into the butchers, fingering the coin in her pocket. Broth her mother needed, and broth she would have, but she would have to save some money to get the doctor to come again. The butcher glared at her as though he had never seen her. Lynne pushed back her damp hair and laughed nervously. He probably hadn't. The little meat they bought came from the grocers and most of it was salted or smoked so it would keep for a long time.

"I need some bones. Something to make broth and soup for some who are sick."

He eyed her coldly. "Wait there. I don't have anything to give away. Can you pay?"

Lynne stepped from foot to foot to generate some warmth. "How much are your bones?"

He tore a white sheet of paper and laid it on the scale, then lifted a large white beef bone to the scale. "Five cents a pound."

"And that is?"

"He scoffed, then threw on three smaller bones. That's one pound."

She nodded. "How much for a chicken?"

She left the store with her precious sack of bones and half a chicken. That left fifteen cents for the doctor and medicine. She tried to remember what he had prescribed Saturday night. She paused outside the pharmacists. She knew she needed some more carbolic acid to sterilize things with. It sounded like sulfur he had made mother drink, but what had he given her for her bowels? If she waited, Dr. Krantz could prescribe it, but perhaps he would want paid to tell her.

Decided, she slipped inside the pharmacist. It was foolish to trust to the kindness of someone as mercenary as a doctor. Hadn't he taken thirty-five cents last night? Today she had far less to offer him. With the children feeling poorly and her unable to work, she might have to doctor them on her own. She purchased a precious ten cents worth of chemicals and left the druggist smiling. It was sulfa drugs and she had a small tin of those and something with magnesium something or other in it for their stomachs as well as the strong chemicals she needed to disinfect the sick room.

Now if she could fetch the doctor, she could return home to her family who needed her. Lynne turned to head back to the other end of town when a large form blocked her way. "My, my, what do we have here?"

Startled, she backed away, glaring up at the imposing figure with the thick German accent. "Hello, Herr Huntmeister. I was meaning to come to your offices."

"Please do child, please come in out of the rain. I thought I saw you walk past earlier. Isn't it lucky I came out to make sure?"

All the time he was edging closer, his voice thick and unctuous with mock concern. Lynne couldn't avoid him without backing down into the mud of the street.

"You are the McKinney girl aren't you? Of course you are." He didn't wait for an answer, merely gripped her elbow, and tugged her forward. Lynne clutched frantically at her packages and started to dig her feet in. Even as he pushed open his office door behind him she fought the panic welling up inside her. She felt like some unsuspecting insect, caught by a spider and being pulled into his web. It would be ridiculous for her to scream for help, but then she would be no match at fighting him. Instantly she quit struggling, instead bringing a hand up to cover her mouth as she coughed dramatically.

"Thank you, you're most kind. 'Tis terrible weather outside, and as you know we all have been so sick. I was just rushing to fetch a doctor for my dear mother."

It worked as effectively as though she had struck him and he let go of her arm so fast that she almost fell back through the open doorway. "Oh, yes, I knew your mother was sick. She complained a little when I was there on Friday a week ago, to collect for the rent."

He said the last, with a husky voice that sounded dirty. Lynne blushed when he added in a low voice. "You know we have a special arrangement to pay the rent, your mother and I."

Lynne felt suddenly hot and uncomfortable. He stepped back from her, waving her toward a chair. "Child, you must take time at least to talk with an old family friend, if only for a minute."

Lynne hesitated. Her instinct was to run, to run as fast and far as she could from this obnoxious man. But the memory of her mother's sobs and attempted confession compelled her to enter and take the chair he indicated. She had to know. Of course, it could be nothing serious, but it had upset her mother so much about being late with the rent. She had to make sure that the man would wait until she could pay again. She tried to steel her nerve, gather her wits. They had to talk.

Calmly, as though she did business with men like him every day, she walked into the office and sank into the chair, letting her wet bundles rest in her lap. The weight of the raw bones was solid and comforting on her knees. She could bolt up like a savage and hit him with the long thigh bone if he threatened her. There was nothing to be gained by panicking, everything by calm negotiation.

"Yes," he walked around behind his desk, positioning his chair cautiously before plopping down into its brown leather cushions. He stared at her with a smirk on his face that Lynne decided could only be called a leer. Slowly he lit a long, black cigar, and then blew smoke toward her. "You are the spitting image of your mother. Only younger, younger, and prettier." He leaned back in his chair and his voice was strangely slurred as he suggested. "Why don't you take off that wet cloak, rest for a while?"

Lynne gripped the arm of the chair tightly, clutching her weapon with the other. How could every word the man spoke sound so evil? "I don't have time. My mother is ill with the fever, and the children need someone at home. I must fetch the doctor." She lifted her hand to cover her mouth in a lady-like cough as the foul cigar smoke reached her.

"Your mother has a fever? I knew she was sick, that is why I didn't come by Friday to collect. But if she is seriously ill, who will pay the rent?"

His words rolled like thunder into the room and Lynne shivered. "I've just come from buying medicine, and I'm sure after the doctor comes she will be better," she blurted.

He rose from his high-backed chair, pacing slowly behind his desk as she talked, his dark eyes devouring her so she felt rigid, like some rabbit being stalked by a big cat. "The rent is already a week over due. If she isn't well by Friday, it will be two weeks overdue. I have people waiting, people who can pay, people who want to rent an apartment now that it's winter."

The threat was real. Money, she had to know how much money they were talking about. "I work for Waltham's, in the sewing room. I earn .90 cents a week, more if I surpass the quota. Last week I earned 1.30. If mother doesn't get better, I can pay the rent."

His eyes glittered, and he smiled at her again. A smile that didn't reach his cold, hard eyes and she shivered in fear. "How wonderful. The apartment rents for seventy-five cents a week. Can you afford to pay seventy-five cents a week?"

Her mouth suddenly felt dry and her heartbeat slowed. So much. How had her mother ever managed to pay so much? How would she manage if something happened to her mother now?

The children. Could she let the boys go to work at the mill, could she let little Mary Anne? She had seen those children, their eyes as old and dark as death, their bodies twisted and scarred as they wound around and around the swinging booms of the knitting machines, replacing thread in the shuttle. Or worse, walking like little monkeys around the cauldrons of boiling dye and starch, balancing to dunk in new ingredients into the vats to keep the consistency constant.

She remembered when one small boy had fallen in. It was the first week she had gone to work, she and her two friends who had come of age the same spring. At thirteen all three were little women, thrilled to be hired at the mills. They had been proud to have real jobs. She would be able to help her mother, her poor mother who had lost so much that winter. Bonnie's situation was similar. Although she had both parents, with ten other children at home, her check would be used to pay bills. And pretty Claire, she had been so excited to have a job with her friends. She had been glad to leave school and though her parents worked and had plenty with just the one child, the money came in handy for buying the pretty clothes she had always wanted.

Then the little boy fell in. Had he been ten like they were told, or younger? It didn't matter. The foreman didn't even hurry. The girls had all three screamed and cried until they had been warned by older ones to shut up. After all, there was no hurry. The child had died within minutes. They waited until the room had cleared before straining him out like some undesirable lump from the huge cauldron. They were told the meat was cooked from his bones and they had to be careful to get every bit of him or it would waste the whole solution.

She bit her lip, staring fixedly at the small brass clock over the huge desk. His laugh came close to her ear, startling her. She tilted her head so that her cloak fell back revealing her soft, brown hair. He was so close she could feel his hot breath on her cheek, smell the sour odor of smoke and evil. "Your mother and I came to an arrangement. If something were to happen to her, I would be willing to continue the arrangement with you."

Lynne turned dark lashed gray eyes to stare into his evil black ones. Her voice was a mere squeak as she asked, her knees bouncing beneath the damp packages on her lap. "What kind of arrangement?"

He laughed, his voice vibrating through her as he reached out a large hand to trace her trembling, heart shaped face. "You are so lovely my dear. More beautiful even than your lovely mother. He leaned forward and her stomach quivered in fear. Such a sweet, innocent flower." He leaned close enough to stick a wet tongue on her cheek and she bolted, no longer hypnotized by his voice.

He laughed and laughed.

Unable to hide her fear, unwilling to surrender, she scrambled for the packages that had fallen from her lap. As soon as they were secure she waited between the door and the chair he now stood over. "What kind of arrangement sir?"

He straightened, staring at her steadily as he answered. "Every Friday I came by the apartment to collect the rent. Every Friday your dear mama lowered her ragged bloomers and let me do whatever I wanted. Then I gave her a receipt and left."

He eyed her flushed face speculatively. "You my precious, you I would be even more generous with."

Lynne turned, struggling with the door. She swore when it wouldn't open and then shrank back when he came up behind her and reached around to open it. "Next Friday, Miss McKinney. Pay the price next Friday or you, your sick mother, your dear little sister, those darling brothers, all of you will be out on the street."

Finally, Lynn reached the doctor's office. When he finally appeared, she pulled the nickel from her pocket, pressed it into his palm and folded the thin, bony fingers closed over it. "I will pay more later, but you have to come now. It is the Typhoid like you warned. And mother is weak, so very weak."

He opened his palm, looked at the nickel coldly. "Insane, that's what I am. To go out in such weather for such a case, I must be insane."

Lynne stood and repeated her words. "I will pay more later."

He laughed, or perhaps it was a cough. As they both walked out into the cold she realized the truth. Her mother had done what she had to for the family. But Lynne wouldn't be beaten by some foul, dirty old man. She would sell the furniture, borrow from friends, even answer an ad to marry a stranger. Never, never would she pay the price her mother had.

CHAPTER FIVE

Boston

Lynne held the bowl and spoon patiently, it was so much like feeding the babies. She could remember helping with the twins and Mary Anne, but it was the two who were lost that she could visualize this morning. Danny with his devilish blue eyes and a long curl of blonde hair that rose on top of his head like a rooster's comb. He had been all swagger and brawn, even as a baby, so much like his father and older brother Sean. He had been almost three when the fever came to take him. Nan had been barely one, a sleepy-eyed angel with red tinged curls. Were the babies both in heaven? Surely they were there, looking like perfect cherubs, but keeping the older angels on their toes with their mischief. She smiled as she tipped the bowl closer, letting the edge extend beneath her mother's chin as she gently fed her the broth.

Doctor Krantz had come and gone for all the good he had done her mother. Yes, she did have typhoid fever, all the symptoms were clear. No, there was no magic cure. With bed rest, liquids, and time, she should recover. Of course if there were complications such as pneumonia or a secondary infection, well then, he could make no promises. If all of that hadn't been obvious to even a ninny, he pointed out that the fever was highly contagious and she should watch the children for symptoms. Of course, he had added, it was highly likely they were all already infected with it, since they lived in such close proximity with the patient.

He had been impatient and brusque and Lynne winced at the careless way he touched her mother. Delicate at any time, now ill, her mother was as fragile as a dandelion puff. Lynne wanted him to leave, to stop his pulling, poking and prodding. Her mother had bit her pale lips to keep from crying out a couple of times and she sighed in exhaustion when he finally finished his examination.

After he left, Lynne was so frustrated and angry, she complained loudly. "What's the point of paying someone your last nickel if they only give you two cents worth of advice, and all of it commonsense?" Of course she didn't add that she had promised him her first earnings when he had laughed at her attempt to pay him. But if it was so paltry, why hadn't he given the money back?

Her mother twisted under the complaints and Lynne swallowed her anger, trying to find something reassuring to talk about besides money. At least her mother's stomach had settled. The apartment was warm, lunch had been cooked and eaten. They had all enjoyed the fresh vegetable soup with its delicious thick beef broth. It was a pity she could only feed her mother the broth.

The rich liquid tilted from the spoon, then spilled down along her mother's chin. It had to be the fiftieth time she had tried. If any liquid was going down, she couldn't tell it by the amount of liquid left in the bowl. Her knee began to bounce, something it automatically did when she was nervous.

"Good, mmm, it's so good mother." For a moment she thought she saw the thin lips move. "That's the way, eat up and get better. You heard Dr. Krantz. You have the fever but you should recover if you rest and get plenty of liquids."

She could feel the red-rimmed eyes staring at her, looking as though she had a hundred questions. She had told her mother about seeing the landlord, but had merely told her he had agreed to wait for the rent since she was so sick. Was that what all the questions were?

"Did you see what a lovely set of beef bones the butcher sent, all heavy with meat and dark red marrow? And a chicken. So fresh and tender, it looks as though it can say 'Cock-a-doodle-do' or cackle and lay an egg. Tonight I will make chicken and dumplings for the children and some nice chicken soup for you."

Her mother smiled weakly at her silly crow and cackle and Lynne smiled in triumph as a little broth slipped down her throat. It was short lived, as it set her mother into an immediate coughing fit. Lynne scrambled to set the bowl down and grab the tea towel to dry her face as she lifted her mother upright. The coughs that racked the frail body brought tears to her eyes and Lynne slipped around to cushion her mother's head and back against her shoulder. Gently she rocked her and patted her back as though she were a small child, crooning soothingly against her face. Her skin was so thin over her temple, Lynne could feel the blood that pulsed blue in her vein there and she tenderly kissed it before laying her down.

As she started to pick the bowl up again her mother feebly raised a hand to protest. "Rest," she croaked.

Lynne nodded and bent to kiss her forehead and pull the covers up to tuck her in. "I love you, mother. Rest now and don't worry. Everything is all right."

She could tell from the way she sank into the pillows that her mother wanted to speak again. But a moment after, her lashes flickered down and she was asleep. Lynne remained standing there for a few minutes, just gazing at the lovely face, so ravaged by illness. She smoothed the silky hair back from her mother's face and wished she could wash and comb it. Combing out each other's hair was always so relaxing for both of them. But even as she smoothed her hair back, the questions haunted her. Was what Mr. Huntmeister told her true?

Asleep, her mother's deep set eyes were softly veiled by purplish eyelids. Lynne could imagine the sweeping lashes raised and the pale gray of her eyes staring into her own gray ones. They had always been close, so close. Her mother never lied. She knew that if she looked into her eyes and asked the question, she would see the truth of his accusations. But how could she ask such a question of her own mother?

A knock on the outer door brought her to her feet and out to check on the children. It was Mrs. Garretty, this time with two over-flowing baskets of laundry and another sad tale. Lynne listened patiently, but when the large woman started giving her orders about how she wanted things starched and ironed, she placed one hand on her hip and held out her open palm. "Of course it will be to your satisfaction, but I'll see the money up front."

"Are you crazy? I've just buried my baby and the other children are coming down sick. I figured with you being home you could do the laundry in your mother's place. She would never have asked for money at a time like this. She be a lady."

The last was said so loudly, Lynne could smell the onions on the hot breath that touched her. "Aye, and my mother, the dear lady, is sick in bed (because of you she almost added) and I cannot go to work, so we need the money. I will gladly do the laundry, and a good job of it, but I must have the money up front."

Red faced, she slammed the door after the woman had called her every name but neighbor. Tom stood up beside her, his anger clear in the red lines along his cheeks, but Jim and Mary Anne only managed to stare in awe after the loud argument. Embarrassed, still angry, Lynne looked round at all three of them. "Well. I guess that's one job I won't have to do today. Can you imagine Mrs. high and mighty this evening though, when she's washed and hung out all those smelly clothes. She'll be a fright to see then."

"She's a fright to see now,' laughed Jim. But by then her whole body will be boiled red like her fat cheeks, her carrot colored hair will be standing on end, and her fingers will be all wrinkly like prunes." He shuddered, then got up to stomp around the living room like a much smaller version of Laura Garretty or was it some kind of troll.

Mary Anne dissolved into giggles, but when Tom played poor Mr. Garretty, coming home tired from his work at the docks, they all became weak from laughter. "Aye, I'm home dear wife." He pretended to look around in a surprised way. "He's expecting to come into a lovely home with his nice hot cabbage and potatoes on the table," he whispered in a stage direction. "But all he can see is a room full of wash hung up to dry, and what's that I see." He peeked around the towels that still hung from their own wash line and screamed in horror as Jim made a big face and came charging toward him, swearing as only a lady like the boiled Mrs. Garretty could do.

They were in a tangle of laughter, both girls hugging the boys to keep them from repeating their performance, when another knock came at the door. She signaled for the children to be quiet and wiped tears from her own eyes.

This time the laundry and money were accepted from the caller and the group set to work. The children cleared away the food and the boys helped her fill the washtub. Afterward, she made them sit quietly on the couch to rest while she stood over the hot washboard and worked on the clothes. Both boys read quietly, but Mary Anne continued to fidget. Lynne finally sent her in to watch after their mother, with orders to force water down her if she woke up.

The afternoon passed peacefully. Two more real ladies brought laundry and gladly paid. Luckily it wasn't raining or snowing so the boys helped her carry it down and out into the yard to hang up. They played quietly outside, standing guard on the precious clothes while Lynne washed the next batch. She cautiously set up the ironing board, taking care not to bump the lines of delicate linens that hung round the kitchen, and placed both heavy irons on the stove top to heat.

Outside, she plucked pins from the still damp clothes and tucked them in her mouth, as she dropped garments carefully into the basket. It took her awhile to master the techniques her mother made look so effortless, but she managed not to spit out the soapy tasting wood. Then she reused the wooden pegs to hang more garments up. The morning rain had ended long ago, leaving the ground only slightly muddier than before. The afternoon was now cold and dry. Not biting or windy, just a still cold that drew the moisture quickly from the cotton. Lynne fussed at the boys running in and out beneath the waving clothes lines for taking a chance on sliding and pulling down the mornings work. Both had cheeks that were red bitten, their eyes feverish bright from their noisy game of war. She ordered them to play inside the building with their stick weapons, but to peek out from time to time.

As she trudged up the stairs under the weight of the clothes she would have to iron, she marveled at the noise and energy of the two lads. She could hear their excited voices rising up the stairwell as they continued to play, changing the rules of combat from battlefield to cowboys and Indians. Inside their fort, they could keep a watch out for pesky redskins that might try to sneak up on the settlement. Each had staked out a nice round peep hole to poke their guns through and she knew the laundry would be safe. Maybe if Mary Anne was rested, she would let the little girl join them.

Lynne somehow managed to prepare supper, watching the chicken cook down while ironing the last few garments. Mary Anne had marshaled their troops and seen to the collection of the last clothes on the line. Lynne pressed the pleated front of a man's dress shirt, the last she had to iron, and handed it to her sister to fold. Without resting, she scooped flour into a bowl and cracked an egg into the middle of it as she watched her little sister sit primly folding the last garments. While Lynne worked the ingredients into a smooth pastry, she watched Mary Anne smooth and pack the delicate undergarments as she removed them from the inside lines. It was clear the little girl helped their mother at these chores on laundry day. Everything was carefully sorted and ready when the messengers finally arrived for the clean clothes.

By the time the last of the laundry was collected, Lynne was exhausted. She sat at the table, staring at the children who had worked at her side all day, neither complaining nor slacking off, until everything was completed. Quickly she bent her head in prayer. There was so much to be grateful for tonight. Together they had earned sixteen cents. True it wasn't enough to pay the rent, but she would figure out something by Friday. Her mother had rested all day, she would soon be stronger. Although Lynne felt unusually tired and achy, she also felt satisfied. Together, they could accomplish anything.

Tuesday was a nightmare. Lynne woke with her head aching and her throat sore. Worse, she had a queasy stomach. When she was finally dressed, she drug her way through the chores. At least there was plenty of food cooked in the window box. With the cold weather, anything they put in it was kept from spoiling. She made tea and porridge, than gave way to nature yet again.

The children felt nearly as badly. When everyone was seen to, she decided to dose them all and debated whether to add sulfur or the magnesium compound to the water.

Lynne set down the tray of steaming broth and tea, then fled to their bedroom. When she returned, her mother stared at her from the tall bed, managing to raise one hand to feel her temperature. "Tend to your stomach first. Use the magnesium." Then she swung slim legs over the side of the bed, the gown bunching nearly to her knees. "Maybe I can take over today."

But Lynne twirled and managed to catch her before she fell. "Nonsense. It's bed rest for you, and for us all."

She was able to get her mother to drink the broth, although she merely sipped the tea. The worst chore of the day was one Lynne insisted on tending to herself. Once she had returned with the clean bowls, she sprinkled the damp white interiors with carbolic acid crystals. Thin trails of smoke floated up filling the bedroom air with a sharp, acrid odor of sterilization.

The children didn't complain. Although it was clear they were not feeling well themselves, they didn't have the queasy stomach yet. Lynne was again telling herself how lucky she was as she wiped the sweat from the kitchen window. It took her several minutes to realize that in the short time since she had returned upstairs, it had started to snow. Dissatisfied at her glimpse of the weather through the small circle, she pressed her forehead against the cold dampness of the glass and raised the window to look out. Snow fell on her feverish brow and she could almost imagine the flakes sizzling as they soothed the back of her open throat.

Tom startled her and she swung her head to look down at him. But the sudden movement made her dizzy. Tightly Lynne closed her eyes and leaned forward out the window again, hoping she was far enough away so that the porridge and foul-tasting tea struck the ground not the building.

Jim yelled, "Oh Gross," Tom made a gagging sound and Lynne backed up to give him room at the window. When he didn't throw up, she thought about pitching him out the opening. Her look must have said so, for both boys quickly apologized.

It was the kind of day that could only get worse. Amazingly it didn't. The weather kept people in, or else the fever. As the children began to sneeze and their noses ran, Lynne decided they were merely coming down with colds. She rubbed their small chests with eucalyptus salve, wiped noses and made them blow good, then left them with handkerchiefs beneath their pillows and snow cooled water on the table between their beds. Once they were all three tucked in for the day and her mother made comfortable, Lynne made a nest for herself on the couch, a book in one hand and a down comforter over her feet and lap. When no one came, she read and dozed.

By supper-time, blessedly, the queasiness was gone. Lynne made chicken noodle soup for them all from the remaining meat and broth. She was grateful when her mother made a real effort to drink the warm broth. She smiled when a soft hand landed lightly on her forehead. Her skin was dry and only barely warm and her mother smiled.

"Good," she whispered, "I was afraid you would make yourself sick trying to do everything for all of us." She patted the bed beside her, and Lynne sat down, tempted for several minutes to lie down to sleep beside her. But her mother was still pale and warm to the touch.

"No, it would be better for us all if I play doctor again." She prepared hot sulfa water for all of them. The yellow powder dissolved, filling the room with the powerful smell of rotten eggs. The children could barely down a spoonful each, and only with their noses pinched closed. Even Jim muttered something about poisoning them all. She finally tucked them all back into bed, and retired to her bed on the sofa to toss uncomfortably through the night. Visions of Mrs. Garretty and the fat landlord played themselves out in her mind. Only in her dream, it was the fat Irish woman who had the special arrangement with the landlord, not her saintly mother.

Somehow she made it through the week. By Wednesday she was well enough to work again, and went to two houses to see about the laundry. At one lovely brownstone, she helped clean up and washed clothes there, leaving when they were hung out on the line, the pennies in her purse. At the other, she brought a basket of laundry home to clean and mend just in time to prepare lunch for the invalids. The children were listless, their noses clogged and messy. She brought all three to the table and set them under a sheet draped kettle. When the croup pot loosened up the congestion, all three began to cough and sneeze. She doctored them and put them back to bed to sleep after mugs of warm broth for their meal.

Her mother obstinately tried to get up to help, but Lynne complained she would be more trouble than help. She gave her mother the job of listening to the sick that she had assigned to Mary Anne earlier in the week. Contented, Lynne worked in the quiet apartment, washing the clothes. Then she hung them up in the apartment to dry, satisfied the additional moisture would help the children breathe.

Only when the room was draped with the wet curtains of clean laundry, did she move light-headed among them. The heat from the coal stove warmed the air until it was smothering to her and she thought about slipping out of her shirtwaist, so heavy with the weight of sweat and spilled soapy water. It was confining, all of life was confining. As she reclined on the sofa, she intended to only rest for a few minutes.

It was Tom shaking her shoulders that finally woke her. Someone was pounding on the door, and all the time she thought it was her pounding head. She stared at his serious eyes, then noticed the runny nose. Only when she had wiped it did she sit up and walk to the door. She couldn't help but notice that Tom was still there, her personal watch dog and protector, as she opened the door. A boy little different than the one behind her stood outside, his cheeks red, his gaze angry. Startled by the time, she promised the messenger that if he returned in an hour, the laundry would be ready. Frantically she ironed and folded, disappointed that she couldn't do it as well as little Mary Anne, but unwilling to awaken the sleeping child.

Tom sat, asking endless questions, barely pausing while she made the answers that he had long ago memorized. "How big is an elephant? How deep is the ocean? How old is the oldest human?" On and on he droned. Only the sound of his voice kept her awake long enough to finish the laundry. Still the messenger returned and had to wait ten minutes before getting his final load of clothes.

Lynne was embarrassed, at her work and the delay, and the boy who had come for the clothes was definitely displeased. What if he didn't bring the laundry to her the next time? Lynne became disgustingly civil and apologetic, but held the purse with its paltry coins closed. Like the tight-fisted doctor, she didn't give the money back. One more day. She had to work everything out by tomorrow.

The children ate without commotion, their colds taking away all their usual snarl and snap antics. Lynne was short tempered, relieved that all obeyed her instantly. For the second night in a row, she slept alone on the fainting couch.

Thursday brought more of the same, but all four invalids insisted on being up and underfoot. Lynne tolerated it, but worried that her mother's not staying in bed might cause a relapse. Slowly, she pushed herself to do up three more loads of laundry. After supper, the children were exhausted and went to bed without protest. By nightfall, Lynne was as tired as though she were a hundred. She couldn't have washed out a hankie, let alone another load of sheets. But tomorrow the landlord would come. Nervously, she tidied up the kitchen. If she hurried in the morning, she might get out to collect more laundry, maybe some mending.

The money had been hard to come by, but she now had thirty-six cents. One of the customers had only been able to pay with produce, but Lynne gladly accepted the food. She had washed the bearded turnip greens and had boiled them along with three of the purple and white turnips. She had even baked bread in the oven, the first time in several days. The customer had brought milk and butter and though she didn't let anyone have milk yet, she made some plain pudding and served butter on the warm bread.

Lots to be grateful for, another very good day. Fortunately, they had coal and the stove was near the sink, so they had plenty of water. It was cold enough outside that some of the neighbor's pipes had frozen. Concerned, Lynne cleaned every container in the apartment, then frantically stood and pumped water to fill them all.

Her mother tottered back into the kitchen and stood with her hands tightly gripping the ladder back of one of the caned chairs as the pipes clanged and groaned. "Bridget Lynne McKinney, this is madness. The children are better, your stomach is better, and I am all but well. Please rest so that I can."

Lynne stared at her, noticing how thin her mother looked, how she shivered in the warm room. "I have to mother, it may not snow again tomorrow." The panic that she felt made her voice quaver and break around the angry words. "The water might freeze. If anyone brings laundry, I have to be ready. I have to make more money. Tomorrow the landlord comes."

Her mother stared at her and Lynne couldn't keep the terrible fear from her eyes. She watched as her mother gasped in horror, then sank down in the chair, covering her face with her thin, white hands. Over the loud clamor from the complaining pipe she heard her mother's keening. She let go of the pump handle and it jumped twice on its own. She barely stepped back as the last of the water splashed into the nearly full washtub.

Quickly she drug round a chair and sank into it, her legs dangling down the sides as she sat spraddle-legged in it, her chin leaning against the top rung of its back. Frantically she pursed her lips in a shushing sound, raising her hands toward her mother's face, but unable to complete the task of reaching over to hush her. It was her mother's hand that moved to clamp in a death grip over her open mouth, the horrible high-pitched sound muffled and distorted by her fingers.

If only the world would stop turning, halt its frantic circling of the sun until she could sleep and everyone could get well again. Her own head throbbed, and Lynne knew the red blush over her face and chest was not from the cold water alone. She had the fever. All the symptoms. It left her light-headed and unable to cope with one more thing. At least she only had a mild case, the sick stomach and sore throat were gone, and by tomorrow her flush should begin to fade. By Saturday, Monday at the latest, she would be able to return to the mill. Her mother could take over at home. But all the reasoning was not enough to prevent the anguish in her mother's eyes, the hot tears that splashed down her cheeks.

There was a choking, barking sound now, and Lynne leaned her head forward so that the weight of it rested against her mother's furrowed brow. She could feel the hot tears on her own face, taste their salt. In horror, she realized the sobs were her own.

Her mother stood up, clutching a hand at her heart, one hand still gripped across her mouth. Her body swayed as she crossed the room, her body making a stiff moaning sound as though she were the string on a harp that someone had plucked too harshly. Lynne watched her through burning eyes as she brought her own fist up to stuff in her mouth. In the sudden stillness she finally heard her mother pull tight the door to the children's room. When she swayed back into view, she didn't come near, merely crept with horror toward the couch.

Lynne forced her legs to hold her as she walked over toward the figure, so small and tiny where she had buried herself in the discarded comforter. With numb arms she reached out to try to hold her, but her mother curled away. "Mother, mother it's all right. It will be all right."

But the only answer was the horrible gasping scream of shame. Lynne sank on the floor beside her, wanting… wanting her mother to hold her, reassure her. She wanted her to tell her that it was all a bad dream. They were good people, hard-working, God-fearing people. They had suffered so much already. There couldn't be more, not now. Outside the stars shown bright, the snow made everything look clean and new. Tomorrow she would get the money somehow, perhaps ask Claire or Bonnie. There were worse things, far worse things. Slowly she realized it was her own voice, calm and clear in the warm room. And her mother had stopped crying and was peeking around the comforter at her.

Quietly, softly she continued to talk. "Of course I have had the fever, do you see the flush on my throat?" She felt her mother's eyes staring uncertainly at her. "But it didn't harm me, I'm almost over it now. And the children are so strong, such stout little things. Not like tiny babies. So the danger isn't very great for them. Isn't it warm in here? Did you hear how the boys were clever enough to get two loads from old Mac for the price of one?"

She cautiously extended an arm to drape across her mother's lap and was satisfied when she didn't pull away. "People have been so kind. I don't know how much you normally make each week, but thirty-six cents seems to me a lot for just washing clothes."

Her mother let the cover drop even lower, slid a hand down to touch Lynne's brow. She still didn't speak, but nodded as though it was most impressive.

"You know Mary Anne is a treasure. Her fingers are so nimble and she knows ever so much about the chores. As soon as she is over her cold, she will be up and helping you run things, so it won't be so hard on you at first."

Her mother started to speak, her lips puckered, and her hand paused. A band tightened around her own heart. She wanted to talk about it, discuss her fears, the truth of Mr. Huntmeister's threats, but she couldn't bring herself to even begin. Just admitting her fear of him had shamed her mother, let her know that Lynne had learned what she had done for the rent.

Lynne wanted to reassure her, tell her she didn't think it was so terrible, that she understood, was grateful, even proud of her mother's courage and sacrifice. But as she hesitated, the tears began to trickle down the pale cheeks in front of her and she merely drew in a shuddering breath.

"Tomorrow morning I will go out early toward the hill. There may be someone whose maid is sick who could use a hand with the laundry this week. Then if I do a good enough job, they might become a regular customer. I have to get out early, don't you see, in order to talk with Claire or Bonnie. The foreman must be truly frantic about my coming back. He always brags I'm the most capable in the sewing room. Did I ever tell you that?"

Her mother was staring at her strangely. At least the horror and shame were fading. "I've been thinking mother. If all of us work at it, not just us women, but the boys can help as well, well there are a lot of chores that we could do in the evenings to make extra money. You know the quilting that some of the ladies do doesn't look so hard. You and I could learn that, and some of the tricks with knitting as well. We could make little pretties to sell in the market. Mary Anne and the boys could sell them on Saturday mornings."

Her mother moved slightly, so that Lynne could lean her head across her lap. Lynne swallowed tightly, her throat raw from the talk, hoarse as she tried to think of something else to say. "It just seems frightening, because we've both been sick. I can't remember you ever being sick before, mother."

She leaned her head back to stare at the woman. A sharp pain of relief swept through her as her mother slipped fingers through her tangled hair. After several minutes she rose, then pulled her mother to her feet. She wrapped an arm around the slim shoulders and guided her back behind the curtain and toward the big sleigh-like bed. She turned and opened the door to the children's bedroom, hoping it hadn't grown too cold in that brief time. Both women stood in the doorway, listening to the heavy breathing of the children within.

It was all back to normal. Lynne helped her mother into bed, kissing her cool forehead as she pulled up the covers. "Go to sleep now, mother. Seventy-five cents is a lot, but we're half way there and I'll get the rest somehow in the morning," she whispered.

She couldn't see her mother's face in the dark, but as the woman curled away from her in the big bed Lynne felt a dark chill pass through her. Once again in the night she heard the soft sobs, choked now against the pillow. With a pain so real it nearly doubled her over, Lynne stumbled back behind the curtain. She didn't have the strength or the courage to make any more promises tonight. For in the empty pain, with the sobs of shame boiling out of her mother, she lost the courage to hope that she could keep them.

CHAPTER SIX

Montana

It was just before dawn. Diamond's scream was his only warning. Phillip rolled, but the rock-hard hooves showered his face with splintered rock as the little bronco galloped into the canyon dangerously close to his head before lifting high against the brush fence. Phillip pulled leather, wiping at his eyes. He saw the furious horse, hung against the top of the fence, and fired two shots into the air.

The mustang twisted, his eyes white in his head, his muzzle pink flecked as he flailed wildly against the barrier and then rolled backward onto the ground. Phillip wondered if he'd hit the animal by mistake but there was a flash of golden hide as the beast scrambled to his feet. Teeth bared, it galloped headlong back out of the canyon. Phillip holstered his pistol and Diamond extended his neck over the fence, pulling his lips back from his teeth in a laugh.

The cowboy dusted his hat against his leg as he wondered if the big horse laugh was for him or the mustang. Irritated, he built up the fire to keep the crazed animal away, in case his humiliation wasn't enough, and then heated some morning coffee.

◇◇◇

Satisfied that the mustang wouldn't be back, he put out the fire and pulled Diamond out of the paddock to saddle. The herd bunched, Phillip headed toward home. Diamond controlled the twenty mares and yearlings with just a snicker, nip or kick. The tall cowboy relaxed, letting the rocking cadence lull him back into a doze as the experienced horse guided them back to his home range.

They were crossing a lazy bend in the river when the first shot whistled from a copse of trees. Phillip dipped to the off-side of his horse even as he fired at the trace of smoke visible against the cottonwoods. Hurrahing the horses to speed up, he still heard the satisfying curse of the man he'd hit.

When two more blasts flew past him, the tall cowboy dug his spurs into the black and Diamond shot from the water, the spray of mud and water splatting against the bank. He didn't pull the animal up until he reached the cover of a large boulder. Taking the Winchester, he slapped the heaving flank of his horse and watched the herd scatter past the rocks and out onto the rolling plain.

For several minutes, he exchanged heavy fire with his unknown assailants. Pinned down, he looked back in disgust. Two of the hard won ponies lay dead near the water. Whoever these bushwhackers were, they weren't Indians. Carefully he reloaded his pistol and rifle, emptying his cartridge belt. Satisfied, he listened as the shots became scattered and then stopped. In a minute, whoever they were, they would try to rush him. Phillip felt his arm shake with the tension of waiting. He eased the rifle down near his leg, settled for cocking the long colts and slowing his breathing.

They both rode out at him, charging the rock and firing wildly.

Phillip rose to a half-crouch and fired both guns, grinning as he watched the two figures fall and their horses veer away from his cover.

He ran forward, firing into each body to make sure they would stay down. In the woods, he spotted the wounded man, holding his shoulder and bellowing for help. Phillip didn't bother shooting this time, just clubbed the man into silence and climbed aboard the remaining horse. As he took off after the mustangs, he prayed Diamond had been able to stop them.

He caught up to the black too soon, the big horse standing with dropped reins. Phillip swore as he looked for dust or hoof marks. He couldn't fault the stallion, he had done what he had been trained to do when both reins were on the ground. But another two days chasing broom tails meant the floors on the cabin wouldn't be in and the horse breaking would now be delayed. That is, if the embarrassed dun hadn't been trailing his lost herd and already reclaimed the mares.

When they finally caught and turned the green horses, they were closer to the ranch than the site of the ambush. Phillip rode one of the captured horses, towing the other behind with the black's extra gear piled on his back. The stallion worked the wild horses into a tight bunch and Shorty held the coral open while they pushed them on inside.

"Twenty horses, you did good, Gant." Banes called.

"You catching them already broke and saddled these days?"

Shorty asked.

Wearily Phillip dismounted and unsaddled both the captured horses before turning them in the coral with the milling herd. The calmness of the broke horses helped the rest calm down and turn to where Shorty was spreading hay near the water trough. In the dropping darkness, Phillip described the ambush.

"Any idea who they were?" Banes asked.

"Not sure. I'll ride back in the morning. I left one man alive. If he still is tomorrow, he'll give me answers."

The two miners stared past the fierce man at each other. For a minute, they said a prayer for the man who had earned his wrath.

CHAPTER SEVEN

Boston

After stoking the burning coals into a blaze, Lynne used the water that sat on the stove overnight to bathe quickly. She enjoyed the early morning privacy of her bath, even though it meant rising earlier than usual. Her chest and stomach were marked with the same erratic spots and splotches that she had seen on her mother only a week ago. But as she scrubbed, she noticed they were a pale pink where her mother's had been scarlet. They would probably be faded and gone tomorrow.

Clean and robed, she peeked in at the children and her mother and was comforted by their sound sleep. She hoped they would still be asleep when she returned. She would make the children bathe when she came back if the journey didn't bring home laundry that would need the water. She placed bread, molasses, and butter out for breakfast just in case anyone woke before she returned.

Only when she was completely warm and dry, did she dress, heating each garment against the stove before sliding into it. Finally she pulled her hood up and slipped from the warm apartment into the brilliantly cold morning.

The sun was barely risen, dark mauve shadows covered the white blanketed yards between the buildings and the main street. Her short boots crunched over the brittle ice crust of the snow and for half a second she was tempted to run across it like a child, pretending to be a bird that could skit along fast enough to not break through. Only after a few slivers of snow slipped down the top of one boot did she search out the hard packed snow of the path through the yard. A stiff breeze blew through a large tree to send a shower of crystalline snow flurrying around her. If Claire had been there, they would have called it fairy dust and made a wish. Lynne pulled her cloak tighter and hurried along the dark section of the path until she came out into the main street.

The shops were dark and empty, the street lamps still lit. Where the yellow glow from the gas lamps fell, the snow seemed to shimmer like watered silk. Up the long avenue she saw a street worker using a long pole to put out the lights, one by one. Impatiently, Lynne shifted from foot to foot, frowning to herself. She should have waited long enough to fry some bacon. But she had been afraid the delicious smell would have awakened the children and her mother. And she couldn't face her mother this morning.

From the stillness, she heard voices in muted conversation. The mass exodus from the tenements to work had begun. It was ten more minutes before she saw a figure that could be one of her friends. Starkly alone, Lynne watched Claire crunching across the snow like a child. Impatiently, she jumped from one foot to the other and flagged her attention. Claire broke into a run and Lynne had to step away and shout a warning before the girl understood why she couldn't come close enough to hug.

"Oh, Lynne, I'm so glad to see you. We've heard some terrible stories about the killing fever. I was so afraid that you might catch it,

I would never survive if something terrible happened to you, too."

Lynne forgot her own caution and moved closer. "I'm fine, just a touch of fever, but I'm already over it. Mother has been so ill though, and the three scamps all have runny noses. I'm hoping they will miss the fever." Hungrily she took in her friends deep green cloak and the bright yellow hair showing around the hood. "You look so pretty, Claire. I've missed you. But where is Bonnie? Come on now, tell me all the news."

"Oh, Lynne, it's terrible news, all of it." She raised a green gloved hand to brush at her eyes. "I've wished and wished you were here to tell me what to do and to make sense of it all. It's as though our whole world has turned upside down and everyone has spilled down helter-skelter."

Lynne saw the little blonde's lips tremble and knew if she didn't make a joke or say something quickly, Claire would be bawling. Then she would never learn what all the terrible changes were. "Nonsense. It can't be all that bad. Why just this morning I was sprinkled with fairy dust so I get to wish any real trouble away. Just tell me slowly, one thing at a time. First, where is Bonnie?"

In their circle of light she watched her friends face flicker through several transformations, the somber look, a twinkling smile, and then the pouty lips again. "Well, you remember she left Tarn Sunday night."

"Yes, she told us Monday. I was worried because she had a bruise."

"A royal shiner. It's iridescent green now, or at least it was last night. Oh, it was a terrible fight. All because she heard he was tom-catting on her, and her five months along."

Lynne nodded encouragement, but stood back toward the edge of the light, making sure even the cloud of her breath wouldn't land on her friend.

"Well, he was waiting for us when we finished work Monday. And he grabbed Bonnie and started to drag her home by her arm. When she kicked out at him he grabbed her by the hair, than knocked her down in the muddy street. I was so angry. I called him such names as my mother would whip me for ... for so much as thinking. All that hateful lot that stand around the pub just laughed and egged him on. We were screaming so loud for help, but no one would come."

Lynne clenched her fists. If only she had been there, she would have taken a board to the thick-headed devil, not hollered for help. Tensely she watched as Claire finished her animated tale. "But just when I thought I might faint from the terror, Bonnie reached out and bit his big thigh. He shook her loose then ... but oh Lynne ... he kicked her. Kicked her and called her the most awful names."

Tears stood in her eyes now, making them opaque like blue marbles in the morning light. Lynne noticed that some were stopping and listening, then walking around the two girls shaking their heads. The street worker cleared his throat, then extended his iron pole up to snuff their light. Amazingly, the light surrounding them didn't seem to change and Lynne wondered if her heart would begin to beat again. Poor Bonnie, poor kind, quiet girl. Tall and plain, but sweet as the day was long. A sin that she'd had to love such a worthless terror as Tarn Micheals. Finally she managed to speak. Her voice harsh with her heavy breathing.

"Is she all right?"

Claire sniffed delicately into one of her embroidered handkerchiefs. "Well, even the worthless men wouldn't stand for that and pulled him off. They were going to hold him for the police, but he broke free and ran away. Bonnie ... oh Lynne ... there was a trail of blood in the snow and two men helped carry her home. Her poor mother went crazy and then all the children started to cry. I couldn't bear it, so I had them take her to my house. My mother is the soul of charity. She sent for the doctor, but the baby died."

"A blessing that. If he were like his father, he would have broken her heart. Now she can heal and get over him. Ooh, if I were just a man, I would kill that worthless devil."

"That's what Bonnie's da said, word for word. He went after the magistrate and tried to file a warrant for murder against the black Irishman for the death of his unborn child. When the law went to question him, he had fled. His friends said he had been talking about going west. Everyone figures that's where he went."

"And Bonnie?"

Claire shook her head and the hood fell back enough to reveal her bouncy curls. "Well, you know our Bonnie. For months now she has known her marriage was a mistake, but she couldn't stop loving that big hulking Irishman. She was hurt and ashamed, of everything being so public, and she cried and cried for the lost baby. But by the next morning she just stopped crying and seemed her old self. She hasn't said anything, but it's clear she's accepted all that has happened, probably sees that it's for the best. She was sitting up for breakfast this morning and ready to go back to work. The poor darling, I haven't had the heart to tell her about the job."

Lynne wanted to see her friend, to rush home and hold her. But would that be a kindness, to give her the fever, and perhaps her brothers and sisters as well.

"It sounds like you've been the good friend she's been needing. Send her my love and explain about the fever keeping me from her. I'll write a note when I get back home. Wish I could send something to help her out, but things are pretty shaky at home."

"Don't worry. I used last week's earnings for the doctor. Who needs a silly corset anyway? And I plan to send my purse over to Bonnie's clan after I collect today. You know I would only buy a new bonnet or something foolish anyway."

Lynne bit her lip. Well, there would be no borrowing from friends today, but no matter. At least both girls were safe for the moment. "What did you mean that you couldn't bear to tell her about work?"

The trail of workers had thinned and Claire looked around in the gray light. "Goodness, look at the time, walk with me dear Lynne."

Lynne followed, still keeping her distance as the girl fled light footed down the snowy path. Together they melted into the gray fog that always surrounded the mill stream, cautiously staring down at their boots as they hurried forward. Lynne heard rather than saw Claire stop just outside the factory doors.

"It's the mill. The foreman laid off Bonnie. Oh, and Lynne, you too. But don't get angry. It's nothing personal. He laid off everyone on the sewing room floor. The rumors we've been hearing about the mill are true. They have decided to close it. Seems they've built newer ones down south. After the war and all, land was so cheap, and we heard they don't have to pay hardly anything, a penny on the dime for what they pay us. Everyone is frantic. Several people are talking about going west together. Even Mom and Pop."

She held the door open so that the harsh light from kerosene lanterns inside set her small figure in dark relief. "I guess we three won't be factory girls anymore, but we'll always be friends. Come at the end of the day if you can, to walk me home. There's so much to talk about. I found another dream man in the advertisements. One for each of us."

The foreman's voice barked and the door snapped shut behind her friend. Once again Lynne wandered through the gray fog as lost as though Claire had been right. Their world had disappeared, and now she had to find a way from these shadows of confusion into a new life. But Claire's family had the money for a wagon and the trip west. How could she manage, when she couldn't even find thirty-five cents more for the rent?

Lynne returned home two hours later, numb with cold and empty-handed. People hadn't set the dogs on her for knocking on their doors, but neither had any of them invited her in for tea or trusted the flush-cheeked girl with their laundry. The trek up the stairs seemed endless, each step harder and harder to take. She dreaded reaching it, opening the door, listening to the sick sounds, or seeing the fear and anguish of uncertainty reflected in her mother's eyes.

Her hand actually shook as she imagined turning the doorknob. What if she just ran away? She could use the little money she had to wire one of Claire's dream men, then accept money from them to travel west. Women did it. She had heard that one of the other girl's at the factory had done it the month before. Of course everyone had whispered it was because the girl's name was worthless. She had given her favors to the wrong sort, someone even lower than Tarn Micheals, for he wouldn't marry her. How terrible that would be, to travel to a new place with lies and deceit between you and the stranger you would marry? She shuddered as she tried to imagine herself on such a journey.

No, there was no way that she would run away. Her family

needed her, her brothers and sister needed her protection, the money she could earn, the food she could bring to the table. The mill wasn't the only place in town that a person could get work. Perhaps she would try round at one of the shops on Monday. By then her color would be normal and she wouldn't be contagious. Full of resolve, Lynne bounded up the last few steps and boldly opened the door.

"I'm home." Her voice sang out, then died in her throat. She heard a croupy cough from the bedroom, echoed by another. But it was not concern for the sick children that stopped her. It was the sight of her mother and the dark figure standing over her that took her breath away. He had already come for the rent.

She wanted to hide her eyes, to scream and swear like Claire would have done, but she couldn't turn away. Her mother's thin gown was pulled down so that one breast was exposed, the end of the hem bunched at her waist. But it was her mother's face that would always haunt her. Her hair stood out in wild tangles, her eyes were wild, the white's visible where her eyes were rolled back in pain, the deep eye sockets purplish black shadows.

Slowly, as though in a dream, Lynne brought her hand up to hide her face. It was then that she heard his laugh. The deep resonant laugh thundered over the quaking figure beneath him and the shocked girl in the doorway. She heard footsteps and turned to see Tom's stark white face, staring from the curtain of her mother's room. Trembling violently, Lynne turned and pulled him back with her, back to the bedroom with the other frightened ones. Jim was struggling to sit up, Mary Anne crying like an infant. Lynne pulled the door shut tightly behind her, gathered their frightened bodies close to still her own frantic heart. She wanted to give way to tears, to childish helplessness.

It was Tom's hoarse voice that brought her out of it. "Aren't you going to help her, Lynne? Can't you make him go away and quit hurting mother?"

It was then that she realized she was crying, holding the twins tight against her, her face buried against Mary Anne's teary cheek. He was right. She was the strong one. She had to do something to help, had to do something to save her mother from more harm, from total humiliation. But she didn't want to leave them, didn't want to be brave and walk out to face him.

Jim pulled loose and whispered. "Listen?"

Mary Anne snuffled and Tom stood up. He was half-way to the door when Lynne rose and placed a hand on his shoulder. "You stay here to protect the others, I'll go out to tend to mother."

"What if he's still there?" Tom asked. She looked over her shoulder to see the other twin holding Mary Anne in his arms.

Lynne swallowed and leaned against the closed door. The room outside was quiet. The maniacal laugh had stopped.

"Stay here!" she ordered fiercely, then slipped through the door.

The room was empty. For a moment, Lynne stood behind the curtains, uncertain if she dared step back into the kitchen where she had seen them. She stared around, reassured by the bulky furniture and empty feather mattress as familiar as her own face. Trembling, she opened the curtain and stared out. The couches were empty, even the comforter she had been sleeping under was empty. She turned slowly, searching, hunting for the tangled figures. The room was completely empty.

Frantically Lynne searched around the apartment, throwing

covers on the floor, peering under the furniture, behind the stove. She ran to open the frosted window, forcing it up to let the tingling cold cool her burning face. The wind made her eyes smart and she blinked them clear and brought a hand up to her mouth. Her mother was there, standing in the yard in the thin gown, screaming in French after the retreating figure.

She slammed the window shut and raced down the narrow stairs and out into the joint yard of the tenements. Faces were beginning to appear at windows and doorways, staring out at the crazy woman screaming in the snow. Lynne was out of breath when she reached her, pulling her cloak free to wrap around the thin, wrath-like figure. But her mother shook her off, strong in her frenzy. Instead of accepting the protection of the cloak she tore at her gown, exposing herself as she pulled the thin wispy cotton away. She was clawing at her face, pulling her hair, scratching her pale flesh until it was streaked with blood. Frantically Lynne tried to cover her but her mother slapped at her, pushed her, until she shook free yet again and flung herself in the snow, thrashing against its burning whiteness. All the time she was screaming and screaming. Lynne knew it was French, but couldn't imagine what she was saying.

It was the elephantine Mrs. Garretty that thrust her aside and with one strong arm gripped the shivering frantic form. She covered her with a blanket and pulled her up. When Lynne stepped forward to try to comfort her, her mother screamed in horror and stepped away. "Leave her to me child. Leave her to me and the other women. Go up and see about the wee ones. This must have frightened them."

Lynne waited, shuddering as she gulped deep breaths. Coward, if she hadn't been such a coward. She could have prevented her mother's flight. But even as she blamed herself she wondered if she or anyone could have prevented her flight into madness. Perhaps the swaggering figure who had debased her once again, demanded her soul to keep her family sheltered, he could have prevented it. In that instant she knew that if she had a gun, she would have killed Mr. Huntmeister, killed him without a moment's hesitation, without a moment's regret. Just as she would kill a snake in the children's bed, as quickly as she would have taken a board to Tarn's head. Some things in this world were so dark and evil, that there was nothing for it but to destroy them or allow them to destroy you. Shivering one last time, she tasted the savage wildness of hate, then let it go as she slipped up the stairs to salvage what she could of her soul by comforting the children.

It had been ten hours, and still her mother lay in the high bed, unwilling or unable to speak to her. Lynne struggled to hold back the tears as she watched Mrs. Garretty run a thin icicle across the pale parched lips of her mother. It made her own chest tighten to hear the labored breathing. The doctor had been summoned by the police to examine the woman after the neighbors reported she had been raped.

Lynne had tried to pretend everything was normal after the terrible morning, but Tom had seen too much to rest until he saw their mother. She wasn't sure what had hurt more. That her mother let someone like Mrs. Garretty help and tend her, or that she withdrew so sharply whenever she saw Lynne. At least she had let the other children be brought to her. She hadn't spoken but had tolerated their tight embraces and tender kisses. She knew it was wrong, but she was jealous of even that.

They hadn't called Dr. Krantz, but one of the surgeons from the local hospital. Mrs. Garretty had protested but Lynne was grateful. The doctor was a young man, but she could see from the doorway how tenderly he touched her mother, how softly he questioned her. Finally he had called Lynne into the room while the other women guarded the sick children on the couch. Both boys were having trouble breathing, their faces bright with fever. But Mary Anne worried her more with her calm, pale lassitude. She wanted to ask him to look at them, wondered if he would want money first.

"Miss McKinney, your mother's condition is serious, perhaps critical. She is despondent and depressed." He cleared his throat, covering his neat beard with his hand as though thinking about how to continue. He looked out past the women in their black gowns, clustered like vultures around the edge of the room. He stepped closer, aware of how emotional the next words might be for the young woman. "I have given her laudanum to comfort her. It will make her calm, help her forget." His voice was soft, confidential as he barely breathed the next words. "I can find no reason for her trauma. No physical evidence of rape. Without physical evidence, I cannot report a crime."

Lynne waited for more, listened, and then whispered angrily. "You mean they won't arrest Mr. Huntmeister?"

The eyes that looked down at her were black as raisins. She could see something in them, was it kindness, pity, or something else. Perhaps he wanted to hear her version of what had happened. She drew herself upright, rubbed at the tears staining her cheeks.

"My brothers are sick, and my sister. I hope it is just with colds. Mother and I have had the fever, typhoid fever, according to Dr. Krantz. If you could, if it doesn't cost ... her voice broke for a minute ... if you would please look at them while you are here. I don't have any money to pay you with now, but ..."

He held a long, slender hand into the air. "The city will pay for this call. Is there another room, where I can examine them without -- he waved his pale hand --without the audience."

She pointed to the door into the back bedroom. In doing so, she stepped closer to her mother's bedside. Just that small motion made her mother twist in agitation and Lynne stepped back behind the curtain, her eyes full of pain. He watched the interchange, placed a hand on her shoulder. "Sometimes the hardest thing to bear is the suffering of others. You are a very brave woman, Miss McKinney."

Lynne turned away, the kindness harder to bear than all the rest. She left the crowded apartment with its curious neighbors and crying children. But even on the landing there was no privacy, as prying eyes stared anxiously up at her. She didn't think she could stand another minute, listen to another filthy question. Her mother would expect her to be strong. If she could only hold on to her courage a little longer, surely her mother would recover her senses. Then she would hold Lynne and everything would be all right once again.

Determined, she breathed deeply and turned back into the crowded room. "Mrs. Garretty, I want to thank you for your assistance, for your kind assistance. But the doctor assures me that my mother will be all right if she is only allowed to rest quietly. If you kind ladies would please return home to your own families, now, I'm sure your children would appreciate your seeing to their needs."

The reaction was mixed. Many of the women looked dissatisfied, one or two asked her questions. Lynne merely pretended to not understand what they were asking and stood insistently at the door. It was Laura Garretty who made the most protest. "Well, I see you are ready to play high and mighty again, Miss McKinney. But you should learn from your mother what the cost of being the proud lady can be."

The others nodded or added their own biting comments. Lynne's cheeks burned with embarrassment for her mother's sake. If only they lived in the country, in a small shack, but a shack without hundreds of busy-body neighbors nearby. But they didn't, and she knew her mother would be disappointed if she reacted to some of the cutting remarks. So she stood, as cool and aloof as her flaming cheeks would allow until the last of the intruders were gone.

As she closed the door, she turned to the sound of applause. The young doctor was staring at her, admiration clearly written across his face. Lynne blushed for another reason and stepped forward to leave the door open into the hallway. He realized the awkwardness of the situation and picked up his coat and hat. He stood just outside the curtains to her mother's room as he pulled on his thick wool overcoat.

"I thought I smelled sulfa and so I gave the children a dose of the solution you had mixed. Do you have any magnesium hydroxide for when ...?"

"Yes, I still do."

"Good, you know when to give it, after the flux begins." At her nod he lowered his head and tapped the tall hat into place. "Watch them. They are weak. With the colds, there is every chance for the complication of pneumonia. I do not want to frighten you, but if they should remain feverish even after bathing, babble incoherently, or go into convulsions, you must rush them to the hospital. Also, watch their color. If their skin should look blue, you must bring them in with all haste."

He looked around the room, noticing the sparse furnishings. "There isn't a lot, but perhaps you could sell your mother's bedroom suite to the curious neighbors. The hospital will no longer accept indigents. You will need ten dollars for the admission of each one of them."

Lynne had told herself she was prepared, but suddenly she sank into the nearest chair. Ten dollars each. There was no way, no way on this earth that she could raise the kind of money he was talking about. Lynne's eyes filled with tears, knew that in just a moment she would be bawling like the silliest baby.

He knelt down, overwhelmed with compassion for the beautiful young girl. He could understand how Huntmeister came to his embarrassing arrangement with the mother. It was not just physical beauty with these women. They were so utterly feminine, so beguilingly helpless. Before he could stop himself, he let his hand slide along the fine cheekbone to tilt the heart shaped face upward. For just a moment, he debated whether he would allow himself to drown in the molten silver of her eyes.

"If you are unsuccessful with selling the furniture, if you find you need funds, I'm sure that I could make some special arrangement." He held her chin a little firmer than necessary, allowed his voice to drop an octave as he whispered the words. Finally he saw her eyes widen in understanding.

He rose abruptly, eager to be gone before he acted rashly and had the police coming to summon him. As her eyes grew cold and hard, he drew out his card and dropped it into her lap. "I will leave word at the desk that I am to be summoned if any of your family is to be admitted. After our intimate discussion in my office, I'm sure that everything will be all right."

He stepped through the door, stared down at the crowded faces, coarse and animal-like. The Irish made him think of pigs, with their pink faces, turned up noses, and coarse coppery hair. But both the McKinney women had classical profiles, soft brown hair and delicate coloring. Even the young children had been exceptionally handsome. How had such a girl come to be born into this sort of thing? It was too bad about the mother.

"Oh, and Miss McKinney. Be prepared for your mother's loss. Once the spirit and mind are destroyed, a body as weak as hers will not linger long. You do not need to rush her to the hospital. Just call for the priest. I would expect the end soon, perhaps tonight. Do you want me to ask one of those kind neighbors to come back and sit with you, perhaps the lovely Mrs. Garretty?"

Dr. Stone looked back over his shoulder at her. Lynne stared up into the black eyes, aware now that what she had seen in them before was pure evil, not pity, not kindness, not even curiosity. A fever of hate swept through her again and she imagined rushing forward to push the tall, bearded Satan over the rail and into his crowd of admirers. But she heard a hoarse voice calling from the sick room and merely rose with unshatterable calm to slam the door in his face.

CHAPTER EIGHT

Boston

Lynne sat in a straight-backed chair pulled up to the edge of the bed. Every few minutes, she reached out and pulled the quilt high around her mother's bare shoulders. Since they had carried her back to the apartment, her mother had resisted any attempts to dress her. When Mrs. Garretty had tried to comb her hair and put salve on her face, she had screamed and swore and pulled more hair out. Only after the doctor had given her the heavy dose of laudanum had she subsided. Still if Lynne moved into her line of vision, she twisted, tossed and kicked the covers off.

All night Lynne made trips between the children's room and her mother's. Mopping a brow, or helping one or the other onto the commode chair that she had moved into their bedroom. Each time she made sure to force a small amount of liquid containing the magnesium compound. She was shocked at how quickly the boys had weakened. Their long muscular little legs and arms were limp as noodles, their faces torched with fever. Mary Anne woke only once during the night, crying because she hadn't made it from the bed in time. Lynne sponged her hot body clean, then replaced the soiled linen with the clean top sheet and a towel.

Each time she returned to the chair beside her mother and tucked the covers. It was the still hour before dawn, when she came back from tending Mary Anne, to touch the covers and find them still in place. Slowly, so as not to panic her, she reached out her own cool fingers to lift up her mother's slender ones. There was no reaction and she swallowed her fears to fold and interlace their hands, the way her mother had done so many times in the past to reassure her. She could feel her mother's pulse in the thin hollow where their hands joined. Softly, so as not to frighten her, she began to talk.

As silently as a prayer, she whispered how much she loved her, how much she felt. Only when she had told her of her dreams, fears, and hopes did she slip her fingers free and hurry down through the still tenement to summon the priest.

Despite the way Lynne had treated them, Mrs. Garretty and the others returned to help prepare the body. Death seemed to destroy all barriers between them. The rituals to be performed drew them, that and the need to have someone when their time came.

She watched from the children's room as they closed her mother's eyes, placing copper coins over them, then firmly tied her mouth closed until the body set. Lynne was surprised that she felt no horror in the rituals, instead felt her heart ease and be comforted as they treated the body with absolute respect. The bedding was removed, the feather mattress dragged down the stairs and into the yard to empty. Lynne stared numbly down through the window as the feathers blew like snow on the ground. When the pillows were emptied, Laura Garretty herself, searched each carefully. She brought back the crown of feathers she found in one. To all it was offered as absolute proof the soul had gone to heaven. Studying the heavy rounded object, Lynne tried to imagine how else it could have been formed.

A white cloth moistened with camphor was spread over her mother's gentle face to keep it from turning dark while parched salt was tied in a sack and placed on her stomach to keep it from swelling. As the children cried, Lynne returned to soothe the living. Mary Anne was shivering with chill and she wrapped her in a heavy quilt to lay sandwiched between the feverish twins. But still she was drawn to the dark rituals.

As soon as the cold body was bathed, her mother was dressed in the stiff black taffeta she had worn three years before to bury her loved ones. Lynne fingered the dark hat and veil that her mother would never wear again while one of the women, Katy Sommers, helped Lynne select a dark blouse and skirt to wear with it to the burial. The young Irish woman had lost her only two children the week before, and while she braided Lynne's hair, Laura Garretty's toddler stood bawling at her feet, burying her face in her skirt and leaving a silvery trail.

Lynne herself removed the camphor and salt pouch, then adjusted the pillow beneath her mother's head, arranged the ribbons at the throat of her gown. A clean sheet had been drawn beneath the body and was already sewn closed on three sides. There would be no coffin. When everything was finished, she helped to bring the children.

As sick as each was, no one thought about keeping them from viewing the body. Lynne carried them into the room one by one. She held them, let them touch the cold fingers, kiss the marble-like cheek. It seemed harder for the boys, especially Tom. Mary Anne seemed unaware of what it all meant.

◇◇◇

Because of the fever, the body couldn't be kept, and the funeral was arranged for the same day. Mrs. Garretty returned home to tend her own sick. Katy Sommers stayed behind to watch the children. Katy's husband bore the weight of the shrouded body, Lynne and a neighbor clutched the sheet at the body's feet.

After a few minutes on the long trek, it started to rain. The two mourners who had helped remained inside the shelter while she accompanied the grave digger. So many had died recently in the slums of the city, that the pauper's field was all but full. Determined, Lynne finally found the markers for her brother and father.

"Here, they left room between them, just in case any others in the family came down with fever that winter. The babies are buried at their feet. Please, can you dig a place between them for Mother?" By the time the hole was ready, the two mourners had left and returned to the tenement. Lynne watched as her mother was lowered into the unhallowed ground. She stared around the gray fogged cemetery, looking for the priest, anyone. A dark clad man walked from the small shed at the edge of the field and she was surprised as two cloaked figures joined him.

She listened to the minister intone the simple ceremony, wished it could have been her mother's priest. Thirty-five was so young to die, but three of her children already slept beside her. Silently Lynne promised her mother that nothing would happen to the three little ones who remained. No matter what it cost her, she would show the courage her mother had, and do whatever it took to ensure their safety.

When the soft words ended she looked up and smiled. The two witnesses were Claire and Bonnie. Silently they followed her from the cemetery, one trailing on either side. Lynne found her voice first.

"I'm surprised to see you here." She turned to search Bonnie's eyes for signs of her own loss, her own fears. The taller girl smiled faintly. "One of your neighbors sent word."

Lynne cleared her throat. "Mrs. Garretty?"

Claire nodded and moved closer. "We needed to talk to you anyway. We're making plans."

Bonnie chimed in. "The Wimberlys are going west in the spring, and Claire has invited me to go with them. We're going to the Oregon territory for free land and young husbands."

Lynne shook her head. "This sounds like one of your schemes Claire. I thought you were going to answer one of those ads for a bride."

Claire shook her head. "Bonnie made me realize how foolish that was. One might agree to marry a Tarn or a mad pincher like our floor foreman."

All three closed ranks. "The children are all three sick or I'd hug you dear hearts." Her voice thickened and she raised a hand to brush her hair back from her eyes. The ground all around the cemetery was still white and glistening, but the falling rain was rapidly forming a film of ice on the cleared, paved streets. "I don't know if you heard how mother died."

Claire extended an arm and leaned a head forward to touch her damp shoulder. Bonnie instinctively reached a hand forward to squeeze her smaller one. "Men!"

It could have been an oath she spat it out so vehemently. Claire raised her head and all three laughed tearfully. "Don't lump them all together. We know they're not all bad. Our mothers found wonderful men to love and marry and we will do the same."

"How?" Lynne sighed. "Just when you think you couldn't meet a more wicked, despicable man than the likes of Mr. Huntmeister or

Tarn, then you do."

Bonnie stepped in front of her, blocking her way. "Who? Has someone done something to harm you, Lynne? If they have, I swear," her brow puckered in concentration. "We'll help you get them."

Lynne stared at the somber brown eyes in the plain, long face and smiled. Claire was trying to edge around on the slippery shoulder of the walkway so she could see Lynne's face as well. "It's not what he did, it's what he offered to do." Again she found it hard to speak, and she drew in a ragged, deep breath then turned her head to spew it out like steam against the cold wet night. "This is ridiculous you know. We'll all three catch pneumonia standing about in this."

Claire pulled her forward and the three didn't stop until they had reached the awning over the corner grocer. The lamp was still on inside and the door unlocked. All three crowded in together. Once inside, Lynne moved over to one side of the corner stove, leaving her friends facing her on the other. Each shook rain from their cloaks and stared at the other. "I have to hurry on home, the bairns are all in torment with this blasted fever."

Claire dipped around behind the counter to give the merchant a coin and came back with a small sack. Bonnie lifted the lid on the small metal skillet sitting on the stovetop and held it as Claire poured the contents into the oiled pan. "Now, you have to wait on the chestnuts. Tell us."

Lynne looked up. She should be crying for her mother, worrying about her brothers and sisters, instead the fear she felt in her chest was for herself. If she started, she was afraid she might give way to self-pitying tears. Bonnie reached across and jabbed her arm softly. "Tell!"

So she did. The horror of her mother's death. The comfort of the neighbors. The unbelievable proposition from the doctor.

Claire listened to the emotional telling wide-eyed, her pretty face twisting into sympathetic or angry faces in turn. Bonnie merely listened. Toward the last, the chestnuts popped. When they smelled the first one scorching Bonnie reached out and opened the lid, shaking out a couple into each of their waiting hands. Then Claire unwadded and reopened the little sack for her to pour the rest into.

Lynne tossed the fiery hot little nuts from palm to palm, relishing their warmth. The others did the same. By the time they had eaten the first ones, the store clerk was calling goodnight to the owner, who was tallying the day's receipts. They lingered by the warm fire, waiting for him to douse the lamps to signal them to leave.

"What are you going to do?" Claire asked.

Lynne gave a twisted smile and shrugged. "I don't know. I just know I promised my mother on her death bed that I would do everything in my power to protect the little McKinney's. It's knowing what such a sacrifice cost her, it makes me afraid."

For something to do, she reached for the tiny bag of nuts. Bonnie was the first to speak. "Sometimes you have to do what you have to do. No one could blame you."

Claire swore, the unlady-like expression far more expressive than the single epithet 'men'. "If only I had enough money, I'd give it to you myself. But now the mill is closed, well, father is selling everything, trying to raise the money we'll need to outfit for the trip west. They say it's terribly expensive."

Bonnie nodded. "You know if I had anything, it would be yours. I'm supposed to go to work at Delaney's next week. It only pays fifty cents a week, but Mom and Dad have promised I can save it up for the trip. I plan to travel with Claire. Maybe you and the little ones could come along too."

The last ended weakly and Lynne shook her head. "No, first I will sell the furniture and anything else of value for the hospital. Perhaps I can ..." but her voice trailed off. There was very little to sell but herself.

The owner doused a lamp and as the girls backed toward the door he called. "Miss McKinney, my wife has been wanting a new bedroom suit. Would you mind if I come up to look at your furniture in the morning?"

Lynne blushed all the way to her ears. "With my wife of course," he added.

She nodded, "Yes, yes, that would be fine." She followed the others outside, tried to figure out why even a kind gesture was so hard to accept. What had her mother told her about pride? What matter all the telling, Lynne knew what it had cost her. She would be glad to accept the owner's help, but could it possibly be enough. Perhaps, perhaps he might go as high as ten dollars, but she would still need so much more. Claire and Bonnie waited and she stomped over to the edge of the lamplight where they stood.

Suddenly, a crazy notion came to her. "Claire, one thing before you go. If you aren't going to be needing those ads of yours for husbands, would you mind letting me have them."

Claire pulled her cape high over her blonde curls. The night was cold, but at least the rain had stopped. She tugged at the gathering on her handbag until the drawstring pulled free and she could retrieve the two yellow papers.

"It's obvious like Bonnie said, a person has to do what a person has to do. But I might as well check to see who is willing to make the highest offer. Perhaps one of those rich, lonely westerners would pay a bonus to get a lovely young bride. Perhaps not, but then what else do I have to lose."

She took the yellow pages and held them in the lamplight, smiling gaily. But her hand shook and her voice quavered.

Claire started to grab the sheets back, but Bonnie held her hand. "Well, it makes sense to me. Perhaps you could go by the newspaper office and make inquiries. It seems to me that if Horace Greeley can say 'Go West, young man, go West!' no one can fault us for going west after the good ones."

The three laughed and for just a moment Lynne felt the faint stirrings of hope. It was so much like the afternoon in the school yard when they had planned to go to work in the mills.

She held out her pinkies and the other two laughed and linked theirs. They raised their arms and cheered. "To Life and Adventure."

The only difference was Lynne had to pull away as the other two linked arms. But into the dark alley and empty yard of the tenements her friend's brave hearts went with her.

Katy Sommers was waiting at the top of the stairwell, eager to go home to her husband. Lynne felt so tired, but the young woman's round face made her lean forward and accept the tender hug of sympathy. Life was hard for everyone, not just her. Self-pity would get her nowhere. Lynne smiled bravely, kissed the smooth cheek and muttered her thanks.

Katy patted her back and leaned down to see her husband glancing their way. "The children are asleep. I used the soup bone to make more broth and did my best to get it down them. It was the only thing my ..." her voice broke and it was Lynne who smiled and gave her a hug this time. "Thank you. Good neighbors mean so much at such a time."

"I know. Your sainted mother was such a help to me when the bairns grew ill. She was a fine lady, no matter what they're whispering. She was a kind, dear sweet soul and you are so very much like her. If you need me tomorrow, for anything, just call. We've all been exposed to the fever so there's no danger, and I like doing for the children. Really I do."

Inside the empty room, Lynne surveyed the damage. All the company had created its own kind of disorder. After she made sure the children were sleeping, she straightened the simple room, pulling the curtain back that had always separated her mother's space from the rest of the room.

Then she cleaned away the painful reminders of death and swept the floors. In the kitchen she stored food in the window box and wiped down the workspace and table with the same dilute carbolic acid she used to sterilize the chamber pots. Finally, when everything had the stringent odor of being clean, she lifted the trunk and carpet bag that had been hidden beneath the feather mattress into the open floor.

Painfully, tearfully, she removed her mother's belongings from the dresser and wardrobe. Each garment she examined, either packing it for herself, folding it to give to a neighbor, or placing it in the rag pile. She was surprised that there were still two good outfits left from before the war. She held up one, a light gray wool traveling suit. It was terribly dated, the small jacket snug-fitting on Lynne, the sleeve edges trimmed with black velvet ruffling. But the skirt was plain and the length right. There was even a tiny bonnet and soft leather shoes to match. The other outfit was a dress, also dated, with its watered blue silk, but at one time it must have been very stylish. Of course her mother would have been unable to wear them around the tenements, but why hadn't she sold them.

The only other thing of value she found was the silver mirror and brush set that her mother had loved so much. It had first been her grandmother's in France, then her mother's. Now it would be Lynne's. No, she put it with the two good outfits. It might bring just enough money, enough money for the hospital. Tearfully, she emptied the last drawer, then leapt up to tend to the children.

Returning, she stared at the pile of belongings, glanced around at the bookcase and books, the two couches. Had her mother really been too proud to sell them, or was she more of a realist than Lynne. The money they would have brought would have paid for weeks of rent, weeks when she could have turned the horrible Huntmeister away at the door. But what would she have done when they were gone. When they sat and ate on the floor like the poorer immigrants, sleeping in pallets on the floor. Would the terrible man have said 'fine, you poor woman, now you never have to pay rent again'?

No, it would only have postponed the inevitable. Her mother had kept the few things that would give her comfort, would make her children's lives better. Lynne lifted the two outfits and the silver brush and comb set into the carpet bag and snapped it shut.

"One does all one can for the living, and then you leave the rest to God." The other thing she lifted and placed in the trunk was the crown of feathers that Laura Garretty brought to give her comfort. She would have to do something special for the ill-tempered woman.

For a minute, Lynne contemplated sleep. It had been such a tiresome day and she had been up all last night. But there was one more chore she had to do. Selecting a torn slip, she rubbed bee's wax from a half-used candle, carefully polishing the bedroom suite until the wood glowed as though alive.

Exhausted, she slept the minutes until dawn.

Mr. Sanders and his wife entered the apartment carefully. Lynne had set bowls of camphor in the front room, had awaken early enough to tend the children and rinse out anything that might smell. All three were ill, but their fevers still dropped when she bathed them with cool water. None had broken out with the rash yet. Mary Anne was no longer having chills.

She smiled as she looked up at the couple standing inside her door. Both wore bandannas across their noses to prevent breathing in any germs. Lynne watched as the thin, bald store owner adjusted his glasses over his nose.

"Good morning, Mr. Sanders. You gave me a start for a moment; I thought you might be a pair of dime novel desperadoes."

"Good morning, Miss McKinney. I hope we are not disturbing your sleep, but I have to open the store and..." Mr. Sanders said with a nervous laugh.

Lynne waved a hand. "Nonsense, I've been up. Come in, come in. This is what I have to sell."

The woman looked as though she had been forced to come along, but when she saw the wonderful bedroom furniture, she was enchanted. It was Mr. Sanders who had to shush his wife so he could make a bid. The first offer he made was for five dollars. Lynne countered with a request for the thirty dollars she needed. Mr. Sanders acted as though she were crazy, but his wife looked ready to pay what she asked.

The bickering might have gone on all day if a scarlet faced Mary Anne hadn't wandered into the room, her small body shivering even while her skin burned hot. Lynne turned her back on them and lifted the small girl up to carry over to the sink. Even with the Sanders behind her, she removed the gown and sat the child in the sink to pump cool water over. Mary Anne squealed and stood back up. Lynne heard Mrs. Sanders gasp and then looked down at the thin chest. The pattern of dark red sprinkled the pale skin from her throat to her groin.

Soothingly she got Mary to sit and to allow her to sponge her body off.

Mrs. Sanders turned and fled down the steps and Lynne cursed her stubbornness at not accepting their last offer of seven dollars. Mary began to cry harder because of her anger and Lynne looked down at the big blue eyes, so clouded with fever. "Oh little angel, what are we going to do now?"

Mr. Sanders cleared his throat behind her. "I know why you need the money Miss McKinney, but I cannot pay more than it's worth. Here, here is eleven dollars for the bedroom set."

He stared as Lynne's calm gray eyes filled with tears. Embarrassed he coughed again. "Here, a dollar more for the sofa and fainting couch. They need reupholstered, but they are good quality. I'll send a boy to fetch them later. Honestly, I wish you and the children the best, but I cannot pay a dollar more."

Lynne pulled a towel around the wet child and draped her against her chest. Before he could think about the offer, she reached out and covered the paper and silver money with her wet hand. "Thank you, Mr. Sanders. I accept your fair offer. Tell your wife Dr. Stone assured me that if there was no contact of flesh or exchange of food or fluids, there was no danger of spreading the germs."

But she was talking to his back as he dashed down the stairs after his wife. Encouraged, Lynn, thrust the money into her pocket. Mrs. Garretty stood at her open door, a rolling pin in her hand. Lynne smiled and called down to her. "He bought the bedroom suit, Mrs. Garretty, you don't have to beat him. But if Herr Huntmeister shows up, feel free to raise lumps."

She was humming as she turned to close the door. Mary Anne's head rolled against her face and she leaned against the hard wood in panic. The little face was burning hot and even as she stared, the blue eyes rolled up as her head lolled back against her shoulder. Lynne didn't wait. She grabbed a quilt to swaddle the child completely as she tugged on her own cloak. On the way down the stairs she called for Katy Sommers.

"Stay with the boys, Oh dear God, please stay with the boys. I'm on my way to the hospital."

"Here," it was Mr. Sommer's firm voice. "I haven't taken the cab out yet. Get her in out of the cold. I can drive you there quicker than you can ever walk. Hurry."

But Lynne had already run through the door and out to the waiting coach. It took only minutes for him to hitch the pair of horses but every second seemed like hours as she tried in vain to get the child to acknowledge her.

Only after she had checked her baby sister into the hospital did she breathe again. A nurse in a white starched uniform tried to shush her out of the way. She didn't leave until she felt Mary's skin after they gave her an alcohol rub and Lynne felt it was cool. Even then she had to lean over and make sure she heard the small heart beating before she would leave. "I'll be back as soon as possible. The boys are ill as well. Are you sure there isn't a discount for families?"

The nurse shook her head, about as sympathetic as the cold cloths she put away, as she tucked the child in snugly. "Are you the Miss McKinney doctor left orders about?"

Lynne's pulse quickened. Abruptly she stood and coolly whispered, "No."

As she walked down the icy sidewalk, she wondered how long she could cling to her pride. If the boys were in danger when she returned, she would have no choice but to hold a private conference with the slimy Dr. Stone, the Satan who had pretended professional concern the night before.

A tall black man stood in front of her. "Be you, Miss McKinney?"

At Lynne's nod he said, "Your coachman said he had to go, he was sorry, but he couldn't afford to be losing his job. But if you need a ride back to the tenements, you should come over to Beacon Street."

Lynne nodded, turned to get her bearings. "No, I'm fine. If he should come by later to check on me, tell him I am fine, and have walked back already to see about the boys. I appreciate all he and Katy have done for us. Can you remember all that?"

She smiled up at him and he gave her a big grin in return. "Yes'sum, I sure can remember any message from such a pretty lady."

She smiled and walked down toward the side of town where she lived. It would be necessary to walk past the <u>Globe's</u> offices on the way back. She straightened her shoulders and smiled yet again. There was only one thing left to sell, and she intended to get the best price she could.

The newspaper office was not what she expected. The floor of offices was above the roar of the printing presses below. One could barely hear anything and she wasn't sure that she could go through with this after all. While she waited for someone to notice that she was there, she pulled the two yellow sheets from her purse. The second sheet had one ad circled by Claire's hand. "Doctor, needs educated woman, to teach school and marry. Apply in confidence..."

A quick scan, revealed only buffalo hunters and successful miners seeking rich and willing brides. The other sheet held the first dream man circled, the Montana horse rancher. Well, better a one-eyed, one-legged miner than a doctor and lecher. Impatiently she shifted from foot to foot.

Finally she was directed to a thin old man for help. She couldn't help feeling self-conscious as the boy who had first spoken to her pointed her out to others. Nervously she lifted a hand to her head. Her hair was hanging in a loose braid down her back, her shirt-waist was still wet beneath her cloak and she wondered if she had even buttoned it up this morning. The way the man was eyeing her and blowing smoke suddenly made her wish she had taken time to primp before coming here.

A faint heart wouldn't help her brothers or herself. Breathing deeply, Lynne walked up and laid the yellow sheets on his desk, then she smiled radiantly. Minutes later, she was following the spindly-back down the stairs and next door to the telegraph office. Even with the door closed, she could hear the drum and thunder of the rolling presses.

"This is most irregular, most irregular. Besides, unless this fellow is in town on business, the odds of you getting an answer back is remote, really remote."

But he blew out the smoke and handed the teletype operator the terse note. "Found bride. Stop. Willing. Stop. If you wire an additional twenty dollars. Stop."

Lynne fingered the thin purse. It was sinful to waste the little money she had on a telegram. If the children recovered, they would still need to pay rent, buy food ..."

But her thoughts were interrupted by the rapid tapping of an incoming message.

"Is she worth added expense? Stop."

Lynne bit her knuckles to keep from shouting. Yes. She looked upward, feeling suddenly as though her guardian angel had to be taking a hand.

The old man who had walked her down, removed his cigar as he laid the short message on the counter. He grinned as he blew smoke into the small room.

"Undo that there braid and shake out your hair."

Suddenly Lynne's excitement was replaced by anger. She couldn't prevent the flush that lit up her cheeks at his speculative gaze. She bit her lip and contemplated leaving in a huff. Instead she closed her eyes and imagined her brothers, burning bright with fever. Quickly she undid the braid and fanned out her hair.

He was staring at her when she opened her eyes. Suddenly the teletype sender leaned closer and whispered something to him. Lynne waited. What would the old pervert ask next?

"Take off the cloak, Miss."

She hesitated, than remembered Mary Anne's white eyes. She unhooked the cloak and twirled it over the counter. Her shirt waist clung to her youthful figure where the fabric was still damp. The top buttons were still unhooked on the blouse and she raised a hand to close them.

The man jabbed his cigar emphatically. "Leave 'em alone."

She dropped her hands to her side. Heavens, she had been looked at before. One couldn't be seventeen and work in a factory without having been stared at good and hard by all sorts. Still, she would have spoken sharply to those men. Now, she merely dropped her lashes and stood demurely before him.

Through lowered lashes she saw the teletypist whisper again. Lynne gritted her teeth. What was this? She wasn't a piece of livestock was she? Then she realized, that was exactly what she was. She prayed they didn't ask her to open her mouth and let them examine her teeth. The old pervert wagged his cigar in a circular motion. Pretending she was flattered by their admiration, Lynne leaned her head back so that her hair flowed and swished down her back. Relaxing, she tilted her head so that her face was angled at his and then smiled sweetly, what she hoped was seductively, as she pirouetted slowly.

When he dropped his cigar, she picked up her cloak and raised her brows.

The next message was one word. "Yes. stop."

When the message was wired, she waited impatiently for the teller to return with the gold piece. The wire for money was emphatic. "Travel west in ten days." The old clerk assured her she would be prosecuted if she didn't do just that. Well the tickets were all paid for, all the way by train and stagecoach from Boston to Butte, Montana. Mr. Philip Gant would get his money's worth. But now she had to hurry to save her brothers.

She raced back up the street and found Sommers. But she

didn't stop to think about the consequences until both Tom and Jim were safely admitted to the hospital. There was so much to arrange, to worry about. For now it was enough that the children were safe. No matter the cost, she could have done worse. At least the Montana man intended to marry her first.

CHAPTER NINE

Montana

It was mid-day when he rode back on one of the rustler's ponies, approaching the cottonwoods cautiously. He began by making supper and tending to the wounded man. After he bandaged the ugly shoulder wound and fashioned a sling, he swiveled on his heel, still in a squat beside the ambusher. He held the canteen of warm water out to tempt him.

"Your partners are dead."

The man grabbed the canteen, desperate for a drink, his eyes wary. Phillip let him take a swallow, then jerked the water away.

"Who sent you?"

The man opened his mouth to gasp like a carp, no words emerging from his dry throat. Phillip let him have a second swallow before tugging it away.

"I don't dare tell you mister," he croaked.

Phillip moved so the bright light shown on his own face, revealing his black eyes and steely features. Slowly he turned his head to indicate the busy buzzards on the two fallen men.

Without a word he rose, hung the canteen over the saddle horn, and pulled free a shovel.

"I brought an extra horse. I can let you ride out -- or dig three graves. Your call."

When the man didn't speak, Phillip quietly went to work stripping boots, gun belts, and money from the now eyeless bodies. The voice was shaky, still dry, but never stopped talking while Phillip dug two shallow graves.

Just as he suspected, it was the rich mine owners known as the four Georgians. Now the dry gulch where they had been working their claim was petering out, they were busy trying to find other prospects, even if it meant bush-whacking a neighbor or sending men to claim jump. It didn't make sense. The four were already millionaires.

The horse rustling was a new piece of devilment. It had already caused him a day's delay and extra work. If he went to Helena to settle up, he would lose the rest of this one. Shorty and Banes hadn't wanted to stay any longer. They were anxious to get back to work at the small silver mine, only staying so Phillip could finish up this business. If he didn't ride this man into town, no one would ever know about the ambush or attempted rustling.

Even if they knew, Phillip wasn't sure it would make any difference. The sheriff had heard plenty of complaints. He hadn't acted on any of them. Phillip drew his gun, worked it onto an empty chamber, and then pointed it at the desperate man.

"Might as well eat before riding out. I see you again," he spun the barrel and aimed between the eyes.

Neither man had much of an appetite. The little shady bank of the river was ripe with the smell of death. Phillip heaved the rustler into the saddle.

"I even hear of your name again …" but the cowboy didn't

need him to complete the threat, it was all there in the dead eyes and clenched jaw.

Phillip slapped the horse's rump and aimed the trouble back down the trail.

CHAPTER TEN

Boston

Lynne sat in the hospital between the two beds. The nurses had finally given up arguing with her and trying to prevent her sneaking in to see the children. Instead, they had given her a pinafore and white starched bonnet in case anyone should see her on the floor and try to bully their way into the wards like the brash young woman. With the fever so rampant in the city, they could use all the spare hands they could find. The young woman was obviously devoted to the children, and since she was helpful in the care of the twins, they let her stay.

The boys went through the dangerous fever and severe chills a day after Mary Anne, so she had been able to stay with the little girl until she was over the worst of it, before having to devote her attention to the boys. When both were stable, she had taken care of some of the last details.

She had returned to the apartment one last time the afternoon after wiring the Montana man. There she had washed up all the dirty bedding and clothes, packed the children's few belongings in clean pillowcases, and carefully crated her father's books. When everything of value was loaded in the coal cart, she transferred it to the Wimberlys.

Claire had welcomed her enthusiastically. After assuring her they would store the things, she had helped Lynne move them into the carriage house. She listened, enraptured at her friends tale of daring. "I can't believe you had the nerve, Lynne McKinney. My, but I wish I'd been there."

Lynne shook her head. "Well, when you don't have a choice, it's like Bonnie said, 'You do what you have to do.'" Claire chimed in on the quote. Lynne sighed, wishing she could hug her dear friend. "There's more I need to ask of you, really from your family."

Lynne was amazed and relieved at how excited the Wimberly's were at the prospect of keeping the children until she could send for them. Since they wouldn't be leaving Boston themselves before the end of May, there was plenty of room and work for them there. Mr. Wimberly had argued, "Why not let the three young ones make the journey with us at least to Ogden."

Lynne knew that with her two good friends and Claire's generous parents the children would be well cared for. "Once we pay for passage with the wagon train, there's no limit to the number in our party. It will be late spring and summer. The children can sleep in the wagon, or in a tent beside the wagon if it's too crowded," he argued.

Claire added, "I've read of families of ten and twelve traveling west in a single prairie schooner."

Lynne promised to send money, if there were any way possible, to help with their transportation.

"Nonsense, those strong boys can help Mr. Wimberly at the foundry before we leave. It will probably be enough to earn their keep on the trip. If Mary Anne is the jewel you claim, she can help me around the house." Mrs. Wimberly argued.

The older couple seemed so pleased at the prospect of having the little ones, Lynne didn't think they were pretending. Claire told her later, "No, really, they've always wanted a large family."

Mrs. Wimberly insisted she wouldn't mind keeping them forever. That was a possibility Lynne's heart couldn't bear. Somehow she would find a way to bring her brothers and sister to Montana to live on the ranch. Surely a man who was generous enough to send extra money, without asking what it was for, would let her have her family join her. But she wasn't sure enough to wire and ask him now. The children would need time to regain their strength. The journey would take nearly three months itself, there would be hardships. But all of their short lives they had been struggling just to survive. And most of the way west was guarded by forts these days. It wasn't as dangerous as when the first settlers went through twenty years earlier. By the time they were near the Montana territory, well, Mr. Gant would have been her husband for six months by then. It would be natural for him to go with her to fetch the children home.

Lynne rose and wiped at Jim's pink brow, pushing his brown curls back from his forehead. Tom cleared his throat and she leaned over to tousle his hair as well. They were both through the critical stages. Another day and all three would be released. When she left them at the Wimberly's, Lynne would have to hurry to catch a train for the journey across country to the arms of her betrothed.

That same night at the apartment, she had loaded her trunk and carpet bag into the cart, then delivered them to the train station. According to the <u>Globe</u> reporter, she would have to come by the newspaper office to pick up her tickets and travel expenses. Someone from the newspaper was required to make sure she boarded the train before handing them over to her.

◇◇◇

Looking around the nearly empty apartment one last time, she felt a deep sadness. Despite the hard times, it had been the only home she could remember. She touched the plain dishes and iron skillet. Mrs. Wimberly had assured her they had more than they could transport already. Everything else that was left, table and chairs, food, dishes, pans, etc. she would give to Mrs. Garretty.

When she knocked on her door the next morning, the woman seemed surprised and a little resentful to see her. She seemed unimpressed by Lynne's gifts.

"So, you found the money to put the little ones in hospital. It's a waste. They all die there, too."

Lynne looked at her worried face and nodded. The baby that had toddled around Katy Sommers feet the day before was lying listlessly on the ragged sofa. She couldn't help scanning the pink skin for the tell-tale splotches.

"There's some food, furniture, and here --this is some medicine I had for the children. The white powder is what you can give for the runs, the sulfa when they have the fever." At the woman's perplexed look she demonstrated. "You put about this much in a pitcher of water, then you give it to them when they need it."

Laura Garretty swiped at her face and stared at her. "Dr. Krantz never left me anything for my bairns. How come he left some for yours?"

Lynne stepped into the room and walked over to where the baby lay. "He didn't. I watched what he gave Mother, then used my last wages to buy the same at the pharmacists. There's also some carbolic acid crystals in a jar beside the sink. Use a little in the water you clean with to sterilize everything."

The woman stared at her back. "And where are you going that you don't need your things? Have you taken up with some man?"

Lynne blushed and laid a hand on the thin child, waiting until she had felt the shallow breathing of the little girl and considered her temperature. Without anger, she answered the accusation. "In a way. I answered an ad from a man in Montana who wants a bride. He wired the additional money for the children to go to the hospital, as well as sent tickets for passage out there."

Mrs. Garretty stepped closer, a look of amazement on her face. "You've gone crazy like your mother, child. There are Indians and who-do artists of the roughest sorts out there. You'll be killed before you ever arrive, and then, well then, he may not marry you first."

Lynne reached over to hug the woman. "I'll be fine Laura Garretty. I just wanted to thank you, for all you did for us and for mother."

She stepped away from the shocked woman and called over her shoulder. "I learned something new at the hospital. When the fever gets so high you can't bring it down with a sponge bath, bathe her skin with alcohol. They used it to save Mary Anne."

Remembering, she felt the same tightening of her throat that had left her brooding and weepy the last three days. Except for when she was with the children, or her good friends, she wanted to give in to her fears and doubts. But when she was with the ones she loved she felt the strangest joy. Their lives had changed so drastically -- maybe it was for the better. She had to try hard to look at the positive side of things. Maybe Mrs. Garretty was right, and she had gone 'round the bend like her mother. At least neither Dr. Krantz nor the sinister Dr. Stone were caring for the boys. A Dr. Leitzensal had been the only one to look in on them. Lynne had finally relaxed. Maybe the young pervert was afraid to show his face, lest Lynne file a protest against him for unethical conduct.

She hummed a song to the boys and watched them smile, smoothing their covers and urging them to lie still. Small arms circled her waist and she grinned down at Mary Anne. The little girl giggled up at her, proud of sneaking past the nurses again. Lynne lifted her up. After she had hugged and kissed each brother, Lynne dropped her down and pulled her starched white over-skirt over Mary Anne's head to keep any of the snippety nurses from seeing her. They had strict rules about girls and boys; even the babies were segregated by sex.

Softly Lynne settled back in the chair, scooping Mary Anne onto her lap and looking up at the two pink faces peering over the edge of their beds. Tom's voice was still hoarse when he whispered. "Tell us again, sister."

And again her soft voice filled the empty ward of the hospital. She was aware of other small heads peering over beds or just turning so they could listen to the soothing stories. "Well, the fever has been so bad. You know that, you three have all had it. Let's look at your spots to be sure." She ran fingers up Mary Anne's tummy first, then when she giggled, she reached up and tickled each boy. Just enough to bring a laugh from each, not enough to get them coughing. "But mother had the fever so bad, she was sick so long, that God sent a chariot down and they carried her to heaven to be with the angels."

"You know even Mrs. Garretty, who doesn't believe anything you tell her, even Mrs. Garretty will tell you it's true. She found a crown of feathers hidden in mother's pillow to show the angels had been there."

It was strange, but Lynne felt just as comforted by the story as the children. Each had tears in their eyes and the same gentle smile on their faces. Softly she hummed a special hymn, "Swing Low, Sweet Chariots," and there wasn't a sound in the ward until she finished singing.

"And tomorrow, because you are such scamps I suspect, you will not go to heaven, but will get to go home with pretty Claire." She twisted the girl in her lap and asked, "You'll like living with Claire, won't you, Mary Anne? She can show you how to dress so pretty." Mary Anne looked anything but certain and Lynne leaned forward to kiss the smooth cheek.

"The Wimberlys are so wonderful. They want you to stay and live with them until I can send for you. And Mrs. Wimberly wants Mary Anne to help her with laundry and cooking." She caught the small little hands in her own. "And Mr. Wimberly wants you two big guys to help him in the foundry, feeding coals to the fire or helping him pour molten iron."

Their eyes lit up and she got a few wow's and several questions before she could continue. "And I will leave tomorrow and go to Montana to marry the cowboy who raises horses." This time all three became excited. "Right, I get to travel by train, and stagecoach, and everything. In about seven days," she leaned down to nibble Mary Anne's ear, "I'll be his bride."

Tom sat up and scowled. "But we don't want you to be anyone's bride yet. He might be mean like Tarn was to Bonnie."

Lynne stared at the serious face and wished she knew what to say to that one. He might also be like Mr. Huntmeister or Dr. Stone. She stared calmly at him and whispered. "No, he's good like Daddy was. You know how sick you three were. I was afraid ..." her voice dropped low, then she looked up and continued. "He sent me money so you could come here and get well again."

"But we'll never ever see you again," wailed Jim. Lynne stood up and looked around, then lifted Mary Anne up to his bed. She turned around and helped Tom to crawl over into it as well.

"I know you're worried, but you have to be brave. You know the story about how Mother and Father met."

"On the boat to America." Tom whispered.

"Right, on the way to adventure and a new world. Well, we will all meet again this summer. Claire and Bonnie are coming west with her parents on a wagon train, and they want to bring you three darlings with them. So I'll go ahead to Montana and get everything ready for when you get there. Then we'll all meet..."

"And live happily ever after," chimed in Jim.

"Right. Now let's have a quick four-way hug and kiss, then it's dreamland for all of you."

Lynne fought to hold back the tears as she felt their young faces and soft lips again. Each one was so precious to her. Finally, she pulled back, leaving her mop cap in Jim's fingers. She gave him a loud smack on the cheek as she retrieved it, then gave Tom one as she gave him a quick swing over into his own bed. She let Mary Anne work at restoring the cap as she carried her to the little girl's ward.

As she tucked her sister into bed for the last time, perhaps forever, she tried to hold the tears for later. That was the real problem with being only half Irish, you could only dream half of the time.

◇◇◇

As she was leaving the ward, she was so busy wiping the tears that she didn't see the figure blocking her way.

"So, Miss McKinney, I see you found another source of funds."

Lynne halted, as aware of why she had stepped into the dark hall as he was. She had wanted to be alone. Quickly she backed up to the door leading into the children's wing.

With her back against the door, she stiffened and glared at him. "You are a fool to threaten me here. My friends have already advised me to file charges against you. If I hadn't been so busy, I would have done so by now."

He smiled confidently, but his dark eyes looked wary, glancing up the empty hallway where she had just searched for some signs of life. "What would you charge me with, offering to assist you and your poor brothers and sister?"

"Propositioning me, trying to use my desperate love for them to take advantage of me sexually, Dr. Stone. Or does a devil like you not know that is a violation of your professional ethics."

He pulled at his beard and again Lynne thought he looked like Satan. "Well, well, aren't you the brave little woman. And do you think a court would believe it was I who propositioned you. When everyone in the neighborhood knew what your mother was, knew what she was willing to do just to pay ..."

He didn't finish the sentence because she reached out and slapped him as hard as she could. The noise reverberated through the hall. A nurse, stepped out of a room and turned down the hall.

He leaned forward, his hand snagging in the hair that had escaped below her nurse's cap. "Such a dear loving sister. So you think this stranger in, where was it, Montana, is some kind of saint. Do you really think he will want something different from you than any other man would?" He moved suddenly, so that his body pressed along the length of hers. "Silly fool. You could have stayed here, kept the children with you." His lips brushed her shell like ear as he leaned even closer. "I would have been happy to set you up in a love nest."

Panicked, Lynne pushed him away as hard as she could. Then before he could grab her again, she shouted. "Do not threaten me again doctor, or I will pursue charges against you with the hospital!"

Then Lynne turned and ran up beside the nurse, moving so the broad figure in the starched uniform was between her and the doctor.

Inside the boys ward, she looked at the concerned woman's face. Quickly she told her what the doctor had asked her to do. The nurse was ready to report it, but Lynne told her to wait. If he left her alone, she didn't want to make trouble. She didn't bother to tell the nurse that he had propositioned her at her mother's death bed, three days before. When she saw his dark face peering through the small window of the ward's doors, she knew he saw her talking. Hopefully, it would be enough to keep him from approaching her again.

Yet all night she kept watch on the sleeping children, moving from one ward to the other. There would be time to sleep on the long journey tomorrow. For now, she would guard them against evil one last time.

Lynne nervously fingered the carpet bag she had retrieved from the baggage claim area. Her back was stiff from trying to stay awake all night, but the evil doctor had made her afraid. A man who would blackmail a helpless woman could also be a threat to children. Only

when she had them moved and settled with Claire's family did she
heave a sigh of relief. Now at the station, she looked around for the
same white-haired reporter who had sent the original telegrams. He
gave her a slim packet and ten dollars. Lynne looked up in surprise.
"This contains all my tickets?"

"No, Miss McKinney. Mr. Gant has wired money to the
various ticket offices. Those are the receipt numbers you must use to
claim your passage along with the letter from our newspaper
attesting to your identity so they will give you the tickets. There is
also a schedule, well, as near as we can tell, a schedule of your
transfer and departure times. Now if you'll hurry, I believe your first
train is about to depart. She tucked the money and objects into her
bag, then pulled the money out again. "The food money."

"Right, it doesn't seem like much, but Mr. Gant has stipulated
that you be permitted to stay in hotels at night and purchase food if
you wish. However, meals will be supplied with your boarding
passes if you choose to take advantage of them." Lynne palmed the
coin into her purse looped around her wrist, then shoved the papers
into the carpet bag she would carry-on with her. That way if the
train wrecked or they were stopped because of weather, she would
have the basic essentials with her.

Nervously she bounced from foot to foot. The older man
smiled at her. "Courage lass, you'll do fine. Mr. Gant is by far the
most generous and thoughtful gentleman we have had advertise for a
bride. As long as he's not disfigured or incredibly homely, you
should have a happy relationship. Thanks to our assistance at the
Globe." He added the last as he handed the pretty young woman up
onto the steps of one of the train cars. "Things have changed a lot
since I was riding one of these. But I still wouldn't ride in the front
or back car whenever there's room on one of the middle cars."

"Why not?" Lynne called as the porter urged her to step back.

He jerked a straight hand across his neck and grimaced. Lynne swallowed and gladly followed the porter's instructions to take a seat. Since she still wasn't sure where the reporter meant danger came from, or how he knew, Lynne took her seat, relieved she was in the middle of a middle car. The sharp toot of the train whistle as it took off sent her heart racing. Gripping the thinly padded bench of a seat, she stared out at the moving platform with its dozens of people and the train yard of busy locomotives.

Lynne noticed several people were staring at her and she dusted the front of her skirt. It was natural for everyone to look at her curiously. Unthinkable, a young woman traveling alone in these times, in these places. But there was no way to have a chaperone. The porter had seemed to take her presence in stride, helping her to find a comfortable seat. The other travelers would just have to tolerate her presence, seemly or otherwise.

Her first destination would be Chicago. From there the line would be called the Chicago-Milwaukee-St.Paul railway. The series of instructions were confusing, and Lynne felt far too tired to read them all. Nervously she checked out her fellow passengers. Satisfied she was the only one on her bench, she slid over so that she could prop her carpet bag between the car's side and the small of her back. Ignoring a woman who gave a disgusted whisper nearby, Lynne repinned her purse inside her skirt pocket, raised her legs and feet to fill the bench. Adroitly she wrapped her legs with her cloak so even the soles of her tiny feet were not exposed, then folded her hands firmly across her lap and the pocket. When the conductor stopped before her minutes later, she let him stamp her ticket and requested primly. "Wake me for any required stops. If there are none, wake me in Chicago."

The conductor looked shocked, ready to deliver a sermon on lady-like behavior on a train. Lynne nodded and let her dark lashes drop closed over sleepy gray eyes. "I haven't slept in days," she yawned, "But if someone needs to share this seat."

He pushed his billed cap back on his head and smiled. A few minutes later a porter came forward with a pillow and blanket and a device that looked like a gate. "Miss, miss." Already Lynne was nearly asleep. He spread the blanket over her and tucked the pillow behind her head and shoulders, opening and locking the gate in front of the bench. "That there's what we give folks for their little ones on long trips. Good thing you'se such a little thing, good thing sure enough." The conductor continued to punch tickets for others who protested the unfair treatment or asked for pillows or lap wraps for themselves.

Lynne awakened when the train slowed about ten hours later. It gave her a chance to look out at the rolling country side just as the sun was getting ready to set. It was the smell of food being hawked along the still aisle of the non-moving train that had caught her attention. Reassured it wasn't Chicago, Lynne straightened, but had to struggle to undo the restraint device before she could sit up. When it was folded, she stiffly stood and walked up and down the narrow aisle-way several turns, surprised at how cramped her muscles felt. Finally she walked back to the unoccupied loo to relieve herself. Inside she could see the railroad ties and gravel beneath the open seat.

When she returned, the gate was gone and an older couple had claimed her bench. She took her satchel and looked around, finally taking the only available seat, next to the woman who had whispered about her when they first boarded.

Lynne inquired about the meal that was to be included and was informed she had slept through it. The same kind porter came back a minute later with a ham biscuit and cup of lukewarm coffee. Lynne accepted it gratefully, then when her fellow traveler complained, she turned to look out the opposite window at the mishmash of train tracks. They were in a place called Buffalo, but she could see none of the huge beasts through the window. Disappointed, she ate in silence as the train cars were unhooked until her car and the three behind it were transferred to a different engine. Then she felt her first thrill of enthusiasm as the train began to speed westward once again.

It took several minutes for the rhythm of the rails and the sound of the train clattering along the track in the still darkness to lull her again. But a sharp elbow in the ribs made her sit upright. Frustrated, she shifted her weight, moved the carpet bag to her other side and leaned against it and the outside edge of the hard bench. Again as she was about to nod off, there came a sharp elbow to her midsection.

More than peeved, Lynne opened wide gray eyes and tried to see the middle-aged woman who was abusing her. Clearly the woman didn't want her to rest. Silently she listened to the melodic sound of the train clacking through the night. She sat as wide-eyed as an owl, staring around at her assorted co-travelers. A lantern at the front and rear of the train car shed dim light, making the dusty windows of the car into mirrors that reflected passengers at both ends of the car. Most were couples. Several were lone men in business suits. In the lantern's golden glow, she could see one passenger busily reading a paper. Most of the others looked as sleepy as she felt. Already Boston and the children seemed distant memories. Her life had changed so much in such a short time.

A buzzing sound made her turn her head. Ready, she smiled mischievously, then sent her own elbow sharply left. There was a soft, rattling breath as her elbow sank into the soft middle. But then another steady snore rose up. The rest of the night she leaned on her snoring companion to doze. The conductor tapped her shoulder shortly after daylight and she looked out to see the sleepy lights of a sprawling city. When the train finally stopped, her nostrils burned, not just with the coal dust from the engine, but the pungent scent from stockyards. Over the clattering sounds of the train she could hear the plaintive lowing of doomed cattle.

Stiffly Lynne struggled to exit, then waited on the crowded platform while the porter brought off her trunk. Chicago was dusty and smelly and she knew she must look little better. She felt gritty and dirty. The station yard had a light powder of snow on it, but the air was pleasantly warm. While she waited, she removed her cloak and shook it out, surprised when a fine layer of black powder flew off. According to the Globe's schedule, they would have a three hour lay-over and she had already decided how she would spend the time. A town this size had to have a soapy bath somewhere.

But the porter who brought her trunk looked around at the still sleeping town. "Ma'am, if'n I was you, I'd just get on the next train I could and go west. This is not the place for no lady, no ma'am."

Lynne followed his narrow black-coated back into the depot, but not before she had cast nervous glances around her. Several of her fellow travelers were casting speculative eyes her way, and there was a very rough looking man in a big brimmed hat staring hard at her, even as she replaced her cloak. So much for rest and exploration. The newspaper reader folded his paper under his arm and walked determinedly off toward a nearby, dimly lighted cafe. Oh to have the freedom of a man.

Inside, Lynne handed the porter her carpet bag to store in the baggage room. There was no ticket clerk in sight. A nice couple walked up to the window, called as though they expected to be waited on. A bespectacled, red-haired man emerged from the baggage room and smiled at them. After he had waited on them, he grinned at Lynne, an especially amused grin. When she handed him her letter and finally the official schedule she had been presented, he laughed. "Mail-order bride. My, my. Well, there is a ticket here for you, marked straight through to Ogden, Utah.

Lynne leaned forward. "I was told there would be numerous changeovers and several tickets to pick up when I left Boston. There must be some mistake, I'm to travel to Butte, Montana."

He studied the schedule, turned his head and spat emphatically. She could hear the splat as it hit a hidden spittoon.

"Well, whoever told you that, they were wrong. I mean, there will be some changeovers and such, but I'm going to go ahead and give you one ticket for all those. It will take you from here to Ogden. Course you could go to Salt Lake if you like. But that would mean more back-tracking for you later. No, Ogden's best. Then from there you'll be taking a stage coach along the Corinne-Virginia City road into Montana. Now that's what's what." He turned around to spit.

Exasperated, Lynne wiped the loose hair back from her face, then reached through the metal grated window to take the schedule sheet back. Reluctantly he let go of it. She had just pulled it forward when she saw black fingerprints on the paper. Turning her hand over, she was shocked to see her fingers were as black as though she had just emptied the ashes from the stove at home.

"Ugh. Do I have black on my face?" She raised the other hand to wipe her cheek.

He grinned at her, then nodded. Frustrated, Lynne folded the piece of paper and turned her back on the clerk. She looked around, but there were no facilities in the depot.

The older woman smiled kindly at her. "There's a pump out front next to the horse trough."

Lynne bobbed her head, then slipped outside. Only when the paper was back in her draw-bag, did she step over to work the pump. It was cold and took several vigorous pumps before a thin trickle of water emerged. The second time she pumped it, she was able to dampen her handkerchief. Only after she had washed her face, rinsed the hankie, and washed it again, did she straighten. Without benefit of a mirror, she stood in the harsh winter light and tightly twisted her hair into a bun. Drawing hairpins from her purse, she secured it above the nape of her neck. Despite her audience, she finished her toilet by rinsing the hankie once more.

Great, by the time she reached her betrothed, she would probably be darker than her porter. But at least if the ticket seller were right, he would be the last one she would have to announce her deplorable state, "Mail-order bride." He had said it as though she were some new kind of marvel. And everyone in the waiting room had laughed about it. Had Dr. Stone been right? Was she headed into the wilderness into the arms of some monster like himself? If so, she could have settled for dishonor and disgrace at home, but stayed behind with the children. Lord but she missed them.

Just as she was wondering if she should wire Dr. Stone for passage back, a group of men on horseback rode along the edge of the rail yard, herding a large group of shaggy, big-horned animals. Her heart gave a leap. They were cowboys, real cowboys. She stared in amazement, raising her hand to shield her eyes against the morning sun that glinted off the animal's horns and their strange spotted coats. The men, the cowboys guiding the animals, looked at her and grinned. It made her think of the ticket-sellers grin. But the lean men had something else in their eyes. Lynne blushed and lowered her arm. The glances were admiring. Not evil or speculative, simply admiring.

Lynne flipped her cloak closed and turned back to collect her ticket. After all, she had two or three more days of coal soot and dust to eat before she could find out if she had made the right choice.

CHAPTER ELEVEN

Boston to Montana

After she boarded the Chicago-Milwaukee-Saint Paul Line, Lynne relaxed and began to enjoy the journey. The seats on the train were far more comfortable, and although smoke still blew back over the train in a black, smelly banner the dust didn't. From the windows during the day, she stared at the changing landscape, thrilling to the broad plains and the occasional glimpse of an animal.

Mainly they passed through barren land. The plains changing little, with only an occasional rocky crest or grove of trees. The rivers they passed seemed wide and flat, as bored by the land as were the passengers. She took pride in being one of the first in her car to spot landmarks or animals. Once they were in a flat area, with nothing but white snow drifts for miles. The train seemed to slow as they came over a rise and the engineer blew his whistle. Everyone collected at the open windows, despite the cold wind, and gasped as an enormous herd of buffalo thundered along beside the train before veering south away from the tracks. As the wind blew past her, just for a minute, Lynne could imagine she was a wild Indian shadowing one of the powerful beasts, ready to pierce it through the heart.

Another time she was the first to spot mountain goats as the train labored up and over a terrifying rocky pass. It gave everyone, especially the children on board, something to do besides hold their breath. If the animals could be so nimble and sure footed, surely so could the powerful locomotive. The scariest time aboard was when they whistled through the dark and the whole train shook, tracks and all. In the morning the conductor showed them a tintype of the bridge they had gone over during the dark at the Green River in Wyoming.

Each day, Lynne carefully wrote a description of all she saw to send to the children. Although it would probably take longer for the letter to reach home than it had taken her to travel west, she knew the children would love it. She enclosed detailed descriptions of the passengers, every possible detail about the train itself and each depot they stopped at, as well as what the strange animals looked like.

Letter writing helped to fill each day and eased her longing for them. Every morning for as long as she could remember she had been the one to waken them, help them dress, keep them entertained. She missed Mary Anne's solemn questioning gazes, Tom and Jim's endless tumbling and teasing. Every word she wrote, she pictured their faces as they would read it. She filled two pages describing the Indians alone, including the clippings from one of the traveler's newspapers about uprisings among the Sioux and Crow. She couldn't help but feel frightened about what she would find in the wilderness of Montana territory. But inside the train other children raced up and down the aisle, everyone talked, smoked and read. It seemed safe, even ordinary.

The only thing she hesitated to describe was the food she ate on the train. Finally, she decided to tell, since at the Wimberly's they were probably having more than potatoes and cabbage every day. Even describing the delicious meals, which sometimes included exotic meats such as antelope, buffalo, or partridges, made her mouth water. Tables pulled down from between the windows and the porters tied on white aprons and carried the food to them on trays resting on white towels. Lynne was enchanted by all the extravagance.

When the train pulled into Ogden, she felt that something important was over. Regardless of what type of man Mr. Phillip Gant turned out to be, she would always be in his debt for this memorable adventure.

◇◇◇

The train change in Utah was far different than all the others. Running off from the depot was another train track, clearly labeled Utah Northern. She couldn't believe what the agent inside the depot had to say.

"No Miss, the track just goes out of town about seventy miles, then stops. You'll have to take the stage on up to Montana, that is, if the road is open."

Lynne had a hard time convincing the man to help her transport her trunk to the stage office, even though it was only a few hundred feet up the street. Finally she had her belongings ready to travel and managed to pick up her stage-line ticket. At least the ticket agent was more hospitable, but not very encouraging.

"Well, so you're the little bride that was ordered by this Montana man, Gant." He looked her up and down as though she were a new trick pony and Lynne frowned, uncertain of his opinion or why it should matter. He laughed at the end, then handed her the transfers.

"Be careful with that ticket Miss. It's worth quite a bit. Stage pulls out on the dot at six in the morning. Your quarters and vittles are paid for already on the road, but you'll need to find a room in town here somewhere tonight. You might run on over to the boarding house and get situated. Place fills up with rowdies sometimes in the evening."

Lynne stared at the man, trying to interpret what he had told her, as she stuffed the transfers into her carpet-bag. "How much is quite a bit?"

"You don't want to know that Miss."

"Yes, I'd really like to know how much Mr. Gant has paid for my trip."

"Well, from here, actually from Corinne, that's about $125.00. Of course that's for nearly 500 miles to get you to Butte. Gant plans to meet up there I reckon, or he would have paid the extra twenty to take you on into Helena."

Lynne stood rooted to the spot, the hood of her cloak dropping backward even as her mouth fell open.

"Hell, that ain't nothing. He paid for your train ticket didn't he, from New York or where ever."

"Boston," she answered coldly.

"Well, there you go, over two-hundred dollars just to get you here. Course you might scrub up better than one of them Flathead squaws, but unless you're a hell of a cook or ..."

He stopped as she blushed scarlet and he saw tears appear in her eyes. "Now Miss, I'm sorry," but by then he was talking to the back of her head.

Lynne navigated blindly, aiming for the boarding house he had pointed out up the street. She managed somehow to bite back the tears long enough to check into her room. Nervously she waited as the woman running the boarding house turned the register around for her to sign.

"Here you go, deary. Sign your name. It's fifty cents for the night, an extra fifty if you want a hot bath."

Lynne stared at her, unwilling to look as foolish as she must have looked to the stage agent. Carefully she pulled the purse from inside her pocket and unpinned it, ignoring the amused eyes of the woman.

She removed a silver dollar and handed it to the woman. "I guess just the room then."

"Well, deary, I don't mean to be unkind. But you look like you could stand the bath, more than the room. Of course if you're moving on to Salt Lake tomorrow."

"No, I'm taking the stage to Montana."

She clucked softly at her. "My, my, aren't you the brave one. Then I suggest you enjoy it while you can, there won't be a chance to clean yourself properly until you get where you're going, and there might not be a place there."

Lynne's eyes widened at the forwardness of her host, then she nodded. "Room and a bath." After all, her betrothed obviously intended for her to travel first class, and she had spent almost nothing during the train trip.

Once in her room, she pushed a hand down on the covers and soft ticking. It had been so long since she had slept in a bed. She slipped out of her cloak and sat on the edge. She was tempted to sprawl out on the wide expanse. But at a light tap on the door, she stood up and watched as a girl came in carrying two buckets of hot water. The girl, who was obviously some sort of Indian, was followed by the woman from the desk with two more buckets. Lynne fell backward onto the simple gold spread in delight and watched them pour the steaming water in while the older woman laid out a towel and a small bar of rose scented soap. "Enjoy it girl. Do you need any help with laying out your things or fetching your supper?"

Lynne sat up, astonished again by the woman's offer. "I think I can manage." But as the woman started to back from the room she called after her. "Is supper included in the price?"

She stared at the young woman, who was obviously little more than a child, and placed both big hands on her hips. "Do you have anyone traveling with you, a mother or aunt, some sort of chaperone?"

Lynne bit her lip, then shook her head. It was the first time it had been asked, but it had been obvious from the first time she boarded the train, that everyone had wondered. That was why after the first night on the train she had sat near older women, or with young families.

"Of course it's included. Take my advice though, eat it in your room."

"Good, then I'd like plenty of everything, but wait an hour to send it up?"

The woman laughed as she slammed the door behind her.

Lynne walked over to the mirror and looked to see what was making everyone laugh so much. Was her hair sticking up, or did she have black all over her face again? The woman staring back at her looked much like the girl who had left Boston. A little dirtier from the trip with its limited facilities for hygiene, but the same gray-eyed girl who had looked at her from her mother's mirror.

She stripped, then sank into the hip-bath, sighing as her aching back and bottom relaxed for the first time since leaving home. That had been the biggest draw back to the trains. There were no real berths to sleep in, and at the rapid pace the trains flew across the prairie, there was no time to stop and sleep in hotels. Only when the trains pulled into scattered stations to take on fuel and passengers, could she even get out and walk around to unkink from all the sitting.

She removed her hairpins, then scrunched forward enough so that she could dunk her head. The water turned gray from the dust. Furiously Lynne worked at scrubbing until her skin was pink, her hair fragrant and clean from the rose soap. Not until the water became completely cold, did she rise from the heavenly bath.

Once dressed in a clean slip, she set about washing out her traveling clothes in the tepid, soapy water. The dark garments that she had worn to the funeral, the hospital, to move, and then to travel across the country, no longer looked durable or usable. Of course she had changed underwear on the trip, and replaced her blouse twice, but still the woman had been right to suggest a bath. Maybe when the clothes were dry, she could borrow an iron from her host and press them into some shape.

Lynne took out her mother's silver brush and mirror, and after working the tangles from her wet hair with the comb, brushed it until it was dry. She couldn't help studying herself in the mirror. Was she funny looking or something? But if she were, why had the landlord and doctor made advances to her. No, she shook her head, then parted her hair precisely down the middle. No, she wasn't old or ugly or silly looking. Surely Mr. Phillip Gant wouldn't look at her and laugh. She stared into the silver-backed mirror in her hand, struggling to keep tears from coming. She would clean herself as best she could the evening before arriving in Butte, then dress in her mother's gray wool suit. She didn't intend to disappoint her betrothed, not after all the trouble and expense he had gone to just to bring her to Montana.

Silently she braided her hair, tying the end of each long braid with a strand of white thread. In the bottom of the case, she had packed her sewing kit, the darning needle and shuttle her mother had used. She was almost through crying and repacking her things when there was a knock on the door.

Lynne sat on the edge of the bed to devour the thin, succulent, roast beef, with its wonderful juices covering lovely mashed potatoes. There were also two thick rolls that smelled slightly sour, but tasted delicious with fresh butter spread over them. The best was a thin slice of white layer cake for desert served with a glass of chilled milk.

Full and exhausted, Lynne pushed the empty tray aside and drifted into a strange dream. In it she was lost in an endless gray fog. She could hear voices calling her from all directions, Claire and Bonnie, the twins and Mary Anne, even distantly her mother's voice. But she didn't turn back toward any of them, just kept wandering through the fog. Hands would reach out to grab her, or someone would laugh loudly. She brushed the hands aside and walked forward through the silvery mist. And with each step she came closer and closer to the retreating back of a tall, well-formed man.

But no matter how quickly she walked, how hard she tried, she couldn't see his face. There was only the gray mist of fog and confusion amid the distant sound of voices.

Lynne had planned to wake in time to iron her clothes for the trip, but the knock on her door was impatient. "The man from the Coach sent a message. They will wait another five minutes, then he's pulling out."

Frantically Lynne sat up. The strangeness of her surroundings, and of the child's voice frightened her. But then she saw the empty dinner tray and swore.

She had barely struggled into her only other skirt and blouse, pulled her cloak on over them and forced her feet into the worn boots. Furiously she rolled the damp clean clothes into a ball and shoved them into the bottom of her carpet bag, mashing them down so the good dresses and precious belongings would stay in. She barely had time to grab the ticket in her hand and make sure she had pinned her purse to her slip before bolting from the hotel room.

The woman came around from the desk smiling after her as she dashed breathlessly up to the already loaded stage. The ticket agent grinned widely and was more than willing to shove her into place among the already crowded passengers.

"Your trunk's loaded. Good luck to you and Mr. Gant. If you're ever in Ogden, be sure to come by and say hello."

The mule-skinner swore virulently and Lynne squealed as the bolting stage threw her back against one of the men in the coach. A woman in black scowled at her as the man opened his arms and laughed.

Blushing furiously, totally discomfited, Lynne squirmed loose from him and switched to the other side, forcing herself between the corner of the Concord Coach and the complaining woman.

Mercifully, the team of a half-dozen horses finally slowed their frantic gallop to a bone-jarring trot and Lynne twisted uncomfortably in the crowded seat. The man whose lap she had been thrown in was still leering at her, while the two men and woman beside him on that side were eyeing her critically. The stage had its own peculiar rhythm, jostling them from side to side, at the same time it bounced them up and down. Lynne knew her bladder would never hold at this kidney bruising pace.

She had grown so used to the easy banter among the passengers on the train, she had thought the stage trip would be similar. But none of the people facing her looked conversational in the least. Lynne twisted just a little more, so that her back was completely along the side of the stage, and her knees turned sideways. The woman gave her an even darker scowl and Lynne tugged to pull her cloak closed over her thin garments. If only she'd had time to iron the others, or at least put on her chemise, additional slips and corset that she normally wore. She didn't even have on stockings and could feel goose-bumps forming on her legs.

For the first time she realized that the coach was different from the train in several other ways. There was no room to pace, they would have to sit, wedged uncomfortably close together every minute of the trip. Second, there was no loo, so she would have to wait until they stopped to change horses to get any relief. But most important, there were no tight-fitting glass windows. The leather blinds were drawn down over the windows, but the stiff breeze stirred up by the frantic pace of the horses, made them flutter. Sitting where she was, there was a definite chilling blast creeping in with each bounce.

Miserably, she looked past her disapproving companion and noticed there were three men on this side of the coach as well. One was a large black man, who rolled his eyes at her, then moved an arm stiffly to tip his bowler.

It was the man who had first caught her, and who kept leering, that finally spoke. Suddenly Lynne realized why there wasn't a lot of conversation on the stage. He had to shout to be heard over the thundering sound of the horse's hooves. "Are you going all the way to Helena?"

Lynne wondered what the polite thing was to do. She clutched at her cloak, moved the carpet bag so it rested on her feet and weighted her skirt down to protect her bare legs from the cold. Her mother had trained her for years to not speak until properly introduced. But on the journey out she had talked and made the acquaintance of some very nice people. Apparently, the west didn't allow for formalities. Finally, she shouted an answer. "Yes, to Butte."

He smiled and it was like the sinister laughs and smiles in her dream. Tired, she turned and spoke to the woman beside her. "Aren't you traveling to Montana as well?" The woman brought a hand up to shield Lynne's face from her view. Shocked, Lynne realized she had been insulted. She hadn't spent any time primping to get ready for the trip again today, but she knew she didn't look that ugly. The woman obviously felt she was too good to talk to the likes of her. For a moment Lynne thought about letting the insult pass, but she hadn't been raised to ignore anything.

"I'm sorry. Did I speak without being introduced to you properly? 'Hello, I'm Lynne McKinney, and you are ...'" Still the woman ignored her. Lynne blushed bright red.

The woman who was part of the couple across from her laughed. "Well, I'm Mrs. Roeder. Don't be offended child, she's a Mormon, they're all a little strange. Maybe she thinks you're some sort of Indian. The red face, braids, and all."

Lynne couldn't help laughing. "I guess I am a sight this morning. It was the first time I had slept in a bed in weeks, and it was so heavenly, I ..."

The woman beside her scowled, but couldn't help but ask. "Where did you sleep, if not in a bed?"

Lynne studied the frowning face, the dark little eyes. Mormons didn't look so different. She couldn't help but wonder if the woman shared the same husband with several other wives. Maybe, once everyone became acquainted, she would dare to ask. Lynne's gray eyes lit up. It would be her first chance to tell anyone about the train trip. "Well, on the train from Boston, there weren't any beds. You just sort of sat and dosed, although one time I did have a bench to myself, and I put my feet up and slept."

"From Boston, you don't say. Such a long way for such a young girl to come alone. Were your parents killed by Indians along the way?"

It was such a peculiar question. "No, I came by train. My parents, my parents are deceased. But no one was killed on the train, how could they be?"

Mr. Roeder shouted an answer. "Wrecks, they wreck all the time. Kill hundreds of people. Could be attacked. We heard there were Indian uprisings throughout the Dakota's and Black Hills. Did you see any sign of trouble during your trip?"

Lynne shook her head. "No, we did see troops loading at Laramie. Several times we saw Indians in towns as we pulled through, but they looked peaceful. They were so interesting looking." She twisted to stare wide-eyed at the woman beside her. "Did you really think I look like an Indian?"

The woman stared at her coldly, taking in the serene features, wide gray eyes, and elfin smile. She timidly reached up a hand to tug at one soft brown braid, giving a snort of laughter as she tugged. Everyone laughed.

By the time they finally pulled up the lathered horses everyone in the coach had become acquainted. Someone had handed her one of the buffalo wraps to help shield her from the cold and Lynne had relaxed enough to almost be lulled back to sleep by the rhythm of the stage.

They unloaded in reverse order and Lynne was shocked when the man whose lap she had landed in reached in to swing her out, holding her up high until her feet landed on a set of planks. She didn't know whether to thank him for the lift or yell at him for taking liberties. Finally she looked back at her satchel and asked him to hand it out to her.

The lay-over had a slant-roof cabin that jutted out from a rock. One couldn't see windows or door until you walked up the plank under the overhanging roof. Inside, the single room had a rough-hewn table with benches on two sides. It was already covered with wooden bowls and in the middle sat a steaming pot of beans and a single pat of butter. Lynne looked around, but could see no partitions or other rooms. When a burly man stepped forward, she asked for directions to the facilities. He laughed and stepped to the door. He pointed to the side and she saw where the line had already formed. The men had already been and most were walking back for their meal. But the dark-eyed Mormon was bouncing uncomfortably on one foot and waiting on the other woman to finish. Lynne picked up her carpet bag and cautiously walked along another plank to the end of the overhanging roof.

She could see why the men took such liberties, lifting the women around. Where her plank ended several of the men were sloshing through boot-high mud. She was just debating what to do when the same oversized man who had been man-handling her the whole trip, laughed, lifted her up and stomped over to set her down on the flat rock outside the divided out-house. Just then the wife emerged, adjusting her skirt and all three women stood teetering about on the same rock. Lynne was relieved to see the burly man lift up the one who had finished and set her down on the plank into the house. Well, if her husband had no objections, then Lynne would have to not be finicky either. She only had the one pair of boots, and although they topped her ankles they would quickly disappear in that deep wallow.

Finally the little Mormon emerged and one of the dark bearded men who had ridden beside her walked out to swing her over to safety. It was a little embarrassing to know they were watching, but Lynne had to hope someone would be there when she finished.

There was little room inside, but Lynne took advantage of the opportunity and finished dressing. Pulling on two other slips and a pair of long stockings. There seemed little point in worrying about her chemise and corset, but she did pin up the two braids so she wouldn't look so much like a child. Finished, she opened the door to see the same big oaf waiting on her. He looked rather peeved and she noticed the horses had already been changed and most of the people were ready to load.

"Reckon we might as well load, we've missed the grub."

Lynne sighed. "Oh, I am so sorry, Mr. ___?"

"Owens. Not near as sorry as me."

He set her up in the coach without letting her feet down at all. The Mormons stood behind him, ready to board. He swore, than turned back into the building. Lynne felt guilty, but also hungry. She hadn't asked the man to stand around waiting on her had she? She didn't even know him. And what type of trip was this if meals were included but not time to eat them. She fluffed her skirt out and wedged her repacked bag at her feet. She had moved the damp clothing so that the dry things were separated by a thin sheet of leather. The Mormons settled beside her, the woman smiling at her. "Very pretty child, very pretty. But weren't you hungry."

Lynne's stomach growled in answer and she shifted to make room, moving her cloak, rolling it behind her to form a pillow in the corner. She could see her big helper if she leaned down. He was standing inside the doorway, bolting down a bowl of beans and using a thick wedge of bread to shovel it down with. It was the couple who smiled at her as they boarded.

"How charming you look. Mr. Owens told us you were already out here. Everything was just about finished, but the innkeeper gave me this for you." She handed a packet of food and a leather bound canteen across to Lynne. The last two men boarding stopped, clearly entranced by the bright smile on her face. The big man grinned and blushed as he wedged his wide self into the small space they had left vacant for him.

Lynne didn't have time to open the packet before the coach bolted into motion again. As soon as its jolting had settled back into a predictable rattle she unwrapped and devoured the chewy, rich tasting bread and crumbly goat cheese. When she'd finished all she wanted and washed it down with the funny-tasting water, she passed the wrapper and remains across to Mr. Owens. "Thank you."

He nodded and finished it off in one big bite. The rest of the trip passed without incident. Inside the coach, it was hard to tell what was happening outside, with the shades down. She had read about the dusty stage coaches, but with the snow and damp weather, their problem was mud, not dust.

The relay station they thundered into that night sat on higher ground. Lynne was able to climb down and maneuver about the yard without help. The sandy soil had soaked up enough of the sun's heat even on such a cold day to melt away most of the snow drifts they had passed in the morning.

She learned at the table, which held more bean soup and bread, that they had already ventured into another state during the hard day's drive. She would have to write the children that she had seen Utah and Idaho, but didn't have a clue as to what either looked like. She was looking around at the room, wondering where they would bed down for the night, when she heard the talk of Indians brought up.

"It's a full moon tonight. Makes sense to move on down the line. Horses know the route and we won't have to worry about any hard roads until we reach the end of the Bitterroot Range."

"Might be Indians around the sulfur springs and smoking waters."

"Yeah, but they won't attack at night."

"Nonsense, we won't get near the Yellowstone until tomorrow night, and that's if we make good time like we did today."

Lynne was fascinated, but knew enough about traveling now to not interrupt men during such a conversation. She would have to wait and ask the women what they were talking about later.

Someone was sent out to harness a new team of horses and the men sat around in the oily light of the big room, smoking, talking and telling stories. Lynne ventured out to the facilities with the two other women, grateful to have their company in the starlit night.

"What did they mean about the smoking waters?"

The young woman's voice carried through the loose framed door clearly. "I don't know, do you Ida?"

The Mormon looked around uneasily, clearly afraid of every motion or shadow. "Some place with hot water and mud that boils. Henry told me about it once." A sharp sound made a horse whinny in the distance, but the night was so quiet, Lynne could still here the hostlers working on changing out the team of horses. "Hurry in there, please."

Lynne extended a hand to touch the older woman's arm. "It's all right. That's just the men working on the team."

But by then the young wife emerged and the woman jerked away. "Indians," she whispered.

Lynne's nerves tightened. The air felt balmy and warm after the cold confinement of the coach all day. She had been looking forward to taking a walk to stretch her legs before sleeping, but it was clear neither of her new companions would want to venture away from the station.

A man called from the door of the station and the woman beside her smiled and whispered, "See you inside."

The door banged shut on the convenience door and the little Mormon bolted past Lynne toward the lighted doorway. Lynne folded her arms around her chest and looked around. It was ridiculous, everything was calm and peaceful. But still she hurried with her business, racing from the outhouse to the stage as she heard the voices of her fellow travelers talking.

"Your satchels loaded Miss." Mr. Owens said and Lynne accepted the big man's assistance in mounting the high stagecoach step.

One of the Mormon's rolled one corner of the blind up on the window beside him, and an owl made a plaintive call that pierced the night like an arrow.

Lynne shivered, grateful to be sandwiched between two big men, just as the woman on the other side had been shifted to sit in the center of her seat. "My cloak," she called, surprised at how high-pitched her voice was.

Someone passed it to her and she managed to wrap it around her shoulders and head. They raised a buffalo wrap across the legs on their side and watched as everyone did the same on the other side. In the moonlight, Lynne could see fear etched on everyone's face. Of course she had shared frightening moments with strangers on the trains, but she hadn't felt so exposed and vulnerable before. If it was this terrifying in the moonlit station yard, what would it be like on the dark trail?

The driver peered through the door. "You men ready?"

She heard someone click a cartridge into a gun, another spin the barrel on a pistol. Her right knee began to bounce, making the stiff buffalo hide rustle. In the barely open window she saw light reflect from the blue barrel of the guard's rifle. Frightened she drew in a deep breath.

The whip snapped like thunder into the stillness. The horses screamed as the driver cursed and yelled at them. As they bolted forward, she let out her breath. Everyone else seemed to breathe at the same time, and they all laughed nervously. But as the flat, empty land gave way to rocks and trees, she clutched her cloak tighter. The trail followed a river and occasionally it glittered silvery in the darkness. She breathed the cloying scent of damp earth as the horses' hooves tore clumps of it from the road as they thundered on and on into the moonlit night.

◇◇◇

Her heart still beat fast and she didn't even smile when someone whispered they were in Wyoming territory. She prayed silently, hoping that she would live to see those she loved again. They were so far away now and with each bounce the coach was carrying her farther and farther from them. All the time carrying her closer and closer to the hidden stranger in her dreams. At some point Lynne relaxed enough to doze, sagging against the shoulder of whoever was beside her.

CHAPTER TWELVE

Montana

Phillip stared around the saloon, wary as always whenever in a crowd of armed men. Once he'd cleared the dust in his throat with a shot of whiskey he looked about for a card game. The place was quiet so early in the afternoon. He'd left the ranch with Shorty and Banes after asking the miners to tend the animals today, and then feed them tomorrow morning before clearing out. He'd expected his business would take a lot longer than it had.

Yesterday he'd brushed and picked the manes and tails before hazing the herd of twelve green broke horses into town. With more time, he could have brought them all but the gunfight at the river had delayed things. Still, he'd kept the better mares at home and had already sold all twelve ponies to the army.

The banks might be unsteady and the economy shaky, but with the Sioux uprising in the Dakotas, the army had a real need for mounts. Now, his pocket full, he didn't want to rush to get changed and ready. Restless, he ordered another drink, still worried about tomorrow. He pulled out a double-eagle and flipped it into the air repeatedly. Behind him he heard the piano player spin the stool before sitting down to plink out a tune.

A golden haired girl, with enough paint on her face to keep a wagon greased and moving for a month, swished his way. Luckily, four dusty cowboys entered, the tallest looping an arm around the whore's waist and spinning her back toward the corner. Phillip pocketed the coin and tilted the brim of his hat at one of the other newcomers.

By the time he downed the drink, he had been invited to a game of poker. Seated with his back against the wall, his eyes on the doorway in case one of the four Georgian's might enter, he accepted the clumsy deal of cards by one of the cowboys. Phillip, kept the cards folded near his shirt breast and scratched his beard between collecting each one.

Four hours later, he sat with a large pile of money in front of him. Two whiskey bottles stood empty in the center of the table. There was a growing rumble from the squinty-eyed, blocky cowboy across from him.

Phillip felt a moment of regret. He had been here before, unfortunately experienced all of it many times. A man didn't live by the gun as long as he had without knowing when he was going to have to kill a man or be killed.

"Damn card cheat," the man shouted.

There was a lot of mumbled agreement.

Reluctantly, Phillip set his hat over the pile of money in front of him. "Boys, it doesn't have to go this way. I've played your game, with your deck of cards, and that you've dealt. I don't need trouble."

Before the man whose hands rested on the edge of the table could tilt it, Phillip swept the hat and his winnings away "Steady," he warned, but as the man shoved, the squinty-eyed cowboy drew.

Phillip fired, hitting the man mid chest. Cornered, he kept the gun leveled at all of them, pointing from one to the other. "Drop your guns and step away, or eat lead."

As expected, the barkeep pumped his shotgun and Phillip sent a shot his way that gouged a new groove in the bar. The man dropped the gun without firing. In the instant silence, Phillip heard the guns drop one by one. Keeping his eyes moving, even pointing the gun at the prostitute who'd first approached him, he backed carefully out the door.

CHAPTER THIRTEEN

Boston to Montana

When they pulled into Idaho Falls in the morning, Lynne was shocked to see clapboard storefronts and houses. The tiny town seemed to still be asleep as the coach pulled up in front of a grand fronted, one story hotel and all the exhausted passengers climbed out. As Lynne disentangled herself from the other passengers, the man grinning beside her tipped his hat. She gave him a cold look as her nose told her there was hot coffee and fresh bacon waiting. Inside she also found scrambled eggs, hot cakes and molasses and this time Lynne was one of the first to sit down at the table.

She heard the big man growling and turned to see Mr. Owens arguing with the one who had tipped his hat to her.

"A man can't help enjoying holding such a sweet little bundle."

It was the driver, Mr. Dodd, who stepped between the two bigger men and forced them to take up opposite ends of the table. Embarrassed, Lynne looked down at her full plate, her appetite suddenly gone. The driver stood over her staring down at her bowed head as though he had something on his mind. She looked up at him through down swept lashes, her face blushing until he swore and walked away.

It was the little Mormon who clicked her tongue and said. "Pay the beasts no mind child, here eat up. It's certainly not your fault there are not enough decent women to go around in this wilderness."

The man who had sat beside the Roeder couple during the trip stared across at the three Mormon's and said what they all were thinking. "There might be, if the Mormon's would settle for just one wife."

Again voices rose in anger and the driver stood up and swore at them as though they were the team of horses he expected to pull together. "Now, I know you folks are tired and your nerves are rattled, but we've got at least two more days of hard travel to reach Butte. If the weather holds and the Indians leave us alone, I intend for us to be there by noon on Tuesday. So don't give me any trouble, any of you," and he glared down to the end of the table where Lynne sat timidly chewing a strip of bacon. "Or I'll put you out here and you can figure your own transport for the rest of the trip."

Furious, Lynne jumped to her feet. "Sir, I have done nothing by word or gesture, to cause trouble on your stage coach, and I think you owe me an apology."

He stared at her, taking his time to study every inch from her mud-splattered dress to the hair that was escaping like soft mist from her crown of braids. Lynne recognized the look instantly and wished she had never called his attention to herself. Great, now she would have three of the big beasts bothering her.

"I have no desire for anyone's attentions. The only reason I am making this journey is to ... well to," as all eyes focused on her she blushed even deeper. "I am traveling to Montana to marry a rancher named Phillip Gant."

There were congratulations all around and both women leaned forward to fuss over the blushing girl. Lynne sank down at the table, wondering what had possessed her to make such a confession to these people.

The older woman patted her arm. "Oh, you precious creature. I wish I could be there for the wedding, but my sons and I are getting off the stage here today. I wish you all the best my dear."

The other woman smiled and patted her shoulder. "It's a shame dearie, we're only traveling to Bannick City. I know you will make such a lovely bride." And she leaned forward to hug her. For just a second, Lynne felt as though these were women she had known all her life. But if they weren't traveling all the way, then she would have to contend with the men who were already squabbling over her.

Driver Dodd was the only one unimpressed. "Well, get your business done folks." He rolled eggs in a flat cake and drizzled molasses in the center. "John get out and help the Mormons' unload their gear. See if the livery can let us have a fresh man as well as new horses and load any cargo that's being sent on."

"Ten minutes, or be left." He thundered past and Lynne tried to shrug the fatigue from her back and shoulders. Hurriedly she ate what she had on her plate, glad to have hot coffee to wash it down. So much for washing up and sleeping a little.

The mild break in the weather seemed to have disappeared; there was a whistling bite of wind as she walked from the hotel toward the coach. As she stepped up into it, she gripped the door and balanced for a minute to stare inside. Two men smiled eagerly at her from one side of the coach, both waiting expectantly. Apparently the black man had gotten off with the Mormons. On the other side, the Roeders had moved down to one end. She climbed aboard and sat next to the wife who again gave her a kind smile. Just before the door was snapped shut, a white haired man was assisted into the coach.

He examined the arrangement only for a moment before choosing to squeeze in next to Lynne. She heard some whispers, then the husband moved to sit across from his wife. Lynne scooted over, again adjusting her cloak and the buffalo robe over her and the other lady before the ride began. She lifted her carpet bag to the seat to keep the older man from scooting against her.

It began to snow about an hour out of the small settlement and Lynne wondered how anyone could survive in the open weather. The driver and the two men with rifles must be frozen. The fine, powdery snow seemed to sift in through the leather blinds at will, and when she shuddered from the cold, the old man beside her laughed. For the remainder of the day's journey, he managed to keep everyone spell bound with stories about blizzards, gold-mining, Indian fighting and fur trapping. When they pulled into a relay to change horses, the riders shifted places so the Roeders were on the same side again, the older gentlemen facing Lynne as he told her stories.

"I can't wait until we stop tonight. I want to write everything down you've told me and send it to my brothers and sister back in Boston."

"You flatter me darling. But is your sister as lovely as yourself?"

"She's beautiful." Lynne's face grew wistful and he laughed.

"Aye, then she must be your twin." Lynne blushed at the compliment, then explained about Tom and Jim and her younger sister.

The other woman was the one to tell him that Lynne was traveling to Montana to get married.

"Truly, now I know every buckaroo in the state, who is this lucky gentleman."

"Phillip Gant of Helena, Montana. Do you know him?"

He scowled at her, then clucked his tongue. "Well, well, so you've come to Montana to marry our Dark Prince."

For a moment Lynne pictured the black man who had traveled with them the first two days and wondered why she had never considered the possibility. Could she do something like that? But how could she back out, whoever or whatever, Mr. Gant turned out to be?

It was Mr. Owens who asked, "What do you mean by that Dark Prince business?" Then he turned toward Lynne. "Are you planning to marry a darkie?"

His tone was as shocked as Mrs. Roeder's face beside her. But Lynne didn't have time to answer, even if she could.

"No, no, he's white, as white as any man can be who lives in this sun baked country. No Phillip's more the morose and melancholy sort, that's what I meant. And this lovely creature seems to be all sunshine and roses."

She asked before she thought about the consequences. "Melancholy, but can you tell me what he looks like?"

Mr. Owens leaned his considerable bulk forward and yanked up the shade over the window. In the slanting gray light from the snow filled air he stared at Lynne. "You mean you don't know what he looks like?"

Lynne looked down at her hands, then back up at the beefy features staring at her. "Not that it is any of your business, but I am his mail-order bride."

The woman beside her gasped, the old timer hooted, and the man who had become overly friendly swore. "I knew, I knew she was just a sweet piece when she went to sleep in my arms the other night." He swore again and Mr. Owens inhaled the cold night air. As the horses labored up a steep incline, the woman who had hugged her like a sister moved to the other side of her husband.

Lynne's knee bounced and her lip trembled as the outraged man let the blind drop down. But even in the semi-dark, she was afraid they would all see the tears of shame on her lashes. Just a civilized business arrangement. She could give them all the arguments she wanted. But to every small mind in that coach only a fallen woman would make such a journey to marry a complete stranger.

This time the journey was endless, the going slow with the driver often resorting to flicking his whip and swearing at the animals. They made it up one grade after an endless struggle by the animals. At the top, the driver dismounted and ordered them all out to walk. "Can't take a chance in this kind of weather with her slipping over the edge."

Lynne gasped in shock to see the narrow wagon road with its shear drop below. Above them, tall, dreary pines whipped in the howling wind. She tugged her cloak as tight as possible and leaned into the wind. The cold flakes burned her skin and stung her eyes and for a moment she was afraid she would slip and fall. The two men who had fought over her hours before, ignored her totally. Just when she thought she would have to beg for help, the slim older man moved along beside her, wrapping the buffalo robe around them both and moving forward to grip the harness on one of the horses.

"Need some ballast, both of us, before the wind blows us

away."

Gratefully Lynne slipped an arm around the thin waist but used her own strength to help him walk down the long grading. At the bottom, they loaded while the coach waited for those who had begun ahead of them to make it down the treacherous trail. The driver Dodd and one of his guards crawled inside the coach. Lynne hadn't realized how much warmer the coach was then the howling wind until she saw their faces. The skin on the driver looked like he had been boiled. The old man pulled out a silver plated flask and offered it to Lynne. She shivered, but shook her head. The old man took a long swig, then passed it to the freezing men. One of them lit a cigarette, cradling his hands around its warmth.

Owens was the first of the others to reach the bottom of the grade and he looked disapprovingly in at Lynne. Irritated, she took the flask back from Dodd and handed it to the old man as though she had been sharing a nip with the others. Finally the big man helped Mrs. Roeder and her husband in and the man he had fought with earlier. The driver and his helper just moved over, but stayed inside the warm cabin. The combined breath from all the bodies packed in close together created a thin film of moisture that coated the leather flaps covering the windows.

"Well, we've got two hours more of daylight, before we get to the station. The way this is coming down, there's every chance we'll lose our way and end up stranded. Course if we sit here, we may end up buried by the blizzard."

He took the flask back from the old man and took a long pull before handing it back and lighting another smoke. No one inside spoke. Lynne's feet were cold, but she kept flexing her toes, hoping they would warm back up.

"Least we don't have to worry about the damn Indians in this.

They won't be out freezing their bare asses in a northern. It's up to you folks, stay and freeze, or try to get on through."

When no one answered Lynne looked up at the driver. "I say we at least try. We might not make it, but we'll know we've tried."

"I second that." The old man said. Lynne was surprised when the others all concurred.

For the next two hours she sat with her arms wrapped around herself, her eyes closed as she prayed. After a while, the rhythm of the coach became smooth enough to soothe her fears and she nodded. But before she gave into her fatigue, she made sure she was not leaning against anyone.

By the time they approached their next stop at Dillion, the terrible, blinding snow had stopped. The road was covered in snow, but it was the powdery kind that didn't pack down or melt. As the horses picked their way along, the old man opened the leather flap and sunshine seeped in to warm them despite the nip in the air. Outside, tall, heavy branched trees marked the border of the road. A tall drift of snow was catching on the right side of the road, as though all the snow were being swept by a giant broom. Lynne stuck her head out through the window, inhaling the sharp clean cold of the air.

The station people were ready to pack up and move on out with the stage coach. The man who ran the place confessed he had seen sign of Crow around the corral, and since his hired hand had run off, he doubted he could shoot them quick enough to scare them off.

Dodd advised him that with the weather what it was, there wouldn't be that much coming through till spring. Might as well close up. They could always rest over at Idaho Falls and take it slow enough to get through with one team into the relay before Bannick.

Lynne couldn't remember being so bone tired. The constant jarring made every muscle ache and it hurt to sit, her tail bone felt so bruised from the long ride. The food was poorly cooked, the beans watery and the cornbread burned and hard. In the corner, she could see the station master's wife sitting holding a bundle on her lap.

Since she was isolated from conversation with the others, she had chosen a seat near the end of the table. Now she rose and walked over to stand by the fireplace and get a closer look at the woman. The woman's hair was long and black, oily blue looking in the fire light. But it wasn't a blush that colored her skin red. What was it the ticket master in Ogden had said? That she might clean up better looking than a squaw. This woman was a squaw. Lynne moved closer still, fascinated by the other's exotic looks.

The woman turned dark eyes on her, as round and empty as an animals. She tried to talk soothingly as she closed the last step between them. "Is that your papoose?"

But before she could reach out a hand to touch it, the woman stood up and screamed and ran from the cabin into the dark night. Everyone turned to stare at Lynne.

"I'm sorry, I didn't mean to frighten her. I just wanted to see the baby."

The driver swore but the station man held up a hand. "It's all right, Seth, she didn't do nothing wrong. Since the baby died of fever, Little Feather's been plumb crazy. I was planning on leaving her behind. Let her go back to her people."

"Poor thing," the wife said.

Lynne sank down onto the vacant chair, reaching down to pick up a tiny corncob doll that had fallen when the woman fled. She stared at it and whispered. "Losing a baby is hard for any woman. I've seen this kind of sadness before."

The big man rose from the bench and started for the door. "Hell, she ain't a woman, she's a squaw."

The old man rose and blocked his way. "There's a jar in the corner if anyone needs to go. Didn't you hear the man say he'd seen sign of Crow?"

It was a restless night. Lynne accepted a bedroll from the station master, then pulled it over into the corner where there wasn't already a bed. She could feel Owens and the other men staring speculatively at her in the flickering light. One more day. Just one more day of this endless journey and then she would meet her husband. But she couldn't close her eyes and sleep. She could hear them talking softly and whispering at the table. Finally the married woman picked up her bedding and pulled it over into the same corner. Her husband placed his pallet outside hers.

"Now, go to sleep, Miss McKinney. We don't want your betrothed to be disappointed in his bride."

Lynne turned her head and stared at her blindly, reaching out to accept the hand the other extended. Suddenly, the tears slipped down onto the coarse blanket of her bedroll and she felt a tide of exhaustion sweep over her. For a moment she couldn't decide which was more wonderful. Having everyone thinking good things of her, or having just one accept her even when they believed the worst?

◇◇◇

The squaw didn't return, so the station master and the driver cooked breakfast. Lynne woke to the smell of scorched bread, with every bone in her body aching. The last thing she wanted was to get back into the coach. One of the stage guards loaded his gun and stood in the door of the station, while the other went out to chain up the team. The light was pale, the sun still not up. When the horses were ready, they shifted in their harness blowing big clouds of steam into the morning air. Both men stood with rifles ready while the women took turns dashing to the single outhouse.

This time there were more men ready to shoot. Lynne sat with an arm wrapped around the other woman as they rode on the floor of the coach. All the windows had the leather blinds pulled up and tied half-open and the cold air seemed to sink around them like a blanket. But Lynne's heart was beating too hard for her to feel cold.

They had been on the road over three hours when the first arrow penetrated the wood and leather sides of the coach. They were driving beside the usual rocks of the road cut and one of the guards fired back. Lynne heard a scream like a child in pain, then looked out of the window to see a row of painted heads running along even with the coach windows. The guns inside were fired so close over their heads that she gagged on the black smoke and her ears throbbed with their booms.

Dust from the road and the thunder of the horses outside made her close her eyes in terror. The wind was so sharp, even the men who were ready to fire, lowered the blinds part way. They rode the same way for nearly an hour when they heard gun fire ahead and smelled smoke. This time she plugged her ears with her fingers and tried to scrunch low so the men who were bracing to fire didn't crush her beneath their boots.

As the driver pulled the carriage to a stop in front of the post, one of the men held the door open while Lynne and the other woman were shoved out and then physically grabbed and pulled into the relay station. The men in the coach quickly followed. Her companion sat down in a heap and began to cry.

Lynne moved toward her but the woman's husband buried her face against his neck and rocked her to and fro. Owens stared at her, but Lynne didn't want to play the helpless female. Quickly she straightened and looked around the inn for something useful to do. One man lay bleeding on the floor, his eyes white in death. In the back of the room a white woman was crying hysterically. Lynne raced to check her out, but there was nothing physically wrong with her. One of the men shouted an explanation. "It's her man lying there dead. Fool woman. Can't anybody shut her up?"

Lynne tried to hold her but the woman pushed her away. It was then she heard the sound of a child crying. A small girl, perhaps the same age as Laura Garretty's toddler, stood holding a broken doll, crying so loudly that she couldn't get a breath. When Lynne knelt to tend to her, she was amazed to see a dark hole on the child's thigh, oozing sticky blood. Frantically she tore her slip to bandage the wound, then gathered the baby into her arms.

The driver and the two guards were shouting over the sound of guns. It surprised Lynne. She had thought the Indian's shot people with arrows and scalped them with tom-a-hawks. But perhaps that was just Mr. Cooper's version of the world. Someone needed to tell these Indians how they were supposed to fight.

The shutters and roof of the building were burning briskly, and cinders began falling on them from the thatched roof.

"Back in the coach," the driver roared. And Lynne and her precious cargo followed the Roeders back into the floor of the coach. The old man had hold of the hysterical woman, but when she tried to run, he calmly clubbed her, then drug her out to join the other women on the coach floor.

One of the horses was hit and its scream was more torturous than that of the woman. Swearing, the men cut it loose and eased the others sideways, freeing the horse hooked beside it and shortening the team. Working frenziedly, the men were able to move a trunk up in front of the driver's post. When one of the guards was shot, Lynne watched him tumble from the top of the stage with horror. But others continued the work until they had stacked enough of the load to provide shelter for one of them on top.

Lynne watched as the roof of the station collapsed where they had all hidden minutes before. Sparks from it must have singed the horses, for they rolled their eyes in terror and before the driver could whip them into motion they were off.

As soon as the coach sailed over the rise and down the road, the world became silent again. The Indians were left behind with the burning station. It was the old man who reasoned it out and had them all sit up on the seats.

"They got what they wanted. An Indian only fights when he has a reason. Maybe his horse has died and he needs another. Maybe the children are hungry and there's no game, so he raids another tribe or a white man to steal what he needs for food. They have twelve horses to ride, and one to cook for supper. Why risk getting shot? They won't be coming after us for a while."

Just as well, the smaller team was already exhausted. Lynne was amazed that they had the heart to continue to run. As soon as the driver realized they were safe, he slowed the animals to a trot.

They didn't make the next relay until nightfall. As the carriage rocked back and forth, Lynne clutched the crying child to her. Softly she crooned a song to her, just as she would have to Mary Anne when she was frightened. In the still night, the sound of her song was so comforting that even when the baby slept pillowed in her arms, the men asked her to keep singing. When Lynne thought her arms would no longer hold the child any longer the woman on the floor sat up and reached for her.

She was crying in a soft keening sound and Lynne let the child slip into her arms. Gently she folded the buffalo wrap around them both and continued to croon until the woman no longer cried.

"You have a wonderful way with children, Miss McKinney," said Mr. Owens.

Lynne was startled, and stared across at the big man. "I'm the oldest girl in a family of seven Mr., Owens. There's not that much to know about them."

The woman who had become her friend reached out a hand to clutch hers. "Why don't you get off at Bannick with us? They can tell your Mr. Gant where you are and he can come to you there."

Lynne shook her head. "Thanks, but I've made this long journey and now it's almost over, I intend to go on in."

They rested only long enough to change the team and to drop off the three who had reached their final station. The old man leaned forward, surprising Lynne with a kiss on the cheek. "I always knew Philip Gant was uncommonly lucky, but after meeting you," He kissed the other cheek. "Any man who gets such a bonnie lassie has the luck of the devil. Perhaps you'll permit me to stop and visit you both in the spring."

Lynne put a hand to her cheek and curtsied at his old-fashioned gallantry.

The driver Dodd asked. "Aren't you coming on into Butte with us old timer.

"No, I think I'll make sure the Roeder's get home safely. You know there are rumors the Indians are up and about."

They all laughed at the small joke. Lynne hugged Mrs. Roeder and kissed her cheek as though she were her dearest friend.

"I wish I could come into Butte to stand up for you at the wedding. But we wish you all the best." Her husband extended a hand and Lynne shook it and even tolerated a kiss from him as well.

◇◇◇

At dawn, the mud and blood splattered coach entered the last post before Butte on the Corinne-Virginia City road. Lynne waited inside the coach to be handed down by Mr. Owens, eyeing the calm little station with suspicion. There was only a tiny plume of smoke to indicate anyone was home. No fire, no arrows, no flying bullets.

The driver stared as Lynne helped the barely conscious woman and her child into the station. He grinned at her, then turned to take her satchel from Mr. Owens.

"In honor of your wedding day, we'll rest and eat here until you've had a chance to bathe and change. Then we'll drive on into Butte."

Lynne smiled and stared into the relay post. "If it is as small and intimate as all our other stops, I may be better off going into Butte as I am."

He laughed, but Lynne stepped into the customary long room

with its big table and benches. The woman inside escorted the other woman and child into the corner where a bed stood ready.

She turned around to stare at Lynne, then smiled. "Well, our feed room's not big, but it does have a door you can lock for a little privacy. And if you can wait until I heat the water, there's a washtub you can make do with."

Lynne was so exhausted, she didn't know if she would have the strength to eat, let alone bathe and attempt to dress. But the others were equally tired, and the food was decent. What had the woman back in Ogden said? "It may be your only chance for a bath." With gratitude she accepted the strong lye soap, clean feed sack, and the dented metal washtub full of water.

Carefully Lynne opened her carpet bag, pulling out the brush, comb and mirror that would be all she had to prepare herself for her future husband. The gray traveling suit was wrinkled from being packed so tightly in the case and the gray hat looked hopeless. Even the leather shoes were damp and mold streaked. Lynne wanted to cry when she saw that the damp clothes she had packed so quickly in Ogden were ripe with mildew. It would take bleach to remove the smell, but she would just have to live with the spots.

She used the corner of a full sack of grain to brush off the shoes, then molded the little hat around the remains of a barely full sack of grain. Smiling and undaunted, she stripped and made quick work of the bath, scrubbing hard with the stringent soap but feeling too exposed in the cold room to enjoy soaking. By the time she had washed her hair, her teeth were chattering. She stood with her feet in the damp water while she toweled off, then bundled her hair in the coarse cloth of the towel. With the care of an acrobat, she tiptoed across the cold stone floor. Quickly she pulled on clean underclothes, hose, and tugged on the little gray boots. The skirt fit perfectly over the only slip she had left clean and she shook out the soft linen blouse she would wear under the tight little tailored jacket.

Half-dressed, she brushed out her hair completely, leaning forward to twist the long brown tresses into a rope which she coiled and pinned on top of her head. As fine as her hair was, she knew it would pillow out as it dried, but the loose style would work if the hat would fit.

The skirt was so dated, it was fuller in the back, pleated down the front. The jet velvet that trimmed the sleeve caps and wrist gave it a touch of style. Lynne tugged on her only gloves, the black kid ones she had used all winter. Frustrated, she peeled them off.

Well, let the men grin, she would have to have a woman to help her do something with the streamers on the blouse and perhaps the station wife would have an iron. How could anyone be expected to travel across America without an iron? She vowed never to do it again.

Lynne stepped out into the large room, immediately aware of all the eyes turned her way. She sat down on the bench edge of the hearth, tilting her head forward so that her damp hair would dry. She heard the low rumble of appreciative male voices. The fat station master's wife nodded toward them. "They all think you're beautiful."

"Good for them, but I feel a mess. I can't do anything with this and everything is so wrinkled."

"Here," she placed a heavy iron near the coals to heat, then smiled and wiped her hands on her apron. "Now for the bow." She smiled at the shy girl, "It's soft and pretty, the wrinkles don't show."

"Something old, something new. The suit was my mother's, the blouse a gift from a friend. Perhaps it wouldn't be as bad, if I knew what he looked like."

"Weddings can be frightening things." She nodded toward the short burley man behind the counter. "Joe there came to our farm in Idaho, just rode up one day. He had a beard and smelled." She laughed and shook her head as she took the jacket and hat from Lynne to press. "Bold as you please, he asks Pa, 'Have you got a daughter grown enough to marry off? I'm looking for a wife.'"

Lynne tilted her head to look at the man behind the bar, then looked at the smiling woman in front of her. "He traded Pa a big horse and a rifle, and my father gave us his blessing. My mother stood in the corner and cried. I was only fifteen. We had to ride down the circuit preacher. Took two weeks before we caught him and could have the knot tied proper."

Lynne stood up and tried on the jacket, buttoning it snugly up the front. The woman snapped the little hat, then added a blue-jay feather from above the fireplace. Lynne tried it on, wrinkling her nose. "Do you think this smells?"

The other woman sniffed, then smiled. "Something borrowed, something blue." She held out a tiny bottle of vanilla, then dabbed it on her finger and touched Lynne's throat in two places.

Lynne giggled. "Nice, but he may think I'm a cookie and eat me up."

One of the men at the table laughed and turned to whisper to the others. Lynne blushed and the little woman touched her elbow.

"A woman needs that sort of time, to get to know a man first, before, well before their real wedding night." She whispered it as she carried the iron and followed Lynne back into the feed room. Lynne helped her lift the washtub and together they stepped to the back door to empty it. In the early morning light. Everything looked so normal, so calm, but Lynne felt in knots..

"I know this is awful, but I think it may be time for my monthly."

The woman leaned back and shook her head. "Well, do say. It can happen like that, and generally does, when it's most inconvenient. You wait here dearie and I'll bring you something to use."

At the door she turned to whisper back to her. "Everything is always for the best, don't you see. It's God's way of giving you two a little time to wait and get acquainted."

Lynne blushed deeper. Well, as long as Mr. Phillip Gant saw it that way. She lifted and smoothed her breasts beneath the soft linen, hating the aching heaviness of them. She could only hope he shared the civilized sensibilities of the station wife.

She packed her carpet bag one last time, smoothed the feed sack over the others to dry and waited. In a few short hours she would climb out of a stage in Butte and into the arms of a stranger. What had the old man called him? The Dark Prince. Morose meant sad, but why was he sad? Would he be like all the other men she had met in her few years, eager to take advantage, slow to offer respect? She had asked for help with her blouse; but she needed help with her heart.

CHAPTER FOURTEEN

Phillip Gant lifted his derby and ran a hand through his washed and combed hair for the fiftieth time that morning, then tried to loosen the stiff circle of his starched collar. He glanced down the street to where the four Georgians held court, but no one was out. From habit he reached up to his face, stopping just before he scratched the baby-white skin that told where the mustache and beard had been.

Ten long days of waiting, fidgeting, working on the house to be ready for her. He had taken the wagon into town for supplies Monday, then lingered. He probably would have frightened her back to Boston if she had seen him yesterday. Living alone, chasing horses and wrestling cows didn't require anything more than good dungarees and a stiff shirt. His hair had been longer than an Apache's and he had a beard that housed more critters than his old collie's fur.

If she didn't make it soon, he'd be out of money. First he had visited Lonagan's and been shaved and curried like a prize pony. Then he'd blown a wad at the Dry Goods. Buying food was all right, but when he looked around a minute too long, the Dutchman had started selling him. He now had a black suit coat that was too tight, a shirt that was too starched, and a hat that made him look like some whiskey peddler. That was only the beginning. This morning the Dutchman's old lady had said, "A lady, you are getting a lady from back East. She will need so many things. Clothes, maybe she doesn't have enough clothes for our cold weather."

He had out argued that one. "There are things a woman needs to run a house, not just clothes." That's where she had him. One old skillet was all he'd had. Now he had enough doo-dads and cooking things to tour the county as a peddler.

Damn, this was a stupid thing to do. If Johnson hadn't ordered a bride in December, this would never have happened. But he and every man in Helena had been jealous when the bald man had helped the beautiful Swede from his buggy. No Nez Perce or Flathead, but a white, white woman. He could visualize her still. She had worn a red cape with fur trim, been nearly as tall as Johnson, and had ice blue eyes, white blonde hair, and two breasts like alabaster pillows.

The fact that Phillip had squatted out the best land on the upper Beaver Head and was running 200 hot-blooded horses on the tall buffalo grass didn't seem so important. Nor did the long ranch house he had finally gotten up before the January blizzard. Not when he and every man in Helena knew what Johnson had spent that cold blizzard enjoying.

Phillip rested a boot on the edge of the horse trough, spitting over its ice flecked surface. Where was she? He had invested over three hundred dollars in getting her this far, and the newspaper agent had sworn she would be here in ten days after he wired her the money. That was the first thing he would ask. What had she needed it for? Probably a new hat or fur-lined cape like Johnson's Helga.

It was already nearly noon and he couldn't afford to stay later than one. The animals hadn't been tended since early morning and he'd told his helpers to get back to the mine, he could handle the ranch. Now he would have to get back soon or bury them when he did. It would take four hours even in good weather to make it back to the ranch, and in Montana, no one was promised good weather.

Out of the corner of his eye, he watched a tall, bearded cowboy edging up the street. Phillip pulled his boot back on the boardwalk so quickly the rowel whirled. The cowboy stopped. Just by swiveling his hip a little, the fancy little coat swung open and Phillip could reach one handle of his colt. He pushed the derby back at an angle and got back to his musing. Montana was a hell of a country come to think of it. Why he didn't move on to Oregon or California was beyond him.

The little gold strike that he had come to mine had panned out three years ago. He had been lucky to find the small vein, but it had played out quickly. By then, he was in love with Montana, the deep valleys nestled between blue mountains, with cold streams full of big trout, and grass a horse could live on all year. The best part was, the horses were already here. Some runty mustangs the Spaniards or Indians had lost, but also big sleek animals that had been lost by unfortunate travelers. The thunder of them in the valleys at night had tied him here forever. He had tried a lot of things in his life, but raising horses was the thing he was born to do.

The saloon door creaked again and Phillip backed up into the opening in front of the Dry Goods store. It was a hell of a lot harder to think in town than out on the range, harder to watch your back. He yanked the derby off, setting it to twirling on his finger, before returning it to his head. Right, the first thing he had tried was soldiering. He had come of age during the war and at fifteen had cried until his mother let him go play soldier. Lord, had he been a fool. Before it ended, he had gotten a belly-full of being shot at and of shooting back and only wanted to get home.

But it had been gone, and he couldn't go back. The big farm, fast horses, the mansion, even his mother and sisters. The war had taken them all. The door swung a third time and Phillip swore. Hurrying, he slipped through the Dry Goods store and out the back. Creeping along the alley back to the sidewalk gave him time to rehearse some more.

He had never liked to make idle conversation. Johnson swore that was what made marrying a Swede so fine. They talked foreign so you didn't have to make conversation all the time. But a woman from Boston. He needed to practice telling some things. Let's see. Then he had let that fat sergeant sweet-talk him into enlisting to fight the Indians. He swore as he remembered how big headed and gullible he was, believing he was the best shot and horseman the big liar had ever seen. So he could fight Indians, looked like that might be useful soon if things got any more stirred up in the Dakotas.

He heard two men approaching and he pulled the silver-barreled revolvers from his holster. Then he had tried cow-herding in Texas, but the longhorns were too dangerous and unpredictable for his taste. After watching a fellow wrangler get stomped and gored, he was ready to move on. Gun-slinging paid more than wrangling, but he gave up the life of a cow-herder when he heard about the gold.

He thought he heard the stage pulling in about the time the first man fired at him. Anxious to be waiting there so he could make a good impression, he opened fire and took the two coming down the alley, one in the shoulder, the other in the foot. Then squatting he spun to take the one in the hip that was sauntering down main street. All three were only wounded, but he hadn't planned on killing anyone on his wedding day. He kept his eyes on them until someone came out to pick them up for doctoring.

He dusted his jeans, loaded and holstered his guns and brushed off his coat. Of course he had been lucky, always lucky. He had been lucky enough to find gold, bank it and get on with something else in life. Plenty of men were still working at panning gold or digging out veins of copper and silver. But freezing water had caused more than one friend to die from pneumonia, and if that didn't get you, some bush-whacker was always ready to plug you for your day's grit.

Seemed like horse ranching might have a down-side to it too, if these good-old-boys were anything to go by. Last night, one of them had gotten upset about losing a hand of poker. Phillip had seen no choice but to shoot first. Seemed like the three remaining men were duty bound to call his hand. He eyed them coolly, his eyes darkening when one still moved. Finally he let people move close enough to help them.

Calmly, as though he met a bride every day, Phillip Gant stepped across to the front of the stage coach line. He could hardly wait to see what he'd paid for.

CHAPTER FIFTEEN

Butte was bigger than Lynne had expected. One and two story buildings crowded both sides of the muddy street. It was also uglier than she had expected, with the remains of snow red and yellow stained from the mud filling the streets. She stared out at all the commotion, then looked across at the woman who had journeyed there with her. The survivor of the Indian attack still looked in shock, her eyes glazed, her cheeks sunken. The baby cried, had cried incessantly. Lynne checked her again, this time finding the tiny girl's leg hot and swollen. She forced the two men riding inside to look at the child's leg with her.

"Blood fever. She'll have to see a doctor quick, might have to come off." One of them offered. Lynne rewrapped the child in the cloak she had given up the night before, then lifted her up to hug and comfort. Could she live in this wild place, have children who would face such dangers.

"No, Miss, you'll ruin your pretty clothes, and you turned out such a treat. Ain't she, Mr. Owens." Owens continued to stare at Lynne open-mouthed and she felt furious at them both.

"Then will one of you men please take her, it's cruel to have a child crying like this and no one doing anything about it."

"What if her mom don't snap out of it?" he asked.

Lynne stared at the vacant eyes once again. "She has to, so they both will get well. It takes time, losing someone you love so much. It leaves a gaping hole that everyone can see through, sometimes in your head, sometimes in your heart." For just a moment, she thought she saw a glimmer of understanding, then the woman turned her head away.

When the coach stopped, the driver was the first to open the door and help the survivors out of the coach. The other passenger descended behind him with the baby in his arms. It left Mr. Owens in the coach with Lynne.

"Miss McKinney, I know you may think this is forward of me, but I cannot bear to let you go without asking."

"Asking what, Mr. Owens?"

"Well," he grinned sheepishly while eyeing her slyly. "Well, if this Mr. Gant don't do right by you, you just have to say the word and I'll marry you myself."

Lynne sat back, as shocked by his offer as by anything that had happened on her journey. She stared across at the oversized man making the serious offer. If Phillip Gant didn't show up today, he would very soon. Even if he was the ugliest man in Montana, she had given him her word.

For just a moment she wondered if she would be better off giving Mr. Owens an evasive answer instead of a blunt no. It would be wise to have something to fall back on. But as she studied him he gave her an open-mouthed grin and she shook her head. At least there wasn't a plug of tobacco in his mouth at the moment as there had been all during the trip. His hair was pale and had thinned until it disappeared on top making the square shape of his head obvious. The worse flaw was the fact that he had held conversation with no one during the entire trip. Could she settle for marriage to such a man? Never.

"Mr. Owens, I'm flattered by your offer. But..." She was formulating an answer that would let the oafish giant understand marrying him would be the last thing in the world she would consider, when a long arm reached into the coach and pulled him out into the mud.

Phillip stood patiently waiting until the driver dismounted. Then he felt his heart drop into his boots. The woman that stepped out of the coach was white, but all the worst things he had feared might show up. She was too heavy, he had always liked women who were well-rounded, but on the slender side. She was too dirty. Greasy dark strands of hair hung down, unwashed and uncombed. Her clothes and face were black streaked. But it was when she turned her eyes toward him that he shuddered. The eyes were empty, dark and still. He had seen eyes like those before, when he'd looked in his own mirror. He didn't need to marry anyone who was as hollow inside as he felt.

When a big man followed her out with a child in his arms, Phillip gave a sigh of relief. The driver turned to stare at him and laughed. "Who run you through the sheep dip and clippers, Mister?"

Phillip ignored him at first, but the man wouldn't be put off. "Throw the bride's trunk down John, I think we've found the bridegroom."

He laughed and took the handle of the large trunk to ease it down. "Well, if you're Mr. Gant, where do you want Miss McKinney's things?"

Phillip relaxed for the first time in two days. He circled his collar with a finger yet again and then took the other end of the trunk to step over to his wagon to load. A man was helping someone limp around the corner and Phillip stiffened, letting his hand return to his gun handle before the driver was ready to put his end of the trunk down.

The driver swore as the trunk slid off the end of the tail-gate. Once he had it back, he looked up to see the cold dark eyes flicker on the man limping past. "Hell, don't tell me that sweet child has come all this way to marry a gunslinger?"

Gant had brushed his coat back far enough to clear his gun hand, now he let it drop back into place. "I'm a rancher."

The driver held up both hands as he backed away. "My mistake, mister. You want me to get the lady out for you."

Gant grinned, his teeth surprisingly straight and white, his eyes softening suddenly. "No need."

He stepped back on the boardwalk and approached the stage. He could hear a man's voice inside the coach, no one else's. He strained to hear, his jaw clinching as he understood the words. The fool was proposing. Swiftly he backed around the end of the coach and flung the outside door open. Two people were staring at each other, the woman pushing him back as the man leaned forward across the seat. He could hear her soft voice of protest, then her startled screech. He wasn't sure if it was aimed at the bear-like man across from her or to protest his intrusion. With one arm, Phillip reached in to give the big oaf a powerful tug through the open door. Then without effort, he sprang up inside the coach and closed the door.

<>
<><>

Whatever he had imagined, he was totally unprepared for her reaction. She stared at him with lovely, soft gray eyes, then laughed softly. "Thank you sir, I don't know who you are, but thank you." She extended a small, ungloved hand and he caught it in one of his large ones. Touching her was electrifying.

"Mr. Phillip Gant."

She blushed and the hand in his trembled. Finally she whispered, "Miss Lynne McKinney."

Mr. Owens was rising from the mud, but before he could touch the door, the driver Dodd and the guard named John, ushered him around the side of the coach. Gant emerged cautiously from the coach, then turned to swing the light bundle of charm down before Owens finished swearing. At Lynne's nod, Gant reached back inside for the tattered, mud-spattered carpet bag. He held his empty arm crooked, and Lynne, still trembling, reached up to take it. When he paused at the loaded wagon to drop the satchel in, he moved so that she was behind him and he could again clear a gun if needed. The three men from the stage stared at him, as full of hate as though they had known him all their lives.

Gant reached up and tilted his derby in salute, then turned around to take his bride's arm again and pull her forward.

Lynne caught a whiff of gun smoke in the air, a sense of danger. She dug in her heels and placed a hand on the powerful arm guiding her. "Where are we going? Where are you taking me, Mr. Gant?"

He raised his hand to point out a door that was clearly labeled "Assayers, Claims Office, Justice of the Peace," then continued to pull her forward.

"Oh," Lynne blushed when she read the third line. "Is there a need to hurry? I thought there would be time to get acquainted, to make sure you found me suitable."

The tall man stood and eyed her up and down. "You're suitable."

"You don't know me at all, and, and I don't know you. Shouldn't I stay in town until we've had a chance to get better acquainted?" This time her voice was sharp, insistent.

"I live fifty miles out. If I had wanted to have to court a woman, I wouldn't have put out an ad for a mail-order bride."

"It doesn't seem civilized."

"This is Montana, not Massachusetts."

They were at the assayer's office. He backed against the door and let go of her slowly so that his fingertips moved down along her arm to touch her fingers. He wondered if he would be able to get his breath so he could talk. Her nostrils had flared and her eyes looked startled. In that tiny hat, with her chin lifted and her cheeks pink, he thought he might have to kiss her on the spot. He wet his lips and inhaled a deep breath. He was shocked by her scent. She smelled of dust, a sweet scent like a cake, and then the rich, earthy scent of being a woman.

"The ranch is four hours away."

She didn't budge, but her hand fluttered and he saw her breathe deeply. It set the little ruffle holding her coat together to moving and his eyes swept her figure for the second time. Maybe not alabaster pillows, but in the tailored suit, she was clearly a fine woman.

"I came in yesterday," he added.

She pulled her hand back and straightened, uncomfortably aware that they were being stared at.

He moved backward, opening the door for her as he stepped inside. She hesitated, a little foot moving forward to peek beneath her skirt, then moving back. She made him think of a new colt, all winsome charm and trembling emotion. He had to handle it right or he would spook her.

"My animals will die if I don't get back."

Lynne swallowed. She was being ridiculous. All this time, all this endless nightmare of a journey, she had been trying to imagine what her husband would look like. Not even in her wildest dreams had she imagined anyone so tall and shockingly handsome. He was lean but powerfully built, all corded muscle ready to spring. His eyes were warm as they swept over her face. It was almost as though he were running his fingers down the straight bridge of her nose, the curve of her chin.

Hadn't she come to Montana to marry this man? Her heart was beating like a wild animals, but he was not proposing to harm her. What had Laura Garretty told her? Maybe he'll have his way with you first. She tugged at the short jacket with her little hands in fists, smoothed down her gray skirt so the pleat was in a line down the center. Then she straightened her back and raised her chin. What was there to fear in this man, with his new coat and shirt and that silly looking derby? Actually his uncertain manners were charming.

He moved backward gracefully, stepping just enough to the side so that she could see the high shelf of the assayer's bench inside and the curious men looking out at her. At her back she knew the road and walkways were filling up, she turned her head to see the loaded wagon where her trunk and carpet bag already sat. What choice was there? Someone like Mr. Owens instead, or the slimy landlord or doctor in Boston. No, this man had been honorable, had sent for her, had offered to make her his wife.

She took one step forward, putting a tiny gray booted foot on the door sill. She heard a gasp from the crowd outside and looked at the gathering throng. How could they be as excited as she was? Did they know she was a mail-order bride?

Lynne turned to look at him one more time. He had removed the black derby and smiled timidly. Inside, the line on his face where he had shaved looked white compared to the suntanned skin around his eyes and brow. His hair was cut close high up around his head, in a line even with his ears, but the top was softly curling, dark and wet looking in the lantern light. But most endearing was the way he raised a hand to run fingers through it.

For just a moment she visualized Tom or Jim standing there, just as stiff in Sunday clothes and with new haircuts.

She tucked her head, then raised it, and gave him a wide trembling smile as she stepped on in through the doorway, firmly closing the door on the agitated crowd outside.

The ceremony was short and simple. First the claims adjuster had them sign the marriage certificate. Both entered their full names, birthplace and date of birth into the register and a clerk copied them onto the marriage certificate. Bridget Lynne McKinney, born June 6, 1859 in Boston, Massachusetts bride of Phillip Andrew Gant, born August 17, 1849 in Louisville, Kentucky married this day, March 5, 1875 in Butte, Montana.

The clerk opened a small book and began to read in a high nasal voice. The words were very simple and she felt disappointed. There was no organ music. The children weren't here, nor Claire and Bonnie. She could hear the noise of the growing crowd outside, see curious faces pressed against the windows. No one looked familiar. The assayer didn't even wear a coat. Her eyes stung as she wished for her own priest.

She stared up at the stranger beside her and felt a new wave of panic. Gently he reached out to take her hand, squeezed her fingers and smiled reassuringly. She relaxed again, breathed deeply, focused on the words. The clerk repeated the words that asked her to love, honor and obey and Lynne managed a soft "Yes." She watched his face as he was asked for his promise to love and cherish her so long as they both should live. His words vibrated through her as he said, "I do."

At the end of the ceremony, both waited nervously. Nothing had been said about a kiss. Lynne watched as the clerk signed his name on both documents, then handed her the copy of the marriage certificate.

"That will be two-bits, Mr. Gant." Lynne watched as he carefully handed the clerk the coins then stopped so that he was facing her. She knew he was watching her, that everyone was waiting. He stood there, not moving, not touching her, just waiting. Finally she swept her lashes up and tilted her head to look at him. He smiled at her, his cheek deeply dimpling. Timidly she pursed her lips and he drew in a deep breath. She couldn't think, couldn't breathe. She closed her eyes as he leaned forward. His lips were so soft on hers, the kiss so quick, that she looked up in surprise to see if it had happened. He smiled again, his teeth strong and white and hungry. For a moment they made her think of a hungry wolf or lion.

Blushing, trembling, she let him lead her back outside where an enormous crowd watched as he swung her up onto the seat of the open wagon. A gangly, gray-haired woman rushed out of a store and held up a sack for them. "For the trip." A little man joined her and both suddenly pelted them with seeds. "For many children." He called and others laughed but the last thing Lynne saw as the horses ran down the broad street was the angry face of Mr. Owens and the worried faces of the stagecoach drivers.

CHAPTER SIXTEEN

The afternoon was clear and cool, but her blood was so feverish, she didn't notice it. The road seemed wider for their wagon than it had for the stage. As she stared around curiously, he nodded to the river flowing beside them. "Red Rock River, joins up with the Beaver Head."

She nodded, noticing the huge cliffs of red rock alongside the road. "Whoever named it was very clever."

He studied her, dimpled again, but said nothing. Lynne shifted uncomfortably on the seat, unsure of how to proceed. But he wasn't disinterested, just quiet. It made her think of talking with Mary Anne. A lot of people made the mistake of thinking the child was shy. But when Lynne asked her about it once, Mary Anne had said she was talking all the time, in her head, and enjoyed talking with people. There was something about the way he rode, the reins comfortably held in his hands, his long legs relaxed against the running board that gave her the courage to continue.

"This is a lovely place isn't it? We were so cooped up in the stage coach, one couldn't see what the country was like at all. Not like on the train ride where you could see everything, quickly," she added and laughed. "But you could see everything. Kind of like riding like this."

When she paused he stared at her, at her lovely kissable lips. For a moment he thought he might pull the wagon up and take his time about kissing her. She was so sweet. But there was still an uneasiness in her eyes and voice. He would need to give her plenty of time.

"You're only sixteen?"

She blushed. "Seventeen, nearly eighteen, but I feel ancient. You're what, twenty-seven?"

He nodded, unable to think what to say next. She had moved back and was studying him like she had at the clerk's office. Her eyes soft, timid, but curious. Oh so curious.

He turned his attention to the road. "You were late."

Her ease evaporated and she sat up nervously. Suddenly the wagon seemed too open, too accessible. "Yes, we were attacked by Indians."

He tensed, slipping an arm around her rigid shoulders, then took the reins with the arm still around her. With the other hand he lifted his rifle. She watched, trembling beneath the strong arm as he cocked the rifle with his left hand, then set it leaning beside his knee. He switched the reins back, but didn't move his arm. Snapping them, he called to the team and Lynne shuddered as they stepped out at a lively canter.

The speed made the breeze pick up and Lynne shivered. The bounce of the seat made her back feel tired and her shoulders ache. He reached behind her, never slowing the team, letting his eyes sweep the trail from side to side. Then she felt awed as he gripped the reins in his teeth and lifted her enough to slip a big wool coat around her. "Slide your arms in."

She did so, letting him hold the sleeves for her like she was a child. They turned a curve and he took the reins in his strong brown hands again and Lynne tilted against his shoulder. When the road straightened, he wrapped an arm around her and Lynne blushed as she felt his hand fumbling over her breast. She brought a hand up in protest and he growled near her ear. "Then fasten it."

Angry at herself for being so stupid, she fumbled with the leather straps, finding it impossible to hook them over the carved wooden buttons down the full length of the long coat as the wagon bounced beneath them. Suddenly she felt warm, except for her ears and nose which were burning. She turned her head, surprised to see he was unfazed by the stiff breeze. When they hit a bump in the road she bounced high on the seat and started to slide but his arm around her snatched her back. "Hold on."

She did, slipping both arms around his waist, then surrendering to the urge to bury her face and ears against his chest. They seemed to continue at the same speed forever. She felt so shaken, she clung to him like a rag doll. Finally she heard the horses blowing and he slowed them down, bringing them first down to a trot, then letting them ease into a fast walk.

Phillip felt her pressed against him, so small and helpless. She was clinging so tightly that he couldn't see her head. The wild ride had shaken the little hat loose and it lay with its brave blue feather on the floor of the buckboard. He breathed deeply, his own panic subsiding. Alone, he would have been unafraid of the Indians. But she was so, he couldn't find the words, but he knew how he had felt at the thought of an Indian harming her. The road emerged into a clearing, the trees and rock cliff left behind.

He looked around, satisfied he could see in all directions for a long distance. He pulled the team up for a rest beside the quiet pool of water and stepped down from the wagon, pulling her down with him.

Lynne uncurled slowly, her legs nerveless beneath her. Her arms still encircled his waist and she leaned against his solid body for support. He brought both arms around her, encircling her body as he pressed her closer still. Where his black wool coat hung open, she pressed against the thin starched whiteness of his shirt. Beneath the solid muscle of his chest, she felt the steady pounding of his heart. Gradually, her own slowed down and she raised her face to look at him.

He moved the arm around her shoulder so he could raise a hand to cup her face. The cheek that had been against his chest was warm, the other icy cold. He cupped her tiny red ear in his hand then lifted her easily against him so that her face was even with his own.

Startled Lynne put her arms around his neck, moving her face so her cold cheek was pressed against his. Her heart beat harder as his lips moved closer, breathing on, then kissing her ear, pulling it into his mouth to warm. She shivered as new sensations swept through her and she turned startled gray eyes to look into his warm brown ones. He pulled his mouth from her ear and throat and stared at the quick-silver of her eyes. Slowly, softly he moved so that his warm lips covered her tender ones. His body shook as he fought for control. She pushed against his neck and he let her slide down the length of him, still keeping her imprisoned, never lifting his lips from her own.

She couldn't breathe, she was drowning. Frantically she pushed against him again. Wanting to breathe, wanting the swirling sensations to stop. When he released her she sank to the cold ground in a crumpled heap, her arms sliding limply along his powerful thighs. The light was fading, the birds calling to one another, in the tall grass an animal moved. He arched back, his body aching to know her, his face turned to the cold air of reason. Finally he looked down at her, so helpless, so submissive. He bent and scooped her up, lifting and carrying her back onto the wagon seat.

He stood beside it for several minutes, blowing like the horses, trying to regain the control he had lost so completely.

When he turned around, he saw her watching him. He had one hand on the wagon seat, one on his hip as he stared at the puzzled expression on her face, the soft bruised look of her lips. He wondered if she even knew what had almost happened.

"Open the sack. See what the Dutchman's wife sent."

Lynne sat up, brushing her hair back from her face. The neat bundle she had made of it this morning had shaken loose. She started to repin it but his voice stopped her. It was that low, deep rumble that made her tremble so. "Let it down."

She pulled the few remaining pins and shook her head, shaking out the long tangle of hair. His eyes were on her face again, those eyes with their sensual glance. Confused, she bent her head and retrieved the sack. She raised it to her lap, then pulled out a tall corked bottle and then one of the chewy loaves of bread everyone seemed to eat out here. There was also a chunk of sharp cheddar cheese. Lynne laughed as she pulled out the last treat. A huge, red apple. She bent her head, inhaling the scent of the bruised skin on it, already savoring the taste of it.

"An apple" she laughed, bringing it to her lips to scratch the skin with her teeth.

He watched, his breath evaporating. Did she have a clue as to how tempting she looked? With her skin glowing, her soft hair spilling around her as she sat primly pillowed amid his oversized-coat and her full-skirted suit. He leaned his head forward and took a bite of the apple where her mouth had touched it. She laughed and brought it back to her own mouth to nibble. He closed his eyes and sank to the ground.

Panicked Lynne screeched as she leaned over the side, half expecting to see an arrow sticking out of his back or one of those dark sinister holes the child had in her leg.

Instead she saw him half rise pulling out of his clothes, tossing the coat and shirt back toward the wagon, skimming out of his shoes, pants and underwear in one move. The wildness of it frightened her, but the beauty of his magnificent body as he dove into the cold water wouldn't let her turn away. Embarrassed, she looked down at her trembling hands. Only after he had emerged minutes later and struggled into his clothes did she dare to look at him. He climbed back into the buckboard, raised the bottle of wine to his lips and worried the cork out with his chattering teeth. He drank it, letting it leak onto his chest where the barely buttoned shirt exposed it.

Lynne turned her back to him, annoyed and frightened. "I thought you were worried about Indians and about your animals starving."

She spoke sharply and he laughed. "So you're ready to go."

She turned stormy gray eyes to look at him. "Actually, I could use a minute of privacy."

He looked around and raised a hand. "This is as private as it gets. You need an ice water bath too?"

Actually she did, but instead of admitting it, she put one foot timidly on the side of the wagon and looked down at the ground. He watched her, not moving to help her down or offer assistance.

She stared down at the ground, wondering how to dismount gracefully when he said, "Use the wagon spokes, but be careful."

She closed her eyes and let go, but managed to land on her feet.

"That's far enough Mrs. Gant."

She stared back in at him, watching him drink the wine and break off a large piece of bread. "I need to walk into the bushes," she said.

He studied the angry eyes, the charming little features. At least he was cold enough for the moment, but there was no way he was touching her again. "I want you safe, stay by the wagon."

She almost fell when her heel caught the hem of her skirt. Gritting her teeth, she worked the fabric out of the way. Furiously, Lynne shuffled to the rear of the wagon, then squatted so she was out of sight. She heard the sound his pistol being cocked at the front of the wagon.

When she walked back around, she was relieved to find him still sitting on top. He seemed totally uninterested in helping her get back into the wagon, either. Irritated, she repeated the procedure of using the wheel spokes to climb back inside.

Lynne sat silently, so annoyed she couldn't speak. He stowed the weapon at hand, but she kept her head bent to hide her fury. Gingerly he placed the bread and cheese into her lap. When he clicked to them the horses moved out at a steady trot. She was determined to remain rigidly on her side of the wagon seat all the way home.

From time to time she felt his eyes on her, wondered what he was thinking. Finally hunger made her eat, although she refused the wine he offered. So this was marriage. She had survived the journey west, but how could she ever survive life with this wild Montana man.

CHAPTER SEVENTEEN

It was inky dark, the stars and moon blotted out by heavy clouds. Lynne still clung desperately to the hard back of the wagon seat. Her spine felt permanently bent, her every muscle ached. Stiffly she dropped down from the wagon, not waiting for her husband to come around and help her. She knew the wagon was completely loaded down, but she doubted she had the strength to move her own body, let alone move so many heavy things.

Phillip Gant watched her, as aware of her now as he had been from the moment he first glimpsed her. He reached back and snagged her satchel, then handed the old carpet-bag and the half-empty wine bottle to her to carry, even as he hoisted her big trunk along his back and led the way forward.

She couldn't see a thing, didn't want to touch him. Instead she dogged his steps closely, surprised when he stopped abruptly in front of her and his voice warned. "Step up twice here."

She did, feeling her way in the strange darkness, not sure if it were even her body that was moving. Her head felt too heavy for her neck and her eyes were barely open as she staggered through the open door behind him. He walked on through the house, not stopping until he reached the bedroom. Suddenly he was glad he had made the bed fresh before he left to pick her up. He let the trunk slide down his back to the floor, took the carpet bag and bottle from her.

"Lynne, your home." He smiled down at his child bride, her

head drooping forward like a little toddler. "Do you need me to help you get undressed?"

The voice was too loud for her, she wanted to say yes, but instead she struggled to open her eyes and managed a simple, "Can do it myself."

But he was already reaching forward and swiftly unbuttoned the dark woolen coat. Once it was removed, he unfastened the snug jacket, inhaling as he slipped it from her and saw the thin linen blouse. It clung to her lovely figure so softly, he almost thought he could see a pouty nipple through the fine cloth. His hand shook as he untied the streamers at her neck. She raised a hand and smacked at his fumbling fingers. "I can do it myself!"

"Good. I'll bring in the rest of the supplies." He turned, set her trunk down flat and flipped the straps to open it. With one hand he worked the bendable fasteners at the front and raised the lid. On the top, lay a nightgown. He lifted it, then hesitated. The material was thin cotton, to him it seemed like gauze. He dropped it back inside as though it were red hot instead of shimmery cool. When he found nothing but more sheer garments he swore. He walked over to his own dresser, opened it and pulled out a flannel nightshirt Johnson had given him after his wedding. He had given all his old mining buddies one, for as he told them, he didn't need them anymore to keep warm.

He held it up and turned back, choking as he watched his sleepy bride. She had unfastened and slipped out of the skirt and blouse. Even as he watched she balanced unsteadily and pulled off her petticoat. His eyes devoured her tempting form, nearly revealed beneath the thin-strapped chemise and soft cotton drawers. One hose rose beguilingly past the knee, the other sagged along a shapely leg. Closing his eyes he opened the nightshirt and stepped forward, holding it open while he said. "Here, slip this on."

As soon as one finger and her pretty head poked through the top, he tugged that hand through, then reached in his own hand to pull the other fingers through the remaining sleeve. He swung her up in his arms, carrying her the few steps to the bed, balancing her light form as he pulled back the covers. He shoved her in, then took a deep breath before reaching under the covers and the shirt to snag and pull off first one sock, then the other. Slowly he brought the cover up to her chin, smiled and sighed as he settled for kissing her smooth forehead.

By the time he finished unloading the wagon, bedding the horses and tending to the other animals, he was beginning to feel the exhaustion of the long day. He shed his own coat and boots, then used the cold water in the bedside pitcher to wash up, splashing his face and scrubbing his hands. After removing his shirt and pants, he hesitated. What if he accidentally rolled over on her? At least if he were wearing drawers, he might not be able to do anything automatically.

Stiffly he lay half-dressed beside her in the bed, listening to her soft breathing. His eyes were closed when she groaned and curved against him. Clenching his jaw, he drew in a deep breath. Slowly he shifted her weight, moving his arm to bring it to curve around her. He was the one to moan as she lifted her head and lay it against the bare skin of his chest.

Tilting his head, he stared down at her to make sure she was really asleep. Perhaps he was mistaken about her. Just because she was young, didn't make her an innocent. Prostitutes in Butte were often very young women. It wasn't something a man wanted to do, but there were times when a handshake wasn't enough. In a country like this, any available woman was pressed in to service, and pressed often.

He remembered the time they had been placer mining, swishing the sand around the big pans, looking for the sparkle of gold in the bright sunlight. A toothless old man had walked up to the creek, grinning at them. Several men lifted guns warily, but all waited. He motioned with his hands and three squaws walked out along the stream bank. Phillip could recall every detail of how their skin had looked, so bright and soft, where they lifted their skirts and squatted beside the creek in full view of the men. The old man had held out a hand and shouted, one dollar. The miners had dropped their pans, fascinated by the display before them. Men started swearing. Phillip remembered being frozen to the spot. The chief clapped a hand and one girl raised her hindquarters in the bright sunlight and held them there in an invitation that couldn't be mistaken. One of the black miners walked across to hand the chief his dollar. After that, they had taken turns with them.

The one he remembered most was the little squaw in the middle. She couldn't have been more than twelve or thirteen. She had squatted there crying, her face streaked with tears and mud, letting the men have a turn until they stopped offering money. Then as quickly as they had appeared, the Indians and their white pimp were gone.

If two of the men hadn't come down with the clap, it might have been a dream. After that, several of the men bought squaws of their own. But Phillip had never been able to get past the smell of bear grease and the flatness of their faces to consider it.

Yet this was frontier country. They had discussed it at a poker game, how Johnson's Helga hadn't been a virgin. The men had agreed that it didn't matter. A woman would pretty much have to leave behind a bad reputation to come to such a God-forsaken country to find a husband. So why did it seem so important to him now? He could make love to her and find out. There should be a difference the first time, the tell-tale drops of blood. Right, if he took her now he would never know.

Even as he wondered, she moved her face against his skin, wrinkling her pretty nose. The urgency of need he had worked so hard to overcome was instantly back. Even as he lay there watching, she opened her mouth and touched his skin with her tongue, then scraped across it with her teeth. Moaning, he turned her beneath him, bringing a hand to her face and sliding his thumb into her open mouth.

"Ouch." He yelled and she rolled back away from him, her eyes sleepy and unfocused. Suddenly a look of terror came into her eyes and she backed away from him in the big bed until she was sitting upright against the headboard.

"What are you doing in my bed?" her voice quivered with indignation.

Phillip wondered if he were crazy or she was. For a moment there he thought she was trying to seduce him, so why had she bitten the fire out of him. "Sleeping?"

She stared at the rumpled hair, the crinkled, disarming face telling its miserable lie. There was nothing sleepy about those dark eyes that roamed across her face like flames. So why did her eyes have to look past to where his bare, brown shoulders and chest were exposed against the white of the sheets. Was he as naked beneath that cotton as he had been today by the river? If so, why did she have the insane urge to fling back the covers, to have more than a brief glimpse? Her heart pounded, as shocked by his nearness as by what he made her feel.

Sanity made her step out onto the cold floor and stand indignantly beside the bed. "Do you have to sleep here?" Her voice croaked and she knew he would take her as some kind of fool.

"It's my bed." His eyes were again sweeping her, wondering what she would do to surprise him next. Johnson's nightshirt hid her tempting body beneath long baggy cotton, and when she started to lift her hand, the end of the sleeve flapped below it.

Stunned, she pushed the sleeves back until she found her small hands. She pushed the wild tangle of soft brown hair back from her heart-shaped face, her dark lashes lifting to reveal shocked gray eyes. "You undressed me?"

His eyes darkened with desire at the mere suggestion. What if he had pulled the last stitch from her body and had his fill of staring at her? She had been helpless to prevent him. He licked his lips, his libido working overtime, imagining removing the form-hugging garments she still wore beneath the nightshirt. When he didn't answer, she walked around the foot of the bed, searching for her clothes. In the dark she stumbled against the chest. He was out of the bed in a moment, scooping a protesting Lynne into his arms and laying her back in the still warm bed.

"Shush," he moved so he held her pinned beneath the covers. "Be still." She made fists and brought them up to pound furiously, cuffing his ears, beating against the warm, heavy muscled shoulders. He laughed, unable to hold back his joy in her as he easily captured her small fists. He raised her hands above her head, then flung a leg on top of hers to hold her down. Her face grew red as she struggled frantically, swearing at him.

The harder she struggled, the harder he laughed, until he finally moved so he lay along the squirming length of her, the thin sheet and coverlet barely separating them. He brought a hand up to hold her face, cupping it so she couldn't bite him, but effectively keeping her from screaming. "Listen."

Lynne felt sudden, overwhelming panic. He could do anything he wanted with her, anytime. Her strength was that of a baby beneath him. Tears leaked beneath her lashes and she hated him for making her cry. He was an animal, a dirty beast like all the others. Only he was the beast she had willingly gone to, trustingly married.

Her tears undid him. The laughter stopped and he grew still atop her. "Shh, darling, don't, don't cry. You're safe. I'm going to let go of you, now don't scream." He saw her face scrunch suddenly and knew she was crying even harder. Before he lifted his hand or his weight from her, he bent to kiss the salty tears leaking from the dark lashes.

The gesture was so unexpectedly tender. Lynne stopped.

He lifted his head, released her arms and slowly rolled off of her and onto his feet beside the bed. "Check. I just gave you a nightshirt to wear over your clothes."

Lynne brought one of her smothered hands to wipe at her face, to erase the signs of her fear. Cautiously she shifted so she could pull one arm back inside the sleeve of the garment.

A minute later, she sat up blushing, incredibly embarrassed by her panic. She turned slowly so that her face was hidden from him, her back to him. Her lip trembled as she tried to figure out what she could say. He must think he had married some crazy person.

"It's too cold for the barn." His resonant voice startled her.

She twisted her neck to look at him over her shoulder.

He leaned forward to lift the covers cautiously. "Move over dear wife."

"You're going to ... to sleep ... in here tonight?"

He smiled, his dimples so disarming, she knew she was being foolish. But still, when she had awaken, his eyes had looked anything but harmless.

"You know, I ... " she didn't know how to proceed. The friendly station master's wife had made it sound like such a sure thing. That he wouldn't be interested in her that way if it were that time of month. But he seemed so much more than interested. And if he kissed her again, like he had today...

He studied her face, read her uncertainty and hesitation in her sudden shyness.

"I understand." He crawled in beneath the covers with her, resting his dark head on the pillow.

Lynne swiveled around so that she could keep an eye on him. When he didn't move, she scrunched down beneath the covers and reluctantly let her head drop back on the pillow. Just lying there, with their faces only inches apart on the pillows, was so strange.

"It's natural for you to want to wait. I understand." His eyes were so knowing, so kind, his voice rich and full of experience. "We'll wait until next week if you want."

She was tempted to ask him, 'wait for what?' but she was palpably aware of what they were discussing. Bonnie had shared enough information for her to know exactly what went on between a man and woman in bed. She swallowed, bringing her arms rigidly down by her sides, staring up at the dark of the ceiling.

She lowered her lashes but continued to look at him from the corner of her eyes. He wasn't pretending to sleep though, just lying there and watching her. In the shared silence, she suddenly remembered the aches along her back, the cramping tightness in her stomach. She curled into a fetal position, still lying facing him.

His expressive eyes flashed with concern and he sat up, putting a warm hand on her shoulder. Again, she was aware of how little he was wearing. It made her want to move over against the sleek warmth of his bare skin. Was that what she had done before to set him off? For she was aware that at times he seemed calm and normal, at others strangely excited. Lynne bit her lip as another cramp tightened her stomach.

His hand pushed her shoulder. "Turn over. Let me help you."

There was magic in his touch, comfort in the soft rumble of his voice. Lynne turned over, her legs still drawn up as her body stiffened even more.

Through the thick cotton of the nightshirt he could feel the tension in her muscles. She was as tightly bunched as a wild horse. He would have to take his time, wait and introduce her slowly to the pleasures they could share. First, he would need to get her used to his touch. At the moment, it seemed to make her jump out of her skin with fright or curl into a ball of resistance.

He fought the urge to move his hand suddenly, forcefully gentling her. Instead he opened his hand and moved it slowly along the tightly knotted muscles of her shoulder. When she didn't flinch, he brought the other hand up and repeated the motion. Gradually he saw her start to let her legs move down. Slowly, soothingly, he worked his hands over the slender body. He ached to slip a hand beneath the coarse cotton, to touch her satiny skin. But that would have to wait. First, would come this casual touching.

Lynne let her body rock beneath the motion of his hands. Wherever they moved and pressed, the tight ache seemed to increase, but as he moved them away, the pain evaporated. She leaned forward on her belly, giving him access to her back. He worked from her shoulders down along her sides, then pulled his thumbs as he moved his hands back to her shoulders again. With each stroke, she felt the same lassitude seep back into her mind that had come on the long journey to the ranch.

As she relaxed, he heard a soft moaning with each pressing sweep of his hands. Each stroke he trailed lower on her back. Finally his hands swept over the first gentle curve of her hips before pulling back. She turned her head sideways. Her eyes were half-closed, her glance suspicious. The next two sweeps he kept them high, felt her shoulders melt beneath his kneading fingers, then as her eyes drooped lower, he ran the hands lower still, covering the full curve of her bottom before starting back.

A tiny drop of drool decorated the corner of her mouth and he smiled, loving her sense of trust. Again he ran his hands down. She moaned and he pressed both palms, filling them with the sweet flesh of her bottom. Still her eyes remained shut. She moved a hand up to wipe the corner of her mouth and he placed his thumbs at the base of her spine, feeling, then kneading the little dimples at the top of each hip. Again she made a guttural sound of pleasure.

When he finally lay back, confident she was relaxed and asleep, he stared miserably up at the ceiling. He had gone too far. Letting his fingers dip along her sides to trace the outline of her firm young breasts, sliding one hand around to caress her flat stomach. Only when his fingers were throbbing with the heat of touching her had he quit. Now he lay engorged and fully awake.

He had given her his word to wait a week. Surely she would turn to him for comfort before then, but if not, he could wait to be sure. He needed to know whether he would be her first lover. Suddenly it seemed more important than anything he had ever wanted to know. But in the dark, he battled with the temptation to slip a hand beneath that confounded nightshirt. He knew she was young and sweet. But on her lips he had tasted passion, had seen it flicker as quick-silver in her eyes. Frustrated, he turned to stare at her profile one more time.

All his life, he had been searching for something of value. Glory, gold, horses, the land. Yet each time he had it, he found it wasn't enough, it wasn't what he wanted. Finding a workable vein when the gold panned out had been thrilling. But his enthusiasm had waned before he'd worked out the last of the ore. By then the horses had called him to this valley. The bachelor cabin he had first erected on the small plot of land had given him tremendous satisfaction. Just a lean-to, but something he had built with his own hands.

When he caught and branded more and more horses, each one made his heart light. Finally he knew he was staying here, not just gathering something before moving on. That was when he had gone after a larger section, proving a claim on it. He had used some of his mining wealth to build his house, a house any man in the territory would be happy to own. Until a month ago he had believed this ranch was all he needed to be happy. Then Johnson had married a Swede and he had realized he needed a wife if he was to going to make a life here.

As he watched her she moved a little and her hair fell over her cheek. Gently he reached out to brush the strands from her face. His fingers caught. Slowly he raised his hand, easing his fingers through the tangled skein of brown silk. Gently he buried the other hand and repeated the gentle motions until his fingers emerged into the air. She turned over on her back and he shifted closer, slipping his hand beneath the soft hair until it rested on the warm softness of her nape.

His eyes drooped from the pleasure of touching her skin. This girl, this was what he needed to fill the hollowness inside. Mrs. Gant was the treasure worth keeping. And soon, soon she would be his in more than name only.

CHAPTER EIGHTEEN

Lynne stretched, then curled. Slowly she opened her eyes, then let them drop again. Sunlight was streaming in from a small window high on the wall. Completely content, her nerveless body felt as though it was floating on a cloud of feathers. Minutes later, she opened her eyes again. The room was strange.

Beneath the one high window sat a single, rough formed chair. Resting on one ear of the chair-back hung a black coat. On the other point, a stiff white shirt rested beneath a black bowler hat. But it was the contents of the seat of the chair that made her sit up. A gray traveling suit was neatly folded with a pert cloth hat resting on top. Draped over the center of the chair back were a pair of pants and a ladies petticoat.

Everything came back in a flash. Married. Cautiously she slid from the bed, tentatively taking a step to test for pain. Bonnie had assured both Claire and her that it was terribly painful the first time. Nothing. This time, full memory of her first night in bed returned. Every detail of her panic and struggle against him. Then she recalled his promise to wait a week. With his mercurial temperament she wasn't sure she could depend on that. She had to hope that her new husband wasn't a complete savage.

◇◇◇

Lynne dressed, took care of her pressing needs, and then

wandered through her new home. On the train from the east she had listened to stories of dug-outs, log cabins, soddies, and tents. In the towns she had seen combinations of each, along with stone and clapboard structures. She had imagined living in each type, planned out how she would manage to keep clean a sod house with its seeping mud and oozing earthworms. She knew many settlers used their wagons and canvas covers along with a few timbers to make a lean-to, and she had fantasized cooking with buffalo chips in a metal stove and keeping house with a dirt floor. A fellow traveler had shared the secrets of making chinking for a log cabin out of clay, not mud, and she could picture doing that each fall, just before the first snows. But she had never imagined this.

Phillip's house was a combination of stone and big timber construction, as thick and solid as any of the relay stations they had visited. The inside walls had been finished with hand-planed boards, eight to twelve inches wide, fitted so close together they seemed to be of one piece. True, there were only two glass windows, both very small and high up, but there were two doors one could open to have a breeze through the entire house. Best, there were floors. Planks, not as well fitted or smoothly planed, but planks to form the floor.

Lynne wasted the rest of the morning shamelessly snooping both inside and outside the house. There was a small, shoulder-high privy at the back of the yard, but it was far from well built. The wind howled through its thin, knotty and curved boards. It was so low, so well-hidden from the house, that she had been afraid he hadn't added one yet. Another tale from a traveler had suggested real settlers just walked to the end of the porch and stood or squatted.

The place had no porch, but there were stones at the front of the house, looking as though he had plans to add one. His house, her new home, had two huge rooms finished, the bedroom and the kitchen. Two rooms were half-built. One had the walls planked but no flooring. The other only had outer walls of stone and logs.

The unfinished rooms were separated from the rest of the house by doors. But the bedroom was closed off from the kitchen by only a thick blanket. Her first morning in the house had been so strange. She had almost fallen in when she opened the door to the last room. It was dark inside and she hadn't been expecting the floor to be down three feet. Cautiously she had lowered herself onto the cold earth inside, pleased to recognize it was a storeroom.

Inside, Phillip had several covered barrels. There was no window, the pale light came in from the half-opened door. She debated opening the barrels, knowing he might get angry. Finally she gave in, cautiously feeling inside with her hand as she peeked in each that was not fastened shut.

Food, one man, and he had so much food. On the wall nearest the door there were shelves, on the bottom shelf were several huge tin boxes. Above them were canned goods. She had to climb on a barrel to be tall enough to reach the cans and read them. One end of the shelf just had cans of milk. That surprised her as much as anything, that a cowboy would get milk from a can, not a cow.

She felt like a thief discovering a treasure vault. All of this belonged to one man and he was her husband. There was meat hanging, a long side of bacon and some big animal, probably a calf.

She had planned all the way from Boston to be a brave, pioneer woman. As she drew ever closer, she began to dream of making a home in the wilderness with nothing, surviving against all odds. She was ready to work at finding the stranger she would marry attractive and eventually finding a way to love the man who would father her children and take in her brothers and sister.

But the house and all its treasure made her heart ache. She sank to one of the square tin boxes and struggled against the tears welling up again. It hurt so much. She couldn't decide why, but it made her hate the man who had so much.

◇◇◇

His voice called through the house and Lynne stopped sniffling. Her breath came in ragged gulps and she put a hand over her mouth to keep him from finding her. She heard the jingle of his spurs as he stomped through the house, then minutes later, she heard him opening doors. She had almost wiped away the last tears when he opened the door above her head and looked inside for her.

The storeroom was so dark, she expected him to close the door without seeing her. Instead he hung there in the opening, listening and staring intently into the gloom. Lynne hiccuped and he dropped gracefully down into the room, poised and listening, his head tilted in her direction. She made another little sound and he let out his breath, stepping directly to where she sat in the corner.

She stared at him, her eyes accustomed to the light. He was wearing a gray, Stetson hat, blue shirt and blue jeans protected by leather chaps. Around his neck was a knotted red scarf. In his jangling boots, he looked so tall and fierce inside the small room.

For a minute neither of them spoke.

"Lynne, are you all right?"

She turned her head away from him, but as usual, he didn't have the patience to ask her anything directly. He knelt in the soft cool soil and grasped her elbows, lifting one as he felt it with sure, knowing fingers. "Did you fall?"

Lynne gulped the air as irritated at her own inability to control her emotions as she was resentful of him for being so reasonable and kind. This time her hiccup was loud. "I'm fine."

She started up, struggling away from his big hands and he moved smoothly to give her room. As she rose, she stepped on her skirt and almost fell. It was then he swept her into his arms and swung her back up out of the room and over the door sill into their bedroom. He made her furious when he presumed to sweep up her skirt and feel her ankles and legs with his warm, callused hand. His touch was mesmerizing. "I'm fine," she finally shouted, pulling her legs away and wiggling out of reach.

But she had forgotten his agile grace as he sprang up onto the floor and leaned over her. "Damn it, talk to me woman. Has someone hurt you?" He extended a hand to touch the tear streaked face and she angrily drew back. But he didn't allow her to escape, instead scrambled around so he was hovering over her, bending to look at her face. Finally he tried to draw her protesting figure into the circle of his arms.

Trapped, Lynne felt the great waves of sadness swelling up again. It was as though the loss of her mother and the forced abandonment of her brothers and sister were just happening. If this man hadn't placed an ad for a wife, then Claire would never have read it and she wouldn't be here now. It was as though everything had become a nightmare for her after Claire read that clipping. And here he sat in his big house with his big land and a room full of food to eat.

Bewildered, Phillip studied her face, watched a tear slip from her stormy gray eyes. Gradually he eased her into his arms. As he stared she dissolved into deep painful sobs. This time he didn't laugh at her fury or grief. Instead he pulled her onto his lap and held her there, rocking soothingly back and forth, crooning her name. Minutes drug by in the quiet house, but she clung to him, to his warm neck, his broad shoulders. By the time she stopped bawling, his shirt was soaked and she was sniffling, trying to regain control.

He tugged his kerchief loose and held it to her face. "Blow."

She did, laughing at herself. She looked up at him, seeing his face clearly for the first time today. In his work clothes, he reminded her of the images of cowboys in the dime novels back home. Against the light shirt, his skin was so tanned it looked brown, leathery. The hat had fallen back at some point and now hung from a snug fitting leather strap, biting into his paler neck. His eyes were solemn as he stared at her and for a minute she felt she could disappear into the warmth she saw there.

He laid a hand on her stomach, pressing softly. "If you're in such pain, I'll ride to get the doctor."

Lynne blushed brightly and lifted his hand away. She was so embarrassed by his knowing that it took several seconds for her to answer. "I'm fine, last night, well my stomach cramps sometimes at first." She blushed again, unable to go on.

He smiled at her, his eyes crinkling at the corners and suddenly she wished she were close enough to drop back in that hole.

"My sisters used to have the same problem. Are these still hurting?" His big hand softly caressed the side of one breast.

She pushed his hand away easily, furious again. "I never told you they were."

He nodded. "They just felt a little tight." His hand caressed the other softly and she blushed bright red. "Guess they have eased some."

Her eyes widened in horror, then something else. "How dare

you? She shouted. "I never gave you permission to ... to touch me there, or anywhere else. When did you?" She felt strangled as soon as she realized the unspoken answer. She backed off his lap and out of reach. "You are no gentleman, sir."

He leaned over her suddenly and she half-lay on the floor to move out of reach. His voice growled the answer. "Right, but I am your husband." He saw the fear rising in her eyes again and pulled back. "I'm not one for pretense and mystery. Now why the hell were you crying?"

"I'm not afraid of you." But as he leaned closer she swallowed tightly, raising hands to push him back if he dared come nearer.

"Tell me."

Lynne swallowed, her muscles quivering from holding her body, rigidly away from his. "So much food." When he looked puzzled, Lynn looked at the open doorway. "One man, but so much food." Her voice caught and she shook her head to clear it, refusing to give into melancholy yet again.

But his dark eyes were on her, searching her somber gray ones, pulling the words from her. "We were so poor. My mother," she couldn't go on. Lynn bit her lip and looked downward.

He waited.

Her head felt achy from all the crying, from the struggle to breathe without smelling him and feel without touching him. She had to talk to ease the charged silence.

In a low, soft voice she told him of her mother's death, about the children she had left behind.

He listened intently, memorizing every word, absorbing the raw emotion in the way she talked about her family. "So that was what the twenty dollars was for?"

She nodded, her face pale and naked beneath the knowing

exploration of his eyes. "It just doesn't seem right for you to have so much."

He clenched his jaw and rose smoothly, pulling her to her feet. "Maybe not. But that's a year's worth of grub down there, for me, two men, and a little spitfire of a bride."

Slowly he stepped out to the kitchen and stirred up the small fire she had started, adding two or three short pieces of wood. "Those men are going to be riding in here in a minute for some grub."

"How? How could you invite company without telling me?"

She spoke with hands on her hips as though she had been scolding her big husband for years and Phillip grinned at her. His eyes glowed, his voice deepened. "I wanted them to see what a beauty you are?"

Lynne was suddenly embarrassed by her red eyes, her mussed clothing. How could one man be such torment? Did he not realize how awkward this would be? Couldn't he have waited to give her time to settle in to everything first? But before she could collect her wits enough to complain they both heard a booming voice.

"Hail, the house.

Lynne stared out their open door and saw two men sitting on horses, staring into the house, grinning at them.

"Come on in. Set a spell, boys," he yelled back and Lynne raised a hand to her loose hair, unsure what to do. She looked up to him for direction.

"We were just arguing about whether to cook antelope or open a tin of sardines and crackers." He pushed Lynne behind his body, giving her time to straighten the garments he had mussed so she could look her best. Then he grinned proudly at the two men who must have been watching for quite a spell from their big grins.

Nervously, Lynne peeked around his shoulder and he pulled his blushing bride back into view. "Talk to them darling."

CHAPTER NINETEEN

Lynne felt strangely content staring at the three men sitting at the table with her. After all the turmoil of the morning, the visitors helped restore her sense of self and well-being. Perhaps it was just flitting around the kitchen cooking. As soon as the strangers had dismounted in the yard, she had pulled out her sense of control. At least the guests would give her a chance to try out her new kitchen.

Already this morning, as soon as her travel clothes had been hung up properly, the suit sponged and dusted, his jacket hung, and the bed made, she had followed her nose to the kitchen and begun exploring. Lynne was enchanted instantly by the big blue stove that dominated the room. Coffee was already made and sat in a pot on the back of the range top. She had poured some and wondered how Phillip had ever been able to make it and bacon without waking her up. While biting the crispy meat, she wondered just how exhausted she had been and what else he had been able to do.

Now, she regarded the men calmly and began to work, confident that she knew where everything was stored and what she would cook. After putting the coffee on to reheat for their company, she placed a skillet with bacon grease on one of the eyes to melt, then strode through the house, calling into the storeroom to her shocked husband.

"Bring up three or four potatoes when you have the meat cut."

Phillip stared up at the woman who moments before had been helpless in his arms. Now she stood with one hand on the door frame, yelling down orders to him. Even as he watched, she pulled her hair back and twisted one long thin strand around the middle to firmly anchor it at her neck so it hung in a smooth clump like a horse's tail down her back. Then she turned and held out her hand to greet Shorty and Banes.

Fascinated, he heard her soft, northern accent welcoming his hired hands as though they were visiting royalty. He worked rapidly, unwilling to trust those two randy cowhands with such a treasure. Pocketing his knife, he filled his hat with potatoes, then vaulted up from the storeroom with the meat. There was no doubt about what his next chore around the house would have to be. His bride needed steps to properly use the storeroom.

The two cowhands were seated at the table on one trestle bench, their eyes tracking Lynne as she busied herself lifting out the thick wooden bowls he used for plates. He slung the meat onto the table and she smiled at him, behaving as though raw meat on the table were normal. He had forgotten how charming she could look when she smiled but when Banes' mouth dropped open he remembered. Irritated at having to share her, he leaned forward and gave her a quick kiss on the lips.

Lynne's eyes showed surprise, but she didn't pull back or act offended. It was as though she knew the kiss was for the men, not for her. She accepted the potatoes and smiled up at him. "I can't seem to find my knife, Phillip."

The way she said his name made his heart turn over. It was an echo of the way his mother always spoke to him, his name said with rich warmth and special affection. Her hand reached out toward him, and only after a moment did he realize what she wanted and hand over the knife to her.

"Could you get me some more water?" She asked, giving him

that same smile and he picked up the bucket and handed it to Shorty who had risen from the table at her request and who was just now putting away his own pocket knife. Scowling, Phillip watched until the hired man was gone.

Lynne shook her head, tickled at his mock jealousy. She turned back to slice thin pieces of potato into the hot grease; standing to one side so as to not get popped. Phillip watched in fascination as she moved the hot coffee over and then turned to place the first steak directly on the hot flat metal eye. He would have waited to use the pan she was frying potatoes in before cooking the meat, but it made sense. Any drippings from the meat sizzling would only drip down onto the wood and make the fire burn hotter.

As quickly as the first potato was all sliced, she flipped the steak, then stirred the potatoes again. The smell was enough to make his stomach growl. He poured out three cups of coffee, then hesitated with his hand on his own mug. If she wanted a cup, then he would have to eat without one. Shorty stepped back into the room, tiptoeing so as not to slosh the water.

"Here go, ma'am."

Lynne smiled at the short man who was nearly as round as he was tall. What kind of help could such a person be on a ranch? She couldn't imagine. The other man was thin, almost concave, but wiry looking. He was so silent, he made her quiet husband seem like a big talker. The way he stared at her with eyebrows raised in his long face made her think of an owl. Neither hand looked like they could do a day's work without collapsing. When she compared them to her husband, both looked like poor imitations of men. Phillip was broad of shoulder, tall, lean and decidedly well-muscled. He had one hand on the back of his head, rubbing the new cropped skin as he frowned at Shorty. For just a second Lynne remembered the intimate way that strong hand had brushed her breasts earlier, and she blushed.

Phillip spoke sharply, and the short man set the bucket down beside the stove and turned back toward the table. Lynne laughed, replacing the cooked steak with a raw one even as she hummed and sliced another potato. She could hear their voices, a rumble of talk about horses and weather, but she could feel all three pairs of eyes on her as she worked. When the third potato was on to cook, she removed the only empty bowl from the table and added flour, water and a little of the bacon grease. This she whipped and raised eyes to stare questioningly at Phillip as she lifted out one of the brown treasures she had stumbled on earlier. A section of wall in the kitchen was not paneled, instead shelves had been placed across the inner timber of the wall. Here she had located the four tins, all the same size. One held flour, another meal, a third salt. There was a large, round metal can labeled "Arbuckle's coffee," amid a florid red and yellow pattern. But in the fourth tin she had found eggs. Not sugar, but eggs.

She had only explored the yard around the back of the house, her new home, so she wondered whether he bought them or if he had a hen. But now, it was enough to have him nod approval as she cracked the egg, then whipped it into the batter.

As soon as she flipped the last steak and removed the potato, she poured out all the extra grease from the pan into the little crock on the back of her stove. Quickly, allowing them merely to brown before turning, she fried the bread.

Phillip brushed past her, reaching up to the top shelf and pulling down molasses. So, he probably didn't even have real sugar, unless there was some in the big barrels in their cellar. He also snipped a big yellow onion from the string hanging from the end of the shelf. Lynne accepted the gift, sniffing it with pleasure, before slicing it to place on the edge of the bowl with the bread.

Only when they were all seated and Shorty had prayed, did she begin to feel nervous again. The men were busy devouring the food, but each managed to mumble praise around big mouthfuls. She sat still, her plate rinsed from the bread batter, now held a few fried potatoes and a small section of her husband's meat. She was surprised they were eating antelope, not beef. But when she asked him, all three men laughed.

"You can sell a beef," Shorty answered, "Antelopes is free, at least to good shots like your mister, ma'am."

Lynne toyed with her food, eating a couple of the crispy potatoes before trying a bite of steak. It was tasty enough, but it took an awful lot of chewing. It also had the same gamey taste of some of the food on the train. Even if it was free, she wasn't sure she could get used to eating wild meat.

She could feel Phillips' eyes on her, sparkling with mischief as she finally worked the bite of meat enough to swallow. "I'll show you how, next time."

She raised her eyebrows. Show her how to cook? But Shorty was talking again. "Oh, yes'em, you've got to soak game quite a bit, maybe boil it awhile in the pan before you cook it. Takes considerable chewing. Not that this ain't tasty, 'cause it sure 'nough is. Best grub I've et since we spent the night at Mabel's." He swallowed off the last with a groan as one of the men kicked him under the table.

Lynne looked down, miffed at their comments, to stare at her plate. Well, if it wasn't good, they were certainly cleaning their plates mighty quick. When she looked up, her handsome husband was gnawing the last of the meat from his steak bone with sharp, white teeth. Beasts. Big, hungry beasts. Suddenly she realized that if they had company every day and she cooked like this, Phillip's supply of food would be gone quickly, way before it was time for him to restock.

She wanted to ask him if they ate here all the time, but as scruffy as the pair were, her husband held them in high enough regard to invite home to meet his bride, and she didn't want to insult them. "I'm sorry gentlemen, but there is no dessert. Perhaps I can manage something fancier for you next time."

"It were good." The skinny man named Banes pronounced solemnly.

Shorty grinned at her. "Well, don't rightly know when that might be ma'am. Banes and I was just working the creek when your mister rode up today and asked us to help round up some more strays. We don't generally ranch, you see, my partner and I's miners by trade." He pronounced the latter as though it were the only dignified profession in the territory.

She turned to stare at Phillip, discomfited to discover his eyes were still fastened intently on her face. Nervously she reached up to brush aside any possible smear of flour. In the meantime, Shorty elbowed the skinny man beside him and whispered. "T'ain't that sweet, him mooning over such a pretty."

Bane grinned at her, displaying two stained teeth. Suddenly she felt irritated. "Well, I'm sure you gentlemen have to get back to your work." She rose abruptly, her full skirt clinging with only one petticoat beneath it. "I have some laundry to do, and I really need to get busy."

Their guests disentangled themselves from the table, bowing to her as they backed toward the door. Phillip flicked coolly appraising eyes over her as he called to them. "Wait, I'll ride too."

◇◇◇

He stepped out, then back into the room, placing a large box on the table that he had carried from the storeroom. "Put this truck away."

She stared at him, surprised by his tone, intrigued by the box. "What?"

"The Dutchman's wife sent it."

Lynne wiped her hands and stepped closer. "A wedding present from her?"

He laughed. "Hardly. Just stuff she told me to buy for you."

He stood there, staring expectantly, waiting for her to act surprised and pleased. Instead she only nodded and finished clearing the table.

Lynne had already stacked the plates and was turning toward the dry sink in the corner, ready to make up suds with the water they had carried in, disappointed to notice there was no pump. "Don't you have water in the house?"

To Phillip it sounded like a full-blown accusation of failure. He again stopped, this time his muscles tensed.

She stared up at him, noticed how the wind had whipped his newly shaved face to a cherry red. Why she hadn't noticed earlier, she couldn't say? But it seemed it was something she should tend to immediately.

His eyes were hard and glittery, but she ignored that, merely sliding the almost clean plates into the large pan of warm water she had moved from the stove to her sink. As he took a step closer, and growled, she stopped her motions and looked up at him. "You need something on your skin. Do you have any salve anywhere?"

Whatever he had planned to say, he forgot as he flashed brown eyes toward the ceiling. "Use grease."

She frowned, but didn't argue, merely dipped three fingers in the warm, almost liquid brown fat. "Are you sure? This will smell and it may have enough salt to ..." At his growl she quit talking and timidly reached up to smear the mess over his red cheeks and jaw.

Abruptly, she heard him expel his breath. Frightened, she lifted her fingers from his face, but he raised a hand to grip her forearm and hold them in place. She dipped her clean hand in the grease and brought it up to the other cheek, slowly spreading it across his face. Already, she could feel bristles where his beard wanted to grow back. They tingled against the palm of her hand and made her knees feel week. She let her fingers trace the grooves along the side of each cheek, moved so her hand swept over the hard line of his chin. Remembering the pale neck, she let her still oiled fingers slide down his throat and around his head to cover the bare nape of his neck, lost in the changing texture beneath her fingers. For a moment, she thought she felt him tremble.

"Look at me." Slowly she raised her lashes to look up into his eyes. "I'll see about steps and a pump. But," and he breathed the word, his voice dropping so husky that Lynne couldn't stand it. She drew in a ragged breath as she stared into the dark liquid moons of his eyes, floating above the whites. "I expect three things from my wife." A shiver passed through her and she lowered her hands from his face.

"I'm sure, Mr. Gant, you expect a great deal from your wife. I knew that you would when I decided to make this journey. I intend to work hard to fulfill my part of the bargain. Of course you must think me some helpless, sniveling female, but I assure you I'm not. Today, today, well that was the first time I've cried over my mother. If so much hadn't happened lately."

"Reminds me."

The words cut her off as he tugged her forward to stand in the path of the open doors. The air whispered past, full of warm winter sunshine. "Never, ever, open both of these together."

Lynne shook her head. "But the cabin needed airing, and there aren't any windows."

"This isn't Boston." He stomped back through the house after closing and locking the back door. Turning, he stared at the small, angry figure caught in a triangle of light and dancing dust motes. Didn't she realize how easily she could be savagely attacked in this country? He hated to scare her, debated how to proceed. She was such a proud little thing, cooking and greeting his friends as though she had been a hostess for years.

Lynne listened to the approaching jingle of his spurs and shivered. It was as though all the surprising warmth of the mild winter day was gone. She crossed her arms in front of her to stop shaking and lowered her head to his approach.

He stopped a few feet away and unbuckled his guns. Lynne shivered as he draped the heavy gun belt around her slender waist, kneeling to adjust the thick leather. When he had pulled it tight, he cut a notch in the tooled pattern so he could force the belt prong through. He rose, drawing one of the long silver guns from the holster.

She gasped and stepped back. He put a large hand on her shoulder and turned her so her back fit against his chest, his long arm with the gun extended out beside her. "One door open." He leaned forward so the harsh words brushed past her small ear in a gust of hot warning. "Watch it. Anybody rides up, hold the gun ready like this." He held it stiffly, pulling his thumb across the top to cock the pistol. "They ride in without hailing the house, you shoot."

She tilted her head to look back at him, but there was nothing light or humorous in his tone. "They call out, you point this at their head, cocked. Then ask their business."

"You're serious. But I don't know how to use a gun. Even if I wanted to shoot them, I'd probably miss."

"Fire. I'll hear it and ride in." He stared down into the alarmed gray of her eyes. "Tomorrow, I'll show you how to shoot." He flipped the pistol down, shoved it into the pocket on his tight jeans.

His hands cupped her head, rubbed the silky hair over her ears. "Don't ask them in unless I'm here."

She swallowed, suddenly aware of why he had been so alarmed when he came home and couldn't find her. He thought someone had kidnapped her, maybe killed, or worse, raped her. As she remembered how he had forcefully examined her, a clear understanding made her shake in terror.

"It's a land of Indians and desperadoes," he pulled her back into the circle of his arms, aware of her rapidly beating heart. "But don't be afraid. I'm working within hearing today. I won't let anything bad happen to you. Soon, you'll be able to shoot well enough to be left alone."

She shivered. And if she never learned to shoot, would she never be left alone? Was she destined to become one of the wounded women she had met on the journey? Bereft of child or sanity? Why had she ever thought this was better than staying in Boston? Would Doctor Stone have been any more anxious to stroke her unprotected body in her sleep? Would the horrible Herr Huntmeister have taken any more liberties or been more of a danger? At least those men only wanted her honor. This man wanted, what did he want?

Lynne pushed out of his arms, turning to stare out the open

doorway at the mismatched pair of riders waiting. Men like these might ride up and she would have to pull a gun on them, shoot them according to her husband. Was that really what was required to survive in her new home?

Phillip let her slip from his arms, aware of her fears and of her doubt. Time, she would need lots of time to adjust. But she surprised him by stiffening her back and turning to stare at him.

"What three things do you expect from your wife?"

He smiled. There was steel in her eyes and a confident tilt to her head. This woman was strong despite her beauty and size. He could hear it in the way she barked orders and questions at him. For a moment he thought about letting her know how angry that tone of voice made him, then decided against it. She would need her strength and confidence here. Spirit was the last thing he wanted her to lose.

"I expect her to make my guests welcome."

She rolled her shoulders and her lips curved into a saucy, half-smile.

"Fine," he answered, "except for telling them to leave."

Lynne shook her head. "I never said any such ..." But at that moment, Shorty hollered into the door. "You want us to wait or go on?"

Phillip moved quickly through the open door and stared at the two men. "Hold your horses." But as his eyes swept the curvaceous beauty inside, he was tempted to have them ride on.

She nodded, looking guilty. "So, that's one thing. What are the other two?"

He remembered the way his mother had railed at his father when he came home from cards or drinking. "Kind words. Sweet greetings and farewells."

Lynne snorted and shook her head. "I'm always kind. I haven't," but at his stern look she turned her head back toward the waiting dishes. She had complained and certainly had failed to greet him at all when he rode up. She stopped, realizing for the first time that each journey was into danger. He faced the same Indians and outlaws that threatened her. How would she feel if anything happened to him and she had only scolded him about her view before he left? "I promise to try."

They heard the raucous laugh of the men waiting outside and Phillip moved back into the shadows of the cabin beside her. "The third thing." He edged closer and Lynne backed around behind the table. His eyes were alive, warm, easily teasing her body into flames with his glances. Finally he had backed her against the wall.

She held out hands stiffly against the heavy muscled wall of his chest. "The third thing is?" She whispered huskily.

"To be kissed hello and goodbye."

She laughed, her eyes sparkling with deviltry. "Oh, it's not enough to just say 'Hello darling,' darling expects a kiss?"

He leaned forward, his eyes dark with desire, his breath brushing her cheek as he moved his head down to claim his due. Lynne giggled and wiggled out from his reach, darting beneath the stove pipe and around behind the stove.

"So, let me be sure I have this right. You don't care if the bed is made, the laundry done, or your meal is ready. You sent all the way back east for some woman who would promise to be pleasant and kissable."

His eyes stared at her, the way her face gleamed with excitement, her eyes sparkled with glee made him grin. Lord no, he wanted all she had just named as well as her sweet young body naked and willing beneath his own. He took a step closer and she squealed and darted nimbly around the room and behind the table.

This time when he caught her laughing body, he held it close to his own. "I want..."

She shook her head and tilted back in his arms, giggling as she said. "Nope, it's three wishes. Everyone knows you only get three wishes. Whether from a fairy, a genie or a leprechaun. You've made yours."

He stopped, so aroused by her squirming body that he was afraid he would be the desperate marauder who ravaged her. "All right."

She noticed his sudden quietness. It was in the stillness of his eyes, the taunt planes of his face and the stiff way he held her body. Unable to stop herself, Lynne raised her face toward his. "You've already had three kisses too."

He raised a hand behind her head, let one trail down to cup her bottom and was rewarded by her gasp. "All the kisses I want, anytime," he growled. "Somehow you've got to make it three hundred dollars well spent."

She stared at him, suddenly aware of the feel of his hard body against her own. His lips hovered over hers, not dipping to claim her lips but waiting. She took one gulp of air then closed the distance between them to kiss him. Not the sweet timid pucker from the wedding. But a soft wild exploration of his lips. Once again dizzy weakness stirred within her, but she knew the men were outside waiting. Firmly she braced her feet and pressed her lips against his. This time she felt his whole body quiver, felt him lean back and gasp. Finally she was rewarded by his confused glance as he backed through the door, setting his hat on his head and pulling the cord tight.

Lynne rested one hand on her hip as she stood in the open

doorway, a bewildered smile on her lips. The heavy gun fell against her leg, the wide belt formed a vee around her hips. She forgot the others, merely continued to stare after him. He still had that astonished look on his face and she ran her pink tongue across her own lips. She laughed as she tasted him -- tasted bacon.

The two men beside him laughed and Phillip blushed as he guided his horse out of the yard between them. Even as he looked back, she was closing the door on the house. His heart was pounding and his body ached as he shook his head. Seven kinds of fool, that's what he was. Would she hold him to only the three things he'd told her he wanted?

In the suddenly quiet cabin, all her self-assurance vanished. Lynne suddenly felt frightened. Without the sunlight, the cabin seemed cold and empty.

"You are crazy." she said out loud. The words echoed around the room and she moved over to stoke up the fire in the stove. Gradually her eyes became used to the light. It was obvious why there were so few windows, but she would have to ask Phillip to make a viewer in the door at least so she could see out. His home was like a fortress and inside she would be safe. But from the doorway moments before she had seen the barn and corral. She wanted to explore them, but even with the gun on her hip she would wait. Maybe when he came home, she could get him to walk her around the ranch and show her where and what everything was.

Industriously, Lynne finished the few dishes, then hesitated. Was she going to stay inside, behind locked doors, each and every day? Is that what the man expected of his wife, total helplessness?

Well, she wasn't about to sit idly by, with dirty dishwater waiting to be emptied, clothes needing to be scrubbed. She let her hand drop down to grip the handle of the heavy handgun. Cautiously she lifted it, pulled back the part he had told her to, and imagined pulling it on someone. The first time, she couldn't, and quickly slid it back into the holster.

Minutes later, she tapped her feet nervously. In the still quietness it would be easy to doze off, to go back to sleep. She could become a pampered, lazy housewife, sleeping all day, rousing just before the evening meal. Again she drew the weapon. This time when she cocked the pistol, she pictured the fat monster who had stood in her apartment over her mother. Suddenly, she was eager to pull the trigger. Satisfied that she could do it if she had to, she rose and emptied the dirty water. Content to be well armed, she opened the back door and walked out to fetch water and tend to other chores.

Even though she searched, she could find no dirty clothes of her husbands to wash. Had he done the laundry himself before she came or taken it into town? As she rinsed out all her soiled underwear and slips, including the petticoat she had on, she tried to imagine that stern looking cowboy with his hands in suds, working clothes along the washboard.

Only when she had strung an impromptu clothesline in the back of the house from a rope she found in his office, did Lynne close the door and wander back inside. The huge box sat on the table, daring her to look. What had he said was inside? Things the Dutchman's wife thought she would need.

It was a wedding present then. Not from the storekeeper's wife, but from her new husband. What kind of man cleaned his house and did his laundry so his new wife wouldn't have to? She leaned against the table, stared at the backdoor, then walked back to lock it. Only when she was completely alone and safe did she begin to unpack the huge parcel.

Each time she brought something out, she tried to imagine Phillip's face while he selected it. She couldn't. He had been robbed. She sat with her elbows wide, glaring at the assortment of heavy cast iron and brass trinkets and gewgaws. There was an iron, but it was shaped like a swan and would probably never get hot enough to even press a handkerchief. A pair of scissors, again cast of ornate brass, were stamped finest seamstress. But she shook her head in bewilderment when she tried to snip a thread with them. He had an assortment of pots and pans, only one of which looked practical. It was made of blue enamel ware, beautiful, but perhaps functional.

Of course there was a tiny bag of sugar. No matter what that cost out here, she intended to keep it. Already she had planned to make stew for supper and a plain, simple white cake.

There was a lovely spice rack, with tiny blue and white bottles, each holding some precious and tempting seed or powder. This she would keep. She had a small stack of her mother's recipes that she had carried here in her trunk. None called for any of the exotic sounding spices, but they did ask for mustard, pepper, and cinnamon. The other nine she would keep and find recipes for.

But the rest of this. She clicked her tongue sharply, repacking tiny glass salt and pepper shakers, perfume decanters, a metal wine rack, and numerous other frivolities. The first time they went into town, she would return these and either demand a refund or exchange them for something more practical.

She repacked the iron last, debating trying to press her clothes with it. No, if it became discolored, then perhaps the dishonest Dutchman's wife wouldn't take it back. There had to be a better way to press clothes. For now, even one of the flat iron circles on her new stove would work, if she could figure out some way to make a handle to move them across the cloth. Disgusted, she packed it, making sure the fragile items were completely rewrapped and inside a smaller wooden box in the bigger crate.

Only after she had everything put away and stew on the stove to cook, did Lynne rest. She would bring in the clothes and bake her cake just before Phillip should be home. As she stretched out on the soft bed, she replayed the events since arriving here. No matter what she tried to do, her mind returned not to the words, but to the feel of his hand, the softness of his lips, the warmth of his body over hers.

For the first time in her life, she had a yearning. A yearning so strong, so urgent, that she wondered if she could wait the week Phillip had agreed to. There was a wildness about the land, but also a wildness about her heart. She couldn't keep the fever of anticipation from making her blood boil.

She had never understood how Bonnie could surrender her honor to a worthless man like Tarn. Maybe she had felt these same strange yearnings. Lynne swallowed. She knew it was the devil that tempted one. All of her life she had dreamed of meeting the love of her life and making a marriage like her parents had. A decent woman did not enter into sin lightly. But there was no sin in having relations with your husband. It was a woman's duty. The sin was in taking pleasure in it. It made her head ache to think about what was right. If only this were a marriage of love not a business arrangement.

<><><>

When she went to check on the stew and start the cake, she

climbed from the bed as awake as when she'd laid down. She hummed as she examined the basic ingredients she had assembled for the cake. The stove was still hot from the stew, but it was a nice, even heat. She had opened the canned milk and crushed the tip of a vanilla bean to add to it. The precious sugar had been added to the flour and the two eggs rested on the table. She reached for the egg to crack when a sound made her heart stop.

In the distance, she could hear voices. But as she tilted her head to listen, no sound came. Someone was in the yard, but they hadn't hailed the house.

Trembling, Lynne looked back through the house and forward. Both doors were closed and locked. Maybe if she were quiet, they would merely look around and then leave. She didn't have to take any chances. Phillip wouldn't expect her to risk her life just to protect the animals in the barn.

Suddenly a voice she recognized said something to the other in an unmistakable Irish accent. Raising the heavy pistol, she stepped forward and opened the door.

CHAPTER TWENTY

Lynne drew a deep breath along with the gun before opening the door. Despite her resolve, the oaths of the three men arguing in her yard were enough to unsettle her. A man wearing one boot, with a large bandage over the unbooted foot, still sat in the saddle. On the ground, half-hidden by his horse, was a nervous, slim blonde man. But it was the broad back and lazy smile of the dark-haired Irishman that made her frown and cock the pistol.

"That's far enough gentlemen."

When the man that was hidden didn't move forward, Lynne squeezed the trigger and fired a warning shot. His horse snorted and pulled away, forcing him to hold onto the reins and struggle to calm the animal, while the man on horseback had a hard time keeping his mount settled. Only when all three were in plain view and she could see they were not pointing guns at her, did Lynne allow her finger to ease up on the trigger. She could still feel the stinging vibrations of the shot along the small bones of her wrist and she frowned fiercely.

"My husband warned me savages and desperadoes might show up. I thought he was just trying to frighten me into his arms for another kiss, but I can see Tarn Micheals he was right." She waved the heavy gun at him, slowly raising it so it was aimed at his angry blue eyes.

"Now, here now, Lynne McKinney, that's no way to welcome

guests. Especially such old dear friends as we are my darling."

Lynne gritted her teeth in warning. "You know I told him I might not be able to shoot anyone, but now I see your black-hearted face, I think maybe I should try it and see."

"What's she talking about?" the man on horseback called out. "I thought you told us she was an old sweetheart of yours."

"Then you men have ridden to your death on the words of a liar." Lynne hissed. "I hate this cowardly fiend. Why don't you ask him about the wife he left in Boston?"

The big Irishman raised his hands in the air and grinned charmingly. "Hush now, sweetheart, you go too far denying all we've been to each other." Suddenly all Lynne could see were Bonnie's dark, empty eyes. Her hand holding the gun shook. Both Tarn and the blonde man on the ground inched closer.

The horse pranced under his bandaged rider, stepping in quick mincing steps. Lynne saw the flicker of movement and stiffened, turning the gun so it pointed at the pale rider who had crept up onto the porch. "My husband is working close to hand and should be here any minute."

She was unaware that her eyes were as cool and coldly gray as the gun she pointed at the man, but she was relieved to notice he stopped, looking from the edge of the porch to the mounted rider.

"Goddamn you, Micheals. Come on, Gunther, let's ride before the devil comes home."

Tarn watched and sidled forward as her eyes swung away from him. In just a minute he would be able to reach out and grab her. Fate had brought him here, had left evidence of her passing like a sweet scent pulling him forward.

As the one gunman fell back and ran for his horse, the big Irishman hesitated. He had ridden into town with the army detail only this morning. But everyone had been talking about the wedding the day before. He didn't know who she had married, but whoever he was, the three of them should be able to deal with one man easily. Still, the man who had brought him here seemed worried and that made him hesitate about slipping a hand out to snag in her long brown hair.

The unit of soldiers had been sent out from the fort to check on reported Indian atrocities along the stage road, and he had been relieved to have a protective escort into the mining town. He had heard about Butte's big spenders in Salt Lake. The fact that the miners had gold and loved to gamble had been enough to send him into the remote, cold wilderness. But each place they had stopped on the hard trail, he had heard glowing descriptions of the little mail-order bride. The descriptions had sounded too much like Bonnie's conceited friend to be anyone else.

Lynne McKinney Gant brought her hand up stiffly, the gun barrel pointing coldly in his face. The threatening gesture made him leer at her, more determined than ever to extract revenge. If it hadn't been for her, her constant harping at Bonnie to stand up for herself, he would still be in Boston. The tall homely girl hadn't been who he would have chosen to marry, but she was a good worker and submissive enough. But Lynne was always filling her with nonsense. Telling her that she was entitled to keep the money she worked for, that Tarn should earn his own, spend his own wages for their room and his drink.

She had probably been the one to tell his trusting wife about the other women. It was her fault he'd had to beat some sense into Bonnie. It was Lynne's fault for butting into his business that he had kicked the pregnant girl too hard. It was the little meddling witch's fault that he had been attacked and run out of town by men he had shared a pint with only hours before. He owed her.

Grinning he stepped to one side, ready to lurch forward to grab her. Lynne's eyes widened, but she turned her body and kept the gun pointed at him.

"That's far enough." The deep voice boomed across the hard-packed ground in front of the house.

The two men who had started to ride out turned their mounts and reined them back into place. Neither was willing to chance being fired at by Gant. The wounded rider was the first to raise his hands into the air, the pale-haired one was slower.

The man on the porch swore, held his hands to his side, and kept them closed in massive fists.

"Move back from my wife." The words were even, but each exploded on the crisp air like gunfire.

Tarn raised shocked eyes to stare at the man on horseback. The blue-shirted rider had half-risen from the saddle, the horse held in check only by pressure from his knees. Tarn's eyes flicked over him appreciatively, noticing the wide shoulders and slim build. He probably had forty pounds on the man, could pulverize him with one hand. So why were the others so frightened? A gray hat hung by a cord from the cowboy's neck, revealing a reddened jaw and ugly haircut. The rider wasn't even wearing a gun belt, merely holding a single revolver in his right hand.

He stared, open jawed at the two quaking gunmen beside him. When he had entered the saloon, weren't these two men the very ones who had been bragging to one and all that they had plans of their own for the little bride. That is, after they killed the bridegroom. It had been enough to convince him to leave the warm bar and sharp whiskey and climb back on that ugly horse yet again.

"You have us wrong," the wounded rider spoke. "We just came

out to congratulate you and wish you and your bride the best. We brought a friend of hers from Boston out to ..."

"Enough." Gant spoke.

Lynne's wrist throbbed, the gun in her hand tilted forward from its own weight. Frightened, she raised her other hand to support her weakened wrist. "Inside Lynne. Close the door."

The voice was so sharp, she raised her head in defiance. But there was something in his eyes, a deadliness that made her swallow. She wanted to argue, to tell him what a snake Tarn was. Would he believe them? Wasn't she to even have a chance to tell him the truth? What if she walked inside, and he were shot? Didn't he think she could help to protect him? The words burned her lips, made her turn stormy gray eyes on Phillip.

His jaw was clenched, his eyes darker, dead black. Frustrated, she flashed another angry glance at Bonnie's abuser, then dropped the gun to her side and stepped back behind the door.

Through the closed door, she heard the heavy brogue and could picture the disarming grin. "We only came out to give the little bride a kiss." Furious, she thought of flinging the door open and screaming all the names that she wanted to call that lying devil. "Lynne and I are old friends from Boston." The last words were said with an oily implication that made her flame to the roots of her hair. The dirty liar. He had tried, but she had never let him within spitting range, let alone kissing reach. But his voice implied even more and she wondered why she hadn't fired and blown a hole through him where his heart should have been.

She waited for her husband to say something. To call the man a liar, to defend her honor. She waited and waited. With every passing minute she grew angrier.

A voice finally spoke. She recognized it as the wounded rider.

"Yeah, I just came out to apologize Gant, for what happened in town yesterday. Me and the boys were still sore about Charlie, that's all. I wanted to come out and apologize, bury the hatchet, and congratulate you."

Still there was silence. Lynne wanted to scream. Was the man she married idiot enough to believe such a story? The man had threatened her. All right, not in so many words. But hadn't Phillip told her to shoot anyone that didn't call a greeting to the house before they dismounted. Well, these three hadn't called out anything. They deserved to be shot. For just a moment she imagined the flash of light, the acrid smell of gray smoke. Ooh, if she were still outside, she could shoot them all. Only she would have four dead men on the ground, not three.

She heard the creak of leather, heard one of the horses snort. Her nerves vibrated, they felt so tense. Finally she heard the soft words. "Ride out."

The thunder of horses was the only sound for a long time. Lynne drew in angry breaths, a cold rage shaking her whole body. She leaned against the closed door, biting her lip to prevent calling out in anger. What would he do once he stepped inside? Would he expect her to cling to his neck, to thank him for saving her from the big, bad riders? She couldn't believe he had allowed men to live who moments before were ready to invade their home, to ... she shook as she imagined what they were probably ready to do to her.

Wearily she leaned against the closed door. It seemed hours before he neared the house. Silently she stared at the abandoned ingredients on the table. Had it been such a short time ago that he had been laughingly chasing her around the room? The thought of baking a cake for such a man made her feel sick.

◇◇◇

Phillip hesitated, still mounted on his horse. He had never wanted to kill a man more, never struggled harder to control himself. But yesterday in town had taught him something. He hadn't wanted to ruin his wedding day by killing. Wounding the men had been enough to stop them, and it had stopped his melancholy. He hadn't been thrown into the dark pit of despair their murders would have caused. Instead of seeing twisted grimaces of dead men's faces last night, he had been able to enjoy the sweet beauty of his brides.

It was time to put the guns away if he was to settle down, be able to provide a safe and comfortable life for a woman. How would such a sensitive creature feel about her new home if every time she stepped outside she walked on ground he had covered with blood?

There was also the shadow of a doubt. The man on the porch was a big, handsome fellow. Obviously Lynne recognized him. What if his story were true? It could easily be the truth. Phillip knew he would never let someone like Lynne ride off and marry another man? Never. He would have followed her out west too. So, if the poor girl had had no choice but to marry for money to save her family the way she told him earlier, perhaps she had feelings for the big Irishman still. If he killed the man, what would she feel for him?

Phillip's head hurt from thinking. All he wanted was to make a safe home for his wife, to have the kind of life he had known as a boy in which to raise their children. Slowly he dismounted, tossing the reins over the porch rail as he stepped up onto the small square doorstep. Soon, he would complete the porch. It only there weren't so much to do just moving the horses down from the mountain pasture before the big snows. Shorty and Banes would probably think he was mad for riding off so quickly, would probably let loose the remuda they had corralled earlier if he didn't ride back. Still he strode toward the cabin door.

When the door didn't give, he drew in a deep breath. Perhaps she was still angry at the way he had sent the men riding. But even if she had feelings for the Irishman, he had no intention of allowing any of the four Georgians into his home, let alone a man that Lynne probably already loved more than she ever would him.

Frustrated, he hit the door a glancing blow.

CHAPTER TWENTY-ONE

Trembling, Lynne backed away from the door as she pulled the latch. Even though she had heard his breathing, she needed to see if the man she had married was all right. The light behind the tall figure in the doorway threw his face into shadow. For a moment she swallowed, worried that it might be one of the other men. But his voice vibrated through the room and swirled through her shaking body.

"Lynne?"

"Phillip," she whispered, then collected herself and strode over to the table. Fine he was alive and well, but she didn't have to talk to him after the terrible thing he had just done.

"I need to get back out to Shorty and Banes." He rubbed a hand against the back of his neck, up through to the unruly curls on top, then back again.

She raised the sifter in her hand, turned the handle on the side viciously as she sifted the flour. "Fine." The word was as indefinite as the whirling flour.

He cleared his throat, set his hat on his head, tightening the cord. "You're all right then?" He took a step closer, letting the light fall through the doorway around him to reveal her features.

Lynne set the sifter down in the bowl, dropping one hand to her hip. With the other she pushed back a straying hair and glared up at him.

He stared at the eyes, stormy gray with rage, and involuntarily dropped his hands to where his guns used to hang. "I'll not apologize for not inviting them in."

"Inviting them in?" She blinked and her mouth fell open. "I expected you to shoot them, or do you think a liar like Tarn Micheals should live to spread false rumors about your wife's character throughout the territory."

His hand flew up to push back his hat and he leaned back on his heels in surprise. Slowly he grinned as he saw her face flame red with outrage and he laughed in spite of himself. "You wanted me to shoot them?"

"So, defending a woman's honor is funny? Well, you weren't here when they rode up and dismounted unannounced. You didn't see the threat in their eyes."

Her voice broke on the last and he closed the distance between them, taking her by the shoulders with his big hands and tilting her so the light reflected from the tears standing in her eyes.

"Damn. I spared them for you." At the confusion in her eyes he growled. "I thought, I thought the big man, that you, that he… hell."

Lynne gasped as she watched the tortured emotions flash through his dark eyes. "You spared him, thinking he was my lover?" She lifted a hand to clutch his upper arm. What sort of man was this? She had heard that westerners were hardened by all the danger and would shoot at any cause. The tabloids in Boston carried lurid stories from the west, of big gunfights, of husbands shooting wives and lovers, of settlers shooting Indians, of cowboys shooting people in bars and over cards and even more lurid photographs of the corpses. Yet this man, this stranger to her, had spared a man he thought was her lover. Had spared him for her sake?

"Listen to me, you big fool. Tarn Micheals's was never…"

Even as she struggled for words, they were interrupted by the sound of men and horses. Phillip pulled away from her and ran from the cabin, darting across the yard and rushing to open the corral as Shorty and Banes drove in a herd of thirty horses.

Lynne stepped to the doorway, her eyes bright with alarm as she watched the stranger she had married swing a gate open and cling to it as the excited wild animals rushed pass within inches of his lean body. She held her breath until she saw him swing the gate closed and drop down on the side away from the snorting horses with their flashing teeth and hooves.

Shorty tilted his hat to her as he slowly rode up to the porch. "Sorry to be such a pest, Mrs. Gant. But we figured your mister would want these animals caught up, not turned loose. Some of these mustangs will need dosing, others might need breaking, or what have you, don't you see. Don't plan to be intruding on your honeymoon don't you know, but well, he asked us to help with the horses."

Lynne blushed at the implication and was aware of the other man riding up to grin down at her also. Phillip turned back in time to catch the two all but drooling over his blushing bride. He crossed the yard in a few quick steps, ready to yell at them, but was stopped by the same vision they were captured by.

In the fading light, she was perched on the small porch, one hand to her throat, the other resting against the sagging gun belt. For the first time he noticed how the dark sprigged dress clung to her youthful figure, the belt molding it around her round hips. Even though it buttoned from hem to throat, it seemed far too revealing. Her brown hair fell thick and soft down her back and her cheeks were pink from Shorty's teasing.

He cleared his throat and she turned, tilting her head just a little. In the fine features of the heart-shaped face, her dark lashes lifted shyly to reveal her silver eyes. At the sight of him she smiled and he felt his heart turn over. For the hundredth time in the last two days, he couldn't believe this woman belonged to him.

Shorty called out a comment to Banes that made him cackle. Phillip felt himself blush until he knew his ears were red. "Best be riding out, 'afore the moon comes up," Shorty cackled.

Lynne spoke into the embarrassed laughter. "Nonsense. Supper is almost ready and I'm baking a cake. Tell them it's all right Phillip, that we want them to stay."

He swept her from head to foot one last time. Blast, why did she have to be so sociable now. He lifted a hand to tug at the mane of Banes jar-headed horse and laughed as her eyes twinkled mischievously back at his. Right, the first of his three wishes. "You heard the Lady, boys, dismount and stay awhile. Besides there's some chores around the house I could use a hand with."

Shorty started to make another comment about certain chores but Phillip's cold eyes stopped him. A chill swept up his neck. Gant was a good man sure enough, but only a fool would cross him. He dismounted, motioning for Banes to do the same.

Lynne had turned back into the house, missing the interplay. Quickly she shook the last of the flour from the sifter, then cracked an egg, eager to let cooking occupy her thoughts. She would still have to convince Phillip about Tarn, but any conversation they might have about such a delicate issue as her virtue might not be easy to control. At least with Shorty and Banes underfoot, she would have time to collect her courage for the inevitable confrontation.

She checked the oven, then slid the single layer of cake into its warm depth. While it baked, she took a damp rag to the table, clearing away any traces of her baking. Phillip and his comrades came into the room carrying lumber and she called cheerily. "Here, could one of you give me a hand. I need this box moved, but you need to be careful."

Phillip motioned the mismatched pair through the door then turned to look at the box he had given her at noon. "Didn't you have time to unpack it?"

Lynne hesitated. If only his eyes would stay warm and liquid, she wouldn't mind talking to him. But now when they were cool and wary, she knew she would have to be cautious how she worded her complaints.

"Yes. It was wonderful. The sugar is in the cake and these spices," she pointed to where the square blue and white bottles filled a shelf, "they're wonderful. I've never received so many splendid presents at one time. But," she fidgeted, crossing her arms and aimlessly scratching at her elbow as she talked. "Well, Phillip, some of it just isn't that practical. I know you wanted to please me,"

"Practical?"

She tapped her toe impatiently, wondering if there was a best way to say the rest. Frustrated, she just blurted out the truth. "I mean really, the Dutchman's wife must be some sort of flim-flam artist. Look at these scissors."

She saw his jaw clench and she stepped forward to pull the heavy, molded brass objects from the box. "See, they won't cut anything."

He took them from her hand and stared at them. Damn right the woman was a con artist, but didn't she know every woman loved gee-gaws and trinkets. Lynne stepped closer, holding out a strand of long brown hair. "Try them."

He took the silken strand, rubbed it through his fingers, and then lifted the awkward shears. Mesmerized, he looked past them to where her somber gray eyes were studying his. "Go on, try to cut it."

Her voice was so confident, so trusting. He stared at the soft pink mouth, pursed in concentration. For just a second he imagined those lips on his again.

"Com'on now Gant. You knows Banes and I's miners, not carpenters."

Trembling he let the hair go, dropped the scissors back in the box. He picked up the box and turned toward the storeroom, calling to the men first, "Just a minute." Then his hypnotic brown eyes were on her, and Lynne drew in a breath. "We'll take them back, next trip into Butte."

Lynne sank down beside the table for a minute, as disturbed by the way just one look could make her whole body feel swollen, as she was surprised and resentful at having their conversation again interrupted. Minutes later, she heard the back door open and the sounds of sawing and hammering. Worried if the sounds were loud enough to make her cake fall, she stepped into the other room just in time to hear Banes give a wolf-like whistle. She looked past the men to the impromptu clothesline she had strung across the backyard. All three were staring at the assortment of undergarments and travel clothes flapping in the cool breeze.

Embarrassed Lynne stormed past, unhooking one end of the line and cautiously reeling them in against her breast. She heard Phillip's cold voice and knew that if she turned back around Shorty and Banes would be working with downcast eyes. But when she did, she was incredibly aware of how Phillip's dark eyes followed her every movement. As she marched into the house his gaze never wavered, and she felt shaken by the realization that he was imagining her wearing those garments. Furious, she stood beside the bed, dropping the betraying garments on its neat covers.

How dare he? She shook as she folded the still damp

underclothes into neat little squares, then turned to hang the tired travel dress and blouse over the open doors of the wardrobe to finish drying. She wanted to yell at him, but with the other two men as witnesses, she merely bit her tongue. Besides, what would he say? Just what he had told her this afternoon, when he had, she swallowed, and sank down on the bed. When he had touched her breasts. 'He didn't have to be a gentleman, he was her husband.' For just a second she sat there, again entranced by the way he could make her feel just by a look or a word.

Awkwardly she rose and placed the damp bundles on top of her travel case. Through the open door, she could hear the thud of the hammer and the men's low voices. They were once again talking about the weather, how the sky was red and that might mean trouble.

Phillip glanced toward the house and Lynne clung to the door frame, keeping out of sight. "Well, if it snows, we've plenty of room for you two to stay."

Shorty swore and tried to look at him. "You crazy or something."

Phillip wondered the same. But if he had to spend another night in bed with all that lovely temptation, there was no way he could keep his word and wait the time he had promised. Even now, he throbbed with wanting her, and that from merely looking at her empty underwear.

Cautiously she stepped forward to stare out at them. They were building a staircase, sawing the wood into matching notches on each side, then carefully fitting flat boards across for treads. Her husband might be forward about handling her body, but at least he was not shy about working. Her eyes skipped the other men, settling on the back of the stranger she had married. Where he was bent, holding the boards, his coarse blue shirt was stretched tightly across his back, his jeans were equally snug across his hips. Lynne swallowed in wonder. If he had any idea how he made her feel? She heard Shorty's comment and cleared her throat.

"Mr. Gant and I would both love to have you stay the night if the weather is a danger. As soon as you're through with the stairs Phillip, I wondered if you could do this as well."

He stared at her, perplexed to find her listening. Cautiously he stepped inside, wondering if he could now change his mind and send the two scoundrels packing.

She stepped back out of reach and he drew himself upright, settling for staring at her. She looked confused, then closed the door. He drew in his breath, choking on her sweet scent.

"See how dark it is inside with the door closed."

He growled in answer.

Lynne shivered at the husky vibration of his voice. "I wondered if you could make a small opening in the door, at about eye level. Something we could cover with wood or leather. That way when someone rides up on the house, I could see who it is without opening the door."

He stood there, his body taunt with anticipation. Nervously she shied away and stepped through the house to the front door. "And maybe a little higher, like here on the front door, or maybe over here above the sink."

She looked back at him, excited by his silence more than by anything he could have answered. She knew he was watching her. How would she ever grow used to his quiet?

"Oh, the cake." The warm scent made her open the oven and

squat down to test it. She placed a finger on top of the brown surface, then sighed and closed the door carefully as her finger left a dent. When she rose to look for him, he was gone.

That night she lay in the bed, tossing and turning. She could hear the men talking, their voices soft and deep in the other room. Somehow they had managed to finish the stairs and drill the holes in the doors as she had asked. She wasn't too pleased at the rough hide covering that Phillip had tacked over the openings, but it was after all what she had asked for. Perhaps she could make an embroidered piece to replace them, or at least to cover the ugly skins. How could they still find something to say? They had been talking for hours now.

She turned to look at the empty pillow beside her, remembering the way his head had looked on it last night. It was true that she didn't have cramps and her body was rested from the long journey, but it didn't mean that she would mind having him there to share the heat or rub her back. The wind howling outside made it seem colder beneath the quilt and coverlet. Disappointed, she turned her back to the mumbled sounds and slowly fell asleep.

◇◇◇

It was late, and the moon stood like a gold plum in the night sky. Phillip cursed fate and the two loud snorers sleeping in his kitchen. He stepped back into the bedroom from the cold trip out into the dark. Only after he fumbled from his great coat and boots, did he slide into the bed. His young bride was sound asleep and he rubbed his cold hands briskly together to thaw. Carefully he scooted closer, not daring to let his cold feet touch her warm ones but willing to steal some of the warmth from the covers. He had thought the wedding would end all his lonely releases, but perhaps tonight would be the last time he would ever have to comfort himself.

He had barely made himself comfortable when she moved, rolling over against his side. He held his breath, not daring to do anything that would set his body into throbbing awareness again. But after several minutes passed, he relaxed. Through the worn cloth of his long-johns, he could feel her warm body.

Carefully he moved his arm, slipping it around to cradle her beside him. The warm weight of her sleepy head moved into the hollow of his shoulder. Exhausted, he nuzzled his face into her soft hair and slept.

CHAPTER TWENTY-TWO

Lynne woke to the sound of voices in her kitchen. She started to get up but a gruff voice whispered, "Don't move."

For the first time since the wedding, she awakened to find the bed occupied. For five nights, she had fallen asleep alone, awakened alone. Not since the first evening had she caught a glimpse of her husband in bed. Now he lay there, his dark eyes watching her, even as she struggled to figure out what was going on.

A pan dropped and she heard Shorty swear, then Banes high pitched answer. Those two, never had she wished more fervently for company to be gone. She frowned in frustration and Phillip laughed. "Look's clear today."

"Good," she sighed as she leaned back against her pillow. "I know they're your dear friends, but honestly Phillip, they are like… like children. Well almost." She didn't need to add, except when they look at me. But he was only too aware of the looks, and had spent a lot of time growling around the cabin like an angry bear whenever he caught them at it.

All three men had worked around the house and barns while the wind and snow blew. Together, they had located a pregnant cow, and after fighting her into the barn, managed to build a stall for her. The plan was to keep her so tightly penned, that she would be used to being touched enough to let them milk her after she calved. Lynne had wanted to cry when she saw how panicky the poor creature was.

Instead, she had taken to talking to the cow a little each day, petting her and feeding her sweet hay.

Whenever the wind died down, the men worked frantically on construction and repairs and had added the front porch and a permanent clothesline in back of the house. There was no plumbing so they hadn't been able to add the inside pump she wanted, but had managed to construct a covered walkway running from the back door to the well and on beyond to the outhouse. It was finished just before the first heavy snow fell and everyone was grateful for how much easier it made the essential trips.

Phillip had also taken the time to show Lynne all the animals and how to care for them, in case he was ever out overnight on the range. He had a pen with three pigs, one a very mean looking sow. The pigs were so noisy and aggressive, Lynne had been frightened of them at first. It was something Phillip appreciated greatly as she ran squealing into his arms the first time one charged the fence. There were eight chickens. He had purchased a dozen, but coyotes had already made off with four. Lynne enjoyed watching them flutter around for scattered corn when she fed them in the barn, but hated trying to steal the eggs from the pecking nesters. Of course there were the restless, wild looking mustangs, but they would soon be gone. The two lovely bays that had pulled the wagon home had stalls in the barn and unlike the cow, already loved to be petted.

She had learned a lot about the ranch in the few days, even watched in horror as her lean husband had ridden on two different mustangs, managing to take the kinks out of one and survive being thrown by the other. The first ride she had been called from the house by Shorty to watch. She had been unable to stay back from the corral, despite the sharp bite of the cold wind and the deep snow around her boots. She had climbed against the rails. As the panicked animal jumped and leaped, large chunks of mud were torn from beneath the white blanket and tossed around the coral. Lynne had stood with her fist in her mouth to keep from screaming out to him.

The second mount had been worse. It had seemed to take an hour to lasso the rough-coated bronco, throw and tie it, then came hobbling and saddling, each seeming more dangerous than the step before. Phillip moved with such grace and ease, handling the wild animal as though it were powerless to hurt him. When he was thrown, Lynne screamed, unable to believe it. But Phillip rose from the snow, brushing snow and mud from his jeans with his hat, shoving Banes and Shorty aside.

Strangely, Banes seemed to have a knack for breaking the horses. Shorty joked it was because he could dig in his heels and the animals just gave up when they grew tired of dragging the long legged man around the corral. Lynne had retreated to the cabin, self-conscious about the emotions watching Phillip work stirred in her. It had to be because he belonged to her, unlike the other men. But surely it was ridiculous to care so much for a stranger.

There was another loud crash from the kitchen and she started to get up but this time he leaned closer and she sank back against the pillows. That was fine for him, but she was the one who would have nothing left to cook with if those two bunglers weren't chased out soon. "What is it?" she asked impatiently.

His jaw clenched at her sharp tone, then relaxed, and she stared in fascination at the dark shadowed, partially bearded face. Less than a week ago, he had been completely clean shaven. She was tempted to reach out and touch it, wanting to feel the prickly texture of it again. Although there had truly been little time for touching or talking in the midst of company, she had felt its ticklish texture when he had stolen kisses. For just a second she stared at the unsmiling lips and remembered the last kiss. They had been in the barn and she had been talking to the bawling cow. Shorty had given the miserable beast the name Beulah, and Lynne had been commiserating with her on being a prisoner when Phillip had walked up behind her.

"Is that how you feel? Like a prisoner." His words had surprised her and she had looked up at him, unable to hide her pouty face. She had shaken her head. "No, I do feel a little sad, wondering how Mary and the boys are doing."

"Did you write them some more today?"

She nodded, looking suddenly shy. He had caught her writing and teased her about sending home a book. But the next day, she could tell he had shuffled through the pages, reading her descriptions of the journey and now of her new husband and home. He encouraged her to make time to write each day. It helped her loneliness to imagine the children's faces, picturing their smiles whenever they should get to read about the sad cow or her husband's strange friends.

He had moved closer somehow, and she had found herself penned between the flat boards of the stall and his hard body. But he hadn't pressed against her as he had on the journey home, merely bent down and kissed her. His lips had been so warm, his beard so ticklish against her hands.

She opened her gray eyes with a start, staring into two big brown ones.

"You started to tell me about the Irishman."

Lynne blinked. Right, she had five days ago. The memory of those threatening riders made her shudder. "You didn't seem to have time to hear me."

"Tell me now."

Lynne shifted uncomfortably, for the first time aware of the fact that she was in her nightgown and he was wearing only his underwear. Outside the blanketed doorway, she could hear the two hired hands arguing. She wanted to protest and climb out of bed to dress but he suddenly rolled on his side, placing his arm on top of the blanket. Lynne stared in fascination at the yellowed cotton sleeve of his thermal underwear, its tight orderly lines stretched and curved over the thick muscles of his arms. The sleeve was pushed high above his forearm, and she noticed the silky dark hairs on the bared skin, the pulsing vein deep tunneled along the inside of his wrist. Nervously she worked her hips over toward the edge of the bed. He smiled at her and followed.

She raised a hand against his chest to push him back and instantly realized her mistake. She could feel the warmth of his body beneath the muscular wall, feel the prickle of the curly hairs on his chest even through the shirt. She swallowed and leaned her head back on the pillow, looking at him for mercy.

"You called him a liar."

Lynne licked her lips, trying to remember how to talk, let alone what to talk about.

Suddenly she remembered the riders and Tarn's comments. She sat up ignoring his closeness. "He's a beast, a lying beast. We were never close."

He drew back, so he could watch her eyes and face more clearly.

"He talked to me, that's all, trying to get me to go out with him, but I refused. He even tried to talk my friend Claire into going out, but even Claire was too smart to go anywhere with him. But Bonnie, Bonnie is my other best friend, she listened." Lynne paused, then whispered. "She ended up having to get married. Then the dog had the nerve to cheat on her and beat her." She paused, remembering the hollow-eyed stare of her friend. "She lost the baby."

The hand she had been watching reached very slowly to merely touch her breast. Lynne dew in a deep breath.

"You weren't lovers?"

She felt her throat tighten, knew she should brush his hand away. The voices outside the door had quieted down. All she would have to do is scream, and one of the two men would rush in to rescue her. She raised dazed eyes and stared at him. "No. Never."

Slowly he moved his hand and Lynne looked down to follow the long brown finger as it traced the outline of her breast through the thin cotton of the gown. Even as she watched, her nipple hardened disgracefully beneath his touch. Breathlessly, she swallowed as he repeated the procedure on the other breast.

Mesmerized, she collapsed back against the pillow. She heard Shorty's loud cackle from the outer room and blushed brightly. "The other men."

He was leering down at her, his eyes dark with desire. "The other men were your lovers?" But she was aware of how carefully he listened for an answer.

"No."

"Never?"

"Never," she whispered, then shivered as he bent his head and opened his warm mouth to suckle her breast through the thin cloth.

A wild quiver of excitement shot through her. Instead of pushing him away, she slipped a hand up to cup the back of his neck and move his head to her other hungry breast. She moaned in pleasure and he raised his eyes to stare into hers, suddenly smiling as he shifted to pull her beneath him.

Lynne swallowed again. She could feel the firm outline of his body pressed against hers and she struggled to resist wiggling beneath him. Phillip groaned and leaned down to kiss her. The full force of his kiss took her last breath away. When he finally drew back, she felt faint. Her lips were bruised, her heart pounding.

Shorty called through the curtain. "Everything's ready the way you asked partner, Banes and I'll be riding on out."

"Thanks men," he called to them and Lynne saw the smile in his eyes, heard the laugh on his lips.

She watched in horror as he climbed from the bed, his long johns failing to hide anything from her. He peeked through the blanketed doorway and she heard the men call back to him as they closed the front door.

"Now you can get up, Mrs. Gant," Phillip said.

Lynne shivered, strangely hurt by his sudden abandonment. He saw the shiver and reached back for his great coat. The old military garment was always waiting on the chair by the bed for the next trip outside, at least since the weather had turned so cold again. Embarrassed, she wiggled back across the bed, finding her shoes under the edge of the bed to slip on before standing.

She was suddenly very self-conscious as she stood and reached for the coat. He held it just far enough away so that she had to stand fully exposed to his gaze, before he draped it around her. She blushed as she shrugged into the heavy layers of wool but she forgot her blush when he drew her forward, sliding into the coat with her. Gingerly he rubbed her body beneath the coat, making sure to rewarm the front of her gown where the damp circles had chilled her. Only when she was once again glowing and light-headed did he steer her toward the back door and the covered pathway.

She was not surprised to find the door swing open as soon as she returned, or to see him latch it as soon as she entered. She was shocked by what she found on the other side. He seemed suddenly shy as he slipped inside the coat again, but this time it was she who let her hands slip over his bare skin. Her eyes widened in delight as she gently explored the many textures of his naked body. Only when she was burning from the joy of touching him did he pull her forward into the other room. Both the Franklin stove inside the fireplace and the blue cook stove were blazing. Between the heat they cast off and the heat he had managed to raise, she found the big coat suffocating.

"So this is what they were up to," she cried in delight as he helped her from the coat and tossed it onto the table. The big wash tub sat between the fires, mist rising from the surface. On the nearest trestle bench, rested a bar of soap and a large, clean towel. Suddenly he stepped around into her line of vision, stopping to stand by the make-shift bath. "You're welcome to go first."

She couldn't speak. He stood there before her, glorious in his nudity, perfectly at ease. What had that ad claimed so long ago, "tall, well formed." He had been far too modest. She blushed, but was unable to keep her eyes from exploring every inch. Slowly she stepped forward, taking up the soap and nodding to the tub. "You first, I don't trust those two not to boil us alive."

He smiled and stepped into the water, breathed in deeply, then gradually lowered himself into the steaming contents. She watched in horror as his skin turned bright red. "Hurry," he groaned and she knelt beside him, dipping a hand into the hot water, bringing out a wet rag to soap into a lather. Years of helping bathe the children kept her from dropping the soap or missing any spot, although she had never enjoyed the chore as she did today. His back and chest were sculpted marble beneath the trail of bubbles and she gentled her hand at the sight of the dark bruise covering his shoulder.

"The horse yesterday," he said, answering her unspoken question. Next she found a small red scar on his right side. "Chickamauga." There was a jagged scar along one rib that had healed white and she ran a soapy finger along it. "Indian campaign, before Sand Creek." His right foot had a dark wound near the heel. "Fleeing Sherman on foot." Another round scar on his left thigh. "Rustlers, at night." Finally she had soaped and inspected everything decent and she handed him the soap and cloth.

He hesitated before accepting them. "Aren't you curious about that too?" The water, still clean, was a soft milky color from the soap so that he was hidden from view. Lynne sat back on her heels and considered the tempting offer.

"Does it have any interesting scars?"

He grinned, his teeth gleaming white in his patchy black beard. "Fortunately, none."

She gave a cavalier shrug and stepped behind him. Embarrassed but aware that there was no way to avoid removing all her clothes if she were to enjoy this opportunity to bathe, she stripped quickly. Not since the morning of her wedding day, had she been able to do more than take sponge baths with the wash basin in the bedroom. Even her scalp itched at the thought of getting clean again.

Nude she lifted the kettle from the stove and checked its temperature, before holding it to empty over his sudsy head. He was just shaking the water from his eyes and reaching for a towel as she put the refilled kettle back on the stove for her own hair. As soon as he stepped out, she sank into the still heavenly hot water, leaning forward to wrap her arms around her knees so she could roll in it and get good and wet.

Disappointed, he lowered the towel from his head and scowled at her. "Pretty sneaky."

She grinned broadly, reaching across for the soap and wash cloth. He made a grab for them but she shook her head. "No thanks. Besides, without the scars, it would be pretty boring." At his disappointed face she smiled agreeably. "You can wait around to rinse my hair, if you like."

He tied the towel around his waist, then walked over to the stove. Lynne smelled coffee, then smiled as he cracked eggs into the skillet. She did her best to imagine he was gone as she thoroughly soaped and scrubbed every inch. Her hair was a major chore. But just as her arms were becoming tired, he pushed her hands aside and knelt to finish shampooing it. Only after he had washed and rinsed it twice, did Lynne start to wonder how she could exit without being watched. After several minutes of sitting folded up in the tub, she reached back to twist the water from her hair.

Disgusted by her shyness, he snorted his disappointment and rose to walk to the other side of the room, standing with his back to her as she climbed out and carefully dried, twisting and drying her hair as well as possible before wrapping the damp towel around her body. Shivering she stepped over to the stove to warm, shifting nervously from one foot to another.

"I'll empty the water later," he called, lifting the flap on the door to stare outside.

Lynne stared at the white foamy liquid. "No need, I can use it to wash out some clothes. Do you have anything that ...?"

He nodded, then disappeared and Lynne hastily gathered her dirty clothes to submerge in the soapy water. She was wringing them out when he carried in his own belongings and the set of sheets. She stared up at him, surprised by his obvious disappointment.

He was staring at her long hair, eyeing the damp towel so longingly, that for an instant she wished she could just remove it and parade around the room as he had done for her. But she couldn't.

He moved a warm plate from the stove to the table and poured her a mug of coffee. "Here, just let them soak for now."

Confused by her sudden desire to be a nudist, Lynne rose obediently and sat down to eat the still warm eggs and drink the bitter brew.

She had barely finished when he walked back into the room, a wide grin on his face. With a flourish he removed his own towel and dropped it into the full wash tub. As Lynne reddened to the roots of her hair and rose to back away, she gripped the edge of her own towel more securely and muttered, "Oh no you don't."

Instead of trying to steal it, though, he handed her a smaller clean one and waited while she wrapped it around her damp hair. Just as she began to relax, he moved closer and swept her into his arms. Shocked, she barely had a chance to squeal before he carried her back to the bedroom. Just inside the blanketed doorway, the unheated air made her shiver. He set her on her feet, and in one swift movement, removed her damp towel and stepped out of reach. Even the evidence of his intentions couldn't prevent her from sliding quickly between the covers of the newly made bed and shivering at the change in temperatures. He nodded, then walked back to throw the towel in the tub and make sure the door was barred.

Lynne lay still, her teeth chattering as she sank into the feathers of her pillow and the mattress. The crisp stiffness of the sheet surprised her and made her move against its unaccustomed roughness. Had he starched and ironed them, or were they new. She slipped a hand beneath the satiny cool smoothness of the pillow. New, if she had to make a guess. Had he bought them for this occasion?

Suddenly the memory of Bonnie's tearful confession about the painful nature of the ordeal about to befall her made Lynn stiffen in fear and grit her teeth. A contract was a contract. She had given her word to marry Mr. Phillip Gant, and even in the Montana territory, marriages were only legal when they were consummated.

When Phillip returned to the room, he found his bride stretched out stiffly in their marriage bed, a look of pain and resignation on her face. Well, he had known this was not going to be easy. He made one more check of the back door, reassured that it was barred against intruders. Then before climbing into bed with the sacrificial lamb, he pulled the dividing blanket back and tied it so the heat from the front room would warm this area as well.

Finally he lit the lamp on the bedside table. Shy or not, he had waited long enough for the unveiling. He slid between the cool sheets, then propped up on one arm to stare at her. The turbaned towel hid the dark hair that he loved. The tightly scrunched eyelids shielded the quick-silver gray of her eyes.

In the dim light, he was conscious only of her smooth, fair skin, her tenderness and youth. If he were to attempt anything with her so frightened, the pain would probably put her off from all the delights he intended to share in this bed. But he had endured a week of torture, tolerated Banes and Shorty for five days, he deserved some pleasure. Grinning mischievously, he pulled the blanket up over his head and stared down at her.

All his good intentions evaporated. His imagination hadn't done her justice. Even with her arms pressed tightly against the mattress along each side, the indentation of her waist emphasized her hourglass figure. Slowly he extended a hand and stretched his fingers to span her slender waist, allowing only his fingertips to touch her skin. She moaned in terror.

The sound unnerved him, almost unmanned him. He waited several seconds before raising up so that he was staring at her beautiful breasts. The skin was so smooth and white, he could see tiny blue veins beneath the surface of one. Gently he blew across it and was rewarded by seeing the rosy flesh pebble and the nipple rise temptingly erect. He repeated it with the other, then leaned down to brush the tender peaks with his lips. She shuddered.

Her skin was silky cold beneath his warm lips. Slowly he breathed against her flesh to warm her, then nuzzled and kissed the soft skin of her stomach, trailing a hand along one shapely leg down to her ankle and back. So many things he wanted to try, needed to do. He could hear her breathing, startled little gasps with each new touch, each warm breath. But she remained rigid and unresponsive. He grew disgusted with himself. This wasn't some hurly-gurly at Mable's, this was his wife. His arms trembled from holding his weight from her.

Softly he lowered his head so his face rested against the cool, flat stomach. His heart racing, he allowed his wandering hand to brush the dark, soft triangle. She made a strangled protest and he sighed. Hungrily he leaned close enough to kiss her there, swallowing her scent and taste in one swift motion. She kept her body tight, gave a hiccup for answer.

Resigned, he straightened up and rolled away. Gradually he steeled himself enough to turn so he could see her face. He lay back against the pillow, his hands clenching and relaxing against his leg. In the lamp's glow, he saw tears leaking beneath the dark lashes. He gave one ragged sigh, before closing his eyes in disappointment. "I'm sorry," he whispered.

At the choked sound of his voice, she opened her eyes to look at him. He lay with one arm raised, his open hand covering his eyes. The heavy muscles in his arm denied the vulnerable position, the black hair exposed made his skin seem too white. For the first time since sliding between the sheets she breathed deeply. Bonnie had been so graphic about her pain, about Tarn's persistence, his almost brutal need to force her to submit again and again. But as she lay there, breathing in great gulps of air, reason returned. This man wasn't going to hurt her. Suddenly he rolled over so his broad back was to her.

Uncertainly, she sat up, the towel falling away from her barely damp hair. She raised a hand to rake through the damp tangles, combing her hair with her fingers. She folded her legs so that she was squatting near the head of the bed, half leaning forward, peering over his shoulder. "I'm sorry too."

He half-turned, surprised to see her sitting there, the covers clutched in front of her. He wondered if he were truly asleep, only dreaming her there. "I know you're young."

The words vibrated over her. Lynne blinked, surprised by how his sympathy was harder to take than his assumption that he could just claim his rights. His eyes were closed, his breathing shallow. She wondered if she touched his arm if he would spring to life, ready to pounce on her as he had this morning. "I'm almost eighteen."

His eyes opened, the gleam in them amused. Amused and hungry. "Careful beauty."

She swallowed at the feral gleam in his eyes, the white flash of his teeth. Disconcerted, she looked away. "I guess I need to get up and wash the clothes before the water cools off."

He lay back, his chin pointed to the ceiling, his eyes and face closed to her.

"I guess I could also start cooking for you and clean up all this mess."

He turned so his dark, empty eyes were on her. "Is that what you think I need from my wife?"

She sighed softly, trembling again from head to foot. She let her lashes drop to hide her confusion. "I don't know if I can," she whispered, her lower lip trembling.

Even with her eyes closed, he knew the terror was back. Slowly, as slowly as though she were a wild deer he wanted to pet, he extended his arm, letting his hand touch her face, his thumb brush downward over her pouty lip. In seconds he rose beside her, leaning forward to take the soft lip between his own. This time she shuddered in a different way. He dropped his hand, let it curve around the inside of her thigh, brush against her innocence. "Trust me, Lynne, trust me to show you."

She looked into his eyes, drowning in their liquid warmth. If he had wanted to brutalize her, there had been a dozen chances since her arrival in Montana. Yet each time he had checked himself, stopped before he hurt her. She did want him, had wondered what it would be like each time they had kissed or looked at each other all week.

If only he loved her. Lynne wanted to scream at her romantic side to be sensible. She had entered into this arrangement, knowing it was business. He wanted a wife, she needed the protection of a husband. They had made an agreement, signed the deed in front of witnesses. She had no right to refuse her husband anything he might want to do with her body.

His smile widened and he stared at her solemn face. "No man could look at you and not want to make love to you, not want to cherish and protect you." His voice was such a thick whisper. "Is it me, my past? Don't you think you can trust me?"

The doubt in his voice was so real she reached out to touch his cheek, stroke across his new beard. "Phillip, I told you about my family, about my life before I answered your ad. All I know about you is what I've learned since I came to Butte."

She blushed and looked confused. "Or what you were telling me when I bathed you."

He laughed, then as her lashes swept up and her eyes stared at him full of questions, he looked away.

"You deserve to know. All my family are dead. My friends are few. Shorty and Banes I can trust, we were miners together. Now I have a ranch, one I intend to make work. What else do you need to know?"

His eyes were dark and full of secrets. Lynne stared at this man who had been so gentle, so careful around her all week. She tried to think why she still didn't trust him. "A man on the stage called you the Dark Prince."

"I've been called that and worse. At night, the faces of the dead haunt my sleep, during the day, the living come after me to seek revenge for their friends."

"Why?"

"I've killed men, killed them for any reason you can name. In the war, later fighting Indians and then working as a hired gun for the cattlemen. I've killed a lot of men."

Lynne shuddered. "It's the west. It's kill or be killed."

"Sometimes," he answered. "Sometimes because you're afraid not to fire or you're ordered to shoot, but sometimes it's because you're so full of anger and hate you want to shoot."

"The men who rode out with Michaels?"

"There's no way I can promise I won't have to kill more. If

those men come back, if anyone tries to harm you…" His face darkened, his eyes became black and cold.

Lynne felt a chill sweep through her. She tried to imagine shooting someone. Hadn't she convinced herself the other day that she could shoot? If it were Herr Huntmeister, Doctor Stone, Tarn Michaels. Didn't the Bible say to think evil was to do evil. Wasn't she as guilty as he was?

In answer, she leaned forward to kiss him again. Breathlessly she pulled away after a second. Slowly she nodded, then gasped as she felt his hand move on her thigh, his fingers softly push back the outer folds on her warm flesh. A shiver of intense delight swept through her as his hand continued to explore her. She wanted to look away, but she was caught by the fever in his gaze as she quivered and sighed.

The room was still cold, but this time as she lay back she couldn't feel the chill for the fever rushing through her. He followed her down, his lips soft on her own, moving until she opened her mouth beneath him. Hungrily he slipped his tongue inside, tentatively exploring her sweet taste. Lynne sighed, struggling to breathe with the dual torture of sweet sensations. When he withdrew his tormenting hand she wriggled beneath him, desperate for she knew not what.

His body covered hers, the warmth of his satiny flesh against her own a delicious wonder. Breathless, she pulled away from his kiss, breathed deeply, then turned back for his lips. But he had bent his head to take her breast into his warm mouth, the pleasure a thousand times greater without the restraint of cloth between them. She moved so that her legs were open, the hard wedge of his thigh pressed against her aching need.

She buried her hands in his hair, let her fingers moved to caress his neck, his broad, strong shoulders as he moved to take the other breast. Desperately she brushed her throbbing lips against his shoulder, his ear, his eye. She cried out in pleasure as he raised his head and claimed her lips again. This time she met the thrust of his tongue with her own, tasted the sweet wonder of his mouth, a million tingling new sensations. Achingly she arched against him, driven mad with the torments he stirred inside her.

When he released her lips she called his name mindlessly as he moved away. He rested on his knees over her, settling so his hips were braced against his heels. For several minutes he drank in the sight of her. Her hair was spread out like a silken fan on the pillow, her eyes flashed silver, her bruised lips, pink tipped breasts and writhing hips told him of her arousal. Gently he lifted her leg so she was open before him.

"Look at me darling."

Lynne felt the pressure of his hand, the urgency in his voice. She didn't expect it when he brought her hand up to circle his manhood intimately. She gasped at its velvety hardness. "It will hurt, but only for a second."

For a moment she felt fear again, but he leaned over her, the warmth of his body pressing reassuringly against hers. His eyes were so tender, so caring as he leaned to kiss her. "Trust me," he whispered against her lips.

The thrust was hard, sudden, and she felt a sharp burning pain. But his lips were on hers, his hand moving to cup and caress her breast, and in confusion, she opened her mouth to his tongue again. As soon as her lips parted he moved inside her grinding against her pelvis, and she quivered with new pleasure, unprepared for the delicious waves of sensation that each gentle thrust produced. She clung to him, drawing him closer and closer, frantically aware that only the frantic pounding of his body against hers could ease the fever in her blood.

His voice soothed her, his hands stroked and guided her, held her hips until her body matched the rhythm of his own. The delicious pleasure intensified, then as her body moved in unison with his, it made her break her lips away so she could croon and scream with pleasure. Only when he had driven her over the edge to glory did she collapse against the pillows, feel his following shudder.

In the still room, there was only the sound of their heavy breathing and thudding hearts. Gently, he rolled over, bringing her sweat dampened body with his and drawing the covers up over them both. Lynne was aware of the pale gleam of sunlight on his dark head beside hers, the waste of oil in the lamp beside the bed.

Slowly, tentatively she reached out a finger to trace the whorling pattern of a dark curl on his chest. "Husband, did you know it would be like that?" she asked huskily.

He laughed, pressing his new beard against her forehead, stretching so his hand cupped her bare bottom beneath the covers. "Wife, I never dared to dream it."

"The lamp." She half-raised from his chest and he moaned and reached over to turn it off. When they were resettled, her head pillowed on his broad shoulder, her body molded to his side, she sighed. "Because if you knew, I would have expected it to make your list."

"My list."

She leaned her head back, rubbed her nose against the bristly new beard. "The three things you wanted from your wife."

"Darling, you are a treasure."

She laughed as his other hand cupped her head for his kiss.

Only after he had released her lips and she was once again tucked drowsily against him did she answer. "That's all right, I'll put it on my list."

He laughed, a deep rumbling sound of pleasure as she smilingly slid into sleep.

CHAPTER TWENTY-THREE

Lynne checked the canister full of eggs, then hesitated. He did seem to enjoy them, but at the price Shorty had told her an egg would bring, she had changed the routine and had fed her tall husband hot cakes or grits instead of eggs with his bacon the last four mornings. He hadn't seemed to notice the difference. Lynne blushed and retied the streamers to the linen blouse. Really, he seemed to notice less and less about the house or her cooking. A bride for three weeks and a day, and Mr. Phillip Gant took her skills as a wife completely for granted.

He stepped into the doorway as though he knew she were thinking of him and gave a low, guttural whistle. Lynne blushed and quickly pulled on the little gray suit coat. At least he took most of them for granted. If she didn't hurry he would have her out of her clothes yet again this morning. As he crossed the room toward her, Lynne wondered if that would be so terrible after all.

He smiled, his bearded cheek dimpling and she drew a deep breath. Wearing the same clothes he had worn for the wedding, he took her breath away. The only change was the short tight beard and mustache that failed to hide his handsome features. Today they would trade the Dutchman's trinkets for some useful goods and get a tintype made of them in their wedding finery. He had promised to let her mail a copy of the picture along with her massive letter to the children, and she couldn't wait to get into town.

"Ready, Mrs. Gant," he asked, his voice a seductive growl. One hand reached out to toy with the bow she had so carefully tied.

Lynne swallowed and grabbed his hand before it could undo more than her good intentions. At his frown, she reached up to give him a quick peck on the cheek. She lifted the canister and surveyed the kitchen. "Ready," she giggled as she scooted out of reach, through the door, and over to the wagon. As he helped her up, a mournful bellow split the air.

"Are you sure she will be all right until we return," Lynne asked, as worried about Beulah as she would have been about Mrs. Garretty back home. Here in the wilderness, the animals were companions as well as livestock. She was surprised at how fond she had grown of them, even the pigs.

He cast the same worried look at the barn, then checked the angle of the sun. "Shorty and Banes are supposed to check on her today. We'll be back tonight." He frowned briefly. "She has feed, water and new bedding." He glanced to make sure the barn was fastened, the house secure but unlocked for his friends. "She'll be all right 'till then."

Lynne accepted the truth of the soft spoken words. She would be as safe as it was possible to be in this country, and she would be no less miserable until the calf arrived if they were here on the ranch or away in town.

The horses were eager to be gone. They stamped and snorted in their harness, and Lynne knew they were as sick of listening to Beulah's sad calls as she was. Two new ponies that were green broken had been tied to the back of the wagon and now they pulled against their lead ropes, making the wood groan. He had explained to her about his money. There was still some in the bank, but most was tied up in the land and the animals. As soon as he trailed animals in this spring, they would have plenty of cash once again.

Lynne had very innocently asked why he had to wait so long to sell them. A simple question had led him to tie two of the tamer mounts to the wagon. If they didn't sell, then they would be more docile to a lead rope she argued. If they did, well, then he could buy seed for hay and her vegetable garden. He always seemed amazed at just how practical she was.

She settled onto the now padded spring seat, wondering if the spring like weather would hold during the entire trip. They were only about two hours away from Helena, almost four from Butte, but it would be easier to take care of their errands in the larger city. Perhaps later in the spring, he had offered, they could drive into Helena so she could see what a real mining town looked like. There was even a smelter in Helena for processing silver ore.

His talkativeness had surprised her. But after the first time they made love, it was as though all his shyness and reluctance to speak disappeared. Relaxed, skin to skin, all the intimacies led to the quiet sharing of past fears, present hopes, future dreams. She had learned all about his life in Virginia as a boy. It helped her to understand his love for the horses on the ranch. She knew everything about the three years he had invested in homesteading the land, building the house, capturing the horses. He still had explained little of his life in the army or working for others, but she knew he would. Every day there was a soft, open time when they lay in each other's arms, completely sated, when it seemed important to share more than just their bodies.

She looked at his face as he clucked to the bays and the team moved forward in a mile eating trot. A man of such contrasts. At times he could be withdrawn, quiet, and solemn. Yet whenever they, she blushed, overwhelmed by weakness at the memory of all his tenderness this morning.

Phillip cast a glance at his shy bride, curious about her quietness and secretive smile. How was a man to resist such sweet temptation? Lord knew he couldn't. He dropped a hand over the one she had placed on the seat back and gave it a pat, even as he returned her smile. Of course if she had remained too frightened of him, tearful at the prospect of each coupling, he knew he would still be denying himself his pleasure. But thank heavens she had such a sensible and giving nature. As though to reinforce his thoughts she moved over on the seat to press against him, letting her soft cheek rest in the protective curve of his neck.

"Mrs. Gant, whatever are you thinking."

Lynne couldn't contain the soft laughter, and she tilted her face to kiss his ear.

"None of that now. We'll never make it to Butte," he said it but turned his head enough to kiss her, even while he kept an eye on the trail.

She laughed, her lips red and sweet from his kiss. Once again Phillip wondered if he was doing the right thing in taking such a beauty into town. When she kept fretting about the children and worrying about their knowing she had arrived safely, he had finally relented. Promising he would take off a day when the weather cleared and go into town to mail her blasted letter. He could even wire them if she would quit worrying. Then she had begun to ask about going along too. She wouldn't listen when he insisted he could trade the Dutchman's wife for whatever she wanted if she'd just write him a list.

He stared down at her bowed head, the gray cap with its impertinent little blue feather. She certainly wasn't afraid to stand up to him. Her bossy tone never failed to surprise him, irritating him as much as when he tweaked the ear of a maverick. And when she argued, "the Dutchman's wife already fooled you once, perhaps it requires a woman to deal with another woman." It had brought him up short, but when he saw the excitement and challenge in her eyes he had let it pass. There was little on the ranch to entertain any woman, let alone a girl from a big city like Boston.

Once he had relented, she had been happy as a bird, flitting around the cabin, humming and singing all the time as she made final plans for the big trip. With the horses all broken, their hooves worked and tails pulled, the remuda had been released to the range around the cabin. A second group had been captured and ready to work before he would have to see to spring calving and gathering the herd. In the fall he expected to have nearly two hundred head of horses and nearly the same number of cows ready to market. He listened to her soft humming, saw the magical smile. Any other woman would need to be blabbing away or complaining all the time, not Lynne. Although she often had to entertain herself during his quiet time, she seemed to accept his need for it.

He slackened the reins, allowing the team to pick their path more deliberately. The only decent road in the territory was the Bozeman, but the Indians had reclaimed that road forever. He was anxious to hear if there had been anymore uprisings since those along the stage route. She had written Tom and Jim, advising them to warn the Wimberlys to wait until late summer before heading west. Gold in the Black Hills had all the Indians restless.

Nervously he kept an eye on the trail, alert for anyone approaching or anything out of place. He hated to make this trip again so soon. Hated exposing her to danger. Although she denied it, he knew she liked being around other people, needed them as much as he needed his quiet. As irritating as Shorty and Banes were, she always seemed to light up whenever they rode in for a meal.

Still, the only time she had been in town, men had caught a glimpse of her, and three had ridden out to the cabin. The memory of it made him frown and check for the guns he wore on his hips. This time, if they so much as spoke to her, he would shoot first, talk later.

Lynne saw the change of expression and sat up primly. As his frown darkened, she wondered what she had done to set him into one of his dark moods. Never rough with her, but the man was temperamental. He reminded her of a sulky child. Fine one minute, the next withdrawn into some dark, angry thought. It hadn't taken her long to realize that talking with him in such a mood was futile. He couldn't be argued out of it or scolded into smiling. She would just have to wait. Occasionally she could ignore the scowls and go on talking and they would leave as quickly as they appeared. But today he seemed determined to frown.

Relaxing, she leaned against the short back of the seat, glad the padding had worked, even if Montana feathers were only wild hay, the cushion and spring of the seat helped her to tolerate the bouncing. Perhaps it was just that she was no longer stiff with fright. Suddenly the rocking motion fell into her hips and shoulder. She stared at her husband, riding stiff and tense on the other side of the seat. Laughing, she stretched out on the padded seat, moving so her head fell into the vee formed by his half-raised leg.

Phillip looked down at her in surprise. Her eyes flashed with mischief as she removed her precious hat and lay in his lap, trustingly looking up at him. Her long dark lashes only emphasized the soft gray of her eyes. Relaxing a little, he let one hand fall to mold one full breast as she giggled up at him. "You're shameless," he whispered.

She moved her head, trying to ignore the press of his tooled gun belt against her ear. "Just tired from all the exercise this morning." He grinned, wondering how many more miles it would be until they came to the wide part of the creek where he had first kissed her. He had spent the first week of their marriage reliving and improving on that kiss in his dreams. He moved his hand back so he could stroke her soft hair that was nestled in his lap. Maybe taking her on a trip wasn't such a bad idea after all.

Finally they drove into town, tying up in front of the Dry Goods store. Phillip looked around the nearly deserted streets, frowning, before he swung her down to the boardwalk, then handed down her precious tin. It made no sense to him, trading eggs and returning the trinkets when they could just buy new. But Lynn Gant seemed to have a mind of her own when it came to keeping track of money. She had been scandalized when he confessed how much he had paid for the lumber he'd used in the house. The fact that she cared about all the little details amazed him. His mother had seemed to have no concept of money other than that his father should not drink or gamble up her endless supply. Relieved to see the store was all but empty, Phillip swung down the offending merchandise and followed his petite bride inside.

The Dutchman's wife, Ida, flew from the back of the room where an Indian woman had been shopping and fluttered up to them like one of the hens in the barnyard. "Oh, Mr. and Mrs. Gant, what a pleasure, what a pleasure. What can I do for you?"

He set the huge box on the counter, then grunted. "She doesn't like any of this, and wants to trade if for something else." Lynne flushed at the look of horror on the other woman's face. Great way to begin this conversation. She stared at him, bringing her hands up to rest on both hips. "Mr. Gant, thank you, but I need to talk with the storekeeper alone. Don't you need supplies or something else?"

He pushed the little derby back on his head as he stared down at her. "You think you can handle business better than I can?"

Lynne blushed, unwilling to be overbearing, unwilling to back down. It was the kind of situation in which her mother would have urged her to use tact and diplomacy. Smiling, she reached out to touch the arm that had only shortly before, lifted and held her skirt and petticoats while she removed her socks and boots, then held her safe from harm while she tested the water in the broad flat bend of the creek. The shiver of delight the ice cold water had caused had been replaced by many others. She could see the vivid memories reflected in his own eyes. "This will be so boring for you, women's things and tiny exchanges. I just thought you might prefer to visit with friends, or perhaps trade the horses."

His mouth didn't change, his lips didn't smile. For a moment she was afraid he would yank her and what he considered her embarrassing box back out to the buckboard. "Please, Phillip," she whispered softly.

He stared at her, saw what it cost her to ask the favor. For one unreasonable moment he felt guilty, then swore. Tapping his hat straight, he leaned forward and gave his shocked bride a growl. "Perhaps I can mail your letter, see about your photograph, and trade the ponies. Do you think that will give you enough time for your shopping?"

Lynne bounced with excitement and impatience again. "Perhaps."

In front of the shocked storekeeper he swept his hat off and held it to shield her as he bent to give those saucy lips a quick kiss.

Laughing, Lynne turned back around to the large woman staring from her to the retreating cowboy. "Yes, it's not that they aren't wonderful. It's that so many of the things are too nice for our little cabin. Have you seen our ranch on the Beaver Head? No, well it's so lovely there. Phillip, my husband, has built the most wonderful cabin, really more than a cabin, a fortress for us there."

Ida nodded and added a few 'ja's, and shook her head to other questions. But she was watching his little bride as though she had fallen under an enchantment. Phillip laughed as he closed the door on the pair. She was right, some things were best left to women.

The Dutchman's wife nodded as Lynne removed the first item from the box, the cast brass swan that was supposed to be an iron. "This is so lovely, just beautiful, but you see all I need is a simple cast iron one."

The woman studied it for a minute, then grinned as she shook her head. "Ja, I see, but it won't be so beautiful."

Lynne smiled. "As long as I can press a sleeve, it will be perfect." While she waited on the iron to appear, she studied the rows of bins and boxes. She hadn't expected the vast variety of choices. Maybe she should have made other suggestions.

Ida placed the small metal iron beside the bright gold one. "You're not a very good trader dearie, the gold cost three times as much."

"Oh," Lynne raised her brows. Slowly she lifted out the middle box and began to unwrap the precious cut-glass cruets, salt shakers and other beautiful but useless items. When she had all of the contents stretched out along the counter, she smiled. "I wondered if I could exchange the iron and these lovely, lovely things, for a good set of dishes and flatware."

Phillip was smiling as he folded the money for the horses into his back pocket. Unbelievable. By far the best trade he had made for horses. It was probably because the Indian trouble and the cold weather had thinned the selection in town, but it had only taken a few minutes of brushing the animals out in front of the livery stable to gather a crowd of interested buyers. The top bidder for the brown was the man called Dodd who had driven the coach to town three weeks before. Apparently he had lost an animal in the Indian raid and had still not been able to find a good replacement. One thing about the wild mustangs on his place, they ran a good size. Not quite as big as the team horses, but far larger than most of the shrubby ponies ridden by the Indians. He had no doubt that the big brown was the offspring of some unfortunate pioneers lost mount. It was docile as well. One of the reasons he had picked these two was their good manners. No one would ever buy a green broke mustang if he were as jittery as most of the rockets he'd left at home.

He learned from the overland driver Dodd that the Indians had gone back to their teepees with the last cold wave. But Butterworth was hiring men to ride shotgun on all their routes.

"Noticed you were pretty good with a gun. You interested in hiring on?"

Phillip shook his head, and patted the wad of bills. "No need. Ranching is a hell of a lot safer and I think it will pay better than most things I've tried."

"Couldn't be that little bride I carried into town for you?"

Phillip's eyes didn't smile and the driver grunted and looked up the street. "There's big doing's tonight. Most of the town is over to Morrison's for the store raising. Guess you'll be riding home to the little wife instead of looking for something sociable."

Phillip shook his shoulders, a sense of unease sweeping through him. He had never had much use for dances, never learned to dance. But perhaps Lynne would hear about it and want to go. Maybe that was what caused the chill to sweep up his spine. He shook his arms, let his hands drop to rest just above his gun butts.

"Lynne's here in town with me. Came in to do some trading while the weather's clear."

"Sure would love to see that lovely thing again." He stared at the dark eyed gunslinger, nervous even about the civil request.

Phillip nodded toward the store and started walking, the stage driver falling into step beside him.

"You know I've transported nearly a dozen of these mail-order brides, but only two of them have been lookers. One was a stunner. Silver-hair and built." He looked around the street, then made the graphic gesture that made Phillip positive he was talking about Helga. "Mostly, they've been some ugly, desperate women. But little Miss McKinney, she takes the ribbon. She was likable, you know. Calm head, easy to look at, easy to get along with. You know some women are so damn tractable, you need a two-by-four just to have a conversation with them, don't you know?"

Phillip nodded, listening with one ear, he paid attention to the street with the other. There were only a few animals tied up in town, fewer people on the street. But there was something in the air. This time he shook his hands out, letting his fingers quiver just above the cold silver of his weapons.

He kept his back to the buildings, his eyes alert as they approached the door. Only when he was sure it was clear inside as well as out, did he hold the door for the driver to follow him in.

Lynne lifted the bolt of blue sprigged cotton to her chin, tilting her head so that the storekeeper could give her an opinion. The last items were lined up along the counter, including the ornamental pots and pans and the large wine rack. The Dutchman's wife couldn't believe she didn't need a wine rack, even after Lynne insisted they had no wine at all. The woman had clucked her tongue in shock and produced several dark brown and green bottles, sliding them into place to impress Lynne on how sorry she would be once it was gone.

Instead, Lynne had chosen a deep square, covered iron skillet, one she could bake bread or cakes in more easily. Then her eyes lighted on the cloth. She sorted through the large stock, choosing two patterns that were both pretty and durable. One was striped with tiny red roses and red birds on dark green vines along its silvery gray. The other was royal blue with yellow, white and red petals scattered in groups of fours and eights.

Both women looked up as the store bell rang. Lynne smiled, surprised to see Phillip back, even more surprised to recognize the stage coach driver. "No, surely it's not time to go yet. I'm still trying to decide. Which do you like darling?" She smiled at the somber dark face, failing to catch the wary, springy quality of his step.

"Take both." His voice brought her up short, searching his eyes for the man she had married. The driver laughed.

"You surely look a treat. You surely do." He scratched his head and Lynne smiled in understanding.

"We're dressed the same so we can get a wedding picture." She smiled and swirled for his appraisal. Then she raised puzzled eyes to stare at Phillip. "Did you have a chance to see about the portrait, darling?"

"Yes. He promised to wait if we hurried over. He has a building to photograph or something."

"Ja, the Morrison's store. Big deal, another store," the

storekeeper complained.

Lynne couldn't understand the change, one moment he was Phillip her husband, the next a cold-eyed stranger. She handed the woman both bolts of cloth. "Six yards of each, and thread, and well, whatever you think I'll need to finish out the order." She looked nervously back over her shoulder, wanting to share all her clever trading with Phillip, certain she should wait until she had them loaded. "And I brought these."

The woman stared at the lovely brown eggs, as though they were not the rare treasures Shorty had told her. But when she gently lifted one out of its nest of wild grass and feathers, Lynne knew the Dutchman's wife knew its value. "Ja, and what would you want for these. I cannot give so much. There is a new store and all."

"Sugar. Just refill it with sugar please."

"Ja, that I can do. You go on and hurry with your portrait. I'll finish this order and see it loaded."

Lynne smiled brightly, thrilled with all she had accomplished, a little wary of leaving the woman alone to load her treasures. She could just imagine finding the sharp steel scissors exchanged for those useless brass ones again, but with the way Phillip was acting, she didn't have a choice.

He gripped her elbow sharply as he walked her to the door. But at the last minute, he saw a fleeting shadow above the four Georgians. He turned to ask the stage coach driver. "Mr. Dodd, would you escort Lynne over to the studio, sir, I'll load her purchases and be right over."

CHAPTER TWENTY-FOUR

Lynne started to protest, but the driver seemed to understand at once. "Glad to. Did I tell you Mrs. Gant what a treat you look? Yes ma'am, a positive treat."

Lynne looked back in time to see her husband gliding quickly toward the back of the store. The driver no more had her part way down the walk then Lynne dug in her heels and protested. "This is ridiculous. Surely I should wait on Phillip. Whatever is the matter with him?"

"Nope, don't reckon you should be waiting out on no street in the open. Best do what your husband orders, lest he has to buy some new two-by-fours."

"Two-by-fours? But she allowed herself to be led and pulled into the darkened door of the studio.

The small man inside was adjusting his pack of supplies, obviously ready to depart. "Well, well, it's about time. I told your husband to hurry. I don't have time to photograph you today. Perhaps you could come back tomorrow." Lynne swallowed hard, trying to control the panic that Phillip's confusing actions provoked.

"Tomorrow."

"Right, tomorrow. Come back tomorrow. I promised to show up in time to photograph the store front raising. My, my, but it's already time. Then there is the dance, and all the couples at the dance. This is just impossible. You'll have to come back tomorrow."

"Today."

It was Phillip's voice. Strong and steady, vibrating through the room and Lynne and the little photographer jumped. "Yes, sir. But hurry, please hurry and take your positions."

Lynne stood to one side as the fussy little man motioned Phillip into a straight chair, removing his derby and fussing about his hair. Lynne opened her drawstring bag and removed the small silver backed comb and used it to neaten his hair, parting it down the center as the photographer instructed. She checked her own face in the mirror, then pushed her hat on straight, brushed the loose strands of brown hair back into the smooth loop at the back of her neck. For a moment, she couldn't stop her hands from trembling. Then the photographer prodded her to stand just behind Phillip's shoulder and positioned her small hands to rest on its wide ledge.

Complaining all the time, he backed up so that the hastily set up camera was positioned correctly. Lynne was aware of time clicking, clicking, clicking on the long-tongued clock by the door as she held her breath and waited. It seemed to take hours not minutes for him to get everything ready. She looked down to see her folded hands, rising and falling with her husband's heavy breathing. Still he made no sound. She drew in her own breath as she noticed the derby now rested on his hand at an odd angle, still held just in front of his right knee.

"Smile, lovely couple, look here, look at the flash pan. Don't move, don't move a muscle. Are you ready? Are you ready? Just a second." He did something to the camera, snapping a long plate into place, then he called to them once again. "Happy thoughts, happy thoughts. Smile."

Shivering Lynne gripped his shoulder and tried to remember the sun-dappled light at the water's edge. For just a second she could see her husband, rising like a God from the icy stream, his eyes gleaming with love and promising glory.

Then a flash of light blinded her and a blast of sound. She was aware of Phillip pulling her down, rolling with her across the floor until they came to rest beneath the window. Breathless she looked up, unsure whether to scream or to laugh. Then he was gone. A dark shadow racing for the rear of the studio as quickly as he had entered it.

She heard the driver's voice, swearing a blue streak as though the room were full of mules instead of one quivering photographer and a tumbled bride.

Dodd worked his way over to her, helping to right her but keeping her head down below the glass pane of the window.

"By golly, did you ever see anything to equal that?"

The small photographer gasped. "I'm not sure how the portrait will turn out madam. There is no guarantee if you move."

"Move you fool, move? Look out there in the street to get your picture."

Impatiently, Lynne forced her head free from the driver's heavy hand and peeked through the bottom of the window into the gray emptiness of the street. A man lay there, sprawled in the dust, a large red stain spreading from the back of what was once his head. The dying man had been fair of hair and slight of build, and she recognized him as one of the riders her first day on the Beaver Head.

"Gee-damn, fastest damn killer I ever saw. You could see it in his eyes, his eyes looked like death. I knew it was all over for somebody, sure 'nough did," Dodd said.

Lynne felt sick. Nausea tearing at her stomach even as she heard the little photographer talking to the driver. He was cautiously exchanging the plate for another one, reloading the flash pan to photograph the dying man outside. "Who was that, whose portrait did I take?"

"You just photographed Butte's Dark Prince of course. The Dark Prince of death himself, Phillip Gant."

"The Dark Prince and his bride," Lynne muttered. From the corner of her eye she watched a black derby roll across the floor and come to rest at an angle against the photographer's tripod. Sunlight streamed in through a tiny hole in the abandoned hat.

Now God was punishing her for her lustful ways. She knew it was wrong, all the wanton desire she felt for this man. Now she knew why. She had married a killer, a son of Satan. . Suddenly all she could hear was the slow click, click of the clock and the strum of icy blood through her veins.

Phillip ran from the studio and back across the alley, dodging the openings onto the street. There were at least two men left, hiding in the buildings, waiting to kill him.

What did it matter now? He tried to imagine her face, her feelings, when she learned what he truly was. He had told her the truth, the week after their wedding, but he had known she hadn't believed him, hadn't understood what he meant. Because he wanted her so desperately, he hadn't protested his guilt, confessed to her his bloody hands. Instead he had taken her as his wife.

He had fooled himself into thinking it didn't matter, that he had bought a bride so he wouldn't have to tell any woman the truth, wouldn't have to see the shudder of revulsion in her eyes. Or worse, see the sick gleam of any creature who would seek out a man like him. There were such women. Drawn as much to his reputation as a killer as by hunger for his body.

Not Lynne. How could he have done it, married such a woman, taken her to his bed, loved her, awakened the fire in her blood, the love in her heart, knowing what type of demon he was? He couldn't even stand himself, how could he ask such a sweet angel to stand him. No, not just stand him, but to reach sweetly for his hands, stand breathlessly on tiptoe to try to taste his lips with her own.

A bullet sang close by his head and he returned to the job at hand. He fired, then lightly he spun the chamber on his gun, replacing the two spent shells, then spun it even as he cocked it back and held it toward where it would mark more deaths. As soon as he saw the large form he rose and sprinted in pursuit, shocked when he tripped over a rope suddenly pulled taut across the alley way. His gun flew free, and he screamed as he tried to force his feet under him so he could continue the chase. He was aware of a man laughing, a man in a small wheelchair in one of the doorways. Phillip turned his head away to avoid the next shot, but it went so wide that he holstered his remaining weapon. Breathing, biting back the pain, he hurled his body forward, knocking the weapon out of reach of the big Irishman.

CHAPTER TWENTY-FIVE

Phillip Gant collided with Tarn Micheals with a fury born of jealous rage and desperation. He kicked his hand so hard that the gun went clattering along the boardwalk. For just an instant the big Irishman considered flight. The man who had taunted him into bragging, who had promised to back his play, lay dead or dying in the street. But then he heard the rancher wheeze, saw the blood on his sleeve.

Phillip didn't expect the force of the blow. It caught him on the side of the head, forcing him to his knees on the boardwalk. Stunned, he shook his head, ready to draw his gun and fire. But the driving knee to his stomach doubled him over. For a moment he thought his stomach would come up with its morning contents.

He felt dizzy with pain. The Irishman was gripping him by the ears, pushing against the sides of his head as though he would crush his skull like a walnut. Over the rush of blood in his ears, Phillip could hear him shouting. "Thought you'd keep her did you? Well, I'll teach that meddling Lynne McKinney to fear me, to know what a real man can do for her." He brought his big knee up in a powerful blow and Phillip knew he was blacking out. But he had to reach her, had to help protect her.

"Hey, you there." The shout was the last thing he heard before fading into darkness. The stage driver rushed up, gun ready, firing after the disappearing brute. Then there was only pain and a great, hollow darkness.

Lynne drew a startled gasp, the sound of gunfire bringing her out of her trance. Phillip was out there. They were shooting at her husband. Had shot into the studio at him, thinking the flash of the photographer's pan would prevent him from firing in time. She heard someone scream, rose to stare out the window as the driver ran outside. She watched in horror as the driver drew his gun and crept along the sidewalk in the direction of the gunfire.

"Phillip."

Suddenly the surprised shouting of the little photographer didn't matter. Heart in her throat, Lynne dashed out. She had to reach her husband.

The driver heard her behind him and extended a hand to bar her way. "Easy now, ma'am. Wait and let me go first, I got a gun."

Frantic, frightened, still she listened to reason and waited. They both arrived in time to see Phillip barreling out of the alley. Even as the driver raced forward, gun ready, Lynne stood mesmerized, watching and feeling every blow that Tarn landed on her husband's face. As Phillip sagged to the rough boards of the walkway, she dropped to her knees in the street. With each savage blow the cowardly Irishman landed, she felt the beefy hand land on her own face, neck, stomach. When she heard the driver's shot, all she could see was the pain and blood on Phillip's face before she fainted into oblivion.

◇◇◇

"What have we here, which one is hurt the worst?"

"The wife, she fainted, reckon that's all. Gant though, could have his head cracked open." In the dark, Lynne struggled to open her eyes.

She heard a woman's sympathetic voice, felt the hand patting her own and recognized the muttered, "Ja, I saw it from the store. The killer man and that awful Irishman. The poor little thing, just a young bride. They were so cute a couple. You should have seen them before."

"Well, at least there is no need to worry about the Georgian. That's one more big cattleman that won't be bushwhacking another rancher." Lynne heard the driver's rough oaths pulling her up from the dark. She had to wake up, had to help them. She had to save Phillip.

But as she struggled to sit up the Dutchman's wife called to the doctor. "Help, she is going to hurt herself, Doctor."

Lynne smelled the cloying scent of chloroform, struggled against the hand over her nose, fought but felt her strength fade. As she fell back into the dark she heard a man's shout. Phillip. If only she could move through the darkness toward him.

In the dark, Lynne floated, drowning in its blackness. Behind her eyes was the red glow of fear. But still she struggled, swam toward the only thing she knew could save her. Somewhere there was a strong brown hand, loving arms to hold her, to keep her safe. The only man she could ever love. If only she could save him from the darkness.

Phillip floated, his mind and soul bathed in blood, the scent of death covering him, pressing him downward. Just when he felt he would fall into the burning flames, he heard her voice. The note plaintive and frightened, calling for him, needing him. Slowly he turned from the beckoning heat, struggled to reach out a hand, clutched frantically through the emptiness of his soul for the voice that whispered his name. His name called with a warmth and tenderness only his mother had used before. Finally he saw a tiny ray of light. With his remaining strength he thrashed out for that ray of hope and felt her tiny hand in his. With surprising strength, the woman he loved pulled him from the darkness.

Lynne leaned over the bed, her loose dark hair framing her heart-shaped face. The big bed reminded her of her mother's, although the massive ends were rough-hewn reddish rings cut from a single mighty tree. She whispered a prayer, then wiped the brow of the dear man in the bed before her and smiled radiantly.

Phillip Gant stared up into soft gray eyes and heard his name whispered again. "Phillip, oh darling you've come back to me."

"I was gone?"

"Yes, for two days now. I've worried that you would be lost to me forever, the way mother and father were."

She moved her hand along the strong arm, bringing it to rest over the slight wound in his right shoulder. It wasn't the wound but the beating that Tarn had delivered that had left him unconscious two days after the gunfight. The Dutchman's wife had been gracious enough to bring them into her home over the store, giving Phillip her own bed. For several hours, he had battled fever, then had slipped into a stupor, but now Lynne knew he was back for good. The fever had broken, but more importantly, she recognized her own dear husband in the befuddled brown eyes looking at her.

"I heard you calling my name, needing me to protect you."

Lynne hesitated. This was the man who had shot and killed a man in the street, another in a room across from the studio. He was the Dark Prince of death. She searched his features for the man she had married. That handsome stranger was lost, in his place she stared at the pale face, bruised and swollen, only one half of it shaven where the doctor had taken stitches along his firm jaw line. His left eye was closed, the flesh around his right eye discolored. His lip stood out, swollen and cut.

She knew his body was just as hurt. She had overcome her shyness in order to make sure there was no permanent damage. Aside from the surface wound on his arm and the damage to his face and head, he had only two bruised ribs and a discolored and tender abdomen. But his eyes were glowing, the confusion falling away as he gripped her hand tightly. "Lynne, you're safe."

"Yes my darling. Safe and ready to go home as soon as you are fit to travel. The doctor told me you have to wait at least a day after awakening before you can leave. Of course the Dutchman's wife may never let us go."

"You two still trading?"

Lynne laughed and fluffed his pillow.

"Oh no, what about the animals, poor Beulah." Again he attempted to sit up and the covers rolled down, exposing the bruised and tender flesh.

Lynne sank down onto the edge of the bed, clucking her tongue at him, bending as he moaned so she could kiss his injured ribs, his bruised stomach.

"A little lower and I may never want to leave." He whispered throatily.

Blushing she leaned forward so she could place both small hands tenderly on his face. "Beulah is safe. Mr. Dodd, the stagecoach driver took our wagon and goods out to the ranch. He promised to stay until Sunday, then bring the wagon back for you. The Doctor thought it might be a week before you were fit enough to travel."

He flexed his jaw and moaned. Lynne released his cheeks, afraid that even that light pressure might have caused him pain. She leaned over to find the glass of water she had been using to moisten his lips and tongue for the past days.

"You look beautiful," he mumbled.

"Shush, now you can be quiet. You look and moan like Beulah sounded when we left home."

"Ouch." he added.

She put a hand behind his neck to half-lift him but at his grimace she let him back. Instead she leaned forward with her small hand cupped to give him another sloppy drink, careful not to touch his sore lip in the process. "Rest, darling, rest."

He caught her hands, then she saw how even his big hands were bruised, the knuckles red and purple stained. "Micheals?" he asked.

She shrugged. "He escaped. But the way he was running there's no chance he'll ever try to bother us again."

His head ached from sleeping so long and from his other injuries. Should he tell her, worry and frighten her for nothing. She sat there, as pretty as ever. "Micheals may well be out there, waiting to see if I survive. Lynne, he may have tried to beat me to death, but he also made threats toward you." He groaned again, exhausted merely by the telling.

"Tarn hates anyone who sees through his handsome exterior to the rotten core inside. He is a coward and a bully. I watched how he struck you. He didn't give you a chance to defend yourself."

He made a wry smile, the fat lip again making him wince. "Mercy costs too much. No one who wants to stay alive ever fights fair."

He felt his eyes falling shut, fatigue robbing him of even the sight of her. "Lay beside me." He whispered it so softly, Lynne leaned down to hear, comforted when his pained voice blew past her ear. "Trust me. Sleep together."

She saw him slip back into the dark and gasped in her own pain at losing him so soon. Softly she removed her shoes, unable to deny him anything. The door to the bedroom was unlocked and she hated to obey. Although the Dutchman's wife generally knocked, she seemed to have to make a dozen trips into the room every day. Each time she always asked if the patient was awake, then urged Lynne to sleep elsewhere while she stood guard.

But Lynne would never do that, couldn't trust the other woman's motives. Even bruised and wounded, he was twice as good looking as the poor little storekeeper she had married. Exhausted, giggling from fatigue, Lynne slipped out of the heavy dress, the voluminous petticoat. Cautiously, tenderly, she slipped between the covers until her head was resting on the pillow beside her wounded husbands.

Tenderly she brushed the flesh above the bandaged arm, then lay still, content to hear his heavy breathing beside her. For the first time in days she could sleep. Tenderly she raised up, moving so that his head was pressed against her bosom. His moan made her wish she were bigger, softer. Another groan made her release him. If it had worked, she would have cradled him in her arms all night long. Instead, she lay there, lips touching the still warm shoulder above his wound until she slept as well.

◇◇◇

Lynne awoke to feel a hand on her throat, softly fingering the cords of her neck, tentatively tracing the blue arteries just below her ears. Alarmed, she opened startled gray eyes to stare into his bruised swollen face, and one open, but blood-shot, brown eye. Relieved, she smiled and was greeted by a tentative smile, quickly hidden by a stiff grimace.

Slowly, leaning into the encircling hand, she kissed the cut above his eye, turned and kissed the swollen eyelids of the other. He drew in a ragged breath and she hesitated.

"No, please, it hurts so good."

Smiling wryly, she even managed to kiss his straight, unharmed nose, his firm upper lip before gently, oh so gently, drawing the swollen lip inside her own.

With her tongue she traced the line inside where it was cut and swollen, pressing gently between her hot wet lips, then at his shiver, releasing it.

He let his hand slide down the white column of her throat as she continued to softly suck on his lip. He pulled at the laces to her chemise and she moved her head so that she was kissing the corner of his mouth, missing the hurt lip. One hand pulled on the soft cloth while the other slipped inside to stroke her cool flesh. This time his groan was from pleasure, not pain.

His hands squeezed her firm breasts, stroked his rough palm

over her sensitive nipples. He felt her whole body tremble and he pushed a hand beneath the loose drawstring of her drawers.

Incredibly aroused, Lynne leaned back away from his body, stared at him even as she felt the muscles in his hot biceps flex against her chest. "No, you mustn't." But a probing finger made her gasp.

He stared at her, growling for an answer, as he slid another finger inside, then used his thumb to torture the sweet throbbing between her legs. Lynne swallowed and clung to the bed to keep from moving against his sore body, her brown hair swaying over the edge of the bed as he continued his torture.

A heavy tread outside the door made him stop to pull her back in the bed. Her eyes were soft, liquid, as she stared at him, her lips red and inviting. Reluctantly he removed his hand, straightened the covers over them as the door opened.

"Ja, you are awake this morning. This is wonderful." The large voice called and Lynne blushed, confused as she nuzzled his hot arm, saw the spot of blood on the bandage even as she felt the surge of blood through her own veins. As she curved cautiously against him, she became aware of the blood surging through him as well.

"Oh. I didn't mean to ... I brought water ..."

Clearly shocked, she stumbled over Lynne's dress as she placed the pitcher of fresh water on the dresser.

"Oh dear. I have ruined your dress."

Blushing, Lynne raised her head up enough to protest. "No, it's all right, it's dirty anyway."

She could feel Phillip shake against her, knew without staring at him that he was laughing silently at her embarrassment.

"Ja, I'm sorry, I didn't think. She opened her closet and withdrew a large, lavender dressing gown. Here, I'll wash this out for you, Ja?"

Lynne fumbled beneath the covers for the laces of her chemise, encountered his fingers holding one end of the ribbon. She intended to get up, to protest and offer to wash her clothes out herself, but his deep voice answered for her. "That would be nice. His thumb stroked her and she squirmed. Thank you."

Blushing, the tall woman clutched the soiled gown and slip as well as the nearly empty pitcher of water. "Ja, ja," she muttered, as she hurriedly backed out of the room.

As the door snapped closed, Lynne pushed away from his embrace, her face shocked and angry. But where her hands pressed, he moaned in pain and she forgot everything but leaning forward to kiss the hurt away.

"This is crazy" she murmured, kissing his bruises beneath the dark, whorling hair. "You're too hurt for this."

He groaned, using both hands to tug the soft cotton down to expose the warm curve of her hips, the sweet nest of damp curls. "I'm hurting too much not to." He moaned, grasping her with one hand as he worked on freeing himself from his clothes with the other.

Lynne wiggled, moving so she propped her body away from him, trailed kisses softly over the bruised ribs, the abraded marks on his stomach.

He gasped in pain and sank back against the pillows, momentarily exhausted.

Lynne watched as he raised his arm, let his large hand rest against his face in frustration. Gently she reached beneath the covers to complete what he had begun. Once free of clothes she crouched over him, her knees braced on either side of his narrow hips.

Holding her body above him, she leaned forward, aware of his pain, his delight as she softly brushed his wounds, then sank to take him inside. He moaned and she moved her hips, delighted when he lowered his arm to touch her bouncing breast. Slowly, gently she moved, as entranced by the passion in his face as by the sensations her gentle rocking brought.

Only when the rhythm carried him forward into a last thrust and he cried out did she feel the tension inside her slip away. Tenderly, she waited, then moved so that once again she lay beside him, this time with her breasts tenderly nestling his head against her own sweat soaked body. After his breathing deepened, she rose to clean herself and him, then redressed his wound. Wearing the oversized gown, she crept down to help her hostess so she would have something to wear again.

She found the tall woman, busy in the kitchen washing out the clothes with some of her own. "Here, I came down to do that."

"No, you should stay with your man while he needs you. I can do this."

"Nonsense," Lynne said. "He is asleep again. I need to fix him some soup, now he is better he will want to eat when he wakes up. Besides, I can't stand to be idle."

Grudgingly the other woman moved aside, admiring the way the smaller woman handled the chore more efficiently. "You seem so young. You do a good job though."

Lynne nodded. "I know a lot about clothes. My mother did laundry the last three years and I had to help her often. Then, too, you can't work in a mill without learning a lot about cloth and how to care for it."

"A mill, what is that."

"The clothing factories, we made clothes to wear-- shirts, skirts, dresses, everything, from thread to finished garment. I worked there three years."

"Really, you seem so young."

"I'm nearly eighteen," Lynne answered as she wrung the last of the water from the small jacket, relieved the woman had at least used cold water. Carefully she pressed the garment into shape on top of a dry towel..

The other woman smiled, raising her eyebrows. "Ja, so very old." She laughed.

Only when Lynne had peeled vegetables under the woman's watchful eye and put them in a pan with leftover lamb and broth, did the other woman get up to leave. "I have customers. The bell not rings, but it is the time of day that someone might come. First, you come with me."

Lynne clutched the wrapper closer, aware of her bare feet on the rough wood floor as she followed the woman into the empty storeroom. The little old man who was her husband was located behind the counter. Curious, he turned around to stare at the pair. The big boned Dutchwoman walked proudly forward with the petite girl trailing timidly behind, her brown hair uncombed and hanging down the length of her back. Entranced, he stared more closely when her movement indicated she was only wearing his wife's old dressing gown.

The tall woman clucked her tongue and stood to stare at him. "The stock in the back needs checking, not here anything needs you to see."

He grumbled but turned away to follow orders. Lynne blushed, hopping from foot to foot, worried that someone might ring the doorbell for real.

"Here. It is something brand new. It costs too much, you see. Besides, there are no womens here to buy the fool thing. Henry tells me to keep it and use it, but I don't know this, this sewing with machines?"

Lynne extended a hand to turn the large steel wheel on one end, watching the needle rise and fall familiarly through the bottom plate. It was smaller, lighter, less powerful than the ones she had used the last year in the factory, but she was surprised at how comforting it felt to touch something she understood so completely. The machine was black, with a beautiful scroll of gold paint along the top and down the front to the wooden desk it sat in. On the bottom was a wrought iron platform. Unlike the steam driven machines, a simple leather pulley went from the pedal to the wheel.

"I can show you how to use it."

The door tingled and the Dutchman's wife looked up impatiently. "Good, I'll have Henry carry it up to the bedroom. You can watch your man and maybe figure everything out. When I close, you can shows me."

Lynne looked over her shoulder at the disappearing straight back. "Fine. But I'll need cloth, scissors, thread. Mr. Dodd took mine to the ranch."

There was a loud laugh. "Ja, everything, of course, I have everything."

Lynne carried the soup up on a tray, eager to see if her tall husband had as much appetite for food as for intimacy. She was almost to the top of the stairs when a loud voice stopped her.

"Miss McKinney. Is that you?" Mortified at being caught in such a state of undress, Lynne rested the tray on the newel post and crossed an arm over the full cotton of the dressing gown to hold it even more tightly closed. Too late, for the big oaf at the bottom of the stairs was blushing as red as the handkerchief he used to mop his face.

"Mrs. Gant." She hoped the words had the proper chill, but he seemed less interested in her words than in her charming state of disarray. "Mr. Owens, good day."

"Mrs. Gant, wait, I ..."

Lynne dropped her hand to clutch the tray, looking ahead to the closed bedroom door behind which her husband hopefully still slept.

"Shh," she called down. "You'll awaken Phillip."

He stomped up the stairs toward her and hastily Lynne lifted the tray and backed along the stairwell until she stood across from their bedroom door. "That's far enough, sir." She spoke sharply and fortunately he stopped.

"I heard what happened here in town, and I came back from the store opening to see if you needed me." His eyes roamed too familiarly along her face, over her loose hair. Lynne felt furious at the man for taking liberties. If Phillip weren't wounded, he would never have dared to approach her.

"Thank you for your concern, but I need nothing that you could offer." She said it in a soft hiss and backed toward the door, trying to maintain the trays balance and her own dignity as she turned the handle on the door.

He leaned forward, his beefy hand on the frame above her head, his voice squeaky and unsure as he said. "I heard he was bad off. If'n your mister should die, I hope you'll remember my offer still stands."

Lynne blushed, full of fury. For two cents she would pour the hot soup over the dumb ox. Just then she heard the loud panting of the little Dutchman as he struggled up the stairs with the new machine.

She wanted to laugh when she saw how the big man backed away in a scramble when the tiny Dutchman came forward. Lynne leaned back against the door, glad it swung open easily beneath her back and she turned to set the tray of soup on the dresser beside the bed. She was shocked when she stared into the pointed silver revolver and brown angry eye of her husband.

Relieved, Lynne smiled broadly. "Good darling, I'm glad you are ready. I've brought soup for you."

Where he had sat up, the covers slipped dangerously low. She stared fondly over the heavy wall of muscle, ignoring the irresistible urge to run her hands over the fine display. Lynne was aware of both the Dutchman and Mr. Owens peering inside the room, afraid to enter in front of the readied pistol.

"There's no need for this darling, you are safe here, now." Calmly she stepped forward and set the tray on the dresser, then gingerly reached out to take the gun.

He held it, his body a study in frustration as he tried to sit upright enough to fire at the two intruders. "Our host is bringing something up I need." She turned to glare at her persistent suitor. "I don't know what Mr. Owens is doing in our room."

She said it so coolly, fighting the urge to giggle as Phillip cocked the pistol and the bothersome pest turned and clambered down the stairs. Only after she had thanked the Dutchman and he had left, did she hold out a hand again. Phillip frowned but surrendered the weapon.

Soothingly, Lynne slid it expertly back into the holster he now had draped over the end of the bed. "How did the gun get here?"

He sagged back against the bed and Lynne placed a hand on the cool skin along his side, then scooted her own body forward to have him lean against her until she had the pillow propped behind him.

"Had to get up," he finally answered and she smiled widely. "I could have waited on you." He scowled and she gingerly kissed his forehead.

As she lifted the bowl of soup and spoon out to feed him, she was aware that he was staring at the robe. "The store owner's wife loaned it to me so I could go down to the kitchen to cook. I was on my way to the room when Mr. Owens spoke to me."

She held the spoon out and he continued to frown, even as he let her cautiously pour it in without bruising his lip. He seemed famished, and Lynne was grateful she had carried up two bowls of the fragrant soup. He had finished almost half of the first bowl when he let a hand drop on her knee. Lynne was unbearably conscious of the weight of his hand on her lap, of all the clothes she was not wearing.

"Enough of that. Eat." He stared at her, then let his hand move just enough to split her robe, revealing her bare, pale legs.

"Phillip, honestly, only the Dutchman's wife and I were down there, while I made the soup." He ignored her protest. She watched as his tongue appeared in the corner of his mouth as he struggled to raise his right hand in the air. Confused, she extended more soup, then gasped as his hand dropped down, forcing her gown open in front. Irritated, she reached out a hand to reclose it and he growled.

Angrily, she rose, rewrapping the gown and retying it, before sitting down again, this time sensibly out of range of his marauding hands. "Listen." She slid a hand under his jaw, careful to avoid the stitches. "If you are going to be so silly because I am here, I'll have the Dutchman's wife come in to feed and bathe you."

"Bathe?"

"Yes, bathe you. Phillip, I want to help you. But I don't intend to repeat the services of this morning again. If I move wrong and something happens to reinjure you, I'll never forgive myself."

He let his eyes close and sighed.

"What?" She set the soup down and moved so she could tilt his face and see into his eyes.

"Others," he muttered. Furious, Lynne jumped up, uncaring as he rolled onto his side and moaned.

"Sit here and rot for all I care. If you think so little of me. If you don't know yet how I feel about you. I would never, ever. Not with any other man. You are so..."

Through the mist of pain he smiled as she paced back and forward in a brisk fury."Tell me, what you feel," he growled.

Lynne stopped, her hand over her heart as she stared in horror at the twisted figure on the bed before her. Frantically she rushed forward, helping to ease him back beneath the covers so that he was lying flat on his back, only his head raised with an extra pillow.

"You old silly," she whispered. "You are my husband. Dark Prince or jealous lover, you have all of my heart."

Her heart pounded frantically as she stared down at him, watched as his jaw went slack and his eyes closed. Had he heard her? Did he believe her or not? She wanted to hear what he had whispered the night before. She loved this man, even now after she had watched him kill men in the street. If he hadn't, then he might be dead himself. But declarations of jealousy or love would have to wait. Phillip Gant was once more sound asleep.

"She found out I can sew," she muttered in explanation as he finally became conscious again.

"Look," she pirouetted prettily for him. He recognized the cotton print she had been shopping for, was it just a few days ago. "She had a sewing machine, but didn't know how to use it. Can you imagine that, not knowing how to sew?"

He smiled, amazed at how beautiful his wife was, how beautiful life was. She wasn't staring at him with hate or disgust. There was no mistaking the soft glow in her eyes. "Good wife," he whispered.

Lynne stopped twirling and stared at him, bringing her hand up over her heart. Tears pricked the back of her eyelids. It wasn't the romantic love story of her parents, but maybe what they had was enough. Finally, everything would be all right between them.

CHAPTER TWENTY-SIX

Phillip was going to be all right. The cracked ribs and blow to his head were already healing. Everything was working out. The stage driver had taken their wagon and supplies to the cabin, promising to stay with the animals and look after Beulah until they could get home. He would be in town Sunday with their wagon and Lynne planned to have him show her how to drive the team so she could get back to her home. She wanted to get back to the new life that had finally begun the week after her marriage.

In other ways, the last couple of days had been wonderful. First she had made the dress for the Dutchman's wife Ida, then one for herself. It was clear that Ida had no interest in learning to sew herself. The next day two women had noticed the dresses and asked her to make some for them. One had been another mail-order bride, a tall, beautiful woman named Helga who spoke little English. Her very tall but plain husband had visited with Phillip while she took his wife's measurements and helped her select fabric for a new gown.

"Lovely," Ida said.

Lynne stared at the statuesque beauty who held up a heavy blue worsted fabric before her. The tall woman was dressed in petticoat and chemise with a snug fitting whale-bone corset tightly cinched around her waist. The wool would be difficult to sew, but Ida was encouraging her to purchase it. Lynne and the store owner had worked out an agreement. Lynne would make twelve dresses up for the woman and her customers. Instead of payment, Ida would mark down the work as payment on the machine. When the last dress was sewn, the machine would belong to Lynne.

Of course she could have asked Phillip for the money, but she felt proud to be able to earn the machine this way. That horrible Tarn Micheals had cost them enough. Luckily, the Irishman had been chased away before robbing Phillip. They could use the money from the horses to buy extra feed and gardening supplies instead of this luxury item that they didn't need. She spent most of the time he slept either sewing or picking out seeds and learning about gardening from her friendly host.

Lynne was so delighted by Ida's generous offer, she was afraid to say anything but thank you. After the mill, sewing was like breathing to her, effortless. The little treadle machine worked beautifully on almost everything she fed through, only balking at really thick seams. With the sewing supplies she had back at their cabin, she knew she could contend with anything that needed to be sewn by hand.

The two tall women talked animatedly together, despite the Swedish girl's lack of English. Lynne was content to stand in the back room, waiting to take whatever they finally agreed upon to sew. Now if she could just learn to ride and shoot so she could help Phillip with the ranch until he regained his full strength. Each day he sat up and did more and more for himself. She had been able to restrain him from what he wanted to pursue, mainly by staying busy over the little sewing machine. She smiled at the thought and the Dutchman's wife teased her.

"This is not such a bad way, Ja, marrying a stranger." The lovely woman she was talking to dropped the cloth and allowed Lynne to reach up to take her majestic measurements. "Gude."

Lynne smiled, then looked at the waiting store owner. "Very good."

"Ja," Ida answered.

◇◇◇

When Lynne returned to the bedroom with the cloth and the measurements, the tall Swedish girl followed. For just a second she panicked when she saw the bald miner resting on their bed. Relieved, Lynne was surprised to find Phillip dressed and sitting up in an armchair by the window.

"There they are. You're right Gant, she's a beauty too," Johnson grinned at Lynne.

Lynne blushed, then stepped through the bedroom door to walk over and stand beside Phillip's chair. She wanted to scold him, but really he did look wonderful sitting there. The eye that had been swollen shut was half-open, the other eye's dark circle was fading to green. She knew the marks on his body were also fading, the wound in his arm firmly closed, but she didn't want him to overdo and risk even greater hurt. They had so much to do at home, he should be resting now. But the men in town had quickly come to wait for Phillip's cautious advice, asking him about mining, about their cattle, or about ranching. Surely if he could help them, he could train her enough to be more than his little bride.

Once again she took her place as his over-protective wife. She knew it annoyed him, but she also knew he would never regain all his strength if he didn't rest.

"Perhaps Mr. Johnson, you would prefer to trade places with my husband. He likes to pretend he is well, but the doctor is concerned about his still feeling nauseous and dizzy when he does too much."

Phillip scowled but Lynne just put the cloth and sewing things down by the machine so he was staring at her back instead.

"Oh, sure thing, sure thing, Mrs. Gant." The gawking man climbed up off the bed and his Swedish bride smiled tolerantly at him as he wrapped a long hairy arm around her. Lynne was a little shocked by his open familiarity with the blonde, even though they were married and it was just in a room with another couple.

She was always confused at the type of manners most westerner's projected. All were warm and friendly, most of the time they were polite, but none of them seemed that refined. Maybe manners were not the daily topic of conversation in the west as they were in the east. She couldn't imagine the Dutchman's wife or the tall miner's bride reading the *Lowell Offering* the way Claire and the girls at the mill had done.

Lynne flicked cautious gray eyes back to Phillip who was still seated. She moved to straighten the bed, making the cover cool and smooth as he reluctantly rose from the chair. Would he scold her again, like he had for her treatment of Shorty and Banes? He moved silently toward the bed, acknowledging his awareness that she merely wanted to help by his keeping quiet and by his stiff movements. Only his last minute drawing of his hands along the chair back to keep his balance, betrayed his continued weakness.

Johnson was the first to comment. "What seems to be broke on you, Gant?"

Phillip allowed Lynne to prop up pillows behind him until he was sitting nearly as tall as the other man had been minutes before on the bed. "Not sure."

"Well, sounds like Doc should have slapped some plaster on you somewhere. Indian Joe had a cracked skull once, as I recall. He fainted dead away and was out for six days. Never was quiet the same when he woke up."

Lynne gasped and turned to face the bald miner. "Phillip was unconscious for two days after the fight."

"Well, I'd get the Doc to slap some plaster on my noggin if'n I was you. Keep things dry in there till the bone sets up good."

There was a short rap on the door before Phillip could answer. "Taken to doctoring have you, Johnson?"

Lynne moved to swing the door wide, grateful that the Dutch couple had such a large room. Even so, the only available chair was now occupied by the bald miner and his buxom bride. Lynne backed out of the way so the doctor had room to walk over to the bed to attend Phillip.

"Now, Mr. Gant, let's see if Doc Johnson's diagnosis is correct."

Lynne watched nervously as the doctor ran old hands over the face and head of her husband. Only when he probed the side of his head, and Phillip swore did the doctor pull his thick fingers away and smile at the couple by the window. "I see, Johnson, you know as much about doctoring as you do about picking a wife." He gave a mock bow to Helga, then lifted his bag to the bed. Over his shoulder he called to Lynne. "If you could bring a pan of water and hold it Mrs. Gant, we should be able to patch your husband's cracked pate as easily as I ever did Indian Joe's."

Lynne watched in fascination as he dumped a small packet of white powder into the water, stirred, and then slowly dropped strips of gauze into the solution to soak. "Coarse, Johnson, forgot to tell you folks old Joe was kicked by a mule and had a big hole knocked in his head. Didn't have much choice but to make him a patch."

Lynne asked curiously as she watched the doctor unroll the

bandage, then carefully roll it back up before lifting it out of the messy solution. "Did the patch work?"

"Only for about two years." He scratched his own head, leaving a sticky white streak along the white tuffs of hair at his temple. "Think he died of the dysentery."

"Snake bite." Johnson added, then shook his head and muttered "dysentery," as though it was the silliest thing he had ever heard.

The doctor nodded. "Right, doctor Johnson."

Phillip shivered as the cold glop ran down his neck and Lynne nervously bounced from foot to foot. Only when the doctor had firmly layered the sticky bandages from brow to the clean-shaven back of his head three or four times, did Lynne relax. She even smiled as Phillip made another face as the bandages were laced repeatedly over his thick curly brown hair, rising turban-like over his scowling face. The doctor finished by smearing his sticky fingers in the gloop and smoothing it over and over the hooded area.

Johnson was the first to laugh out loud, then Helga joined in. Lynne raised a hand to hide her own smiling face but Phillip growled as she swung the now empty pan away at the doctor's command.

"Reckon those little cracks in your ribs have quit aching by now. Girl, quit giggling and get me some water to wash up a little."

Lynne dashed from the room and returned only a few minutes later with a clean pan of water. The doctor twitched his fingers in the air as though the small wide marvels would set if he didn't keep wiggling them. Quickly he dunked them in the basin and scrubbed for several minutes before removing them triumphantly, once again pink and fat.

Lynne stared at where Phillip had removed his shirt while she was gone. She cast gray, cool eyes toward Johnson's bride in warning as the big Swedish girl grinned at the display of muscle and warm flesh. Johnson noticed the same appreciative leer and rose abruptly, all but dumping his wife on the floor. Startled she straightened and didn't look back as he tugged her from the room.

Relieved, Lynne stepped around the bed and sank into the now empty chair. Phillip was watching her, his eyes golden brown with merriment at her obvious jealousy. His wry smile faded as the doctor ran strong hands over the dark matted hair covering his chest, then changed to a frown as the man folded a knuckle and thumped his rib cage like a ripe melon.

Lynne winced in sympathy and the doctor stared at her heart-shaped face and gave a chuckle. "Hurts you too, does it." He repeated the motion on the other side, but other than a grimace, Phillip didn't react. "Healing nicely." He pushed his hand along the washboard stomach, and Phillip's eyes darkened in pain.

"Ah, thought so. It's not the busted noggin after all, making you queasy, it's you're still pretty bruised inside." He looked over his shoulder at Lynne, smiling kindly at the worried face and sad eyes. "Don't worry, Mrs. Gant, he'll be good as new in another week or two. It's your job though to make sure he has plenty of bland food to eat and nothing but bed rest. Keep him off any bucking mustangs and away from any restless longhorns and he should heal good as new."

He straightened and cleared his throat and Phillip looked directly at Lynne as he reached to unfasten his pants. Blushing furiously, Lynne scooted out of the room, chased by the laughter of both men.

Only after the doctor had packed his little black bag and left, did Lynne turn back to the bedroom. Phillip was under the covers, sitting upright. His brown nude torso made her wonder if he were nude underneath as well. Nervously she closed the door before walking back across to sit in the chair. The spring air blew through the open window, billowing the white curtains inward around her.

Phillip sat, angrily aware of the added weight of the wet plaster on his head. Doggone if he wouldn't get even with Johnson for suggesting it. He stared across at his petite bride, perched nervously on the caned chair by the window like a bird ready to take flight. One knee bounced beneath the full skirt of her blue dress, making the stiff cotton rustle. The white curtains curved around her, revealing then hiding her lovely face. They emphasized the dark richness of her brown hair, piled softly on top of her head. He watched as beneath arched brows, her long lashes lowered over the stormy gray of her eyes. He felt himself harden impatiently at her shyness.

"Lynne?"

Mesmerized, Lynne stared across at him. The doctor had gone, but the bandage he had fashioned still wasn't dry. Against the whiteness of the cloth, Phillip looked darker still. In the soft light, he looked deliciously dangerous. Despite the raw stitches over his jawbone, the raccoon like circles around his eyes, his brown eyes glowed luminously. She shivered as the air became cooler with the fading sun.

"Come here, wife," he whispered huskily.

Lynne shook her head, pursing her lips to form a wordless 'no.'

"Why not?" He asked, grinning wryly.

She swallowed, uncomfortable with the subject, breathlessly aware of his hand poised above the woven bedspread. If she didn't speak soon, he would probably throw back the covers and come after her. Nervously she eyed the closed bedroom door, then turned to look out the window at the sudden sound of voices in the quiet street below.

The voices carried clearly into the soft silence of their bedroom.

"Thanks, Doc, I'll bring Helga by tomorrow."

"Mighty quick work if she's expecting already."

Lynne could almost see Johnson's grin of pride, the tall blonde's laughing blush. She felt Phillip's eyes on her, caressing her as intimately as though she weren't primly covered by the sprigged blue cotton day dress. Raising a hand, she plucked at the soft ruffle on the high collar, moved to stroke her throat where his hungry eyes roved. She folded her hands in the full gathers of the skirt over her lap, fought the urge to pull the long sleeves over her hands.

He moaned and she raised shy eyes to look at him. His head was leaning forward, his shoulders curved as though in pain. Panicked, she bolted to him, hesitated by the side of the bed. He remained slumped there. Cautiously she extended a hand to touch the bare skin of his shoulder, felt an electric quiver in her stomach at even that brief contact. She leaned closer, surprised by the clean alkaline smell of the wet plaster. He tilted his head back so she could once again see the hunger in his eyes, feel the scalding desire in his next breath.

"Lynne."

She sank onto the bed beside him, letting her hands roam over the same broad muscled chest the doctor had so cruelly thumped moments ago. "But darling, you're still so hurt," she whispered in one last argument. Then she gave into her own need, shivered with the pleasure of touching his warm flesh, stretched silkily over solid muscle, covered by coarse, tingly hair. She wanted to fold him in against her, ignore the wet bandages, help him relax against her own willing body. But each pass of her hands made his muscles tighten, the flesh tense from her teasing touch. Breathless, she let her fingers brush across his face, felt the thousand bristles of his unshaven face and trembled. He turned his face into her hand, moved his warm lips in the center of her palm until she gasped in shock as she felt a similar sensation between her legs.

"Oh Phillip," she moaned, then pushed against him, undeterred this time by his moans since she had watched the doctor use even more force to restrain him. "You're too hurt for this."

He leaned close enough to brush her cheek with his lips and Lynne felt the cool dampness of his head dressing. "Stop. Your cast."

Sighing, he collapsed against the big wheel of wood that formed the headboard.

Lynne breathed deeply, looked across to see him smiling at her. As he raised a hand, he wiped the wet plaster from her hair. "The only thing that causes me pain darling, is knowing that you are so close to me and so unreachable."

Gently, slowly, she leaned forward on her knees and moved so she could kiss the fading bruises around his eyes, the rough edge of the cut along his chin. As she began to trail kisses lower and lower over the warm flesh of his arms and chest she felt a heady sense of power as his breathing became more ragged.

He didn't protest when she lowered the sheet, merely let one hand reach out to snag her rich heavy hair. Only when her lips dared to brush his tenderest flesh did he protest. Lynne drew another breath, then let her tongue reach out to torment him further. She felt his whole body shiver against her even as he moaned. She let her head press against his stomach, closed her mouth over him.

He lifted and pulled her face away as he brought her hand up to close around him. She gasped as she felt him pulse in her hand, the warm spill of seed through her fingers. The seed that should be growing inside her. Beneath her cheek she heard the heavy beat of his heart.

She moved so that her face was even with his, her head resting against his shoulder, her nose pressed against his chin. He lowered his mouth to claim hers, whispered against her eyes. She couldn't understand the words, but knew the meaning, had heard the echo of her own love and excitement in his heart beats. Tomorrow they would go home. In another week he would be well.

Dodd brought the wagon around to the front of the store, made another trip inside to carry down Lynne's sewing machine. He had already placed the new plow, seeds, and hardware in one side of the wagon. The other was full of the mattress he had carried out that morning, only now it was folded in half to make room for the additional supplies. He wondered how they would deal with it when they got home, then turned to stare into the intense eyes of the handsome cowboy leaning on the hitching post in front of the store. If the big hat hadn't sat at an odd angle, one would have never known this was the same man he had helped carry to the doctor's the week before. The body was lean and powerful, dressed in a pale cotton shirt that showed a pencil thin stripe of white against its muted blue.

He grinned as he saw the little bride emerge from the door beside the tall wife of the Dutchman. "Ja, Ja, but you will have so much to do, sure you are you don't want to stay longer. There's plenty room. You're no trouble, eithers."

Lynne smiled, shielded her eyes to look out into the bright light of the street beyond Ida to where her stubborn husband rested so nonchalantly. Even with the absurd hat, she was aware of the white bandage that smothered his dark hair. He acted as though it were not there, shifting his gaze from one side of the street to the other. This morning he had dressed completely as soon as the first sunlight crept through the window. He wanted to stand guard, to make sure everything went right. She had argued that he should be back in bed.

His teasing answer had made her keep quiet until Dodd finally arrived with the team. Phillip had wanted to rush down to help the other man, but Lynne had at least been able to prevail on him to merely stand guard. She was aware of what his exertion cost him, had been only too aware of how quickly he had fallen asleep after supper last night. She had every intention of following his doctor's orders about diet and rest. She wanted a well husband, not a crippled one.

Dodd sweated and strained to lift the sewing machine into the rig. All three men swore at the same time as the machine tilted crazily. It was only Phillip's quick dart forward that kept the machine from falling out of the wagon onto the dusty road. Lynne clutched Ida's hand as Phillip caught the machine in one hand and helped to lift it back onto the wagon, his face darkening in pain from the sudden movement. It was ridiculous, his refusal to ride home in the back of the wagon. But even as she fumed, she darted a glance around the busy street, checking on who was watching. For a moment she thought she saw Micheals, but then she realized it was just a shadow.

She clambered into the wagon unassisted, knowing that if she didn't Phillip might strain himself again helping her. He said nothing as he moved between Dodd and the wagon to climb up on the padded seat beside her. Gravely he took both reins in his hand, then turned without a smile and lifted a finger to touch the brim of his hat in salute to those who watched. Lynne smiled, relieved to finally be headed home. Merrily she waved back at the strange woman who had become her friend in the past few short days. The stage coach driver lifted his battered hat to wave and shouted the team forward.

Lynne turned to brace her feet in the floor of the wagon for balance as they jolted forward, glad to be away.

Tarn watched the wagon pull out. He had been ready to make a move on the gunman, certain that he must still be injured from their last fight. Then he had watched him leap from the rail to grab the heavy machine as though it weighed a feather and his self-assurance vanished. He didn't fear the man if they were to come together hand to hand. But he didn't fool himself into thinking he was any kind of gunman. Especially not as fast as the devil Lynne had married.

If conditions were right, he was ready to attack again. If anything, their encounter the week before had strengthened his confidence in his ability to beat the tar out of any man fool enough to marry a bossy woman like Lynne McKinney. Of course, the poor man didn't know what she was like before she arrived, or he probably would have settled for one of the numerous Indians or tarts this town harbored.

Let them have time, this rancher would discover what she was really like. Then with any luck, he might set the dark haired lass loose. In a town as rough as this, she might be glad to turn to a familiar face. There had been a time when he had fancied the bit of goods himself. She had a fine little body, an almost angelic face. If only she didn't feel she had to put every man who came near her in his place.

Well, whether he threw her out first, or Tarn had to kill the black eyed gunman, the snooty little woman would be fast on her back beneath himself and then a long line of others. There would be time to make Lynne and Gant pay. There was plenty of time for everything. He merely had to be patient.

By the time they were safely out of town and a few miles down the road toward home, Phillips stomach and ribs were hurting, not to mention his throbbing head. Damn that devilish Irishman. He was confused, relieved that the man hadn't dared to attack them, angry that he hadn't had a chance to kill the bastard once and for all. A large rut in the trail made the wagon jolt and he gasped, then swore again. Now she would really let him have it.

Lynne lifted her long lashes to cautiously study the man beside her. He was pale beneath his tan, grooves ran from his aquiline nose along the corners of his mouth. Were they from his injuries or from his constant frowning? In his lean face, they gave him a predatory look. If she hadn't lain cradled in his arms only hours before, even she would never believe he had a gentle, loving nature.

Silently she looked around from the rocking wagon seat, studying the even pace of the bright red backs of the horses pulling them. If she said nothing, allowed him to play macho man just to travel home, what was the point of her nursing him all week. So when the wagon passed from broad, open road to the sheltered groves of cottonwood, she spoke.

"Phillip, aren't you going to show me how to drive a team?"

For several minutes they rode in silence, then he tilted his head at an angle to study his little bride. The horses were both graceful, well trained mounts who also worked well as a team. Her hands were small, but he knew she was no reed to be broken by the first breeze. Both her hands and back were strong, as he could attest if any needed convincing. He had planned to use this time while he was healing to train her in the ways she would need to survive in the Montana territory. Foremost among these survival skills were the ability to shoot and ride.

She had come to him full of excitement and youthful innocence. Boston and her trip west had been very educational, but she knew far too little to defend herself or escape. If anything happened to him, how could he expect her to protect herself in this dangerous, unpredictable land? At least he had to show her how to handle and control the horses.

He jerked back on the team, then as they pulled up, he handed her the reins. Ignoring the tenderness in his shoulder, he managed to lean forward to wrap a long arm around her. Gripping her small hands in his, he fed the reins through her fingers, talking softly the whole time. "You have to hold them securely, but not jerk on them unless you really want them to stop. They're a good team to work together, but when we start up the pass, they may seesaw."

She raised eyebrows, excited at the possibility of driving the team herself. "Seesaw?"

"Yeah, one may pull and the other loaf. Then you need to snap out the reins over the back of the one that's loafing."

"All right."

He smiled, surprised at how delightful it was to watch her

smile. "You're ready?" At her answering grin, he snapped the reins and yelled the team into motion.

Only after they had topped the first grade and she was still poised and in charge did he relax and sag against the back of the wagon seat. Lynne kept the team to a gentle rocking gait, surprised when she felt his shoulder sag against her. Half standing, she rose on her feet to pull the team to a halt.

Phillip sat up, alarmed at their stopping. She turned to smile at him confidently. "No arguments. Please climb into the back and rest. Or don't you believe I can handle the horses?"

Phillip scowled, then allowed his own eyes to soften at the loving gray in hers. He leaned forward, gave her a little peck on the cheek, and then carefully climbed over onto the rolled mattress in the back. Sighing he relaxed, content to allow her to take them home.

CHAPTER TWENTY-SEVEN

Even the daylight seemed green. Lynne hesitated inside the barn, staring out at the morning. She had already managed to feed the animals, had given up on gathering the eggs. The chickens had turned vicious in the week they had been gone. Before she had been able to cautiously remove eggs, even when the hens were in the nest, but not today.

A loud bawling made her turn back inside with a smile. The little calf was again demanding to be fed. Lynne walked back to the stall, overwhelmed by even the rich, acrid smell of the barn. It was so good to be back home. Cautiously, she extended a hand to pat Beulah's wide horned head, then scratched earnestly along her heavy jaw and under the soft fold of flesh beneath her neck. The cow mooed contentedly.

The calf had careened behind his mother on her approach, but now it emerged from eating, licking his wet muzzle to watch the proceedings. Lynne hummed contentedly and held her left hand inside the railing, just within his reach. Beulah rolled one eye to watch the calf then tilted her heavy head, so Lynne could reach the other side of her face.

Cautiously the little one touched her fingers with its soft nose, then backed so quickly he half-fell into his mother. He made a strange noise and Lynne smiled, but continued to stroke the cow. Beulah made a soft call of demand to the baby and he edged forward along her side. Lynne watched as the huge gray tongue worked to clean the little one. He rocked under the pressure as she washed from one end to the other. It made Lynne's own heart tighten, suddenly missing Mary Anne and the boys with unbearable fierceness. She started to turn away when she felt the calf's wet tongue against the back of her hand.

Reassured by his mother's scent on her fingers, he nuzzled the strange soft fingers, would have nipped them it Lynne hadn't curled them into her palm. Delighted, she managed to rub the incredible softness of his face, trail a hand along the young back and shoulder before he took flight and Beulah snorted in warning. Laughing at the way he kicked his hind legs into the air as he twisted away in panic, Lynne felt her heart ease. The children were fine, would be with her soon. And oh, would they love the animals and farm. This little maverick would be half-grown by the end of summer, but there might be other babies for them to enjoy.

Singing, she emerged into the sunshine and crossed quickly to the house, halting only when a dark shadow filled the doorway. Phillip stood with an arm wrapped around his waist, hunched forward as though to protect himself from the new day. His shirt was open down the front and Lynne felt the usual desire to stroke the hair darkened skin exposed. But his posture made her hesitate. He was leaning against the door frame, his bandaged head starkly white even against the pale wood. His dark eyes looked wet amid the hurt colors of his face.

After the long trip to the cabin, he had been moaning in agony. That despite the doubled mattress Dodd had placed in the back of the wagon. Lynne had dismounted, determined to comfort him, but he had sworn and forced her away. She felt that hurt again as she remembered how hard it had been to release the team, then lead the pair inside the barn to unharness through her tears. Unloading the wagon had been even harder. He had insisted on helping and each step he took made her feel white with shared suffering. They had managed to unload the mattress and return it to the bed, although dragging it to get it back in the house. She had added sheets while he staggered past to the privy. Only when the last of the tools were stored in his office, did he finally agree to sink back on the bed.

But all during the long night he had resisted her help, lying there so close but so remote. It was as though he were locked away from her with his pain and something else. All during the night she had listened to his mutterings, his woeful sighs and moans. As soon as the first rays of light appeared through the small window she had escaped the bed into the routine of chores.

Now he stood there, watching her. She controlled her need to ask how he felt, what she could do to help. Instead, she talked of the inconsequential.

"Isn't it a lovely morning? Everything is turning green." She spun, pointing to the distant edge of trees, then to the few blades of grass in the area between their house and the barn.

His gaze seemed to soften as he looked at her and she felt the first glimmer of hope. "The calf is so perfect. He let me pet him this morning. Do you want to come and pet him too? He's awfully shy, but so curious. I'm sure he would let you."

He barely shook his head and a wave of pain forced bile up his throat and made him wonder if he could even make it back inside the house to the bed. She didn't deserve this. He stared at her, the gentleness in her voice, the tenderness and excitement. He turned away suddenly, repulsed by what he was, what he had done to bring such a beautiful creature to share such misery.

As he staggered back inside, Lynne clutched her hands together. If only he would let her help, not shut her out of his dark world. She heard him cough and gasp. Was he drinking again? Last night after she had finally drifted into an exhausted slumber, she had awakened and heard him in the other room, drinking. He must have had a jar hidden in the spare room. She shuddered with revulsion. It was the only thing that she couldn't stand. There had been plenty of men in the tenements who drank. Men like Garretty and Michaels who would drown their sorrows in a bottle, while their poor families ran around hungry and without decent clothes. Then they would take their rage and bitterness out on those they should have protected. Heaven help her if she had married a drinking man and ended up with a drunken bully like Bonnie's.

Nonsense. Lynne shook her head to clear away all her doubts. Phillip Gant was not like any of them. The three weeks before the trip into town, he hadn't had anything to drink. It was just to dull the pain. After all, it was something she wished she could do. Doctors. That quack in Butte didn't have a clue of how to treat Phillip. If he was still this sick on Friday, she would have Shorty and Banes ride to Helena for their doctor. Something could be broken inside, he could be dying. A tremble of fear swept through her. "Nonsense," she whispered.

Once more firmly in hand, she entered the cabin. Keeping her voice light, she set about making breakfast, talking to him as she worked.

"Guess you'll have to settle for porridge, the hens wouldn't let me get a single egg. Something must be wrong with them." She waited, expecting him to laugh and tell her she needed to be braver the way he had the first time she had gathered eggs. The silence worked on her nerves.

"I'll write the children today about our trip and about the calf. Then I guess I'll work on the dress for Helga. I wish she'd chosen a lighter grade of cloth. Honestly, if the weather continues to grow warmer, she'll melt when she wears it this summer." She pictured the cool, over-endowed blonde melting and smiled in satisfaction. By now though, Helga had probably heard from the doctor that she was expecting. Lynne probably should leave room in the waist and the side seams in case the woman's size had changed when they made the trip to Helena to meet them in three weeks.

She set the can of molasses on the table, poured a cup of black coffee for each of them. Only when the oatmeal was in bowls waiting did she walk through the silent house to look for him. He was lying on the bed, his back to her, his body curved into a cramped circle of pain.

Lightly she stepped closer, as afraid of startling him as she had been of the calf this morning. Gently she sank onto the edge of the bed, slipped a cool hand beneath his shirt. Even as she stroked the tight muscles, she felt pleasure at the satiny feel of his skin. She leaned forward and brushed his ear with her lips as she whispered, ever moving her hands to knead the bunched muscles. "Do you remember when you did this for me?"

Phillip half rolled, unwilling to turn enough to stop her. For the first time since they left Butte, he felt some of the tension drain. His eyes covered her face as his mind relived the first night he had shared a bed with this beautiful woman. At his smile she shifted to kiss the corner of his mouth, moved so her lips were buried in the softness of his neck even as her strong young hands massaged away some of his aches. It would be so good if he could love her, bring those wild cries of pleasure to her lips. But he wouldn't start that. He couldn't bear to have her give him release again when he was unable to bring her body to the same point. He closed his eyes so she couldn't read the disappointment in his own.

Lynne sensed the change in him. Sighing, she let one hand rub the base of his neck, the other the base of his spine. "Come on, time to get up. If you wait much longer the porridge will turn to rock."

She rose from the bed, after giving the back of his neck a soft kiss. "Now that Beulah has milk, you'll have to show me how to get some. It would be nice to have in the coffee or over the cereal in the morning if the hens are going to continue to be so selfish."

He rolled flat, smiled up at her. She was wearing her old dark shirtwaist, her soft brown hair drawn back from her sweet face in a single fat braid. For a moment he noticed the rise of her young breasts beneath the dress as she waited impatiently. Maybe he wasn't as hurt as he feared.

She must have seen the gleam of lust in his eyes for she smiled. "That can wait too. I've got so much to do this morning and I need to clear away the breakfast dishes to get to it."

Reluctantly she backed out, brushing the hanging blanket aside. She wanted to stay and help, but knew he wouldn't take it, would become angry at the offer. Instead she waited in the other room, trying to close her ears to his muffled groans of pain and oaths.

His shirt was buttoned and he looked all right when he came through minutes later.

Lynne was surprised when he bowed his head first. "Thank you God for everything. Amen," she whispered softly, feeling hopeful once again. "I would have sliced some bacon, but the doctor told me to keep everything bland, no spices, no grease."

He nodded, then set his teeth against the pain. He would have to remember not to do that. Instead he spoke. "Right, this is good." He didn't want to say he hated gruel for breakfast, instead sampled it, and was surprised at how good it tasted with the dark bite of the molasses. Maybe the only thing that was wrong with his stomach was the Dutchman's wife's cooking. He looked across at his bride. Lynne was a much better cook, a better wife in every way. Her soft girlish voice continued and he smiled, delighted to just be sharing the meal.

"Do you think old Dot taught the others her tricks? I mean she's always pecked at me, but the others had never done a thing. But when I tried to lift one of the younger hens, she bit the fire out of me. See."

She held out her tiny hand and he took it, turning it so he could see the red mark, the circular bruise on the back of her hand. "It's early, but they're probably setting. Six days away, the little clutch of eggs piling up made them all want to be mothers."

Lynne drew her hand back, and laughed. "Little chicks, I've always wanted little chicks. Mr. Sanders used to sell them every spring. I mean Boston is a big city, but everyone still needs eggs and there is usually enough room for coops if you have a backyard. But of course the tenements weren't allowed to have chickens, but they were so cute."

He laughed, astonished by her enthusiasm for even the smallest thing. The sound chased the last of his somberness away. He might still be weak and sore, but another week or so and he would be back to normal. Without Lynne, he would have probably fallen into a deep melancholy and stayed drunk until he was better off dead. But she was so...

She stared at him and swallowed. The laugh had been so real, so deep. This was the man she had married. She didn't need food. She could live forever on the warm glow in his eyes.

One of the horses whinnied and snorted and Phillip rose from the table in one lithe move, the sudden shift bringing a groan from him. Angry at his weakness, he swore as he pulled the gun down from over the fireplace. Only when he emerged out of the cabin did he stop swearing. A pair of young Indians were riding out of the corral with two of the remaining mustangs. Furious, Phillip yelled for Lynne to stay put, then darted across to close the gate on the last three animals even as he fired the rifle after the thieves. The sound of the rifle made both Indians scream high wild cries of delight.

Lynne shivered, opening the door as soon as they were gone and running out in the yard carrying the belt and revolvers to him.

Furious, he continued to pace up and down swearing. He turned black eyes on her. If he hadn't been mooning over his bride again, then he might have heard them in time to save the horses. Geez, and he would have to spend days rounding up more, then weeks breaking them.

A sharp pain in his head made him stop and draw a deep calming breath. Who was he kidding? He couldn't ride, could barely run out of the cabin. By the time he was ready to ride again, the horse herds could have drifted. Even if he caught more, he was in no shape to break them.

"Will they be back?" she asked in horror.

He stopped long enough to study the signs. There had been only two in the raiding party. Boys by the size of them. Robbed by a pair of children. But if they rode back with the horses and not even a scratch, then others from their camp might come riding in for the remainder.

He looked at the house, the barn, the remaining livestock, finally at his wife. "They were Ute's. Not usually this far north. I've got to go after the animals."

"But you're still hurt. The doctor said no riding. Phillip you know you're too sick." But he was ignoring her, strapping the gun belt around his lean hips as he strode into the barn to saddle one of the bays. Lynne saw him pause to lean against the rough planks of the stall and caught up with him.

"This is crazy. You can't do this crazy thing."

He stared at her, his eyes hard and black. They had the same lifeless coldness that she had first seen in Butte. Only now she knew what it meant. She folded her hands and brought them up to her mouth. She wanted to hold him, order him to stay. She wanted to pull her Phillip from inside this stranger, this Dark Prince of death.

He stepped around her, quickly and efficiently proceeded to saddle the big bay. Frightened, Lynne slipped into the stall next to him, watching each thing he did, copying it clumsily on the remaining horse. The animal protested her intrusion with a loud, angry whinny and Phillip's head swung up too quickly to see what she was up to. The sudden motion made him dizzy and for just a second he clutched at the horn on his own saddle, clung there until the   spinning   stopped.

"Lynne." He started to yell, paused long enough to throw up. She used the precious seconds to force the bridle onto her horses head, to look back at his saddle to see what he had done with the strap thing.

Angry, she led the reluctant beast out. Normally she would have been terrified to come this near to one. But there was no way she was going to let Phillip try to ride out alone. Someone had to be there to bring him safely home in case he fainted and fell out of the saddle. It might be dangerous, but she was not going to let him go alone, and she knew she couldn't stop his going.

Finished, he straightened, shoved the rifle in the saddle holder, and then led his nervous horse out. She was standing there, her eyes gray storm clouds of fear and anger. "Here." He handed her the reins of his own horse, struggled to smooth the blanket, straighten the saddle and tighten the cinch on hers. When it was ready he stared at her. "Have you ever ridden?"

She thought for a moment she could lie and say yes, but she saw the concern behind the question and shook her head. "But I learn fast."

He swore again, then took the other set of reins. Furious, he bent and swept her skirt up between her legs and fastened it over the belt loop like he had seen so many women do to ride. He swore when she swayed woodenly beneath his touch. He dropped both reins, then pushed her over to her own horse. "There's no time for you if you're afraid. Stay here."

Her little chin trembled, then she bit her lip and squared her shoulders. He felt the stiffness leave her spine. "Put your foot in my hand." She did and in one swift move she was on the back of the tall horse. The animal shifted nervously under her and he knew she was feeling another wave of panic. He used his calm voice to settle the horse, felt her settle down as well. "Grip the side of the animal with your legs." He pushed on her bottom, making her roll her eyes in question, as he checked her seat.

Only after he'd mounted, did he reach over to hand her the dropped reins. He brought them together, draped them in her right hand, jerked a bit of mane and put it in her left hand. "Whatever else you do, hold on. He'll follow Bob and me. Just don't let go."

Then he was out through the door and she was riding. The animal had followed as he said, carefully keeping even with Phillip's mount. Her initial fear was replaced by wonder and excitement. She was riding. Not just riding. Galloping in pursuit of Indians. The wild grass was still brown, but in places the new green leaves underneath showed, giving it a strange velvet appearance. Looking down made her feel dizzy. So instead she looked straight ahead, awed by the way the ground seemed to be gobbled up beneath the animals racing hooves.

They rode over the next hummock before they saw them. Lynne felt her assurance disappear and her horse almost stumbled. Phillip brought both animals to a standstill. For the first time she looked across at him. His face was covered with beads of sweat, his skin was chalky white. In one motion, he brought the rifle to his shoulder.

The little Indians had paused beside a stream and one had switched his blanket to the back of one of the spotted horses. They were so intent on what they were doing, they seemed to be unaware that the real owners had arrived. Lynne swallowed in horror. One of the boys was little older than the twins, the other a little younger than Sean had been the last time she saw him alive. She heard Phillip cock the rifle and wondered if she would be able to stand it if he shot either of them.

She screamed in protest. At the same instant he cocked the rifle, the half-broke pony raised his heels and twisted. For a second the boy hung on, the next he was flying through the air. He landed with a sickening thud and the other boy's laughter died.

Phillip lowered the rifle, looked at Lynne, motioning with his hand to circle them. Aware that there was little time, she obeyed, glad her horse understood the directions of what was expected of them better than she did. It was the first time she had actually been in charge of navigating. But as the savvy horse swung wide on the two horses, she realized who was really making the decisions.

Only when they had circled around them, did Lynne draw a

breath. She dared to look at Phillip again. Some of his color had returned. He held the rifle ready on the two boys, both of whom were on the ground. "Easy now." His big voice boomed. But Lynne knew it was the long black barrel that held them prisoner. The big boy was cradling the younger one, whose arm hung useless by his side. He made a fierce face at them, but Lynne noticed he had no weapon other than his long knife. For several minutes they stared at each other.

Phillip lowered the rifle and motioned with its barrel. "Go."

The boy swallowed, as surprised by the decision as Lynne was. She watched as he helped the younger one onto his small pony. It was then that she saw how thin the tall boy was. He was only half as wide as her own brother had been. Her heart twisted as she thought of all the food they had on the ranch. Obviously these boys had never known that kind of bounty. Even in Boston, as bad as things had seemed, they had never had to go hungry.

She fought the urge to climb off her big horse and hug these terrible savages. Instead she waited beside her sick husband until the young raiders had disappeared.

"Hurry, let's get these back before the rest of the tribe shows up."

Lynne smiled, amazed to see Phillips own grin. Relaxed, she was relieved to see his back remain straight as he cut his horse over to head back an animal dumb enough to follow the wild Indians.

Only when the animals were all safely back in the corral and the two saddle horses back in their stalls, did either speak.

Phillip closed his stall door, stood and scuffed dirty straw over the place where he had deposited his oatmeal earlier. Lynne patted the animal that had been so useful moments before, surprised at how such a little thing as riding could involve so many emotions.

"You're a natural." He breathed into the heavy silence.

Lynne smiled with pleasure. "I loved it. She tugged impatiently at her skirt and released the full folds of cloth. "But I think I need a different riding outfit."

He extended a hand, impatient to draw her into the shelter of his arms. "You can borrow my pants."

She laughed, imagined herself flapping around in the long-legged breeches. Letting her arm encircle his hips, she realized they might fit if she shortened the legs. "Maybe if you have some old worn-out ones, I could cut part of the leg off."

He grunted in answer. "We'll see. Now I know you can ride, I'll have to let you do it some everyday, if only to work the horses."

She looked back at the restless animals and tucked her head, leaning closer to him until the hard butt of his gun made her pull away. Dancing in front of him as she backed from the barn she had to ask. "Would you have shot them?"

They were both outside in the bright sunlight. He paused with the rifle cradled across his arm and stared at her young face, knowing he should never tell her the truth. "Yes."

All the pleasure faded from her eyes at his answer and he swore and brushed past her into the house. But he was unsurprised to have her follow him inside, hear her yell at him.

"No, you couldn't have. You didn't. Twice you had them in your sights and you didn't. You're not a cold-blooded killer."

He felt pain in a different place than his head for the first time this morning. There had been no questions from her about the shooting in town. He knew she had doubts, wanted to ask a million questions. Was that why she hadn't? Because she didn't believe he was a killer. But as he placed his rifle over the fireplace he brushed his eyes, tried to brush back the memory of all the bloodied faces from men he had shot.

Quietly he walked back to clear the table for her. Lynne took the bowl from his hand, paused with one hand on her hip, tried to see into his face. "You couldn't have shot a couple of boys. Tell me you couldn't have."

But his lifeless black eyes told her the real truth. Shocked, she nearly dropped the bowl. But lightning quick, he caught it in his hands, set it back on the table. He stepped forward, tried to pull her into his arms. She backed away from him, shook her hands out beside her. "They were just children. Poor, starving children." She walked with her back to him to look out at the now quiet yard, heard the reassuring sounds of the animals in the distance.

"The one boy, the littlest one. Do you think he'll be all right?"

Again he removed things from the table. She had said she needed it cleared to work. What was it she wanted to do? Sew?

"Maybe. If they set his arm right."

She followed him with her eyes, tried to resolve the deadness in his voice with the kindness of his action. He didn't know himself. Couldn't see himself the way she could, that was why he had lied to her. "But they don't have doctors, surely they don't have splints and plaster and bandages the way our doctors do. They won't be able to help him at all will they?"

He removed the molasses, used the feed sack she had dried with yesterday to wipe at the circles the cups and bowls had left. "They're not ignorant. Their doctors will use branches and wet leather to make a brace. It might heal right."

She stepped back toward him. "Leather wouldn't set hard like this." She reached up a hand to touch his head and he breathed deeply for the first time in minutes.

"Harder, and it draws up as it dries. Rawhide strips work better than these rags. Then they'll give him willow bark tea for the pain and in a few days, he'll be ready to steal horses again."

"Is that why you could shoot him, because of the horses?"

He looked at her, looked beyond her toward the animals and barn. "Nope."

Softly she stepped closer, moving into the circle of his arms where she had wanted to be all day. He leaned forward, letting the weight of his head rest on top of hers. "They were such little Indians," she protested.

He wrapped arms around her, wanted to avoid the truth, but knew he had to tell her. "There are others in their tribe. If they came in with horses, the others might come back for the rest. For you." His voice cracked on the last and she tilted her head just enough to kiss him. It was firm, definite, but didn't change into the passionate one she wanted. Before she could move against him he released her.

"Best get your chores out of the way, you need to learn to shoot this afternoon." He turned toward the back room and Lynne wanted to ask him what he would be doing but he answered before she could. "I need to sleep now, so I can stand watch tonight. Keep the door open, the rifle handy. If you leave this room, close and lock it first."

With those cold words, she felt a somber chill sweep down her back. He would have killed them, but only to protect her. She wondered if all the Indians were as poor as these had looked, but his voice had been a command. He had to sleep, not answer questions about Indians. With a confidence she didn't feel, Lynne took out the blue cloth and pattern she had made for Helga. Only when everything was laid out to work did she take the rifle down from the hooks and stand it beside the door, ready to fire. She might not hit anything, but she could use it to protect her own life, to protect him.

Maybe later, she could get him to show her what willow looked like so she could get him some bark. And if leather strips worked best, maybe they could use them to replace the bandage that quack had made in Butte. Wanting to ask him if there were any trees nearby, she stepped to the opening lifted the blanket. He lay on the bed, still dressed, with his dirty boots resting on top of the bedspread. At least he had removed the spurs. Tiptoeing closer, she noticed he was already asleep. His face was drawn from the pain, and she wondered what the ride had cost him. What had the doctor said, no work, no wrangling? Sighing, she left him to sleep.

Dropping the blanket, she went back to the task of cutting out the dress. When that was finished she checked on him again, slipped past to cut meat and bring up vegetables for supper. When she had the meat in the oven to cook, she worked at basting the dress. The yard remained quiet, a soft breeze stirred up a dust devil. Weary of sewing, she took out paper and wrote the children, quickly filling six lined pages with descriptions of the gunfight, the new calf, the pitiful Indians, her first ride on horseback. When her pencil was worn to a nub, she squinted and looked up. The sunlight was fading. It would be dusk soon.

When Lynne checked on him once more, she was surprised to see his eyes open as soon as she lifted the curtain. The rest had done him good; his color was better, the long grooves beside his cheeks less noticeable. Once again she realized she had married a handsome man. His brown eyes smiled and she blushed. It amazed her how just his smile could make her heart race. Confused, she dropped the blanket and waited outside in the kitchen for him.

"Ready?" He growled.

Lynne felt her stomach tighten, drew a deep breath and stepped on out into the yard.

He paused, sniffing the rich smell of pot roast, unbelievably starved for it and the pretty girl in the door. Rifle in one hand, cartridges in the other, he stepped through to find her waiting on him, her eyes silver and mysterious. At least his head was clear of pain, his stomach calmer. She stepped skittishly out of reach and he laughed.

"Woman." If only the doctor had realized what temptation he would have to resist in waiting a week before enjoying relations with her. How had he phrased it? No exhausting work at all, not even sex.

Lynne stood at the impatient tone, dropped her dark lashes to hide the desire bubbling in her. She followed meekly as he led the way to the side of the house away from the barn, took time to set empty cans along a rotting log before coming back toward her. She watched, drinking in the beauty of his motions as he bent and moved, relieved to notice he was less stiff than this morning. Maybe the ride had helped?

He stepped back toward her; aware of the greedy way she was studying him. Might as well get this over with first. He handed her the rifle, asked her to shoot. She stared at the first target, fired, yelped in pain and let the rifle tilt toward the ground.

Only when he was behind her, his arm holding hers straight, the rifle butt braced against her shoulder did he lean his face forward and whisper in her ear. "The doctor said no relations."

She half twisted, her eyes full of shocked innocence.

He smiled at her protest. Turned her back around and repositioned the gun. "Concentrate on shooting only." But he was aware of the sweet weight of her breast against his arm, the way her rounded hips molded against him despite her full skirt. He leaned his head closer, steadied her toward the target. Whispered in her ear, "Squeeze slow." But he wanted to do far more than help her learn to shoot.

This time the can moved and she squealed in delight. He sighed as she left the gun in his hand and ran forward to retrieve the can. She held it up in the sunlight, turning it so he could see the holes, then repositioned it on the log. When she started to move back in front of him, he swore and stepped clear. He broke the rifle, made sure she had plenty of shells, then handed it to her again. "Take your time, I'll be impressed if you hit it on your own."

She repeated the steps, tried, missed, tried, missed. Finally on the third shot, she fired and was rewarded by seeing the can fall. He was standing there, a hand over his eyes, his breathing ragged. Concerned, she stepped closer.

"Phillip." He nodded. Shook himself and stepped away again. "I'm going down to the creek to cool off. Concentrate, don't waste shells."

He was almost past the house when she called out to him. "Bring back some willow bark and don't be long."

He squinted back toward her, amazed at how glad even her bossy tone made him feel. He looked around, then back to the trim little figure. Everything looked so safe, the smoke from the chimney, the restless animals snorting as the scent of gun smoke reached them. Had she accepted the need for shooting children? He never had, had left the army so as to not have to follow orders to shoot women and children. But if she were in danger, he would. Now the question was, could she ever shoot at someone to protect herself, to protect him.

CHAPTER TWENTY-EIGHT

Under the trees by the creek, the light was lost among soft shadows. Phillip sank to his knees and dipped a hand in the water to sip, then looked at his red fingers. The spring melt had turned the usually shallow, warm pool into ice water. So much for cooling off, but here in the peaceful tree line, the distant thunder of Lynne's rifle was enough to ease him. Besides, with them sleeping in different shifts, it would make temptation much easier to resist.

He waded among the trees, searching for a willow among the stand of cottonwood and aspens. Suddenly he stopped. Clearly marked in the damp creek bank were tracks. Tracks from unshod ponies and moccasins.

Enthusiastically, Lynne finished firing, managing to at least hit each can before the cartridges were gone. Hopefully Phillip had more shells in the house, or the Indians were going to stay away. She broke the rifle the way he had shown her, then loaded the remaining six shells before trooping back toward the house. The sun was dipping over the mountain range, touching each blue and white shoulder with purple fingers. Lynne paused to watch, feeling her soul fill with the color and peaceful beauty of the scene.

Inside the cabin, she was disappointed to find Phillip had not returned. As she replaced the rifle on its rack, she noticed the old

Spenser was gone from below it. Of course, Phillip had returned and taken it with him. Perhaps he was hunting. The antelope was nearly gone and it would be nice to have some fresh meat. With Indians about he may have needed it to feel safe while he was cooling off. She smiled, remembering the reason he had left her. He would be home before dark. Singing, she set to work baking bread to finish out the meal.

Bob snorted and he dropped off, holding a hand over his muzzle to signal the big stallion not to whinny. There were only four tee-pees. He felt the same emotions the young Indians stirred in him. These were not members of a war party, only desperate people trying to survive.

Warily he led the horse with its load of meat into the clearing. An old squaw was the first to notice him, but instead of giving a warning, she merely tracked his approach with blue filmed eyes. Only when he was in the middle of the village did a brave rise to bar his way, rifle in hand.

Phillip raised both empty hands, making it clear he meant no harm. Children and more old people stepped forward. At the end of the temporary village, a single tee-pee stood apart, smoke rising from the top of its ornamental sides. Slowly, so as not to startle anyone into regrettable action, Phillip led his horse and his offering forward to present to the chief or medicine man.

She heard steps on the porch and let the skillet rest on the stove, the bread still inside. Running she started to swing the door wide, ready to welcome Phillip with a warm hello and kiss. But the sound of another footfall made her hesitate. Nervously she backed away from the door, stepped back to the wall and removed the rifle. The bolt had been thrown on both doors, but in the stillness she heard a hand on the outside, tugging at the latchstring.

Indians. Frightened, Lynne wondered how many were outside. She wanted to look, but her heart was pounding so hard she was afraid she would not be able to peer through the small opening. What if they had Phillip?

It was so dark, even pressed against the door she could see nothing. Finally she heard one of the horses whinny from the barn, heard Beulah's loud bellow. Without hesitating, she placed the gun against the opening and fired.

There was a loud shuffling of feet on the porch outside, the eerie scream of pain from the direction of the barn. Shaking, she again peered through the hole, avoiding the smoking edge of it. There were three of them, moving like shadows in the twilight. Two were helping a third that they held between them and she was relieved to notice they were only taking their own, big-ribbed horses. Lynne could not help but wince as she saw them lift a short man onto his horse. She expected to hear the whiz of an arrow, the sound of rifles firing back at her. Instead she noticed without wanting to that the wounded one fell forward onto the neck of his horse and the other two seemed unable to hold him.

It only took a minute to decide. She opened the oven to remove the enamel ware baker, turned the cornbread out into a pie tin and set it down on top of the bubbling pot roast. Holding the hot roaster in the feed sack on her hip, she lifted the bolt on the door and stepped through, depositing the meal on the porch before stepping back in and grabbing the rifle.

"Wait." The three riders turned at her voice. Shaking, she knew that if they chose to fire at her, she would be as dead as any of the unfortunates along the stage trail. One man helped to steady the wounded rider, backed both horses out of range. The third man sat staring at her, his face shrouded by the dark. Lynne motioned toward the food with the end of her rifle, the way she had watched Phillip motion to the boys earlier that day.

The Indian dropped to the ground silently, approached the porch warily, his hands held clearly out to his side. He stared at the girl, then the smell of the meat roast told him the rest. Warily he lifted the food and turned to vault back onto his horse's blanket. Holding a hand up he turned and all three rode out of sight.

In the village, Phillip had deposited the young steer and most of the tribe were busy skinning and butchering the kill. The medicine man stood aside as Phillip peered down at the broken boy. The arm had been set, but the branches were short and curved. Wordlessly he pulled the thin planks from his saddle underneath his rifle and handed them to the chief, pointing to the arm with them. The old Indian stared at him in surprise, then grunted and bent to rework the brace. At his command, others brought the cowhide and began to work it to remove raw strips of leather.

An old woman tapped the back of his head and Phillip winced. The others laughed and whispered in turn. Only when the boy's brace was reworked did the medicine man walk over to touch the white bandage himself. Phillip wished he understood Ute, but in broken English and a little Sioux, they were able to talk. While the medicine man cut and removed the mysterious white bandage from his head, the old woman watched. As soon as it was gone, Phillip smiled as she put it on her own head and ran around in a circle laughing.

He was ready to ride when the three braves returned. Instinctively he drew his pistol and pointed at them as the tired warriors lifted a wounded brave between them and carried him toward the medicine tent. When he saw the enamel pan, Phillip swore. But before he could fire, the old squaw with the white bandage stepped between them. In broken language he asked the questions, swore in surprise at their answer. Only after he had shielded his weapon did the two bring their wounded companion forward.

She sat with the rifle across her lap, the lamp burning behind her shoulder. Tired and hungry, she rinsed an unpeeled potato and stoically gnawed on it from time to time. Worried, she berated herself for the hundredth time. What kind of pioneer wife was she, to feed the men who might have kidnapped or killed her own husband? For if Phillip were all right, he surely would have returned by now.

Indians were marauders, thieves. Hadn't she heard nothing else on the long trip west? So why did she feel she had to feed men who had come to steal from them. Once again she said a prayer.

She heard the sound of the rowel on the porch before anything else. Swallowing, brushing at tears of relief, she ran to hold the bolt on the door. At his loud rap, she swung it open, then flung herself into his arms.

Phillip held her to him, felt the strum of her heart against his own. With the palm of his hand, he molded her features in the darkened doorway, used the same hand to turn her mouth beneath his own. Only after the long, sweet kiss was over, did he release her. She still clung to his neck, but he brought hands to her waist to lift her away from him. Teasingly he began.

"Enough of that. Let's eat, I'm starved." He brushed a hand across his mouth to hide his smile as she looked confused. "Didn't I smell pot roast earlier?"

Nervously Lynne backed toward the stove, looked at the cool top of it where only the old coffee pot and the empty skillet remained. Fool, why hadn't she thought to make more food? In the hour, or was it two, that she had sat here waiting for his return, she could have made another meal. True there wasn't a roaster, but she could have cooked something in the pan.

The doctor had emphasized that she should only serve him bland foods, but to make sure he ate every meal, ate good, and took it easy. In the flickering light she stared at him, tried to decide how she could ever tell him the truth. It was then that she noticed. Where he had removed his hat, his brown hair was clearly exposed.

"Oh, here's the bark for tea. My head is killing me so if you could make it soon."

Wordlessly she turned and scooped up a small pan of water and set it on the stove, then added wood and shook out the ashes to stir up a blaze in the fire box. All the time she worked, she stole glances toward him. Cautiously she took some bark from the small leather pouch on the table, rubbing it between her fingers to break into papery shreds on top of the smooth water.

"I was worried, you were so late coming back." She tried, but all her wasted worry for this smiling brute gave the words an edge.

"Where were you?"

He studied the familiar pose, both hands on her hips, her brows raised in question, her quick-silver eyes studying his every expression. It would be fun to aggravate her more, drag out the drama. But there was an edge to her glance that made him cautious about teasing her too much.

"I saw Indian sign down by the creek. Came back for my gun and Bob."

She bit her lip, the vision of the scraggly Indians fresh in her mind. "Did they surprise you while you were bathing?" Suddenly she could see the three men, lying sprawled and dead on the banks of the creek. For some reason, it made her heart pound. Why, when Phillip was safe?

"It was too cold to bathe, even for me. Snow run-off." He wrinkled his nose, dropped a hand to his stomach and rubbed it. "Aren't you going to get me some grub?"

Flustered, Lynne turned back, opencd the empty oven, held a hand over the simmering water. If she had any eggs, she could scramble some, serve them with bread. If she had any bread.

"There's not any." She winced, waited for him to yell. Instead he looked hurt, rose to his feet and picked up his hat. As he settled it on his head, he eyed her with disbelief. She watched in amazement as he stepped out the door, letting it bang closed behind him.

For several minutes she waited, her hand over her pounding heart. The food had seemed so unimportant before. How could she explain to him that she didn't think, had only wanted to make up for her crime of shooting one of the pathetic strangers? Food was the only thing she had had to offer. Could she convince him how much it hurt her, how sick she felt, knowing that she had wounded a man, hurt him, maybe killed him. What if he were the father of the little boy with the broken arm? Surely Phillip would forgive her.

He stepped in through the door, straight to the stove, setting something down. She moved aside as he entered, turned in amazement to see the bright color of the blue and white metal pot on her stove. The bright speckles seemed to glimmer through her tears. Had he known all along? Had he killed them and recovered her pan? Did he think that would please her, his lightning reflexes against three poor starving Indians?

Righteously she stormed toward the stove, lifted the lid from the pot and turned to shout at him. He was laughing. For a moment she wanted to hit him with the pot lid, but his head was hurt enough. Then she realized something was wrong. Turning she looked into the almost empty kettle. In its cool bottom rested her pie pan. As she lifted it out, she was surprised by the two red steaks lying inside.

"Now, if you'll fry me some meat, I'll tell you my tale. When dinners on the table, you can tell me yours."

Too astonished to argue, she set to work, salting the thick steaks, then dropping them into the big skillet. She snagged an onion and couple of potatoes to slice up.

"Like I said, I saw tracks. Saddled Bob and rode them down. Too dangerous having Indians around and not knowing where." He noticed how wide her eyes were, how intense her curiosity, even as she tended to getting his meal.

"How did you get the pan? Did you shoot them?"

He ignored the flashing knife in her hand, stepped over to pour the hot headache potion into a mug. He stared down at her, even as he drank it, amazed at how angry she was at the thought that he might have hurt one of her Indians. Hell, she was the one who had shot one of them, not him. "Nope."

She let her lashes drop to hide the anger in her eyes and he dipped to kiss her cheek, even as he refilled the cup. Only when he was seated back at the table did he continue to talk.

"They're a poor lot, that's for sure. You seemed so worried about the boy and all, well, I took some decent planks, figured I'd leave them on the edge of their camp. Indians are great scavengers."

She left the stove, dropped onto the bench across from him, too excited to wait any longer. "Did you see the little boy? Was he all right?" She swallowed, then brought her hands up to cover her mouth. Only after breathing deeply did she manage to mumble. "What about the one I shot?"

He leaned forward, pulled her hands down, squeezing gently. How could a man deal with a wife who had such a tender heart? It made a fellow feel all squeezed up inside.

"They're both fine," he croaked, then cleared his throat. "Now see to my dinner before you burn it." Lynne brought his hand to her lips and kissed it, then laughing nervously rose to turn the meat. He used the time to wipe his eyes. The strange tea was making them water.

"Yeah, medicine man had seen to it like I told you. But there wasn't any decent wood. He seemed grateful for the planks."

"You waited and watched, after you left the wood." She put down the onion, lifted her apron to blow her nose. Darn onions always made her eyes water.

"Not exactly." He watched her, wondering if she knew how kissable she looked when she cried. "There were only a few of them, so I rode in to camp to see for myself."

She dropped her apron and raised a hand to her throat. "They might have killed you."

He laughed. "A dead shot like me?"

She shifted nervously, stabbing at the steaks, removing them from the skillet and adding the onion.

"Anyway, I'd spotted a young steer on the ride over. Took it in sort of as a peace offering. Poor people. They've been decimated by white men, now by the Apache's, Crowe's and other Indians the whites are forcing onto their land. Their peaceable folks mainly. But they don't have a lot of options left."

She sliced the potatoes quickly, eager to finish cooking and sit down beside him. "Is that where you got the willow?"

"Yeah, old man told me their sorrows while he tended the boy." He raised a hand to brush through his curly dark hair and again Lynne wondered about the bandage. "Even mended my cracked skull right. Laughed at what a bungle job the quack in Butte made of it."

She nodded. "Then he must be a very smart medicine man. Did it still hurt on your ride home?"

She filled a plate with the steak and onion, carried it to him as she fried the potatoes. While beside him, she examined the thin strip of leather that bound the base of his skull and traveled around his forehead. Satisfied she finished cooking.

He was quiet while he ate and so she talked. It was surprising how easy it was to tell about shooting the man. Remembering how he leaned over the horse's neck wasn't easy. He lifted his fork from the plate as she added the potatoes, his eyes dark and knowing. "You did right. They might have been war-like Apache's or murdering Crowe's. Besides, a hungry man is a dangerous man. Out here, you don't get to take all day to decide before you shoot."

She sank onto the bench across from him, stared down at her

food and knew she could not eat it.

"He was all right?" she asked.

"Your shot creased his skull. If it's as hard as mine, he should be on his feet tomorrow. They're just plumb fagged out with hunger, that's why he fainted." He tilted back on the bench, full from all the food, uncertain if the red meat would remain on his stomach.

In the silence, both could clearly see the ragged Indians. He dropped a hand to play with her small fingers. "That was a foolish thing you did, carrying food outside to them."

She tugged at her fingers, but he kept them trapped. "More foolish than riding alone into their camp?" she asked.

He shook his head, folding her small hand inside his own.

"What will happen to them?"

"Well, that depends on how you feel. I don't have any wranglers, and spring calving time is here. Figured if they'd stay and work, they could take a beef as they needed, stay long enough to plant some vegetables and grain."

He studied her, relieved by her big grin.

"Oh Phillip." She slid from the bench and onto his lap, circling his neck with her arm.

"You know most folks will figure we're plumb crazy."

"Most folks don't matter. It's the Christian thing to do." She pressed his head against her chest, rubbed through the dark curls.

He buried himself there for a minute, let an arm circle her waist even as he rested his head on the soft pillow of her young breasts. A man could grow awfully soft with a woman to encourage him in his foolishness.

He set her off his lap, rose and grunted. "I've got to tend to Bob, see to the rest of the stock. You eat missy and get some sleep."

"But now the Indians are our friends?"

He stared at her, mesmerized by her dark lashes, her soft pouty lips. How could he explain it wasn't Indians he was afraid of? "Best to be sure."

The Indians were full of surprises. Phillip had warned her they were like children, but she still could not get over in how many ways they were the same. Even the oldest ones were shy and trusting. They were quick to figure out what she wanted if she asked one of the squaws to carry water or help plow the field. They never complained or argued. But if she turned her back they would stop working and sit down to talk among themselves. It was a good thing she had grown up the oldest girl in an Irish household. She felt no qualms at setting them back to work or scolding them when they did something wrong.

The Indian children were full of laughter and mischief. Unlike her brothers and sisters who had always been given chores, the older Indians didn't seem to expect their children to work. All day they played, running in circles, stalking young rabbits, teasing the calf or wild horses. One would have thought the boy with the broken arm would have been enough of a warning for the rest of them, but several times Phillip or one of the braves would have to stop working to rescue one of the young boys from the corral after being thrown by one of the green broke mounts. Phillip never seemed surprised or upset by their actions, just smiled at them, wiping the dirt from the children and letting them loose.

The older Indians were great with the animals. Riding even the greenest horse until it would follow their wordless commands, answer to just the pressure of their knees or heels. Lynne rode out with the group once to secure some of the cattle. Phillip planned to brand the new calves and had argued that he was well enough to ride with them. Lynne had argued if he was still too ill to share her bed, he was too ill to be herding animals. It shocked her when he laughed and let her ride off with the two Indians. She actually felt foolish in her cut-off jeans, with his revolvers belted around her waist. But she was proud to be able to ride back with six cows, two of which were still heavy with calf.

By the end of the week, they had all become used to each other's ways. The women no longer clucked their tongues at her funny clothes, the braves no longer shook their heads when Phillip made her stand and shoot at targets. It seemed as though they had always been part of the Gant ranch.

When Shorty and Banes rode up to the ranch, their necks stiff and hair bristling, it was Lynne who laughingly welcomed them, reassured them of their harmless neighbor's ways. But the Indians were wary of the other white men and seemed to vanish from the ranch while they were there.

"People will talk." Shorty warned.

Phillip nodded, relieved to be able to do so without feeling a sick quivers in his stomach. "Some always do."

"Indians like to run sheep." Banes added, as though it were the worst thing that a person could ever do.

"Usually do."

"You could hire white men, there's good men in Helena, not all have work."

"Plan to see about hiring some next week. Lynne and I've

promised to meet Johnson and his Helga there next Friday. There's a dance or something, they wanted me to take Lynne to."

Lynne placed a large pie on the table. It was made from dried fruit, but already Banes' eyes were glittering and he had lifted his knife and fork in his hands beside his empty plate in anticipation. "You never said anything about the dance."

He raised his brows, dimpled in confusion. "Wasn't sure you'd want to go?"

"Not go dancing, but I love to dance."

He laughed and eyed the other two men. "Figures."

"You mean you weren't going to take me if you could get out of it."

She had set her hands on her hips, and the warning of danger was clear in the stormy gray of her eyes.

Shorty spoke for all of them. "Reckon that there warm apple pie tastes mighty good. Especially with some of that there milk."

Lynne looked at him, then caught the way Banes was eyeing it, his mouth all but drooling. Angrily she sliced it into four big quarters, heaping a big piece on each of the crusty miner's plates. Phillip let his tongue slip out and smooth his lips.

She didn't put any on his plate. He watched as Banes poured the cold milk over the pie and felt his own mouth water. She was capable of serving the whole thing to the two worthless bums.

"I don't know how to dance."

She dropped her hands, all the anger dropping away as quickly. She shoveled a slice of pie onto his plate, handed the pitcher of milk to him before sitting down beside him on the bench. "Well, you taught me to shoot and ride, I'd love to return the favor by teaching you."

He gulped, scooped up a bite of pie to sample before she could move it away. "There are always so many rough men at dances, very few women."

Lynne sat still, accepted the information, and turned to see Banes tilt his plate to drink the last of the milk and pie from it. Without hesitating, she sliced the remaining quarter and offered him a wedge.

"You don't feel well enough to protect me?"

He blushed, staring at the determined set of her little chin. Hell no, he could protect her, he just didn't want to share her. Especially when the other men knew how to dance and he didn't.

She tilted her head, let her chin rest in her hand as she studied her suddenly shy husband. She ran a finger around the edge of the pie pan, brought the thick sweet juice up to lick from her finger. The warm taste of cinnamon and sugar blended with the rich fruit and she claimed the remaining piece before Banes could ask for another.

Phillip stared at her, his eyes darkening even as his blood stirred. Impatiently he turned to stare at Shorty and Banes. "Reckon if you two are fed now, you could ride over the south range with Running Wolf and Sly Otter and bring in the cows who wintered there."

"You want us to work with them heathens."

"Yeah, if they'll put up with you two."

Shorty looked about to argue, then noticed the way Phillip was swallowing his pie and staring at his bride while she slowly chewed a bite of her own. He elbowed Banes. "Let's leave these two love birds to fight and coo. You and me got to earn our feed."

Neither bothered to get up to see their guests away. It was Lynne who spoke first. "Don't you think it's about time you let me teach you something?"

"You, teach me?" He growled.

She scooped the last bite of pie up, held it in front of him, and then slowly licked it from the spoon. She watched his hand shake as he studied her mouth.

He left his pie half-eaten, moved to pull her onto his lap and hungrily licked the pie from her lips. One hand moved to close over her firm young breast and he groaned as she let her own tongue tangle with his. For a moment he thought about clearing the table and taking her there, but she suddenly laughed and pulled free of his arms and roaming hands.

"First we dance, then you can test how well you're feeling."

Growling, he stood, ready to pull her back against him. She might protest at first, but her blood ran too hot to deny him.

As though reading his mind, she stacked the empty plates, reaching for his own. He snagged the abandoned pie. "Fine, I'll wash dishes while you finish your dessert. Then we'll practice dancing.' She said it as though he had nothing to say about the order of things and he grinned, rubbing the place where the rawhide strip had been for so long. Hell of a thing Johnson had warned him, to see a grown man bullied by a young slip of a girl. Laughing, he finished his pie and decided to accept his fate.

CHAPTER TWENTY-NINE

The trail to Helena was broad and well graded. The team of bays worked the ground as though they were thrilled to be free to run. Lynne drove the team for the first few miles, then gave the reins back to Phillip. He amazed her. Even her father would not have allowed her mother the freedom he showed her. Whatever she wanted, he merely shook his head, then did everything in his power to get for her. A woman could get drunk on the power of that kind of love.

She stared at his strong profile as he took the reins and guided the team toward the town. In the back of the wagon was the gown she had finished for the Swedish bride, as well as her latest long letter to mail to the children back east. Phillip had given her a box number the children could use to write her and she was more excited about the possibility of news from home than about the dance tonight.

Of course, she did have a new dress that she had made for the dance. Phillip had fussed when he had first seen it, and she had sewn a ruffled yoke from the gray material to fill the wide expanse the original gown had bared. After he had all but devoured every inch of flesh that was exposed by the gown, she had seen the reason in his argument. It looked more like a dress an old maid school teacher might wear then a rancher's young bride, but he had sworn it was still beautiful. He swore she was beautiful a lot lately. She laughed, turning to look at him shyly.

"What?" he growled, instantly excited by her blushing laugh.

"I was remembering how beautiful you told me my new dress looked."

He frowned. "Far too pretty for you to wear to a dance with a bunch of drunken miners. I'm crazy for letting you talk me in to this."

"Why? You dance beautifully. You'll be the best dancer there by far."

He smiled. "You made a great teacher."

After a few minutes, he looked across at where she sat, still softly smiling. "But what was so funny about my saying your dress was beautiful?"

She leaned against his arm, her eyes silver with laughter. "I was only wearing my petticoats when you said it."

He laughed, slipping an arm around to pull her closer. "That's why I enjoyed the dance lessons so much, you little nymph."

The streets were full of carriages and horses and Lynne was too excited by everything to sit still. Instead she swiveled on the seat, turning to look for their new friends the Johnsons. Phillip concentrated on navigating through the heavy traffic, waiting until they were in front of the Hotel Helena before pulling the team up. He jumped down and secured the reins, then turned to swing Lynne down to the boardwalk. He could not help but notice the men turning their way after catching a glimpse of the lovely woman and he hurried her inside to register. Only when he had her secure in a room upstairs did he return to take the wagon and horses to the stable.

Lynne paced the hotel room, furious at being shut away. She walked across to pull the blinds on the window and open the upper pane. The view of the hectic street was so exciting, she debated disobeying Phillip and walking down to meet him. What harm could it do for her to walk around town and visit the various stores? She had been able to do so in Butte without his complaining. Ida had even recommended that she visit the dry goods store here in order to take orders for more dresses to sew. How could she do her work if Phillip didn't want her to leave the hotel without him?

Even as she peered down at the street, two men across from the hotel looked up at the window and yelled. She watched in astonishment as two others rushed over to join them. Lynne smiled in amusement as the shortest man in the group waved his hand at her. The motion was like that of a small child who had just learned to wave bye-bye and it made her laugh. Quickly she waved back and the group below hooted and hollered.

The commotion drew others and she wondered what they were so excited about. It wasn't like she was the only woman in town. She could see two women standing along the street. One of them looked like Shy Fawn, the young Ute back at the ranch who was the mother of the boy with the broken arm. Fawn often came to the cabin to help Lynne in the garden, showing her how to make hills and rows and plant seeds.

The other woman was boldly dressed in a low-cut, yellow dress and for just a moment Lynne wondered if she were one of the women who worked in the many saloons they had passed on the drive into town. Even as she stared from one exciting stranger to another, the crowd's attention was diverted from her window. She followed their gaze and noted the stunning couple walking up the street. Helga in a bright red cape was strolling with her arm linked with that of Mr. Johnson.

Lynne leaned out the window and waved down to them. "Hello, Hello. Up here, Helga."

The tall Swedish girl stopped and tilted her head back to look up to her and smiled broadly, then raised a hand to wave. The red cape fell open to expose her stately figure and the crowd of men watching gave a collective gasp of pleasure. Johnson swore profusely and brought the cape back around her shoulder. Helga laughed in amusement at his possessiveness. Chuckling, Lynne backed into the room, knowing that Phillip might scold her if he caught her leaning out. But it was so much like watching a stage comedy, observing the actions of the residents of this unusual city.

When the impatient tap at the door finally came, Lynne rushed across to open it, only hesitating at the very last moment. "Who's there?"

"A devoted admirer, Miss McKinney."

Lynne leaned her back against the door, then took a steadying breath. She looked around the deserted hotel room, at the suitcase and carpet bag that waited to be unloaded. Surely Phillip had packed a hand gun in one of the two. But she didn't have time to search through it now. Besides, she remembered Mr. Owens voice from the stage. The large man had been most persistent, but always a gentleman. She hesitated with her hand on the doorknob, then reached up to remove her little gray hat, withdrawing the long steel hat pin to release it from on top of her neatly combed chignon.

She slipped the pin in her skirt, just beneath her hand as she opened the door and smiled. "Why, Mr. Owens, I did think I recognized your voice."

She stood blocking his entrance and smiled up at him. "But it's

Mrs. Gant, don't you remember, Mrs. Phillip Gant." She said the last for emphasis and extended a hand to shake his.

He looked into the hotel room, smiled lewdly and thought about stepping through the doorway and showing her a little mining town appreciation. At least if her gunslinger husband weren't home. "Mrs. Gant, of course, of course. And is Mr. Gant home."

Lynne stared down the hall behind the tall man, delighted to see the Johnson's just reaching the landing. She called to them, then stepped back and opened the door. Owens still hesitated, stared into the empty room beyond before entering, closely followed by the tall couple. Lynne felt shorter than usual and looked around the room, wishing there were somewhere for her guests to sit.

Mr. Owens walked over to the chair by the window, stared down and waved to the mob below who gave out with several unsavory cheers. The Johnson's looked around after Helga gave Lynne a little hug and decided to sit on the edge of the bed. Lynne was just closing the door when Phillip came bounding up the stairs, swearing as he came. He pushed his way in past her, then whirled around the room and ran over to the window to yell a few choice words at the crowd. Owens leaned forward to allow him room, then slipped surreptitiously from the chair to stand near the head of the bed on the side opposite the Johnsons.

Lynne heard the crowd mutter and then the noise from the street below began to fade. He turned to stare at her, his eyes black and flat. When she flashed angry eyes on him for his rude entrance, he swept past her to the big man huddling at the head of the bed. Helga smiled nervously and Johnson laughed out loud. "Well, a big hello to you too Gant."

Phillip snorted and stood, his hands dropping from the guns beneath his coat. "Sorry Johnson, guess I just don't like having a

town full of randy miners hollering obscene things up at my wife."
He flicked angry eyes across at Owens before stepping back toward
Lynne. He held out a possessive arm but she sidestepped his
embrace and stood glaring at him.

"That doesn't excuse your conduct. I'm sure the men did not
mean any offense to me."

He stared at her, took in the bright color in her cheeks, the cool
gray eyes. "I hadn't expected to return to a full hotel room, either."
He growled and watched the color spread into a rosy glow as she
ducked her head. The last few miles of the ride, he had proposed
doing a few things in the room that only honeymooners were
permitted to do. She shrugged her shoulders in apology, then
stepped closer.

This time when he held out his arm, she slipped into its
protection.

Helga laughed gaily. "So pretty."

Both looked across at her, surprised by her English. It was
Johnson's turn to look embarrassed. "Yeah, well, I figure how she's
going to be a mother, she'll need to learn her some good English to
teach the sprout."

Lynne beamed at the beautiful blonde and rushed over to hug
and congratulate her. "I wondered if it might be wise to leave some
extra room in your dress. Here, let me show it to you."

The two women stood talking by the dresser. Phillip held out a
hand to shake Johnson's hand and congratulate him. Owens moved
cautiously from the corner and extended his hand as well. "Way to
go, Mister, that sure didn't take you long."

Both men glared at him and the big man dropped his hand and
backed toward the hotel door. Lynne looked up and smiled as she
watched the clumsy man fumbling for the doorknob. When Phillip

took a step forward, the other opened the door and slipped out with a less than hearty good-bye. Helga said something in Swedish and Lynne smiled. Some things needed no translation.

Three hours later, they returned to the hotel room alone to get ready for the party. The Johnson's had promised to come by their room when it was time to leave so they wouldn't have to worry about finding the place. Lynne stared at the tub of hot water that had been rolled to the room and filled by room service in their absence. As much as she had enjoyed the trip around Helena and the meal in the Hotel dining room, she was relieved to be rid of the Johnson's for a few hours.

She looked shyly over her shoulder as she heard Phillip turn the key in the lock. She again removed her hat, this time leaving the pin in its cloth as she stripped off her gloves. She watched him strip out of his black suit coat as he walked across to lower the blinds on the window.

She laughed as she rushed to unbutton the long row of buttons on her blue day dress, laughing louder as Phillip mirrored her efforts on his white shirt. Both finished with all but their boots and socks and sank on the edge of the bed to struggle with them, laughing harder and harder with each move. Impetuously he pulled her against him, smothering her laughing mouth with kisses. Lynne grew still as his kisses grew more ardent. When he dipped his head to her breast, she lifted her little gray boot and trailed it against his bare calf. He smiled wickedly at her and sat up on the bed, rolling her to sit spread legged across his lap. Smiling she crossed her legs behind him on the bed, pulling closer until they were joined.

Languidly she leaned backward, her lashes sweeping down to veil the molten silver in her eyes. He moved sharply and her eyes flew open. He smiled, his teeth white and sharp and hungry and she gasped with delight.

They had made love, bathed, slept, made love again, then half-bathed in the cool water before dressing for the party. Even so, Lynne hated to leave the privacy of their room and join the others. Since the Indians had settled in on the ranch, they no longer had the privacy they needed, someone always seemed to show up to interrupt any intimate moments. Also, she doubted she had enough energy to dance around the room once, let alone the dozens and dozens of dances Helga had warned her about.

"Theze men, thezes danzing fools."

Johnson had added. "Well, they don't have enough women, so a real lady is a treat for any of them. It's considered unforgivable to keep a wife to just yourself, when everyone else has to dance with a fella."

Phillip had scowled. Lynne wondered if he would be able to handle watching her dance with friends and strangers. He had always seemed jealous, even of Shorty and Banes paying compliments to her. She hoped he would leave his gun and gun belt behind.

When they both stood ready, she leaned gently against him staring at their reflections in the mirror. He was dressed in his starched white shirt and black coat, a thin string tie around his neck, his hair carefully combed and parted, his face clean shaven. He tapped his new brown bowler and smiled at her.

She made him think of a porcelain doll, her features and gown were so perfect. He gazed lovingly at the silver striped gown, her hair draped heavily against her neck after being drawn up and down in a smooth swell that she had fastened with the pearly combs that had been her mother's. The gray matched her eyes, her brown hair and dark brown lashes emphasized her cool beauty. Phillip swallowed, unsure if he could bear to watch anyone dance with her.

He bent to store his guns in the dresser, then drew a pistol and made sure the chamber was loaded. When certain, he took the handbag she had carefully sewn to match her dress, and slid the weapon inside before drawing the strings. He handed it to her, watching as she frowned at the great weight.

"Maybe we should just stay home."

He smiled, his lips pursed to consider it. "Probably should, but since you've ridden this poor horse to death, reckon we better go out and dance a while to rest him up." She swung at his arm, delighted by his suggestion, when there was a rap at the door.

The dance was being held in the empty floor of a new building. It was obvious from the bar and mirror at one end that it would soon be a new saloon. But the city fathers had offered the hall for a dance and the few ladies in town had leaped at the possibility to decorate it with spring blooms and pine boughs. A platform had been erected at one end, and a band was already tuning up. The bar was serving its original purpose, and although one end had been appropriated for cake and punch, the other held a wide variety of jugs and jars that had been provided by those attending the dance.

One interesting feature of the dance was a stack of tea towels that were being doled out as guests arrived, carefully tied around half the waists to mark the "heifers" at the dance. Lynne and Helga joined the dozen women near the far wall. They waited in anticipation for the first dance, which would be couples only.

Lynne eyed Phillip's tall, slim form in the room full of barrel shaped and spindly men. Her stomach tightened with anticipation. Even though every dance they had practiced at home had ended with them both crazy with desire, she had been impressed at the beginnings of each by his natural grace and ear for music that made them step together whether dancing a waltz or a polka. She felt flames sweep up her neck, just imagining those lewd performances within the closed doors of their small cabin. Looking around, she was convinced that she had married the handsomest man in Montana. The ladies beside her were just as nervous, following the conductors instructions, they sorted themselves out into a single line.

She looked up as he stepped into line across from her, his dark eyes glowing with appreciation. She smiled at him, then placed her trembling hand into his. She was surprised to feel his palm was damp, his hand trembled, as he positioned her hand on his shoulder while she tried to get ready. The heavy purse thumped against his side. Without hesitation he shoved it beneath a suspender and inside the waist of his pants. Lynne frowned, then raised her hand to his shoulder again.

The five men in the band began playing and the group swept out across the big floor in a Virginia reel. Suddenly the setting disappeared and Lynne was carried away by the magic she always felt in the arms of her lover.

Phillip smiled down into her eyes, as entranced by the beauty of her heart-shaped face as by the grace with which she circled the floor in his arms. When the dance ended, he drew her instinctively close into his arms and leaned to kiss her forehead. They stood there clinging, as all the others changed partners, including Johnson and Helga. A man timidly reached over to tap Phillip's shoulder and he gave the man a dark glare. But all the others stared at Phillip in disapproval.

Johnson called to him. Reluctantly he relinquished her, staring with the threat of death in his eyes as the shorter man moved into position. Lynne wiped her hands on her skirt, then placed one on the small man's shoulder, the other hand in his as the band struck up Turkey in the Straw. This time, the caller led the group in the calls for the square. From time to time, Lynne managed to catch Phillip's eye. Grumpily he stood by the bar. Lynne frowned as she realized it wasn't the end with punch and cake.

Her partner was changed with each call and she was surprised when she ended the rapid dance facing the same little man. The next to step up was nearly Phillip's size, with warm, ingratiating manners. She noticed how his face changed to a poker blank as Phillip gave him his familiar scowl. She smiled, then sighed as they swept around in a rapid Polka.

When a waltz was announced, she was relieved to line up and see her husband elbow the stuffy Owens out of position across from her. The man started to protest, then turned to angrily stomp from the floor. She grinned and then squealed as Phillip swept her off her feet to lift and swing as they started off. Then she became stiffly polite, annoyed by his drinking.

He noticed and complained. "You think you could watch me dance with dozens of pretty girls without getting jealous."

She tried to imagine it, but grew so angry at the thought that she refused to smile at him. "Who, Helga?"

He shrugged, "Helga, the girl in yellow, the other in pink.

Anyone but you. Wouldn't you feel jealous?"

Lynne waltzed and then scolded. "You can dance with one of the men if you are so unhappy about the line moving."

He snorted then reached across to kiss her full on the mouth before letting go of her hands and backing out of reach. She pretended to be shocked, but enjoyed the tribute.

By the tenth dance, she understood what Helga had complained about. By now most of the heifers had been drafted and pulled out onto the floor to complete the numbers. The room was hot from the crush of bodies and everyone had grown damp with perspiration. Waves of heat and odor threatened to suffocate her. Some of the men smelled too sweet, from fancy colognes and toilet water. Others smelled of leather, smoke, horse sweat and the foul fumes of the smelter. The floor was so crowded, she lost sight of Phillip in the hustle. It was then she looked up to see a dark handsome man facing her. Only it wasn't Phillip.

As Tarn Micheals drew her across and led her in another rapid polka, she closed her eyes and trembled, but not from excitement. She hoped Phillip was watching. If the tall Irishman knew how many times he had complained about the treacherous attack in Butte, he would never have shown his face inside the dance hall.

She managed to raise her head and her voice to shout and proceeded to scold the Irishman before breaking free and heading toward the edge of the floor where she had last seen Phillip. The tall man had no intention of letting her go. He caught at her arm and would have pulled her back onto the floor but a strong hand blocked him. Before he could react, a heavy weight swung out and struck him on the side of the head. Lynne watched in horror as blood sprang from the big Irishman's head, rapidly covering the floor in wet spray.

She looked up, shocked to see the fury in his face as Phillip drew her off the floor. She would have pulled away again but he managed to loop his hand around her waist and lifted her off the floor like a giant sack of potatoes.

Only when he had toted her to where the door opened onto the cool clear night air did he set her down and Lynne exploded in anger. "How dare you attack an unarmed man, even an animal like Tarn Micheals?"

He breathed, shaking his head in the clear air, trying to shake free of the three whiskeys, the fever that came from watching his bride dance around the room without him.

Trembling with anger, she reached over to grab her purse, ignoring the additional red color, then stepped out into the cool air. "Humans are better than cave men, or haven't you heard of civilization."

She heard the noise before she saw him coming. Owens was charging like a bull from the other side of the room where he had been drinking. His head was lowered, face red with whiskey and rage. Instinctively Lynne reached inside the tight drawstrings of her bag. Phillip spun to face the sound, gracefully ready with a solid right fist that brought the head up, followed with a thudding left that hit the big farmer in the middle and raised him the rest of the way.

Suddenly someone inside screamed. There was a shot and Lynne watched, clutching her stomach with her left hand as others screamed and shouted and the floor was cleared. As though in slow motion, the big body of Owens was falling backward. For a second Lynne wondered if it was he who had been shot, but then another bullet hit the door to the right of Phillip and just above her own head.

Phillip froze, his hands to his side, ready in his gunman's pose, his hands hanging above empty air. Lynne didn't hesitate, sprang forward beside him, the gun cocked and ready. Tarn stood, bloody and reeling, and fired again. The bullet tore across the top of Phillip's ear and he raised a hand to protect what was left.

Lynne fired.

Another woman screamed and the men at the dance divided into two lines, armed and unarmed, pushing the real women to safety behind them. Lynne stared in at the wounded man. It seemed to take decades but he was crashing to his knees, his head already bloodied, his mouth calling obscenities and curses even as he fell, his guns continuing to fire even as his body thudded lifeless on the dance floor. Somehow Phillip had taken the gun from her limp hands, reached for her but Lynne was running forward.

In shock she knelt on the floor, her knee dipping into the spreading pool of blood as she pushed at the big shoulder to turn the body. Phillip had entered the dance hall, the gun once again tucked at his waist. In disbelief she stared at the dark circle that covered the front of the Irishman's shirt, leaned down to push the blood back inside the gaping wound, heard him whisper a name as he died.

She squatted back on her heels, shocked to hear the high, keening wail that split the silence. This time when Phillip tugged at her, and lifted her into his arms she did not struggle. Instead she pushed in against his neck, tried to close her mind to the dark sight and smell of death.

CHAPTER THIRTY

Helga sat beside the bed, a damp cloth in her hand as she wiped Lynne's face clean. Somehow, someone had removed the bloody, sweaty dress and she now lay beneath a thin sheet in only her underclothes. The chemise lay loosely tied, her breasts heaving as the terrified voice that had awakened her died down. Frantically, Lynne opened her eyes, stared at the tall buxom blonde and searched for Phillip.

"Where is he?"

"He is gone for doctor."

Lynne raised her hand, saw the blood on her fingers and shivered in revulsion. She sat up, moving as though the hand were some threatening object, not part of her own body. Sensibly Helga took the hand and dipped it into the basin. Entranced, Lynne watched the clean surface of the water change to red.

The men entered without either woman hearing them. Phillip was shocked by the wild, disheveled beauty of his bride, the crazy look in her eyes as she stared at the basin Helga held. He was not sure he could bear to hear the dead man's name on her lips again, knew he could not bear to leave her alone.

The doctor raised bushy brows and gave a drunken salute to Phillip's wife's charms. For once, the words did not provoke the killing cloud that had blinded him all day. He had donned his gun belt as soon as they were back in the room, and automatically he checked to make sure the handles of both weapons were in reach.

The doctor caught the warning, drunk though he was, and stepped forward slightly sobered to tend to the girl. He gave a leering smile to the beautifully formed Helga as she rose to move out of the way.

The doctor sat on the bed, took Lynne's wrist as though listening to her pulse, then leaned forward to place his grizzled head on her half-bare bosom, his lips forming a loose smile. Disgusted, Phillip jerked him up and threw him out the door. Johnson stood in the hallway and shoved the humbug in a spin down the hall. Then Johnson welcomed Helga into his embrace, wrapping her bright red cloak around her. Lynne closed her eyes in revulsion at the color of the cape and began a soft whine through barely open lips.

Phillip closed and locked the door on all of them. Now she was awake, maybe he could reason with her. But her eyes held a new fear, a distant place where he knew she now walked all alone. Groaning, he ran a hand through his thick hair, let his hand rest on the gun belt before unbuckling and hanging it on the chair.

It was his fault that she had killed a man. Even though she had told him she did not love the Irishman, just the sound of her high wail of grief had made him ache with the possibility that she had cared for the man without knowing it.

She had even called out that clown Owens name in her unconscious terror. Sighing, Phillip looked around, then walked over toward the bed.

Through her blurred eyes she saw the tall dark man approach the bed and a scream of terror tore from her throat as she thought Tarn Micheals was walking from the grave, heartless and bloody, to seek revenge. His hand reached out to grab her and she screamed and screamed again, struggling against this new terror.

Phillip brought her body beneath him, her mouth under his hand, smothering her scream. She struggled until she was breathless and he stared at the whites of her eyes, the head twisted back from him. Sighing, he released her mouth, heard her ragged gasps for breath. Then felt her soft body dissolve into sobs as he kissed her cheek, muttered her name over and over again.

Lynne was lost in darkness. Everywhere around her bodies whirled and spun to wild music, jarring against her over and over as they danced away. First her mother swept by, eyes blind in madness, body nude and streaked with red where she had tried to claw the blood and shame from inside herself. Then the faces of her brother Sean and her father, moldy from the grave, beautiful strong bodies crushed and mangled beneath the heavy weight of the wall that had fallen on them. Next she saw a blonde cowboy, his hair soft, eyes cold blue, thin body shivering with anticipation as his slim hands hovered over his guns. But as he whirled by, the back of his head was gone and blood and gore dripped down over his shirt.

Some of the dancers she could put no name to. Even children were at the ghoulish dance. Her own lost little brother and baby sister, golden then stained red with death. Babies, distorted and blotched with fever, whirled from where they had been abandoned in mass graves. Settlers, pierced with arrows, riddled with black wounds promenaded past. Even Indians danced, young and old, some pierced with bullets, others with tiny bodies broken at odd angles. Lynne turned, trying to keep each from drawing her into a dance, searching the crowd for the face of the man she loved.

Finally from the darkness a tall figure emerged, Darkly handsome, wicked charm showed in his dimples as he smiled at her, then pulled a tall, shy Bonnie past. Only when that dance was over, did the apparition turn toward her. She struggled past him, past the big buffoon that had grabbed at her on the stage. He bellowed and fell away, backward into the darkness and she was drawn into the arms of the apparition. He grinned down at her, his laugh loud, his lips moving to utter vile curses, and when she put a hand up to push him away her hand sank into the bloody hole where his heart should have been.

Phillip lay beside the sweat soaked girl, listening to her rambling and moaning. Had he not journeyed to this same dark place dozens of times in the past? He knew the faces she was seeing, the horrible parade of dead and dying. Even in his fear for her, he did not know if he could journey there again.

But her body was heaving, her sobs tearing at him, finally her scream was in his ear and he was running, running into the darkness to find her. He brought her body beneath him, his lips covering her throat, her eyes, and her petal soft skin as he desperately called her name.   Wildly she clung to him, moved so that her body covered his, her limbs tangled and squeezed and drew him close. Again he rolled on top, thrust deep inside her, called her name.

At first Lynne saw the stranger, the Montana man who had ordered a bride. But as she walked closer she saw more than new clothes, the bad haircut. When he smiled, his eyes were dark and cold as death. Frightened, she wanted to turn back, to run anywhere but toward his arms. She smelled gun smoke, heard men scream, then saw him stagger toward her in the dark, his head strangely white, and his face beaten and bloodied. Even his beautiful body was bruised and streaked with pain. But he was calling for her, calling and crying her name. Confused she reached out, tried to see past the black emptiness of his eyes.

Softly she felt the brush of wings, whispering through the air, shushing her and guiding her back from the terrors. She heard her mother's soft voice crooning to her from a great distance, then a deeper voice, male and strong and alive.

From nowhere there was a cloud of feathers spilling like snow over the ground, covering the blood and the emptiness with light and warmth. Hungrily she clung to her husband, found his name on her lips, swirled and danced with him in fluid grace among the glowing world of white. Everywhere was new and clean and perfect, suddenly green with life and promise. And among all the light she saw the warm glow of love in the golden brown of his eyes and felt at peace.

Finally she was safe. Phillip had brought her from darkness to glory once again.

EPILOGUE

The twins, Tom and Jim, and Mary Anne would be arriving at the end of September. She had drawn solace from the letter so many times in the past months that it was a wonder the paper held together. Still she sat at the hotel table writing, intent on sharing each of the events since the last letter.

The battle at Little Big Horn had occurred in June. Fortunately Tom had gotten her first letter and had written that they would follow Phillip's advice and wait until the end of summer before beginning their journey. Since July she had not had another letter. Since Custer's defeat, scattered bands of Sioux, Cheyenne and Crowe had crossed their lands. Perhaps because of their own little band of Indians, the nomads had never attacked the ranch, taking only an occasional cow or horse as they crossed. Lynne always grew furious and fussed about the thefts, but her gentle husband Phillip would only smile and say he was glad to get off so easy.

There was a light tap on the door and she opened it to the same shy Indian who had brought her bath water on her first journey through Ogden. As soon as the girl left, Lynne stripped out of the dust-laden shirt and jeans that she had worn on the trail. Even though her body had grown hard with the exercise of riding daily on the ranch, driving cattle from the Beaver Head down the Virginia City-Corinne Road had left every inch of her sore and aching.

Only when she was in the tub did she lift the paper and pencil to continue writing. She heard the key turn in the door, barely glanced up to see her handsome husband striding excitedly into the room. She ignored him, merely sinking lower in the tub to escape his roaming eyes and finish her latest letter. The tablet was full of them, none mailed after the July departure date by the Wimberlys and their precious cargo of loved ones.

Phillip laughed at her and sank down behind the tub to lather her back as she leaned forward and finished. She had wanted to let the children know that most of the Indians she had told them of would not be going back to the ranch. Now they were back in Utah, they planned to find their own families. Only Running Wolf, Broken Wing and Shy Fawn would be returning to the Beaverhead with them.

Phillip took the tablet away as she added the date at the end. "I sold the cattle. The army is looking at the string of horses. It should be enough to buy another section of land."

She leaned back against him, smiling up to kiss his scratchy chin. He let a hand dip to circle her breast, then compared it to the other. Both were definitely larger. He nibbled an ear, dipped his soapy hand along the slightly rounded curve of her stomach. He felt a special thrill, wondered if she had any suspicion of her condition. Of course he probably should have left her back in Montana, but he could not bear to think of her alone in the cabin with only scattered and untrustworthy neighbors to look after her. Even if she was a dead shot, she was too precious to trust out of his sight.

He had just been haggling with the livery stable. They had a new buggy with spring seat and suspension drive. It was expensive, but he figured if it would cushion such a special cargo, he would buy it for her and the children's trip back home.

Lynne stared at him, her eyes a warm liquid gray. She took the soapy cloth from his idle hand, reached up to wash at the grit lightening his tanned face. He snorted in surprise and she laughed. "What will we do if they don't come?"

He swept a thumb to brush back silky strands from her forehead, smiling as the dark hair changed her small face into a heart. He bent to kiss her lips, ignoring her protest.

She twisted from him, listening for his standard answer. "We'll wait a month, if they don't come, we'll journey down the trail until we find out what happened to them."

Satisfied, she leaned forward, eager to see if two could fit into such a small tub.

The cavalcade of settlers plodded along the broad street, clearly interested in the town's tall store fronts. Lynne bounced up and down beside Phillip on the high buggy seat, her knee rattling the stiff cotton of her first store bought dress. He had argued that if she could sew and sell them, then the least she could do was help some other poor woman make a living. It was beautiful, the lilac fabric drawn up in intricate flounces in a vee down the bodice, the skirt heavily gathered. She had protested it made her bodice and bottom look far too ample. Phillip had argued valiantly such charming assets could never be too ample and she had blushed and purchased the dress. It was the wide seam along the sides, the hidden ribbon to let out at the waist that had sold it to her.

She blushed and wormed her hand into his for reassurance. Phillip wrapped one arm around her, squeezing her hand, aware as never before how beautiful his glowing bride was. Suddenly her mouth fell open and she squealed as though shot. Phillip paled but she was pulling free, scrambling down, and running. Frightened, he pushed back the dark coat to clear his guns and dropped down to stare at the passing wagons to see where the danger was coming from.

One of the wagons had stopped, the oxen yoke held on either side by two boys, more men than boys, their shoulders wide, bodies iron hard and muscled. The crazy thing was both were staring at his Lynne, their mouths open, screaming in return. Two women broke from the wagon and ran toward her but it was a small girl, slim and brown with soft blonde hair that darted from nowhere to beat all of them to her.

Only when she had swept the girl into her arms and turned back to see him did Phillip breathe again. Both faces were so much alike, their soft brown cheeks streaked with tears of joy. He watched smiling and easy as the two boys joined their sisters. Then smiled again as he recognized her friends Bonnie and Claire, though dusty and worn, they were just the way she had described them during those long nights when he had tried to ease her homesick heart. Two men riding with the wagon train watched the women and he knew her friends would both have interesting stories to share with Lynne later.

Now, now her heart would be full and happy. There would be no missing pieces to fill with shadow and doubt. All her heart had finally journeyed westward to him. If it took him a lifetime, he would do all in his power to make sure all of her dreams would come true.

THE END

ABOUT THE AUTHOR

J.R Biery, is a retired teacher who loves to write fiction. "I enjoy stories about wonderful people who get slapped in the face by adversity and discover who they really are as they overcome the challenge."

DEAR READER

I hope that you enjoy this historical romance, From Darkness to Glory. The characters and incidents are composites from stories of the west and the imagination of the author.

I have done my best to edit this text, but if you find errors, I apologize. Please send me your comments or suggestions at biery35@gmail.com

If you enjoyed this novel, I would appreciate your help. Please post your kind review at

http://www.amazon.com/review/create-review?ie=UTF8&asin=B00LG1ZPMK

OTHER WORK BY J.R.BIERY

Full-length Novels

The Milch Bride, http://www.amazon.com/dp/B00JC6DOLK

From Darkness to Glory, http://www.amazon.com/dp/B00LG1ZPMK

Killing the Darlings, http://www.amazon.com/dp/B00IRRMO2A

Edge of Night, http://www.amazon.com/dp/B00J0LLQC6

Will Henry, http://www.amazon.com/dp/B00K5POM0O

Chimera Pass, http://www.amazon.com/dp/B00KALJYRY

Potter's Field, http://www.amazon.com/dp/B00KH7Q8C0

He's My Baby Now, http://www.amazon.com/dp/B00N1X6ZFW

Shorter Work

Ghost Warrior, http://www.amazon.com/dp/B00M62NBEC

Happy Girl, http://www.amazon.com/dp/B00MHHXMEA

LONGWOOD PUBLIC LIBRARY
800 Middle Country Road
Middle Island, NY 11953
(631) 924-6400
longwoodlibrary.org

LIBRARY HOURS

Monday-Friday	9:30 a.m. - 9:00 p.m.
Saturday	9:30 a.m. - 5:00 p.m.
Sunday (Sept-June)	1:00 p.m. - 5:00 p.m.

42090357R00208

Made in the USA
Middletown, DE
02 April 2017